The PEACEMAKERS

AN AMERICAN FAMILY PORTRAIT

Book One:
THE PURITANS

Book Two:
THE COLONISTS

Book Three:
THE PATRIOTS

Book Four:
THE ADVERSARIES

Book Five:
THE PIONEERS

Book Six:
THE ALLIES

Book Seven:
THE VICTORS

Book Eight:
THE PEACEMAKERS

JACK CAVANAUGH

The
PEACEMAKERS

RIVEROAK®
Good News in Fiction

COOK COMMUNICATIONS MINISTRIES
Colorado Springs, Colorado • Paris, Ontario
KINGSWAY COMMUNICATIONS LTD
Eastbourne, England

RiverOak® is an imprint of
Cook Communications Ministries, Colorado Springs, CO 80918
Cook Communications, Paris, Ontario
Kingsway Communications, Eastbourne, England

THE PEACEMAKERS
© 2006 by Jack Cavanaugh, second edition,
previous ISBN: 1-56476-681-0

First edition published by Victor Books in © 1999.

Cover Design: Jeffrey P. Barnes
Cover Illustrator: Ron Adair

This story is a work of fiction. All characters and events are the product of
the author's imagination. Any resemblance to any person, living or dead, is
coincidental.

Printed in the United States of America.

1 2 3 4 5 6 7 8 9   Printing/Year   11 10 09 08 07 06

Scripture quotations are taken from The King James Version and Geneva Bible of
1560, both of which are Public Domain. The author has modernized some terms for
easier understanding. Italics in Scripture have been added by the author for emphasis.

ISBN-13: 978-1-58919-072-6
ISBN-10: 1-58919-072-6

LCCN: 2006925519

To Greg Clouse,
my editor, my friend

For all you've gone through to complete this series of books,
you deserve a lot more than to have this book dedicated to you.
But this I do with warmth and sincerity.

ACKNOWLEDGMENTS

As always, there are many people who have had a part in the making of this book—this one probably more than any other since my own background and experience have without doubt colored my understanding of the historical events.

To those of you—far too numerous to mention—who have had a hand in my spiritual and academic growth, from the depths of my being, I thank you and pray that God will reward you richly.

Thanks to Peggy Phifer of Las Vegas, a writer friend I met on a Christian writers Internet workshop; for it was she who suggested the title for this book.

Thanks to Roger and Andrea Palms for sharing yourselves and the fruit of your research on the Jesus people with me. It is always enjoyable making new friends.

Thanks to George and Dorcas Taggert for loaning me your book on Billy Graham and, more importantly, for introducing my books to so many readers through your book fair ministry.

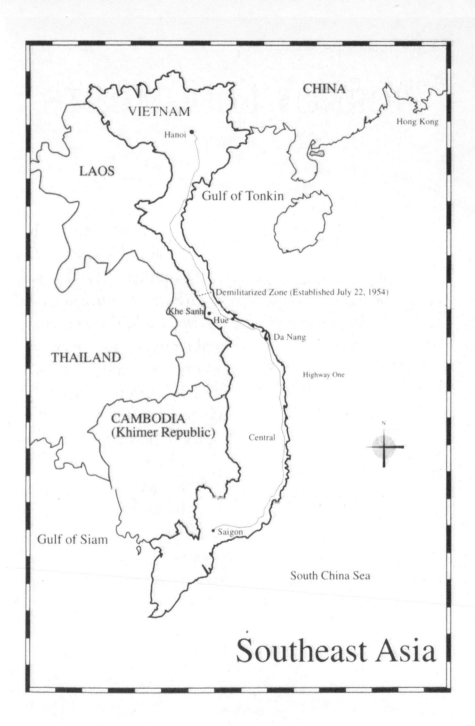

CHINA

Hong Kong

VIETNAM

Hanoi

LAOS

Gulf of Tonkin

Demilitarized Zone (Established July 22, 1954)

Khe Sanh

Hue

Da Nang

THAILAND

Highway One

CAMBODIA
(Khimer Republic)

Central

Gulf of Siam

Saigon

N

South China Sea

Southeast Asia

1

"I'm not going!"

Paige Morgan took her stand in the center of her bedroom, hands on hips with three paint brushes jutting from her left hand. A white canvas with a charcoal sketch waited to receive its initial dabs of color. At least half a dozen art books lay open atop an unmade single bed pushed against the wall. Each book was open to a print of a Marc Chagall painting.

In the corner of the room a table stereo belted out a Jefferson Airplane tune about pills that made you larger or smaller, and about chasing rabbits and posing questions to a ten-foot-tall Alice.

Paige's father stood in the doorway. Pulling tight a conservative blue-striped necktie, he said, "It's Sunday. This family goes to church on Sunday. Now get dressed. We're already late."

"I'm twenty-one years old," Paige replied. "I'm old enough to make my own decisions."

Her father scowled. "As long as you're living under my roof, young lady, you'll do as I say! We'll wait for you in the car."

Paige didn't move. The brushes in her hand quivered, betraying the calm, resolute image she was attempting to portray. She laid the brushes aside on the easel tray. Calmly, deliberately, she picked up a rag soiled with streaks of paint and linseed oil. As casually as she could manage, she wiped her hands. "I'm not going," she said.

Her father's eyes narrowed. A burning red color crept up his neck and into his face. The color frightened Paige. Father was the easygoing sort. For his face to color like this meant he was really angry. Leveling a stiff index finger her direction, he said, "This is the last time I'm going to tell you. Get ready for church!"

"Nat, dear, what's all the commotion?"

Paige's mother appeared behind her husband. Now it was two against one. Paige's resolve began to waver.

Although Allegra Morgan was ten years older than her husband, she looked younger. Fashionably thin, she had shoulder-length blonde hair that curled under and bounced when she walked. She had a dignified old-world European demeanor about her so that when she spoke with a native French accent, no one seemed surprised. The surprise came when they discovered she was blind. For a woman without the benefit of sight, Allegra Morgan showed uncommon poise.

She sniffed the air. "Paige, are you painting? It's time for church."

"She's not even dressed!" her father groused.

From Nat Morgan's point of view, this was true. The battle between father and daughter over her appearance had been raging for nearly a decade. In his opinion, her dresses were too short, her hair too high, and the style of both were outrageous. At the moment, while Nat was attired in a conservative charcoal gray suit, Paige stood barefoot in frayed cutoff jeans and a tie-dyed T-shirt.

"Paige, dear," her mother said, "are you not feeling well?"

"She's feeling fine," Nat answered for her. "Or maybe I should say she's feeling her oats. Your daughter is no doubt allowing herself to be brainwashed by the radical drivel of that bunch of hippies she hangs out with at UCRD."

"I'm not being brainwashed by anyone!" Paige cried. "This is how I feel. And I think you should respect that."

From farther down the hallway came a voice. It was her brother.

"Hey! What's going on? We're gonna be late."

Travis popped up behind his parents. With sandy blond hair, he was tanned, solidly built, and a good head and shoulders taller than either of them. He wore a tan suit with a narrow black tie. When no one answered him, he shot his sister a puzzled look.

Paige moaned inwardly. *Great! Now the whole family is here.* She wanted to crawl under the bed. Instead, she continued to wipe nonexistent paint from her hands.

Ever since the spring semester of her freshman year at the University of California at Rancho Diego she knew this day would come and had dreaded its arrival. Now that it was here, it was harder than she'd imagined it would be. Maybe she should just give in and go to church with them. It wasn't as though this private little protest was going to change the world or anything.

Then, she remembered the campus rally that had prompted her decision to make a stand. She remembered the long line of brave young men as one by one they burned their draft cards in protest of the war, risking imprisonment for what they believed.

A sudden rush of resolve bolstered her courage.

To Travis, Nat said, "Son, this is none of your business. Wait for us in the car."

"But this *is* his business," Paige said. "Don't you see? That's the whole point. He's the one being shipped out. How can you go to church so glibly today and then tomorrow send your son halfway around the world to be slaughtered?"

"Paige!" her mother cried.

"That's enough from you!" her father roared.

Paige jumped at the force of his voice. Only once before had she seen her father this angry. Travis was in junior high school at the time. He came home wearing an Iron Cross around his neck. For Travis, it was a surfer symbol; for his father, it was a reminder of Hitler and Nazis and the Third Reich. The medallion quickly disappeared and nothing was ever said about it again.

"Paige," Allegra said calmly, "this isn't about politics and war. This is church."

"No, Mother, you're wrong. The two are one and the same when the church celebrates sending young men to a senseless war. It's beyond me how can you worship God one moment, then sentence your own son to certain death, or disfigurement, or at the very least two years of hard labor. No civilized society would impose such a sentence on its criminals, let alone its innocent young men."

"Your brother is serving his country," her father shouted, "just like I did when I was his age."

Paige countered: "It's not the same. Travis is nothing more than a political pawn. What sense does it make for us to say we're fighting for freedom and justice if we strip our own young men of their personal identities and freedom in the process? The politicians are sending young men to Vietnam against their will. Travis doesn't want to go. Nobody does. What about his freedom?"

Nat's finger jabbed the air repeatedly. "Listen, young lady, I was ducking bullets in a foxhole long before you were born. This isn't the first generation of American men who are being asked to risk their lives for liberty and freedom. So don't you stand there and tell me I don't know what I'm sending my son to do."

Allegra interrupted. "Nat, this isn't the time for this discussion. We're late for church. Paige, are you coming with us or not?"

Three faces awaited her response. And Paige loved every one of them. That's what made her decision so hard. She didn't want to hurt them.

"No," she said softly. "I'm not going with you."

"I suggest you spend the time thinking long and hard about what you're doing," her father said. "You're not only letting down your family, but you're letting down your church and God. Think about it." He disappeared down the hallway.

"Travis, would you please assist me?"

Paige winced. Her mother's request cut her more deeply than her father's anger. Blind since birth, Allegra had not the slightest difficulty navigating around the house, except when she was extremely hurt or upset. And Paige knew her mother well enough to know this was not a play for sympathy.

Travis extended a crooked arm to his mother. At the same time he gave his sister a sympathetic half smile. Moments later, she heard the car doors slam and the sound of an engine roar to life then fade down the street.

She was alone.

The house was so silent, it was unnerving.

With a shaky groan she slumped onto the edge of the bed. As she did, one of the art books slid over the side and flopped to the floor. It fell open to a page that bore the representation of one of Chagall's better-known paintings—*Adam and Eve Expelled from Paradise.*

Paige chuckled at the irony. Her stomach was one large knot. She breathed in deeply in an attempt to calm herself. A ragged exhale proved the effort unsuccessful.

It had to be done, she reasoned. How could she let them—all of them—send Travis to Vietnam without some kind of protest?

She tossed the soiled rag at the canvas. It hit with a thud, then slid to the floor. She never had intended painting this morning. The canvas, the brushes, the art books merely gave her hands something to do while she listened to the familiar Sunday morning sounds as her family got ready for church.

Now what should she do? Her eyes roamed aimlessly across the walls of her bedroom, which were heavy with posters. One of the larger posters had a solid blue background with red psychedelic letters.

Bill Graham presents
Jefferson Airplane
and
Grateful Dead
in concert
Fillmore Auditorium,
San Francisco

Beside it was a poster that bore a picture of a simplified flower in primary colors. It read:

War
is not
healthy
for children
and other
living things.

From the stereo in the corner, the guitar chords of Jefferson Airplane wailed a tune about a time when truth had been found to be lies and when the joy within you dies. The song's refrain floated around the room: *Don't you want somebody to love? Don't you need somebody to love?*

Her tension found its release in tears.

Don't you want somebody to love? Don't you need somebody to love?

She reached for a tissue from a box on her bedside stand. She dabbed her eyes and wiped her nose. Then, picking up the princess telephone, she dialed a number. After several rings a recognizable voice answered.

"Well," she said, "I did it."

Nat sighed. It seemed the whole church had but a single question on its mind.

"Where's Paige?"

It was Elmer Odell's turn to ask the question. A horseshoe-bald man with a spattering of freckles on his forehead, Elmer held out a printed order of service to Nat, thus fulfilling his role as church usher. Elmer was one of the mainstays of the church. While European cathedrals had stone gargoyles guarding their entrances, La Jolla's Church on the Bluff had Elmer Odell. Rain or shine, year after year, Elmer was there. An old navy captain, the church usher's sharp, stony facial features sometimes resembled that of a gargoyle, especially to younger children who seemed to fear him. But over the years Nat had found the man to be warm and personable.

"Paige wasn't up to coming this morning," Nat replied.

This was the excuse Nat had settled upon. He didn't want to lie, but then neither was he willing to admit to the world that his daughter had chosen to turn her back on everything she'd been taught to believe. So he'd formulated this excuse. It was vague, but not untruthful. He'd used it on Paige's friends in the parking lot when they first arrived, and it was the answer he'd given Paige's Sunday-school teacher when they passed each other in the breezeway. So far everyone had accepted the excuse without inquiring further. But Elmer Odell wasn't just anyone.

"Classes haven't started at UCRD already, have they?" he asked.

"No, not yet," Nat replied. He shifted his attention to the printed sheet in his hand while continuing toward the sanctuary.

"She's not ill, is she?" Elmer asked.

"No. She isn't ill," Nat stammered. "Thank you for asking. It was just that … well … she just wasn't up to coming today."

"Ah!" Elmer said knowingly.

Nat hadn't the slightest idea what conclusion the usher had arrived at, and he didn't care, as long as it concluded their conversation.

Stepping into the sanctuary, he scanned the pews for his wife. A waving arm on the third row from the front caught his attention. His mother. Allegra was seated to her left and his father on her right. In all the commotion Nat had forgotten he'd invited his parents to join them this morning.

Feeling conspicuous, he walked the length of the center aisle. Why had Allegra allowed them to sit all the way up front? She knew he preferred sitting in the back of the auditorium. He slid into the pew beside her.

Before he could say anything, Allegra took his arm. "Mother and Father wanted to sit up close," she said softly.

"Hello dear," his mother said.

Nat greeted her and reached over both women to shake his father's hand.

"What's all this about Paige?" his mother asked.

Nat grimaced, not knowing how much or how little Allegra had already told them.

The electronic organ resounded, doing its best imitation of a pipe organ as the choir filed into the loft. The service was beginning. As the choir launched into a spirited rendition of the "Battle Hymn of the Republic," Nat turned his attention forward, grateful for the respite from his mother's question.

He felt something tapping his forearm.

It was his mother. She was reaching across Allegra.

"You didn't answer me," she whispered. "What's all this about Paige?"

Nat pressed his lips together, perturbed by his mother's persistence. He whispered back at her, "She didn't feel up to coming today."

His excuse prompted a scowl, and Nat knew he'd made a tactical error. A vague excuse may put off friends and Sunday-school teachers, but to a grandmother it was no excuse at all. Worse, it was tantamount to telling her to mind her own business.

Nat's mother sat back in the pew, clearly displeased. Donning a feigned neutral expression, she turned her attention to the choir. Nat sighed. He'd have to apologize to her after the service and try to explain himself.

Travis appeared at the far end of the pew. With a half smile of an apology for being late, he sat next to his grandfather. Nat's father leaned over and whispered something into Travis's ear that made him laugh.

Their church was a small one with a membership of not more than fifty families consisting mainly of bankers, publishers, jewelers, land magnates, and the like. They were an elite congregation from a wealthy neighborhood who worshipped on a priceless bluff overlooking the Pacific Ocean.

The site had been donated to the church by a land developer on his deathbed, the act of a desperate man trying to bribe his way into heaven. And while the majority of the congregation openly doubted the man's attempt would be successful, they willingly accepted the land. On it they built a picturesque white panel sanctuary complete with steeple, bell, and arched stained-glass windows. They named it, appropriately, The Church on the Bluff. It soon became a favorite of Hollywood directors. In its two decades of existence the church had already appeared in a half-dozen feature films.

On this particular Sunday the morning service had a patriotic theme, this in honor of Travis Morgan's eminent departure into military service. Keith Rawlins had been given a similar send-off only six months earlier. These two men constituted the church's total contribution to the armed forces. All the other available

young men managed to escape military service with student or
medical deferments.

Rawlins was two years older than Travis and had, for a time,
dated Paige when they were both seniors in high school. Athletic,
confident, and a natural leader, Rawlins was something of a
poster boy for the church. Everyone proudly claimed him as his
or her own. They eagerly followed his progress through training
camp and insisted his first letters from Vietnam be read from the
pulpit.

The choir's opening choral arrangement came to a goose-
flesh-raising crescendo. Dabbing his brow with a white
handkerchief, the choir director turned to the congregation and
announced a series of hymns. The congregation stood and sang in
succession "Onward Christian Soldiers," "God Bless America,"
and the national anthem.

It was a struggle for Nat to keep his mind focused on the
songs. The confrontation with Paige kept rushing to the forefront
of his mind. The more he tried to bury it, the more he thought
about it, and the more he thought about it, the angrier he became.

How could she stand there and say those things? She didn't
really believe them, did she? That was not his daughter. They had
taught her better than that. To respect authority, for one thing!
And how dare she accuse him of taking Travis's induction into the
army lightly! It took little effort for him to recall the horrors of
war. Casablanca, Anzio, Rome … his friend Murphy's death …
these were not distant memories. Besides all that, confound it,
didn't Paige realize that the liberal rhetoric of hers was aiding the
advance of communism?

What had gotten into her? This was not the same young lady
he'd sent away to college a year ago. This was not his daughter.

The pastor approached the pulpit. A man in his midfifties,
Pastor Carl Lamar's white hair was combed straight back. He

wore gray-framed glasses and was thick of waist, just shy of being portly. Soft-spoken, over the years the man had interpreted his ecclesiastical role as that of a benevolent father with a large extended family. And while he wasn't an accomplished preacher, Nat found him to be an effective spiritual leader.

"As most of you know," said the beaming minister, "this is a special day for our little church. For the second time in a year, we are sending one of our own into military service tomorrow. And from what I've heard of his family's history, who knows? Maybe he'll straighten out this whole mess overseas single-handedly!"

While the congregation responded with generous laughter, Travis blushed.

The minister continued: "Travis Morgan. Would you please stand so that our people can see you?"

With shy reluctance, Travis stood. Though he was in excellent physical shape, he moved as though the effort pained him. Nat was reminded how much the boy had grown in the last few years. His shoulders were broad from swimming, his skin was tanned and his hair bleached from endless hours in the sun. Following high-school graduation, Travis had worked as a lifeguard at La Jolla Shores during the summer, then in a local surf shop during the fall and winter months. The beach and surfboards had been the sum total of his life for the past two years. During the middle of his second summer he was promoted to captain of the life-guard team. Two weeks afterward his draft notice arrived in the mail.

The congregation honored Travis with warm applause. He was well regarded in the church. Nat particularly noticed the way the high-school girls stole glances at him, then whispered among themselves and giggled.

"And now the parents," Pastor Lamar said. "Nat and Allegra Morgan, would you please stand with your son?"

Nat glanced at his beautiful wife. She reached over and took his hand. Together they stood and acknowledged the applause of their friends and neighbors.

"Aren't we missing someone?" the pastor asked. "Where's Paige?"

Nat stiffened.

"She didn't return to UCRD already, did she?"

"Umm … no," Nat stammered.

"I hope she's not ill."

Nat looked around him. The applause had died out. He found himself wading in a sea of faces, all of them staring up at him. An image of Paige flashed in his mind. She was standing defiantly in the middle of her bedroom in shorts and a T-shirt with paint-brushes sprouting from her hands. Nat felt his face growing warm. Clearing his throat, he said, "No, Paige isn't ill. She … um … is unable to attend church this morning."

Pastor Lamar seemed to sense Nat's discomfort, and none too soon. But the damage had been done. Paige's absence hung heavy in the air. Unresolved—for he really hadn't explained her absence—and uncomfortable. And Nat was certain this wouldn't be the end of it. He could expect another barrage of inquiries from well-wishers and busybodies alike following the service. Paige's rebellion was an irritation that just wouldn't go away.

"Nat," the pastor continued, "I see your parents have joined us for this special occasion honoring their grandson. And although this isn't the first time they've attended our church, there may be some who haven't met them yet. Would you introduce them?"

While Nat motioned for his parents to stand, Allegra and Travis took this as their cue to sit down. Nat's mother stood read-ily; his father had to be coaxed. "This is Johnny and Laura Morgan. They live in Point Loma."

As Nat and his parents began to sit down, Pastor Lamar suspended the action with his outstretched hand.

To the congregation, he said: "While all of us know Nat Morgan to be a world-class photographer for *FLASH!* magazine, you may not know that his family has a long and distinguished history."

Nat treated the comment as a compliment. He nodded his thanks and began to sit down again. The pastor prevented him.

"Correct me if I'm wrong, but your father fought in World War I, did he not?"

"Yes, he did," Nat replied. "He was a pilot."

Nat motioned to his father to elaborate.

"59th Pursuit Squadron, France," was all Johnny said.

"For which he was awarded the Distinguished Flying Cross and the Croix de Guerre," Nat added.

Johnny Morgan shooed away the applause that erupted from the congregation.

"And your mother," the pastor prompted, "I understand she too saw action during World War I."

Laura didn't share her husband's shyness. Answering for herself, she said, "Yes, I did. Alongside Johnny's sister Katy. We were nurses and drove ambulances."

"Close to the front?" the pastor asked.

"That's where the wounded were," Laura replied with a polite smile. She and her husband sat down. Nat started to join them.

"And Nat, you served your country during the Second World War."

"Yes. Third Infantry. North Africa and Italy."

"And you met your lovely wife, Allegra, behind German lines?"

"Correct. She was part of the French resistance, not only during World War II but also as a little girl in World War I." He looked down at his wife and smiled. She sat straight and proud, smiling, her face forward and fixed.

To the congregation, the pastor said, "For those of you who don't know this couple's story, I encourage you to corner them sometime and drag it out of them. Theirs is a saga of courage and faith."

Nat did his best to hide his displeasure. A private man, he didn't appreciate the pastor's open invitation to pry into his life. Nevertheless, he smiled and began to sit down.

"Wait, wait! I'm not finished with you," the pastor said good-naturedly.

Nat straightened himself, wondering why the pastor seemed determined to prolong his discomfort.

"I also understand that your family has been represented in every major war in our country's history. Is that true?"

"Umm … yes, I believe that's true," Nat said. He glanced down at Allegra. She was nodding her head affirmatively.

"We've already acknowledged we have representatives from the two major wars of this century," the pastor said. "How about the Civil War?"

Nat looked to Allegra. Again taking his cue from her, he answered, "Yes, I have ancestors who fought in the Civil War."

From her seat Allegra added, "Three Morgans fought on the Union side. They also mounted a daring rescue to save a fourth son, Willy Morgan, from Andersonville Prison."

Nat glanced at his parents. His father in particular seemed concerned that Nat himself was unable to recall these details. The Morgans took great pride in their family history.

"And the Revolutionary War?" the pastor prompted.

Again, Nat was unsure.

Allegra smiled. "Twin brothers," she said. "One an English patriot, the other a colonial patriot."

At this the congregation and the pastor laughed.

"Sounds like the Morgans were hedging their bets on that one. And your family goes back how far?"

"Umm, 1600s," Nat replied.

Allegra said, "Drew Morgan was the first of the family to arrive in America. He sailed aboard the *Arbella* with Governor John Winthrop. They arrived June 1630."

"Well, I can see who the historian is in the family," chuckled the pastor.

Nat tried to sit down.

"And isn't there a family Bible?" the pastor asked.

Nat straightened himself. "Yes there is."

"And how old is it? Over 300 years, isn't it?"

Nat did some mental calculating. "At least 330 years old," he concluded.

"I'd like to see it sometime."

"It's very fragile," Nat said.

Allegra spoke up. "The Morgan family Bible has an interesting history itself. For years it was lost among the Narragansett Indian tribe; many years later, it saved Nat's brother's life when it intercepted a piece of shrapnel during a B-52 bombing run over Germany."

The pastor shook his head in amazement. "What a glorious family history," he said.

Nat started to sit down.

"And now it continues with a new generation," the pastor said. "Travis, stand again with your father and grandfather that we might see three generations of Morgan history."

To the enthusiastic applause of the congregation, Nat stood with his father and his son. This time, however, he felt no embarrassment, only pride.

2

Limbo. Hanging between two worlds. Claimed by both, living in neither. That's how Travis felt as he sat on the beach, his last night as a civilian.

Sitting opposite him on the far side of the fire ring was a bare-chested, skinny, high-school sophomore with big ears. Travis could see the boy sporadically through the flames. He was strumming a guitar and singing, "I've Got Peace Like a River." A dozen or so adolescent girls in flowered two-piece bathing suits and guys in baggy swim trunks joined in, their faces lit by the fire's orange flame.

Travis sat with them but he was not one of them. He was an adult sponsor, enlisted for the outing because he was a trained lifeguard. They were all younger. Just kids. And while he was only two years older than some of the seniors in the group, it felt like decades had passed since he'd been a member of the church youth group. They all looked so young. Was that how he had looked to Paige and Keith?

The scene changed before his eyes, as though Dickens had sent one of the Christmas ghosts to show him shadows of his past. He was sitting at this same fire ring, but looking through younger eyes. Keith Rawlins was the guitar player then; he was also the president of the youth group, the one who always led the devotion, the one who told the funniest jokes, and the captain of the winning team whether they were playing volleyball, keep away, or running relay races. Keith was the guy every girl liked and most guys wanted to be like.

Paige sat close to Keith, clapping her hands to the rhythm of the music and singing. She was smiling. Happy. The two of them were the ideal couple. The darlings of the church youth group. Everybody expected them to marry soon after their high-school graduation.

For Travis those were carefree days. He was happy just to tag along. Keith treated him like a little brother. Every Sunday afternoon they either played football in the park or went to the beach or dreamed over cars in used car lots. And Paige acted differently when Keith was around. She seemed to forget that Travis was her little brother and treated him like he was a human being.

Those were the days. Back then his greatest concerns were passing U.S. history, waxing his surfboard, getting his driver's license, and working up enough courage to ask Diana Purdy out on a date. But those days were long gone, mere shadows of a life that once was.

Travis blinked his way back into the present. He stared at the crackling flames. Lately, even the present seemed to be fading before his eyes. One more sunrise and his life would change in ways he could only now imagine. His future was fixed; it merely awaited its appointed time. He was the property of the United States Army, signed and sealed. Delivery would take place in the morning when he reported to the induction center.

It was hard for him to fathom what it would be like. In just a few hours he would be swallowed up by a foreign regime that regulated itself with stacks of manuals filled with alien regulations, rigid protocol, traditions, and rules. He would eat and sleep with people he'd never before met in a place he'd never before seen. He would rise when they told him to rise, do what they told him to do, go where they told him to go, and kill the people they told him to kill.

This was what disturbed him most. The idea of killing.

Some of the guys he'd talked to were dreading the loss of their freedom and privacy, or the rigorous boot camp training. Not him. He dreaded the weapons and what they expected him to do with them.

He'd imagined the scenario a hundred times. No, not imagined. It was much stronger than that, more like a vision or a trance. He saw himself looking down the barrel of a rifle, resting its sights on the chest of an Asian man thirty feet away. He watched the man move, breathe, speak to a buddy, smoke, look casually from side to side, and brush away a fly—totally unaware that he was living his last few seconds on earth, that in just a few moments a metal projectile would be launched at him, one that would rip through his chest and lungs and heart, leaving him gasping for breath as he crumpled to the ground and watched helplessly as his life's liquid drained from his body.

In Travis's mind's eye his finger would tremble as he pulled the trigger, his shoulder would feel the rifle's kick. He would watch in horror as the man's head jerked backward, his eyes expressing astonished pain. The man would clutch at his chest as though he was trying to rip the bullet out before it did too much damage; but it was always too late. The man's legs would fold, drained of the strength that had supported him since infancy; his arms would fall limp and he would collapse to the ground, a lifeless tangle of flesh.

Every time Travis imagined this horror—every time without fail—the man's eyes remained open. Staring skyward. Locked in place. Frozen in this way, they were prevented from searching for his killer. So they waited. And waited. It was as though they knew the man who fired the shot would come to them, as though some natural law decreed that a man's killer must stand over his vanquished victim and look down at him.

And Travis would find himself gripped by an invisible force, led against his will to the place where the dead man lay, compelling him to look down upon his victim. And as he entered the dead man's field of vision, Travis would stare in horror at the yellowed, fixed eyes, and they would stare back at him. Accusing him. Convicting him. Haunting him. Until Travis's hands shook and his knees grew weak.

Then, a new horror would strike him, one born of the realization that he was about to faint. He knew he was about to fall on top of the man he'd just killed, like a tree being felled in a forest. The ground rushed up toward him and there was nothing he could do to stop it.

The next thing he knew, he was cheek to cheek with the dead man. The man he'd killed. He could feel the man's still-warm skin and smell his rancid breath. Revolted and half-crazed, he would try desperately to push away, to climb or roll off the dead man, but something held him down. Some unseen force pinned him there.

And then he knew. This was his punishment for killing another human being. He was being forced to witness death close up—to lay against the dead man that he might feel the man's joints stiffen, that he might feel the man's skin draw taut against his bony frame, that together they might share the flies that buzzed over them and feel them crawl unhindered on their exposed flesh.

In his dream Travis would scream, but no sound came from his mouth. Death was silent. Those who lay with the dead were forbidden to make a sound.

Whenever Travis had this nightmare or vision he would tremble for days afterward. The dead man's yellow stare haunted him for weeks every time he closed his eyes.

And if all this anxiety came from merely imagining what it must be like to take a life, how could he ever bring himself to actually do it? And if he did, how would he survive afterward? He could refuse. But the army frowned on that sort of thing. And how would he ever face his father and grandfather? The Morgans had a proud military heritage.

So he told no one of his visions or his fear. And though he harbored no childish fantasy that somehow he'd manage to escape the nightmare altogether, he figured that when the time came he would find it within himself to do the right thing. If other guys could do it, so could he.

Distant high-pitched screams snapped Travis's attention back to the beach. Seasoned eyes squinted into the distance, searching for the source of the screams. Three fire rings down from them children were chasing each other in and out of the surf. Splashing water. Squealing. Shouting. Having fun.

Nine times out of ten that's all screaming ever amounted to on the beach, kids having a good time. Still, he'd been trained to check just to make sure. One never knew when the childlike screams would turn to screams of terror.

He spied a man and a woman sitting in lawn chairs next to the fire ring closest to the kids. They seemed oblivious to the shouting, more intent on their conversation. Typical, but not wise considering no lifeguards were posted on the beach after dark.

Around the youth campfire the singing had stopped momentarily. The skinny guitar player had asked for song requests and was instantly bombarded with responses. He fended them off with an uplifted hand.

"I have an idea," he said. "Since it's Travis's last night, why don't we let him choose the next song?" Folding his arms across the top of the guitar, he engaged Travis and said, "What'll it be, soldier?"

A circle of adolescent faces swung Travis's direction.

"I don't really have a favorite." Travis demurred, somewhat embarrassed by the attention. "Let someone else choose."

A chorus of objections rose along with the sparks from the fire. They weren't going to let him off that easy.

"All right," he conceded. "How about 'I've Got Peace Like a River'?"

Hoots and groans and laughter were heaped upon him.

"Earth to Travis," the guitar player laughed. "What do you think we just finished singing?"

"Oh. I was ... my mind was ..."

Travis felt his face flush. He laughed with them. They howled and carried on more than the mistake warranted. It didn't bother him. Many of them were junior highers. And they were laughing out of relief that it was Travis who had done something stupid and not them.

Someone said, "Since he's goin' to 'Nam we should sing 'Ballad of the Green Beret'."

Travis winced playfully at the suggestion. "How about 'California Dreamin'?" he suggested.

The guitar player rustled through some loose pieces of sheet music that he kept anchored under a rock. A couple of guitar chords later, everyone was singing again. Travis caught some of the junior-high girls stealing glances at him. He lowered his head and chuckled. Girls their age preferred older boys, a fact that had irked him no end when he was that age. Now that he was older, he realized he needn't have worried. Guys his age weren't interested in junior-high girls.

As for the laughter, he could live with it. At least it broke the spell of the killing vision and brought his mind back to the beach party. Looking at the surf and speckled sky he realized he would be a fool to let his last night in California slip away.

He was on the beach—the place he liked better than any other place in the world—with a cool breeze blowing in from the ocean. White-capped breakers looked almost mystical the way they rumbled out of a black sea and spread their foam across the sand.

Three fire rings distant the squeals began again. Travis instinctively glanced in that direction. Something was wrong. This time the squeals were different. Deeper. Frantic. Not squeals at all. Screams. Screams for help.

Travis bolted that direction, his feet tossing sand into the air behind him.

"Jori! Oh, dear God! Jori!"

The woman he'd seen earlier conversing by the fire stood screaming knee-deep in the surf as she searched the waves. She held two small boys, one in each arm. The boys shouted with her in a heart-wrenching trio. The younger boy repeatedly glanced up at his mother. He was crying at the sight of his mother's tears.

Farther out in the surf stood the man she'd been conversing with. Travis assumed he was the husband and father. He stood in water up to his torso. He too was shouting against the sound of the crashing waves. He ventured farther into the water. Tentatively. By inches. Wanting to plunge into the waves. But something was holding him back. He probably couldn't swim.

Travis hit the water in full stride. Small explosions of water erupted beneath each footfall. He charged past the woman. "I'm a lifeguard!" he shouted. "There's a pay telephone at the tower. Call for help."

The woman looked at him, her face a portrait of motherly fear. "My little girl! She's way out there! She can't swim! Please hurry!"

"I'll get her!" Travis shouted without breaking stride. "Call for help!"

The water was up to his knees. High stepping, he made every effort to keep his forward momentum going. When the water reached his waist, he dove into an oncoming wave. Surfacing behind it, he started swimming.

In no time he reached the father who was now standing shoulder-deep in the surf. If the situation weren't an emergency, Travis would have laughed. Against the dark sea the man's bald head looked like a volleyball bobbing atop the surface.

Travis grabbed the man's arm. "Can you swim?" he shouted.

Eyes filled with fear stared back at him. Frantically the man shook his head. "My daughter's out there!" He pointed beyond the breakers.

"I'll get her," Travis shouted. He pulled the man backward until his feet could touch bottom. "Go back to shore!" Travis shouted. "I'll get your daughter!"

The man rose and fell with the swells. "She's way out there! How did she get so far out?"

"I'll get her," Travis repeated. "Go back to where your feet can touch. I don't want to have to rescue you too!"

Travis plunged seaward into the dark liquid with powerful strokes. His progress was phenomenal, aided by the very current that created the tragedy.

Even at night Travis had recognized the rip current. Often called riptides or undertows, they looked like a muddy river flowing away from shore. This was the sea's way of recirculating the water that had been pushed ashore by waves. Surfers, rafters, and weaker swimmers, if caught in one, could be carried out to sea.

Travis lifted his head to get his bearings. A full moon overhead brushed the undulating surface with white highlights. Anything white appeared luminescent. *Thank God for that*, Travis thought. The last he'd seen the little girl she was wearing a white T-shirt over her bathing suit.

Still there was no sign of the shirt or the girl ahead of him. He looked back to shore. A crowd was gathering at water's edge. No one was entering the water, and there was no sign of emergency vehicles. He was on his own.

Except for the emergency it was a perfect summer night at the beach. The water was nearly as warm as the air temperature. The sky was clear with an impressive array of stars on display. The moon shown brightly. It was the kind of night that cast mesmerizing spells over people. Poets and songwriters had tried to capture its allure for centuries.

These thoughts occupied Travis's mind for but a split second. There was a little girl out here somewhere. He had to find her.

Travis could feel the current pulling him out to sea. He stared at the murky brown water, trying to see through it. It was thick with sand and too dark to see but a few inches beneath the surface. He felt all around him with his arms and legs. Nothing. Had he gone out far enough? Had he gone too far? With only his instincts to guide him, he lunged seaward and swam farther from shore, letting the current carry him.

His muscles were warm with effort, just on the edge of tiring. He pulled up again. Treading water, he turned full circle. Still no sign of the girl. What was the name her mother used?

He shouted. "Jerri! Jerri! If you can hear me, wave an arm! Shout! Do something so I can find you!"

He listened. Beyond the breakers the smallest sounds were accentuated on the water. He could hear clearly the lapping of the water against his chest and his own labored breathing. But little else. Any sounds from the shore were masked by the soft distant crash of breakers.

It was surreal. How many hours had he spent in the water? Yet never had he experienced anything like this. Peaceful. Beautiful. Distracting.

All of a sudden he felt incredibly alone in this watery world, as though nothing else existed but him, the ocean, the stars, the moon, and the sky. The difference between him and everything around him was that all the other elements held their position in this universe effortlessly.

He was the only thing drifting.

He had to exert effort against the ocean-bound current simply to maintain his position, his life. The sea was working against him. Soft invisible hands pulled at him. It was a deadly beauty in which he floated. Should he stop resisting for just a few moments, the sea's hands would pull him under. And the stars and the moon above would do nothing to prevent it. To them, should he perish, there would be one less speck in the universe while they continued day after day, night after night as though nothing had happened, as though he had never existed.

He couldn't let that happen. To him, or to a little girl.

Travis plunged beneath the surface and swam farther out to sea. He was running out of time.

His arms were aching now. Swimming became increasingly difficult; staying afloat was an effort.

Then, he saw something. Something white, just ahead, floating beneath the surface like some ghostly apparition. Travis lunged for it.

A white T-shirt!

It was the same size the girl was wearing. He grabbed for it. The shirt was empty. There was no little girl in it.

A sense of dread swept over him. He began to fear the worst.

Surfacing, he trod water, turning in circles, staring into the muddy blackness, shouting the little girl's name, searching with his arms and legs. All the while the current pulled him farther out to sea.

There was nothing left to do but dive. But with visibility less than a foot, all he could hope for was a lucky break.

"O Lord ..."

That was all he said. He trusted God to fill in the obvious.

Taking a deep breath, he went under. He swam blindly, feeling his way inch by inch. He stayed under until he could suppress his instinct to breathe no longer. Breaking the surface he took another gulp of air and went under again.

Time was running out for the girl. He was losing hope. She had been under too long. A dozen lifeguards could search the water all night in these conditions and not find her. It was over. A few days from now the *San Diego Union* would report that the body of the little girl had washed ashore, found by someone taking his morning walk along the beach.

But Travis couldn't bring himself to give up. His lungs screamed for air. He surfaced for breath and tried one more time. He turned in quarter turns. He saw nothing but sparkling flecks of sand against a murky black background. He began to ascend.

Then he saw something. It startled him.

His heart lurched and pounded wildly against his chest. His lungs felt as though they would collapse upon themselves. In the murky water was the alabaster face of a little girl.

Her eyes were closed. Her expression was serene. Her pale skin was luminescent, and her hair spread out and waved gently in the current. Particles of dirt and sand speckled her forehead and cheeks like glitter, highlighted by the ghostly whiteness of her complexion.

Travis needed air. Badly. But he was afraid to surface. He might lose sight of her. He reached out. The current pulled the girl away from him. He reached again, this time managing to grab her. The girl's flesh was cold and slippery. Furiously Travis kicked for the surface. Moments later they broke through the boundary separating water and air.

His arms and legs screaming from effort and lack of oxygen, Travis gulped air greedily. He indulged himself for only a moment. Instinct took over. He did what he'd been trained to do. Keeping the girl's head above water, even though she was not breathing, he raced to get her on dry ground.

He swam parallel to the shore. This indirect route would take longer, but it was necessary to escape the rip current. Inexperienced swimmers try to swim against it, to fight the sea one-on-one. These were the fatalities. The only way to keep from becoming a victim himself was to slip out of its grip.

Once he was free of the current, Travis swam for shore. The current had done its damage. They were a good distance from the beach and he was tiring. His arms and legs felt like burning rubber. His lungs were on fire. Choppy waves slowed his progress. Several times he inhaled and swallowed water. The salt burned his throat, making breathing even more difficult. As for the little girl, he might as well have been towing a rag doll.

Finally Travis reached the breakers and the surf began to carry him and the girl toward shore. It was no easy ride though. Travis fought to keep himself and the girl level. The surf wanted to send them tumbling ashore.

He caught a glimpse of several people running into the surf to assist him. The girl's mother and father were among them. The mother was hysterical at the sight of her child, limp and lifeless in Travis's arms.

Exhausted, Travis felt the ocean bottom with his feet. He stumbled forward several more yards before falling to his knees in the surf. A second later half a dozen hands grabbed him and helped him to his feet. Someone attempted to take the girl from his arms. He wouldn't let them.

He tried to say, "I can save her!" But all that came out of his mouth were garbled words and sea water.

Again, someone tried to take the girl from his arms.

He pulled her away. This time the words were understand-able. "I can save her!" he shouted. "Stay back! Give her room!"

With people still assisting him, he made it out of the water. He laid the girl in the sand and knelt beside her.

Opening her mouth, he checked for any obstructions in her airway. All around him people appeared with gas lanterns and flashlights, all of them shining down on the girl. Her face was turning blue.

Tilting the girl's head back, Travis pinched her nose. He placed his mouth against hers and puffed short breaths into her. He did this while checking the girl's abdomen to see if the air was having any effect. The little girl's belly rose and fell with each puff.

But she didn't breathe, and she didn't stir.

A portion of the crowd parted as firemen arrived on the scene. The firemen observed for a while, saw that Travis knew what he was doing, and let him continue.

The girl's mother was on her knees near the girl's head. Her husband stood behind her, his hands on her shoulders. The mother was praying aloud.

"Dear God, save my little Jori! Don't let her die, dear God, don't let her die!"

So Travis had heard her name wrong. Between puffs he began to use it himself.

"You can do it, Jori! Come on! You can do it!"

She'd been underwater a long time. There was no sign of life in her as she lay motionless in the sand.

"Come on, Jori!" Travis shouted.

The church youth group stood among the others watching. Travis could hear the voice of the big-eared guitar player mutter-ing something. Probably a prayer. Travis needed all of those he could get.

He bent over and puffed again.

There was a stirring. A gurgling sound came from the girl's throat followed by a geyser of water that spilled down her cheeks.

Travis turned the girl on her side so she wouldn't choke. More water came out. She coughed and took a raspy gulp of air. Coughed again. Then another breath. The little girl started crying. Color returned to her cheeks.

A cheer went up all around Travis. He slumped to a sitting position while a multitude of hands slapped him on the back.

The firemen moved in. A couple of policemen were close behind. A gurney appeared as they prepared the girl for transport to a hospital.

"Good work, son," one of the firemen said, stepping between Travis and the little girl.

Travis barely had enough strength left to acknowledge him.

The beach party was over. The kids and the sponsors had all gone home, all of them anxious to tell their parents about the night's drama and the church's new hero.

As little Jori was being taken away, her parents heaped a thousand thank-yous upon Travis. The girl's brothers looked at him like he was Superman.

Travis lagged behind at the request of the police. They needed his statement for their report.

"I understand you're a lifeguard," the police officer said.

"Yes, sir."

The officer wrote on his pad. "Lucky you were here."

"Yes, sir."

At the officer's request Travis described the incident while the policeman took down everything he said, interrupting occasionally to ask clarifying questions. When the policeman was satisfied, he flipped closed the cover on his pad.

"That should do it," he said. "If by any chance there are any more questions, I assume I can reach you through the lifeguard station."

"No, sir. This is my last night in San Diego."

"Last night?"

"I've been drafted. I report for duty tomorrow morning."

"Oh?" The officer opened his pad again and made an additional note. Flipping it closed again, he said, "Think you'll go to 'Nam?"

Travis shrugged. "A good possibility."

The officer slapped him on the shoulder. "Nothing to worry about," he said. "You have a good head on your shoulders. From everything I've heard tonight, you're one cool customer under pressure. You'll do all right."

"Thank you," Travis said. He only wished he were as confident about his future as the police officer.

3

Paige had spent all day Sunday in her bedroom, venturing out only for a bowl of soup shortly before noon. Pastor Lamar always preached ten or fifteen minutes past twelve. She could have waited longer since the church was having a potluck dinner in Travis's honor, but she didn't want to take the chance that for some reason one of them might come home between church and the potluck for something.

The afternoon dragged by at a torturous pace. Her parents and Travis didn't return home until after two o'clock. Paige stayed in her room with the door closed. No one came knocking, which was fine with her. She listened to records, flipped through her art books, filed and polished her nails, and second-guessed herself.

Would it have been so wrong to attend the church service? What a silly thing to take a stand on. What had her protest accomplished? Nothing was changed because of it, only that now her parents hated her. And Travis—did he hate her, too? She'd told herself she was doing this for him as much as anyone. Did he realize that?

Come morning he would be gone. Paige knew she had to talk to him before he left. She had to make him understand why she did what she did.

But as the day passed, the possibility of talking privately with Travis looked increasingly unlikely. He had breezed in and out only long enough to grab his swim trunks and a towel before heading to the beach, or so she gathered from the muffled conversations through her closed bedroom door.

The thought of a youth beach party prompted memories of the days she was in high school. She thought of Keith Rawlins and smiled. It had been a long time since she'd thought of him. It was hard for her to imagine he was in Vietnam.

The thought sobered her. Vietnam. Keith could very well be dead. An image of Keith lying facedown in an Asian rice paddy brought tears to her eyes. Though she no longer had romantic feelings for him, she had fond memories. Besides, no one deserved such a fate. Not Keith and certainly not Travis.

It's a well-established fact: War kills young men.

Allen West, the leader of the student movement at UCRD, had shouted those words during his rally speech. Paige remembered the moment with satisfaction. Thousands of protesters had packed the student square. It had been their most successful demonstration to date. When Allen said those words, the entire square erupted in pandemonium. It was a powerful moment.

As always, Allen reveled in the adulation. Only it wasn't his words he was speaking. Not many people knew it, but Allen was only the mouthpiece at the demonstrations; Del Gilroy was the creative genius behind them.

Paige wished Del were here with her now. He would know what to do. Several times today she'd wished she could talk to him, but he was in San Francisco and she didn't know how to reach him.

Another of Del's quotes came to mind.

Unless our combined voices force change, they are nothing but noisy gongs that fade in the night.

What had her private little protest accomplished today? Nothing. Travis was still going off to war. She was nothing more than a noisy gong.

Paige paced back and forth in her room. "This is one voice that's not going to fade in the night," she muttered.

※

Headlights flashed across her bedroom curtains. Paige peeked out the window. It was Travis. Paige looked at the clock beside the bed. It was 9:21.

She gave him time to come into the house. Placing her hand on the bedroom doorknob she paused to take a deep breath. Then, she opened the door and headed purposefully down the hallway.

She found her younger brother seated at the kitchen table. A half-eaten hamburger, fries, two tacos, and a chocolate shake were arrayed in front of him. An empty, white Jack-in-the-Box bag lay nearby.

"Hey, howzit going?" Travis greeted her between chews.

Paige shrugged sheepishly. "Rough day," she admitted. Pulling out the chair next to him, she sat down.

He grinned. "Yeah, you stirred things up pretty good this morning. Fry?"

He held the small white bag of french fries toward her. Paige never would have told her brother this to his face, but she was struck by his good looks. Strong. Intelligent. Sensitive. All the more reason to do what she was doing.

"Thanks." She took one of the fries and bit the end. "Is this your hero's dinner?"

Travis's face reddened. "You heard."

"Mom told me," Paige said. "Mrs. Truitt called about an hour ago."

Travis nodded. He took a huge bite out of the hamburger.

Paige smiled. "I take it daring rescues make a person hungry."
Her brother shrugged. "Where's Mom and Dad?" Travis asked.

"Mother's in bed. She has one of her headaches. Dad was called into work, something about missing negatives."

Travis chewed and nodded, nodded and chewed. He seemed preoccupied, which wasn't surprising considering what had happened tonight combined with what was about to happen to him tomorrow.

"Can you talk about it?" Paige asked.

"The rescue?" He'd said it as if it were too boring to relate.

"Of course, the rescue!"

In a very monotone voice, Travis narrated matter-of-factly how he noticed something was wrong, charged into the water, found the little girl, and gave her mouth-to-mouth resuscitation.

"Just another day in the life of a superhero," Paige deadpanned.

Travis smiled. He knew she was poking fun at him. "That's what I do for a living." He took another bite, then corrected himself. "Did. That's what I did for a living."

He offered her another fry. She took it. "Have you and Mom talked?" he asked.

"About this morning?"

Travis nodded.

Paige lowered her eyes. "A little. Her headache was pretty bad."

Allegra Morgan was subject to migraines. When she was younger, in keeping with her fighting spirit, she would refuse to give in to them. As she grew older she learned that it was a battle she couldn't win. She found that if she succumbed to them early and went straight to bed, they didn't last nearly as long.

"What did Mom say?" Travis asked.

It was Paige's turn to shrug. "She said she was disappointed. That despite my political misgivings I should have been there for you. You know, support the family and all that."

Travis finished his hamburger and reached for a taco. He gave little indication that he was even aware he was at the epicenter of the family argument.

"Were you hurt that I stayed home this morning?" Paige asked directly.

Travis shook his head. It was an honest reaction. If he was covering up, she would have known it.

He said, "It bothered Dad, no end, though. Everyone kept asking him where you were."

"Who asked him?"

"Grandma and Grandpa."

Paige winced. "I forgot they were coming."

"All your friends. The pastor."

"The pastor? When?"

Travis chuckled. "During the middle of the service."

"No! Really?"

Travis nodded.

"Dad must be burning!"

Travis turned his head sideways to take a bite out of the taco. While he was chewing he said, "I'd lay low for a while if I were you."

That's exactly what Paige planned to do. There were only two more weeks before school started. For those two weeks she planned to become invisible.

But first there was something she had to do for her brother's own good. While she worked up her courage to begin, Travis finished one taco, took a couple of long draws on his chocolate shake, and reached for taco number two.

"How do you feel about going into the army tomorrow?" Paige asked.

"The way I see it, it's sort of like the measles," he replied. "It happens to some people. When it does, you can't avoid it."

"That's just the point!" Paige said, her passion rising. "You *can* avoid it!"

"It's not a big deal. Just two years. I'll serve my time, then get on with my life."

"That's assuming you still have a life! What if you lose an arm or a leg? Do they hire one-legged lifeguards?"

"Nothing will happen to me."

"How can you be so sure?"

"I can't. But I'm not going to drive myself crazy worrying about all the things that might happen." The killing vision came to mind. He'd never told anyone about it. He shoved it deep into the closet of his mind. He wasn't going to tell Paige about it now.

"What if I told you that you didn't have to go?"

Travis laughed. "Are you tight with President Johnson or something?"

"No. But there are alternatives to going."

Travis nodded philosophically. "All right, I'll hold my foot steady and you shoot it."

"I'm not joking."

"I think you are."

The passion within her was hot and rising. What kind of a country raised its young men to be so flippant about guns, and shooting, and war?

Paige persisted. "I know some guys at UCRD," she said. "They can get you to Canada."

"Canada?"

"Just get up tomorrow morning like you're going to the induction center. Instead, go to UCRD. Baylor Hall. Ask for Jim Green. Tell him who you are. He can see that you get to Canada."

Travis stared at his sister in disbelief. "You're suggesting that I run for it?"

"I'm serious about this."

"But I could never come home!"

"But you'd be alive!"

Travis had stopped eating. He was considering it. She could see it in his eyes!

"No," he said. "I couldn't do it." He slurped his shake.

"Why? Because of Dad?"

Travis thought before answering. "Yes, because of Dad. And Mom, too."

"But they don't understand what's happening over there! This isn't our war!"

"It *is* our war," Travis replied. "It's our war because America has made a commitment to halt communism. And it's my war because I'm an American. When our country set out to stop Hitler, Dad did his part. And Mom did her part for France. How can I do any less?"

The back door to the kitchen swung open. Their father walked in. Everything about him indicated he was in a foul mood. His tie was pulled loose, his dress shirt was wrinkled, his coat was draped carelessly over one arm, his hair was mussed, his eyes red, and his face was a dark scowl.

Paige's timing couldn't have been more ill-advised. Coming up the back walkway, Nat had heard, "Hitler ... Dad ... Mom ... France ... how can I do any less?"

"What are you trying to do now?" he thundered. His opening fuselage was leveled directly at Paige.

"Travis and I were just talking," Paige said.

"Just talking?" he challenged her. "Or just trying to brainwash your little brother?"

Paige stood to better fend against his attacking posture. "If there has been any brainwashing done around here, it's been done by you!" she shouted. "You've raised your only son to believe 'My country, right or wrong.' And it's going to get him killed."

Nat tossed his coat onto the table, knocking the fast food bag and empty wrappers to the floor.

"There are some things in this world worth fighting for!" he yelled. "And I'll not stand by while you try to turn my son into some kind of coward or traitor." He turned to Travis. "What has she been telling you?"

Travis took a conciliatory tone. "Dad, calm down. We were just talking. Nothing has changed. I'm still joining the army tomorrow."

Nat's hardened features softened slightly, indicating a measure of relief. But it was reserved only for Travis. When he looked at Paige, everything about him hardened again. With a voice that could crush granite, he said to her, "I want you out of my house."

The blow staggered her. She was too stunned to reply.

Travis interceded, "Dad, I told you. Nothing has changed. We were just talking."

But Nat wasn't listening. His eyes fixed steadily on Paige, he swept up his coat from the table and said, "Tomorrow. By noon. I want you out!"

Travis stood. "Dad, you're overreacting!"

"I'll not have a communist sympathizer under this roof! Tomorrow. Noon!"

The rage inside Paige built until she thought she'd explode. She knew better than to say anything, but she couldn't help it. The words blurted out before she could stop them.

"John Wayne would be proud of you," she said. "Shoot first, think about the consequences later. Well, you probably just signed your own son's death warrant."

The verbal blow registered. It took Nat a moment to recover. When he did, he glared at Paige with a look that could kill. But he said nothing. As quickly as he appeared, he disappeared into the back of the house.

For a long moment there was only silence.

"Whew!" Travis said, plopping back into the kitchen chair. "I always thought you were the smart one."

"I know," Paige said, already lamenting her retort. As her anger was subsiding, it was replaced with tears.

"What are you going to do?" Travis asked.

"What can I do? I'll pack up and get out."

"You could talk to Mom in the morning."

Paige wiped tears away. She shook her head. "No, it's probably better this way."

"Where will you go?"

Paige shrugged. "Don't know yet."

"You could always come with me and join the army."

Paige looked at her brother. It was just like Travis to say something like that. He punctuated it with a silly grin. Paige started laughing and crying at the same time, which only made both of them laugh harder.

She placed her arms around her brother.

"Take care of yourself," she said. "Don't do anything stupid, like try to be a hero or something."

"Don't worry about me," he said. "I'll come back."

She held him tight. It was the first time she could ever remember hugging her brother. And her intuition told her that it would be the last time, too.

4

Paige pressed herself against the passenger door. She couldn't get away from The Suit soon enough.

The man behind the wheel had given her his name and occupation when she climbed into the aging Cadillac, but at the time she'd been too distracted to remember it. Her thoughts had been diverted by Travis and his ridiculous "my country, right or wrong" philosophy, her father's anger the night before, and his ultimatum.

He threw me out of the house!

She still couldn't believe it. She'd fully expected him to come to her room later that night, or early this morning, and rescind the order. An apology was expecting too much from him. The more she thought about it, the more she expected him at least to talk to her through her door and say something like, "Well, since classes start in two weeks, you can stay until then."

But he never came. Neither did her mother.

It wasn't as though this was the first time he'd blown his stack over their political differences. He'd shouted things like, "I can't believe a child of mine would ever spout such stupid liberal nonsense!" and "As long as you're under my roof …" or "As long as I'm the one paying for your education.…"

This time was different. This time there had been no laments, no threats, just the order to get out.

Come morning she went to the kitchen. Her father was there. He didn't speak to her. He didn't look at her. He refused even to acknowledge her presence.

Well, if that's the way he wants it, she'd concluded, *that's the way it will be.* She returned to her bedroom, packed a suitcase and her backpack, and left the house.

Thankfully, she'd encountered no one in the hallway or living room when she walked out. Travis had already gone. She'd heard him leave before the sun was up. And her parents were some-where in the back of the house, which was fine with her. She didn't even want to see her father again.

Mother was a different story. She'd made no apparent effort to talk to Paige. That was troubling. Maybe her father forbade her to intervene. Just as well. Saying good-bye to her would only make leaving more difficult.

Paige hauled her suitcase and backpack down to where La Jolla Shores Drive intersected Ardath Road. She'd considered hitching a ride from there. The traffic flowed heavily toward the interstate, making it a good place to catch a ride. That is, unless your name was Morgan and your old man had just thrown you out of the house. In that case, it was too conspicuous. Too many people she knew passed through that intersection every morning. Many of them from church. Catching a ride with them would raise embarrassing questions, such as:

"School doesn't start for two more weeks, does it?"

"Why aren't your parents driving you back to school?"

"Does your mother know you're hitchhiking?"

Then, being good church members, they would feel obliged to report back to her parents that they had given her a ride, which would cause them even more embarrassment. She cared little whether her father was spared any embarrassment, but she saw no reason why her mother should suffer on his account.

So Paige walked the lengthy Ardath Road ravine uphill to Interstate 5 where she hitched a ride on the northbound ramp. That's where The Suit picked her up.

Ordinarily she wouldn't have climbed into his car. The moment she opened the door she felt bad vibes. But a highway patrolman had just passed by heading south on the freeway. He'd given her a good, long look and was undoubtedly circling back to hassle her. So, leaving her better judgment on the freeway ramp, Paige tossed her belongings into the back seat and climbed into the car.

The Suit reclined leisurely against his door with one hand on the steering wheel and the other stretched across the back of the seat. His wheel hand sported a wedding band that he tapped against the steering wheel as he drove. The instant Paige's door slammed, he stomped on the accelerator and the car lurched forward with more sound than power. There was something wrong with the car, as it needed the entire downward slope of the entrance ramp to reach freeway speed.

The Suit's coat hung open, exposing a protruding gut that rubbed the bottom of the steering wheel. A dirty horizontal line marked his white shirt where the steering wheel rubbed.

Paige guessed The Suit was some kind of salesman. Her backpack had landed upon stacks of blank invoices, and her suitcase tipped into a box of some kind of record books. There were other boxes that were closed. She assumed these carried his product.

"Looks like this is your lucky day, little lady!" the man shouted over the loud engine. His voice was oily and his teeth yellow. As he spoke, his gaze moved deliberately from her eyes to her chest.

Paige did her best to ignore his rude stare. "How far north are you going?" she asked.

"LA. You?"

"UC, Rancho Diego."

"Ah! A coed!" The man seemed pleased.

Paige shifted uncomfortably in her seat, closer to the door. The armrest had a sticky feeling to it. From the looks of it, so did the dashboard. Bits of hair and fuzz were stuck to it. Below, a protruding ashtray overflowed with cigarette butts.

The Suit reached into his front pocket. He pulled out a pack of cigarettes and offered Paige one.

"No thanks," Paige said.

"Sure?" The pack remained extended toward her.

"I don't smoke," Paige said.

He gave her a look of disbelief.

"I don't!" she insisted.

"All coeds smoke."

"I don't."

"You probably prefer something smoother. Sweeter. A reefer, maybe? I know a place where we could—"

Paige shook her head. "No thanks."

"Hey! Relax! I'm no narc. I may look older, but there's no generation gap here, baby. I'm cool. And I know what goes on at those university frat houses. Hey, I'm with ya! I'm all for free love!"

"All I want is a ride to the campus," Paige said.

"No sweat. Just tryin' to be friendly." The Suit lit his cigarette. He inhaled deeply and stole another glance at Paige's chest.

This wasn't the first time Paige had hitched a ride from The Suit. Not this one in particular, but others like him. They were pretty much the same. Middle-aged. Married. Usually salesmen, sometimes a businessman or a manager of a small company. Without exception they tried to impress her with how hip they were. Their sentences were laced with words like *"groovy," "rap,"* and *"mellow."* Pop phrases like *"far out"* and *"blows my mind"* fell generously from their lips. Some of the worst ones wore clothes with psychedelic colors that bulged in all the wrong places. The very worst of them wore cheap rugs to cover their middle-aged baldness.

In return for a ride, some of them would brazenly hit her up for drugs or sex. Others, like this one, would sneak glances at her chest when they thought she wasn't looking. It was a game to them, the goal of which seemed to be to ascertain if she was wearing a bra. They were usually harmless, lookers only. Paige wondered what this guy's wife and children would think if they knew he acted like this on the road.

She turned her attention to the passing scenery. The Carlsbad exit was fast approaching. Open fields lay beyond. There was a restaurant. A car dealership. An energy plant on the other side of the road. It was much like this the entire stretch between San Diego and LA. Mostly scrub brush interrupted by small cities, an occasional lagoon, or a glimpse of the ocean here and there.

There were those who predicted that this cement artery would one day be an unending procession of businesses and industry. She hoped not.

There was a flower farm around here somewhere. In the spring you couldn't miss it. Brilliant rows of yellow and red and orange flowers rose and fell with the terrain. Paige occupied herself by looking for it.

She remembered the first time she caught sight of the colorful array. She gasped audibly. Her family was traveling up north to see some relative. When her mother heard her gasp, then learned what had prompted it, she insisted they stop. Paige described each row to her mother. Her mother called the place God's perfume factory. To Paige it was an enormous magic carpet.

When it was clear they had gone past the flower field without any sign of them, Paige concluded it was too late in the year for flowers to bloom. Pity. She could use a little magic in her life right about now. Instead, there was the odor of The Suit's incessant smoking.

Thoughts of the flower field made Paige think of her mother. Paige wondered how she had reacted to her daughter's sudden departure. When had she found out? Paige couldn't bring herself to believe that her mother knew about her leaving and yet made no effort to say good-bye. It would be just like her father not to say anything to her until it was …

Paige felt her blouse slowly being pulled off her shoulder. She grabbed it.

"Hey!"

The Suit was pinching the cloth between his fingers, leering at her with his yellow smile.

"Come on, honey!" he oozed. His face was twisted in a wicked grin. "You know you like it. You think I haven't read about all them wild *orgies* on them college campuses?" He pronounced orgies with a hard "g" sound.

"I don't care what you've read," Paige said. "Keep your hands to yourself!"

"Listen, sweet thang, I'm harmless enough. Just think of me as your sugar daddy. Treat me right and I'll take real good care of you."

The Suit was inching toward her, alternately glancing at the road and her chest. He tugged harder on the sleeve of her blouse. Paige checked the speedometer. They were going 70 miles per hour. This guy was crazy! What did he expect to do while traveling at this speed?

She slapped his hand away. "Pull over and let me out!"

"Just give me a little peek and I promise I'll be good."

"Pull over, right now!"

Paige backed as far against the door as she could. On the other side of the metal barrier the pavement was a blur.

"You're not going anywhere," said The Suit. "It's just you and me, babe."

Paige looked outside the car windows for help. Someone to signal. To her horror, traffic was light. Where is a cop when you need one? She considered grabbing the wheel; maybe she could force him to the side of the road. Too risky. She glanced at the keys in the ignition and wondered what would happen to a car that was switched off while traveling at 70 miles per hour.

"Look, honey, what's the problem here? Hey, I admit I'm no Sean Connery, but I know how to show a woman a good time."

"Let me out!" Paige shouted.

He winced and recoiled a bit. The volume seemed to hurt him. She'd found a weapon!

At the top of her lungs, she shouted, "Let me out! Let me out! Let me out! Let me out! Let me out! Let me out! Let me out!"

The Suit pulled back, covering his right ear with his free hand. Out of necessity he kept his left hand on the steering wheel, leaving his other ear exposed.

Paige continued her ear-shattering litany: "Let me out! Let me out! Let me out! Let me out! Let me out! Let me out! Let me out!"

By now The Suit was cringing. His eyes winced back the pain. "All right! All right!" he shouted back at her.

Paige stopped shouting but kept a wary eye on him. She remained ready to loose another barrage if needed.

"That hurt!" The Suit whined. "I have sensitive ears."

Paige felt no sympathy, nor did she express any.

"Hey, I'm sorry," said The Suit. "I didn't mean anything by it. I just thought the two of us could have a little fun, that's all."

Paige wasn't appeased. "Let me out at the next exit," she said.

"Look, no harm done, OK?" he replied. "I'll drop you off at the university and that'll be that."

Paige studied him. He seemed contrite. Besides, who knew how long it would take for her to hitch another ride? And she could always start screaming again if he made any more advances.

"All right," she said, cautiously.

The Suit smiled a conciliatory yellow smile. "Fine," he said. Then as Paige turned away, out of the corner of her eye she caught him stealing another peek at her chest.

UNIVERSITY OF CALIFORNIA,

RANCHO DIEGO

NEXT EXIT

The familiar green freeway sign was a welcome sight. Thirty minutes had passed since the shouting incident, and The Suit had behaved himself just like he'd promised.

Dutifully, he steered the old, creaking Cadillac onto the inclining freeway exit ramp to an intersection. A McDonald's restaurant claimed the near corner of the intersection, while a self-serve economy gas station was situated on the far corner. Were they to turn right or proceed straight ahead they would pass a line of small businesses before entering the town and suburbs of Rancho Diego.

Instead, The Suit turned left and crossed the freeway overpass that led directly onto the university grounds. They passed a vacant white guard shack, the first indication that the campus was closed for summer break. In the distance multistoried buildings were nestled amongst eucalyptus trees and a variety of evergreens. Beyond that a cool ocean breeze rushed to greet them.

The UCRD campus was the most beautiful and most photographed of all the University of California campuses. It perched on a spacious bluff overlooking the Pacific Ocean. Large floor-to-ceiling picture windows in the library provided a stunning panorama of coastline and surf. And if that wasn't distracting enough for students, a half-dozen whitewashed pavilions lined the edge of the hundred-foot-high bluff with benches and tables for outdoor study. An unmarked rutted dirt trail snaked down the side of the bluff to a private cove where students surfed and sunbathed during the spring and summer months.

Large academic structures that were built to accommodate thousands of students and faculty stood hauntingly silent and empty. Here and there solitary wanderers could be seen; otherwise the campus was deserted. To reach the dorms and student apartments, a person had to drive or walk through the campus and past the sports and military complexes to a hilly expanse nearly half a mile away.

Paige had given The Suit verbal directions how to get there. The Suit, however, took a wrong turn. He veered left down a steep and narrow roadway that led to an auxiliary parking lot used mainly by commuter students.

"What are you doing?" Paige said.

"I'm following your directions," said The Suit.

"No you're not. I told you to stay right."

"You said left."

"I did not! I distinctly said right."

The Suit shook his head in bewilderment. "I could have sworn you said left. Sorry, my fault. Where does this lead?"

"To a parking lot."

"Is there a place where we can turn around and head back up the hill?"

Paige didn't answer right away. She was trying to evaluate the driver's intentions.

"Is there a place to turn around?" The Suit asked again, looking directly at her.

"I suppose," Paige replied.

The car reached the base of the decline, and a wide expanse of black macadam stretched before them marked with faded white parking lines. Wooden posts as thick as telephone poles lined the western ridge. Heavy chains stretched between the poles to complete the barrier that protected cars from going over the side of the cliff.

The Suit steered wide, giving the indication he would circle around and head back up the way they had just come. Then, without warning, halfway around the circle he pulled into a parking place, switched off the engine, and pocketed the keys in one smooth movement.

Paige didn't demand an explanation. None was needed. It was clear he'd planned this. Just beyond the nose of the car and the chain barrier the earth gave way to a precipitous slope that ended against a rocky shoreline. There were no other cars in the isolated lot. Having walked the roadway above, she knew that anyone looking down at them would see only the top and hood and trunk of an aging Cadillac. The only way anyone would see them would be if they came up the beach trail at the far end of the lot or if another car drove down into the lot. Considering that the campus was closed, either event seemed unlikely. Her only chance was to get out of the car.

She reached for the door handle. It worked easily. Too easily. The latch didn't engage.

"I've been meaning to get that fixed," said the grinning suit as he scooted toward her.

The window! If she could get it open maybe she could squeeze out. She searched for the knob. There was none. Only a metal tab. The windows were electric and the engine was turned off.

"It's time to pay up for the ride," said The Suit.

Paige's back was against the door. She tried to swing her legs up, to get them between her and The Suit.

Too late. He was already close to her and easily pushed them aside. Steadying himself with one hand on the sticky dashboard, he leaned toward her. There was a hungry look on his face, much like she imagined a starving man would gaze at a steak. Only his gaze rested on her chest while a clawed hand reached for her blouse.

If she couldn't escape, she might be able to fight him off, but for how long? The only thing left for her to do was to scream. It wouldn't summon help; they were too far distant from anything. Besides, the pounding of the surf against the base of the cliff drowned out most sounds. The scream was her only weapon. It had backed him off once. Maybe it would work again.

She took a deep breath and let loose with all her strength. For a split second it worked. It startled him. Hurt him.

Wham!

The Suit's open hand slapped her head against the window glass with such force that she would be surprised if the glass didn't crack.

The double blow—to her mouth and the resulting hit against the window—choked off the scream.

"Don't ever do that again!" The Suit shouted. "The next one will be even harder!"

Paige could feel her lip swelling. When her tongue explored the area, she tasted blood.

The blow had dazed her. She was vaguely aware that The Suit was searching for something under the seat. She was conscious enough to care what he was doing, but not enough to do anything about it.

The next thing she knew he was stuffing something into her mouth. A rag. It was stained black and smelled of oil. Now she tasted the black on her tongue with bits of dirt and straw and gravel. The Suit rammed the rag deeper into her mouth until she gagged.

Her head was pounding. The toxic odor of the oily rag made her want to wretch.

The Suit had positioned his body in such a way so as to pin down her legs. With one hand he held her shoulder against the door. His other hand was coming at her again.

She screamed and squirmed.

The sound was muffled. Useless. He had position on her. Her struggling was equally useless.

Still, The Suit apparently felt the need to rap her in the mouth a second time. The blow made her bite down hard on the rag. She swallowed more of its grime.

Paige began to cry.

The Suit grabbed the top of her blouse. It was the slip-over type without buttons or zippers, gathered at the neckline with elastic. He was stretching the elastic down over her shoulder.

Suddenly, the door gave way behind Paige. It had opened so unexpectedly that she fell out of the car from the waist up. Had her legs not been pinned down, she would have tumbled out of the car completely.

The opening door took The Suit by surprise too. His face plopped against Paige's stomach.

Whack! Whack! Whack!

Unsure exactly what was going on, to the sound of some kind of whacking and The Suit's cries, Paige managed to pull the soiled cloth from her mouth. Everything was upside down to her. The bright sky and sunlight assaulted her face, blinding her. However, she was aware that someone was standing over her with arms flailing. One of them held some kind of weapon that made a dull thud as it repeatedly hit The Suit on the head.

"Get off of her! Get off! Now! Get off!"

The voice was feminine. The screams were male—The Suit.

"Off! Off! Get off!"

Long blonde hair flashed in the sunlight with each blow.

Pushing off of Paige, The Suit retreated back to the driver's side of the car. The moment Paige's legs were freed, she began to slip unceremoniously off the front seat and onto the parking lot. Almost oblivious to her presence, her rescuer followed The Suit into the car, not letting up on him for a moment.

Paige pulled herself into a sitting position. It was then that she recognized her rescuer. She knew the girl only as Terri, a student at the university.

Terri was thin to the point of anorexic. She was wearing a two-piece bathing suit. A towel lay nearby on the macadam. At the moment she was wearing only one sandal. She was using the other to pummel The Suit.

"Back off!" yelped The Suit. "Back off! Ow! Stop that!"

But Terri had no intention of backing off. She had crawled halfway into the car and was still clobbering Paige's assailant with her shoe like she would a cockroach.

Paige got to her feet. Her head was still swimming in pain; her vision was blurred. It was as though she were looking at things underwater. But what she saw made her feel good.

The Suit was reaching into his pocket for his keys with one hand while trying to protect himself from sandal blows with the other. He managed to pull the keys from his pocket. But no sooner had they emerged than Terri whacked the back of his hand. He let loose a howl. The keys dropped to the front seat.

Deftly, Terri snatched them up and backed out of the car.

The Suit opened his door and climbed out, rubbing his hand. Speaking across the top of the car, he said, "Hey! Come on! Give me the keys!"

Terri looked at Paige. "Are you all right, Paige?" she asked.

Paige grinned in spite of her pain. "Thanks to you."

The Suit started to make his way around the front of the car.

Terri stepped to the edge of the pavement and cocked her arm, threatening to throw the keys over the side of the cliff.

The Suit froze. "Hey! Don't even joke about that! I have an important meeting at five o'clock!"

"Paige, is there anything in the car belonging to you?" Terri asked.

Paige looked at Terri with a mixture of amusement and admiration. She'd always thought of the girl as a stereotypical dumb blonde. Yet, here she was in complete control of the situation.

Climbing into the Cadillac, Paige retrieved her suitcase and backpack. She set them down a good distance from the car.

"All right," said The Suit. "She's got her stuff. Now let me have my keys!"

"Next time you give a girl a ride, you treat her like a lady, understood?"

"You're nuts!" shouted The Suit.

Terri threatened to toss the keys.

"All right!" shouted The Suit.

"All right what?"

"Next time I give a babe a ride I'll treat her like a lady!" The Suit was perspiring heavily.

"Promise!"

The Suit cursed. "Will you just give me the keys!"

"Not until you promise."

"I promise!" shouted The Suit.

Terri gave him a hard stare. Then, she whirled the keys over the cliff as far as she could throw them. The Suit stared in horror as he watched his jangling keys tumble all the way down into the surf.

"We'd better get out of here," Terri whispered to Paige.

Terri slipped her sandal on and grabbed her towel. Paige slung her backpack over one shoulder and grabbed her suitcase. They half-walked, half-ran across the parking lot.

Paige looked over her shoulder. The Suit wasn't following. Apparently he'd had enough of Terri for one day.

"Why did you throw the keys over the cliff?" Paige asked.

Terri grinned. "I thought he needed a little time to think about what he tried to do to you."

5

With each step Paige's knees grew increasingly weak. It wasn't the climb up the hill from the lower parking lot that was causing them to fail. Her emotions were catching up with her. An unsteady hand reached up and touched her lip. It was swollen, tender, and sticky. She pulled her finger away. The tip was dotted with blood.

"Let me take a look at that," Terri said.

Stopping in the middle of the deserted campus street, Paige turned her face toward the bikini-clad girl. Terri was shorter than Paige; she had to stand on her toes to examine the lip. Paige helped her by bending down slightly.

"It's split," Terri said. "Hurts like the dickens, doesn't it?" The girl's fingers hovered over the lip during the examination, but didn't touch it. "How's the back of your head?"

Paige felt her head and winced. There was a definite knot.

"Come over here." Terri led Paige to a tree beside the road where there was a curved cement bench sitting in the shade. Terri sat Paige on the bench and walked behind her to get a better look at the injury.

Paige felt hesitant fingers pulling aside hair from around the bump. A finger touched it.

"Ow!"

"Yep, it's a bump alright. Not too bad. I've seen worse." Terri chuckled, "I've *had* worse."

She walked around the bench and faced Paige.

"Are you dizzy?"

Paige took stock of her equilibrium. She felt dazed—was that different from dizzy?—and tired.

"I think I'll just sit here awhile," Paige said. "Don't let me keep you, Terri. You've been terrific."

Terri plopped down on the bench beside her. "I'm in no hurry," she said.

Paige smiled weakly, grateful for the company. She realized that fatigue was only partially responsible for her weariness. The incident had left her feeling vulnerable. Scared. It was her hands that betrayed her. They were trembling. And not only because of The Suit.

"Hitchhiking, right?"

"Huh?"

Terri was leaning forward with her hands on the edge of the cool cement bench. Her shoulders were hunched. She spoke with her head lowered, as though she were addressing her feet.

"Hitchhiking. You were hitchhiking," she repeated. "I've been there." Nodding toward the lower parking lot, she added, "I recognize the type."

Terri's admission to hitchhiking didn't surprise Paige. She had frequently seen Terri riding around campus in a variety of vehicles—on the backs of motorcycles, in the beds of pick-up trucks, and in cars of all conditions, sizes, colors, and shapes. The girl got around.

Terri said, "You know you're in trouble when they start staring at your breasts."

Paige glanced over at her. The girl had been there, just as

she'd said. "This guy would sneak peeks at me when he thought I wasn't looking," Paige said.

"Ooo! They're the worst," Terri exclaimed. "Just when you've concluded the guy gets his kicks by copping peeks, he pounces."

Looking back on it now, Paige realized The Suit probably had the whole thing planned. He seemed delighted to learn she was a coed, talked her into staying in the car all the way to the campus, then pretended he didn't know his way around the place. The Suit probably knew all about the isolated lower parking lot. Paige felt so dumb.

"If it hadn't been for you," she said, "The Suit would have been all over me."

Terri laughed. "The Suit? That's what you call him? I like it!" She said it again as though it was fun to say. "The Suit. It fits!"

Paige laughed and winced. Laughing made her head pound.

"I hitched a ride from a guy just like that about a month ago," Terri said. "*My Suit* was from Cleveland, and he gave me a black eye."

"Really?" Paige stared at Terri's eyes. Sure enough, she saw a slight discoloration beneath the girl's left eye. "Had to beat that one off with my sandal too. That's why I like sandals. They slip off easily. And I always get the ones with hard heels. The harder, the better."

"Well, I for one am glad you and your sandals came along when you did," Paige said. "And first chance I get, I'm going shopping for my own pair of sandals. Do they make sandals with spiked heels?"

Terri laughed. "I just happened to be down at the beach getting a little sun. Nothing else to do around here with everything closed down. This place is dead!"

From the deep brown of Terri's skin, Paige guessed this had been a daily activity for most of the summer. Her face was so deeply bronzed that it exaggerated the whiteness of her eyes and teeth.

Terri continued, "At first, when I saw the car rocking back and forth, I thought that you were, well, you know."

Paige knew. She felt her cheeks color.

"Then I thought I heard a scream, but I wasn't sure. It was a real dilemma. I certainly didn't want to intrude or run for help if you were doing what I thought you might be doing."

Paige was amazed at how casually the girl spoke about it. Anybody passing by might have thought The Suit and she were eating ice-cream cones in the car.

"But then it bothered me to think someone might be in trouble. And I didn't want to stand by and do nothing if someone needed help. I mean, what if I was too late?"

Too late. Paige shuddered at the idea.

"Then I heard your head slam against the window and I knew you weren't exactly cooperating with this guy."

The mention of the blow seemed to aggravate the pain. Moreover, scenes of what happened inside the Cadillac flashed in her mind. They were graphically vivid.

Then it dawned on her. She had almost been raped! Thrown out of her house and raped all in one day! It was all she could do to keep back a rising tide of emotion. Pushing tears and images aside, she asked, "Are the dorms open yet?"

Terri shook her head. "Not for another week. That's right. You live in the dorms, don't you?"

The last thing Paige wanted to do right now was relive her fight with her father. "By saying the dorms aren't open, you mean they're not assigning rooms until then, right? People still live there, don't they? Summer students? Resident assistants?"

Terri's head shook side to side. "They're locked up tight. The university's fumigating."

"All of them?"

"Yep."

Paige could hold back her emotions no longer. Two pioneering tears tracked their way down her cheeks. Once the trails were blazed, a pair of steady streams followed. Could the day get any worse?

Terri's eyes brimmed with sympathy. "Where are you coming from?" she asked.

"San Diego."

"No sweat. I'm sure we can find someone to give you a ride back home—"

"No," Paige said. "I can't go back. My old man ..."

A wave of heavy emotion cut short her sentence. It was one thing to admit to herself what had happened between her and her father. Telling someone else was entirely different. Somehow, the telling memorialized the event, made it part of history. After that, there was no going back. It could be told and retold, discussed and interpreted, but it could never be undone.

Paige inhaled deeply. It had to be done sometime. She said, "My old man kicked me out of the house."

Terri was clearly stunned. A thin smile creased her lips.

Paige was hurt that Terri found her pain amusing.

"Oh honey," Terri cooed, "I'm sorry. I didn't mean to make light of your getting kicked out. It's just that it took me by surprise. I mean, you're not the kind of girl who gets kicked out of the house. I mean, look at you. I've always thought of you as having it all together. You're a good student; I've seen your paintings displayed, you're talented; you have friends; you dress conservatively, you, you ... well, you're just not the type of person who gets kicked out of the house."

Paige dabbed her eyes. "Well, whether I'm the type or not, it happened. I came here hoping to live in the dorm. If nothing else, to sleep on someone's floor. Are your sure nobody's living in them?"

"Positive," Terri replied. The tone of her declaration rang with confidence.

Paige lifted her hands in a helpless gesture and let them fall limp in her lap.

"You can come stay with us," Terri offered.

"Us?"

"Yeah! You know, that old white two-story house on Shores Drive. There's plenty of room. In fact, if you want, you can stay in Del's room."

Paige's heart jumped at the mention of Del's name. "He went to San Francisco for the summer," she said.

"He's been back and forth," Terri said matter-of-factly. "Right now, he's away." She gazed at Paige questioningly. "Don't the two of you have a thing for each other?"

"Yeah," Paige said.

"Then it's settled!" Terri said. She popped up off the bench. "Come on. Let's go." She held out her hand to Paige. Once again the girl was coming to Paige's rescue.

Paige lifted her aching bones off the cement bench and took Terri's hand. At least one of her problems was solved. But then, in its own way, what she had just heard created new problems.

If Del had indeed been living in Rancho Diego, at least part of the summer, as Terri said, why hadn't he called her? He'd told her he would be living on the road and in the street all summer. And what would Del say when he returned to find her living in his room? Would he be pleased, or would he think she was trying to push him into something he wasn't ready for? And how would they handle the sleeping arrangements? By sharing his room, would Del also expect her to share his bed? Would he think that's what she wanted?

Paige's head hurt too much to think about these things right now. All she knew was that at the moment she needed a place to crash. She surrendered to the pull of her unlikely bikini-clad heroine down the tree-lined campus street to the house on Shores Drive.

The house on Shores Drive was a three-bedroom white clapboard two stories high. It served as the living quarters for about a dozen people. The exact number was difficult to ascertain due to the frequency with which its occupants came and went.

Originally, the house had been the single residence of an elderly couple who rented out the two upstairs bedrooms to college students. When the couple passed away within months of each other, their only son—a criminal lawyer living in Santa Barbara—allowed the entire house to be taken over by students. Whether this was by design or long-distance neglect, none of the current residents knew, or cared.

Not all the residents were students of the university. There were those who came and went while passing through town. Sometimes they stayed a day or two. They chipped in what they could for the food they ate, but most were simply looking for a place to crash for the night.

There were others who were former students who flunked out or were kicked out of the university for nonpayment of fees and, sometimes, for disciplinary reasons. Preferring the life of a university town over that of their hometowns, they stayed on, usually getting jobs as gas-station attendants, fast-food servers, or any other of a number of minimum-wage jobs in Rancho Diego.

There was a third group of residents who were neither former students nor hitchhikers. These were attracted to the campus—and the house on Shores Drive in particular—because the house had a reputation of being the headquarters for the radical student movement in Southern California. The two linchpins most often associated with this arm of the national movement were Allen West and Del Gilroy.

Paige's Del.

Wooden steps badly in need of repair led up to a spacious front porch. Nearly half of the entire right side of the third step was missing. During the school session this sometimes caused minor delays as residents were forced to take turns ascending and descending the one good side. Some threw caution to the wind and leaped up or down, whatever the case may be.

Terri stepped aside as two barefoot coeds wearing cutoffs and tie-dyed T-shirts bounced down the steps. They called her name in greeting as they passed. Terri checked the door to see if there were any more of them. There weren't, so she made her way up the steps. Paige followed, stepping cautiously on the third step.

To their right a couple lounged on a porch swing. The guy was tall with broad shoulders and big feet. His only attire was a pair of blue jeans worn through at both knees. Sitting slumped in the swing with his legs stretched out in a leisurely manner, he balanced an acoustical guitar on his bare belly. He plucked softly on its strings.

The girl next to him reclined the length of the swing with her head using his leg for a pillow. Her legs were propped on the armrest while her feet extended well past it. She had long straight hair that looked as though it had never seen a curl in its life. She wore a loose, flowing summer dress with an empire waistline. The sweeping folds of the dress hung over the edge of the swing and dusted the porch as they went back and forth and back and forth. The girl's attention was on a small wildflower that she twirled with her fingers. A few of the tiny petals had fallen onto her midriff.

The guitar player caught Paige's eye. He winked at her and flashed a grin that the big bad wolf would envy. Had he pulled a knife on her, Paige would have felt no less threatened. Terri didn't see his overture. Neither did the woman on the swing. Her eyes remained fixed on the flower.

Paige closed what little distance there was between her and Terri. She whispered, "Do you know that couple?"

Terri shook her head. "Never saw them before. Why?"

"No reason," Paige said, hurrying across the threshold. "Is it safe here?"

Terri responded with a quizzical glance. "Sure," she said. Stopping in the doorway, she turned to Paige. "The Suit wouldn't dare follow you here. Trust me. I know the type. By now, if he's fished his keys out of the surf, he's halfway to LA. He'll want to put as much distance between him and you as possible."

"Oh! You're talking about The Suit," Paige said.

"Of course, I'm talking about The Suit! Who else would I be talking about?"

"Oh, nobody," Paige said. She was embarrassed. She was overreacting and she knew it. "I was just … I mean, I'm still shaken up about the whole thing, that's all."

Terri smiled an understanding smile, then led Paige into the house.

The front door stood open. It was open when they approached it, and Terri made no attempt to close it after entering. Now that Paige thought about it, the two girls who passed through the portal gave no thought to the door. It seemed to be something of a symbol of the house's transient clientele.

Most striking to anyone entering the house was the huge American flag that covered the ceiling from corner to corner. It was tacked up in such a way it appeared to be billowing in the breeze. The room itself was spacious. Its walls were plastered with posters of rock concerts, rock groups, antiwar slogans, pro-drug messages, peace signs, movie stars, airline color photographs, and psychedelic art. The room's only furniture consisted of a well-worn couch that faced the fireplace. Overstuffed chairs closed off each end, making it an ideal gathering place for small groups. At the moment it was occupied by a single male who was draped sideways over one of the chairs. He was sleeping, his mouth open in a very unattractive way.

On the other side of the room a heavyset male lowered the arm of a portable stereo down onto the spinning disk. A moment of scratching sounds gave way to an explosion of guitars and drums as the Rolling Stones belted out their familiar complaint that they couldn't get any satisfaction. The stereo's speakers were stretched six feet to each side of the turntable, as far as they would reach. The heavyset male sat on the floor between them, his back turned to Terri and Paige.

In the corner another male was curled up on a sleeping bag. Like his counterpart on the chair, he seemed oblivious to the loud strained voices on the recording.

Ignoring the guys and the music, Terri casually motioned for Paige to follow her. There were two exits to the large room: One went to a kitchen, the other led to a hallway and stairs. Terri led Paige up the stairs.

As they ascended, they passed through a haze of cigarette and pot smoke. Upon reaching the second floor, they turned and walked the length of a walkway. At the end there was a bedroom door painted with a large, yellow peace sign. Terri swung it open and motioned for Paige to go inside.

"This is it," she said. "Del's room."

"You're not leaving me, are you?" Paige asked.

Terri's eyebrows slanted in sympathy. "I have to meet someone."

"Can't you stay for just a little while?" Paige's hands began to tremble again. She felt the fear rising inside her like the incoming tide. She hated feeling this way, like a foolish little girl scared to be away from her mommy. But hating it didn't make the fear go away.

"Sorry. I have to go," Terri said.

Paige pursed her lips in an attempt to hold in her emotions.

"I'll only be gone an hour," Terri said. "Maybe less. I promise to come back as soon as I can."

Paige nodded reluctantly.

This brought Terri's hand to Paige's cheek. It was gentle. Soothing. Warm. Tears of sympathy filled her eyes. "I know how you feel," she said. "And I hate doing this to you. But it's something I have to do."

Now it was Paige's turn to cry. "Forgive me. I'm normally not this emotional. I … I really don't know why I'm acting like such a baby. And you've been so kind to me already."

"I'll be back as soon as I can," Terri promised.

Paige forced herself to smile. She turned and entered Del's room alone.

The curtains were drawn. A soft shadow covered the room and its contents like a dark dusting of snow. There was a single bed with no bedclothes pushed against the wall to the right. The bedclothes had been tossed into the adjacent corner, pressed down in the center like a nest.

A heavily scarred chest of drawers was shoved against the wall on the left, a dusty frameless mirror perched on top. A veritable junk pile had accumulated at the base of the mirror—keys, pencils and pens, rubber bands, paper clips, socks, opened packs of gum, empty wrappers, a banana peel, the empty shells of sunflower seeds, a broken shoelace, sticks of unburned incense, spare change, and a wrinkled photograph of Del and Allen West standing side by side in some unknown park at an unknown gathering with an unknown band in the background. The two men were flashing the peace sign at the camera with their fingers.

The photo brought a smile to Paige's lips. Del and Allen were an unlikely pair. One tall and handsome, the striking image of a leader with an easy, charismatic smile; the other, short and wiry with a struggling beard, bowed legs, and a pained expression that served as a smile. Just from looking at them it was difficult to imagine that the two would have anything in common. Yet here they were, the leaders of the Rancho Diego student movement, a movement that was beginning to attract national attention.

Paige placed the photo back where she found it. She noticed a drawer missing from the chest. It lay upside down on the floor in the corner near the bedclothes, its contents spilling out around its edges. On one side of the inverted drawer there were stacks of periodicals: the *Los Angeles Free Press*, *Rolling Stone*, *Whole Earth Catalog*, and a variety of comic books, mostly *Superman* and the *Fantastic Four*. On the other side of the inverted drawer was a stack of three books: *Siddhartha*, by Hermann Hesse; *Stranger in a Strange Land*, by Robert Heinlein; and *American Power and the New Mandarins*, by Noam Chomsky. Apparently Del was using the bottom side of the drawer as a desk.

Walking to the window and pulling the curtain aside, Paige took in the view in front of the house. All was peaceful for now. A solitary figure ambled down the street toward the campus.

With a sigh Paige let the curtain fall back into place. Crossing the room she closed the door. She tried to lock it, but the lock didn't work. Neither did the latch. The best she could manage was to hold the door closed for a moment. This was the only way she could keep it from yawning open by itself.

She plopped onto the bed. It supported her but not without a squeaky complaint. Spilling out from beneath the bed were loose papers, single sheets of newspapers, soiled clothes, shoes, empty food bags and cartons, and cigarette butts. Paige kicked at these with her feet for a little while, then, lifting her feet onto the mattress, she fell backward and was nearly engulfed by its softness. Overhead, a naked bulb swung at the end of an electric rope.

Paige closed her eyes. At first there was nothing but blessed darkness. Then, gradually, as her rational mind released its grip, images of The Suit played in her mind. His leering eyes and yellow teeth; his clawlike hands, reaching for her. Groping. Striking.

She heard a noise in the hallway and bolted upright. Her head swirled with pain and cottonlike confusion. There was enough rational thought for her to know it probably wasn't The Suit. But what about the guitar player in the swing? Her heart hammered. She stared at the door. Had it moved? The crack looked larger than before. She listened and stared. Afraid to breathe, to make a sound.

When the door didn't open and she hadn't heard anything for what seemed to be a sufficient time for evil to present itself, she slowly and quietly swung her legs over the side of the bed. It creaked with creaks that to her sounded as loud as the Stones album blaring downstairs.

She waited, half expecting the guitar player to burst through the door. He didn't.

As quietly as she could manage, she made her way the rest of the way out of bed and to the door. She rested her hand on the knob. Slowly, she enlarged the crack, just enough to see out. There was no one on the walkway or stair landing. The door to the other bedroom was open. She could hear people talking in low tones inside. Suddenly, someone burst up the stairs.

She gasped at his sudden appearance.

Carrying a six-pack of beer, he bounded up to the landing and into the second bedroom. The door slammed shut behind him. All was quiet again, except for the jarring chords of the Stones.

You're acting like a child! Paige scolded herself.

She closed the door. It yawned open. Going to the chest of drawers, she removed the frameless mirror and scooted the chest against the door to keep it closed.

Squeaking her way onto the center of the bed she lay down. Her chest rose and fell rapidly. Was it fear or exertion from moving the chest of drawers? Maybe it was a combination of both. She closed her eyes and tried to think of something pleasant. She envisioned a deserted stretch of beach with a gentle surf and setting sun. The air was cool, almost brisk. She could feel the sand spread beneath her feet. Shadows were long and the colors deep. Unexpectedly, images of The Suit tried to crowd in. She pushed them aside. Then, the guitar player in the swing popped into her head. She pushed his image aside too. She concentrated on the sun. The surf. The sand.

After several minutes she was calm. Minutes later her breathing was rhythmic. She fell asleep.

A gentle rap on the door woke her. Her heart froze.

"Paige? It's me. Terri."

Groggily, Paige rolled out of the bed and shoved the chest of drawers aside to let Terri in.

"Did I wake you? Oh, I'm sorry!"

Paige waved aside the apology. "I was just resting," she said.

Terri stepped inside the room and looked at the chest of drawers. She said nothing. The expression on her face indicated she understood.

"Are you ready for the grand tour?" Terri asked.

Paige ran her fingers through her hair. "Give me a moment to comb this mop," she said. "You know, first impressions and all that."

For the remainder of the afternoon and into the night, Terri introduced Paige to life in a campus commune. With the rooms open the way they were, it was difficult to ascertain who slept where with any constancy, except for Del. He alone commanded a room of his own, insisting he needed time alone to think and plot strategy, and as his status was growing to legendary proportions, everyone was willing to give him his space.

But the relaxed sleeping arrangements did not mean there was a lot of promiscuity. Such a thing was not conducive to group living. A girl tended to stay with one guy for an extended period, and once it was clear they were a couple, others respected their relationship. Indiscriminate sex would only serve to disrupt things.

Paige learned that there were two married couples living in the house and one university professor who had left his wife and family. At least that was his side of the story. According to another source, it was she who had kicked him out.

As for finances, each member of the house contributed as much money as his allowances from home would permit, or as much of his salary as he could spare. From this kitty the rent was paid first. After that, the money went for food and household expenses.

The cleanliness of the house and the quality of the food rose and fell with the talent and interest of the house's female members. The food was usually good to excellent with an emphasis on health items: whole wheat banana bread, rice dishes with Indian spices, and casseroles or dishes that made the most of the budget, like spaghetti. Meal hours were usually breakfast at noon and dinner at midnight.

At the house marijuana was as common as beer. Other drugs were used on occasion, but were frowned upon since they greatly altered the lifestyle and personality of the user and inevitably led to trouble.

For the most part, hospitality was common, too. When the residents were introduced to Paige as Del's girl, she was instantly accorded the respect given Del. It was during a discussion at dinner that she learned that Del and Allen were currently in San Francisco, purportedly to meet with Abbie Hoffman himself. The entire house was anxiously awaiting their return.

Paige also learned that as the new semester approached, plans for a variety of campus disruptions were already underway: a draft-card-burning rally, an administration sit-in, and a variety of campus pranks. She was given a copy of the student newspaper that was written and printed at the house, *Bold and Free*. Del was the general editor. The publication was a strident voice calling for social revolution and dedicated to the collapse of modern American society.

Following the midnight meal Paige once again went upstairs to Del's room. Terri offered to escort her. Paige declined. After meeting most of the residents of the house, she was feeling more secure. Not secure enough, though, to leave the bedroom door open.

After pushing the chest of drawers against the door, Paige put on the long nightshirt that served as her pajamas and curled up on the squeaking bed. Because of all the strange new sounds in the house, it took awhile for her to fall asleep, but sleep she did.

A noise woke her.

At least she thought it was a noise. Maybe she had dreamed it. Either way, it was sufficient to trip her heart to pounding and cause her eyes to fly open.

The first thing she noticed was the dresser. It had been scooted back, enough so that the door stood halfway open! Her pounding heart gave way to full panic.

She sat up.

Someone was in the room with her. She sensed his presence before she saw him. She heard a shuffle in the corner. A sniff.

Whirling in the direction of the sound, she saw a man sitting in the corner, cross-legged, Indian style. He was using the inverted drawer as a desk. With one hand he held a flashlight; with the other, a pen with which he wrote on a single sheet of paper.

The reflected light from the paper was enough to make out his features: deep-set, dark eyes, a thin nose, and a struggling beard.

"Del!" Paige cried.

6

Nat's nightmare always began in war-torn Germany. He stood in the middle of a bombed-out neighborhood. As far as the eye could see, row after row of houses were reduced to rubble. Cement steps led to nowhere. Gray smoke rose eerily from charred remnants. The once thriving community was giving up its soul.

Take good care of Allegra.

The voice came from nowhere. He recognized it.

Josef!

Josef the German, which made him an enemy. Josef the Christian, which made him a brother and a friend. Josef, Allegra's intended, which made him a competitor.

"Josef! Where are you?" Nat said.

Take good care of Allegra.

"Where are you? Are you hurt?"

I won't be going back with you.

"Josef! Tell me where you are. I can't see you."

Take good care of Allegra for me.

Plunging into the rubble that once was Josef's home, Nat lifted boards, overturned brick and stone and burnt furniture in search of his friend. He could sense time was running out. Josef was dying. As strange as it seemed, Nat could *feel* the life ebbing from Josef. And as it did, he too was weakened. Planks and brick flew every direction with his effort.

As his strength waned, his desperation escalated. All of a sudden he stopped. Josef was dead. Nat could feel it. A part of him died too. The loss was as real to him as the loss of the use of an arm or a leg. Nat attacked the rubble again. If he could just find the body, maybe, just maybe …

"Nat? Nat!"

Allegra?

Nat stopped digging. He listened.

"Nat!"

He straightened himself and looked in the direction of the voice.

Allegra!

She was as young and beautiful as the day he first laid eyes on her, standing in the middle of the cobblestone street, rubble strewn all around her feet. With one hand she reached toward him. A puzzled expression framed her face.

"Nat?"

No! She shouldn't be here. It's too dangerous.

The roar of heavy aircraft rumbled overhead. Nat looked upward. B-29s. They were in bombing run formation. Even now he could see bombs dangling from their underbellies like deadly strings of black pearls.

He tried to shout to Allegra. To warn her. To tell her to find cover. But his voice was as dead as Josef.

Unable to call to her, he tried to get to her. His feet could barely move. They were entangled in the rubble. Only with great effort could he lift one, then the other. All the while, the strings of bombs fell toward them.

Using his arms to help lift his legs, he slowly made his way to Allegra. He tried calling to her again. At the same time Allegra was calling to him.

"Nat? Help me! Help me!" Her voice was frantic.

Nat yelled for her to run, but no matter how hard he tried, no sound came from his throat. He motioned frantically with his arms. She didn't understand.

Why didn't she run? How could she be unaware of the danger? Couldn't she hear the bombers overhead?

So this was how they would die. Odd that it would be in Josef's neighborhood. But then, was it so odd after all? People die in war; so do cities and countries. This once beautiful town, vibrant with people, alive with music and games and laughter, was a trophy to war's destructiveness. Now it was a killing ground. And Nat and Allegra were its next victims.

Just as Nat was breaking free from the rubble and just before the first of the bombs hit, people appeared from nowhere. Stout German women pushing baby carriages. Men in suits striding to work, puffing purposefully on cigars, their minds preoccupied with business. Children, holding hands, laughing, giggling, playing silly games. Movers carrying furniture. And in the midst of them all stood Allegra. Nat's hopes rose. Maybe one of them would save her. But how could they? They seemed just as oblivious as she to the death that was about to rain down upon their heads.

KA-BOOM!

The first blast was close. It knocked everyone from their feet and tipped over the baby carriages. Little blanketed bundles rolled into the street.

The force hurled Nat a good three feet backward. He landed on his seat and rolled on the scorching macadam. His cameras, strapped around his neck, clattered against the paved street. Where had they come from? Instinctively, he checked the cameras for broken lenses and cracked cases. Then, he remembered Allegra.

A fireball rose to the sky from the crater where the bomb impacted, a wicked-looking black plume of smoke billowing beneath it. The blast had made a direct hit on a '62 Chevy, completely destroying it. Flames climbed hungrily over the car's frame, devouring anything that would burn. The heavy smell of burnt rubber soured the air.

Nat looked frantically for Allegra.

She was nowhere to be seen!

He scrambled to his feet. The weight of the cameras banged against his chest. All around him people were getting up from the ground. No longer were they carefree and casual. They scurried in every direction seeking some kind of cover. And, oddly still, they were no longer Germans. They were black. Poor black.

Another explosion rocked the street. A second plume of smoke rose skyward. Gunfire followed. Something struck Nat's ankle. He looked down just as the sidewalk exploded next to his foot. Chips of concrete splattered his pant legs. His ankle stung again. He ducked for cover beside a brick building, not knowing where the building came from, only grateful that it was there to provide him cover.

Cautiously, he peered around the corner looking for Allegra. The street had changed. It was no longer European rubble. Now it was a wide thoroughfare lined with earth-toned, stucco bungalows with wrought-iron bars covering nearly every window and door. Like its German counterpart, this street was a scene of utter destruction. Windows were smashed; smoke poured from building interiors; car fires and trash cans blazed out of control. A young black boy emerged from a storefront carrying table lamps his own size. He ran awkwardly down the sidewalk. Suddenly the sidewalks were filled with people. Everyone was toting something. TVs. Stereos. Radios. Three hefty men emerged from one storefront with a refrigerator on their shoulders.

What was this place? Nat looked around him. He spied a street sign.

Avalon Boulevard.

He recognized the name. Not only did he know where he was, but when. Los Angeles. Watts. It was August 1965. The city was an inferno. The streets were sweltering from summer heat and racial hatred.

Nat had been sent there to photograph the riot, which had entered its third day. Two days previous Marquette Frye was behind the wheel of his mother's Buick when he was pulled over by police for suspicion of drunk driving. A scuffle ensued when his mother, Rena, and stepbrother, Ronald, interfered with his arrest. All three were arrested and taken into custody.

A crowd watching the arrest of the black family by white officers grew to nearly one thousand people. Shirtless young black men began hurling rocks at the officers. It was all the spark that was needed to ignite the powder kegs of hatred that had been stockpiled in Watts for years.

"Burn, baby, burn!"

Nat spotted three black men who were looking to do violence the same instant they spotted him. They altered their course and came straight toward him, shouting obscenities and racial slurs. When their hands weren't making offensive and threatening gestures, they were clenched tightly for a fight. One of the men was carrying a bottle filled with gasoline. A rag spilled out of the bottle's mouth. The three men stopped their advance long enough for one of them to ignite the rag. With two running steps the bottle-bomb was hurled at Nat.

Nat ran as fast as his legs would carry him. He heard the bottle crash against the wall behind him. An explosion followed. Luckily, he had managed to stay far enough distant that he escaped major injury, though pieces of hot glass nicked his ear and right arm deeply enough to draw blood.

Nat glanced over his shoulder. The three men were running after him. They were young and unencumbered. He was middle-aged and heavy with camera equipment. Already he was wheezing and his legs burned from exertion. Fear drove him. He tried not to think about what they'd do to him if they caught him.

Another scene played out in his mind with the rapid click, click, click sequence of a camera shutter. A white truck driver was being pulled from his rig in the middle of an intersection. A swarm of black youths surrounded him. Kicking him. Punching him. Beating him until he was senseless. Nat had recorded the act with one of the cameras that was now dangling around his neck.

His pursuers were closing on him. The racial slurs they hurled at his back were louder. All three of them were close enough now that Nat could hear their labored breathing.

Nat knew he wasn't going to escape this time.

It wouldn't be like Anzio, where, in the battlefield trenches, his best friend was killed and he was spared. It wouldn't be like the Nazi prison train from which he escaped. It wouldn't be like the French forest where he witnessed the execution of German spies and managed to get away. He'd escaped all these times and more. After all that, he thought it ironic that he'd die on a California city street at the hands of three street toughs.

The more he thought about his fate, the angrier he became. What was wrong with this picture? This was America, for crying out loud!

His toe caught a crack in the aging macadam. He stumbled. His arms flailed about wildly like two out-of-control windmills. He fought desperately to retain his balance. If he hit the ground now, he was dead.

Despite his efforts, Nat nose-dived. Twisting to one side, his shoulder hit first. He tumbled. The street scorched his bare skin.

The cameras that hung around his neck banged alternately against the street and his ribs. As he rolled to a stop, he remembered what had happened to the truck driver. He covered his face with his arms and hands to ward off the coming blows. It was a fragile defense at best against the fists, feet, bricks, boards, and whatever else the three rioters would use to bludgeon him.

But no blows came.

Curious, Nat peeked past his flesh-and-bone defense. What he saw hurt him worse than a thousand blows.

The three men—their chests heaving, sweat pouring down their faces and dripping from their chins, their eyes yellow with rage—were holding Allegra and Paige and Travis. Nat's heart seized.

How had they gotten hold of his family? Hadn't he told Allegra to run? Why hadn't she listened? Now Paige and Travis were in danger, too! No. This couldn't be happening! Things like this just didn't happen in the land of the free and home of the brave.

Nat stretched a pleading hand toward his captors. He offered his life for the safety of his family. The three black men showered him with vitriolic abuse. He begged them not to hurt his wife and children. They laughed and mocked his pleas. This angered him. He changed tactics. He swore vengeance on them should they harm his family. In response the three black men dragged Allegra, Paige, and Travis into the middle of a deserted Avalon Boulevard. They informed Nat that they were going to kill his family one at a time while he photographed their deaths.

Nat charged at them. A distinct click and the sudden appearance of a switchblade pressed to Allegra's throat cut short his attack.

Then, to Nat's amazement, Paige heaved a frustrated sigh of disgust. She directed it at him! Calmly, she left her captors' side and approached him. Even more incredibly, the three black men made no effort to restrain her.

"Father," she said using her heavily exasperated tone that sooner or later surfaced in all of their arguments of late, "they're only asking you to take pictures. Is that so hard for you to understand?"

Nat couldn't believe it. Paige was one of them. How could she be sympathetic to them?

"Look around you!" he shouted. "Is this the kind of country you want to live in?"

Allegra and Travis stood passively with their captors, as though bored with the whole thing.

Paige rolled her eyes in exasperation. "Father, as usual, you're making a mountain out of a molehill," she said. "Here, let me help you."

Moving beside him she lifted one of the cameras from around his neck, a 35mm single lens reflex. She raised it to her eye and looked through the viewfinder and focused on her mother, brother, and their captors who all smiled at her. Then, she handed the camera back to her father.

Motioning beyond the captors to the burning buildings and looters behind them, she said, "Use f/22 for depth of field. We want all the street activity in focus." She glanced around, assessing the light. "It's bright enough, don't you think? You might want to check your light meter, but I think there's enough light."

This was ridiculous! The riot. The hostages. Paige's traitorous behavior. Allegra's and Travis's casual attitude about the whole thing.

"Father, don't be such a stick in the mud," Paige protested. "These young men only want to kill us. It's not like it's the end of the world."

Moving behind him, Paige peered over her father's shoulder. "If you shoot the scene a little off-center," she said, "you can pick up the burning squad car on the sidewalk."

He didn't know why, but he raised the camera to his eye. He saw rioters. Looters. Burned-out buildings. Vehicles ablaze. And thick columns of black smoke. He focused on the steely hatred in the black men's eyes. Their muscles tensed; they were ready to do violence.

Paige returned to her captors. "You can kill us now," she said.

One of the men gripped her arm hard. She let out a squeal of pain.

Nat sighed in resignation. *Why not? It's what everyone seems to want. Just take the pictures*, he told himself.

Nat's nightmare ended the same way every time—with him dutifully taking pictures of a burned-out Watts and thinking how similar it was to Josef's hometown in Germany.

"You were restless last night," Allegra said.

She stood beside the kitchen counter in her robe holding an empty coffee cup. Behind her the coffee percolator strained to complete one final eruption.

"Yeah," Nat mumbled. His muscles felt as though he'd been hauling bags of dry cement all night long.

"You had that nightmare again," she said. It was a cool comment, not a question.

Nat had long ago given up trying to understand his wife's uncanny intuition. He just accepted it. When they were first married he thought it was an attribute she'd developed to compensate for her blindness. When he mentioned this to her, she laughed and said it had nothing to do with blindness. She was a woman. She'd made the statement as though no further explanation was needed.

"The nightmare was different this time," he replied.

"Oh?" Allegra turned to the counter and poured a cup of coffee. "This time Paige sided with the rioters."

Allegra turned and handed the steaming cup to Nat, letting him come to it. Her face showed no reaction to this new revelation.

"Thanks," he said, taking the cup from her.

"There's cereal on the table. Toast is in the toaster."

Nat set the coffee on the table. He looked for strawberry jam. Not finding any, he went to the refrigerator to get some.

"Don't you find that a bit odd?" he asked.

"What?"

"That Paige would side with the Watts rioters."

"It was *your* dream. Paige had nothing to do with it."

Her comment didn't set well with him. Of course Paige had something to do with it. The dream merely reflected her anarchistic political leanings. Part of him wanted to say something to this effect, but a greater part of him didn't want to get into it this morning.

Grabbing the jam, a plate, a knife, and the toast, Nat sat at the kitchen table. Allegra joined him with only a cup of coffee.

Nat glanced over at her and quickly forgot what he was doing. For a mother of two grown children, Allegra was incredibly beautiful. He'd always thought she was too classy for him—never more so than now. After all these years in the States, she still had a European air about her. She carried herself like an empress. Her speech was crisp and clear and exotic. Nat knew her well enough to know that she could lose the French accent any time she wanted; why she retained it, he wasn't sure. Maybe it was her way of retaining a portion of her heritage. Maybe she did it for him. Who knew? All he knew was that after all these years he still loved hearing her voice.

He also loved being alone with her. Allegra had a way of making everything around them blur into insignificance. When they were alone, the universe became nothing more than a backdrop to their existence. These were the times he loved most in life, and they came all too infrequently; the memory of which only made these times when she was angry with him that much worse.

Sitting at the table with toast in his hands Nat felt an incredible urge to drop everything and lead Allegra by the hand into the bedroom where they could pull the bedcovers over their heads and shut everything else out for a week, maybe a month. No job. No children. No worries. Just the two of them wrapped up together so tightly it would be next to impossible to tell where one of them started and the other one ended.

"I called Paige's friends," Allegra said, breaking into his thoughts.

"This early?" Nat grumbled. Her comment shattered his growing romantic spell. He tried not to let disappointment creep into his voice.

"She isn't staying with any of them."

"Hmm."

"I also called the university, thinking she might have gone there."

Nat took a bite of dry toast spread with a thin layer of strawberry jam and munched it thoughtfully.

"The offices were closed. So were all the dormitories."

"Hmm."

Nat took another bite of toast. Allegra had been furious with him when he told her about his altercation with Paige. He'd debated with himself for over an hour the night before whether to wake her or wait until morning. Then, when he did wake her, she immediately went to Paige's room. She found Paige's door closed and the light off.

To make matters worse, Allegra's headache medication caused her to oversleep. By the time she awoke, both of her children were gone. Travis to the army. Paige to who knows where. Allegra was devastated.

She set down her cup. Her voice was heavy. "I'm worried about Paige," she said.

Reaching for a napkin, Nat wiped crumbs from the corners of his mouth. "She's capable of taking care of herself," he said. "Take you, for example. You were a member of the French underground long before you were her age. The times and situation were a lot more dangerous then, yet you managed to survive."

From the frown on Allegra's forehead it was clear the comparison didn't impress her. "I survived only by the grace of God," she said. "I was one of the fortunate ones. Many girls didn't survive."

"Last I heard, God is still in the business of watching over people," Nat said. "We'll just have to trust him to watch over Paige." He regretted the comment even as he was saying it. It was one of those statements that sounded good in the mind, but once it was spoken, sounded absurd.

The chair scraped angrily across the floor as Allegra pushed away from the table. She turned her back to him and walked over to the kitchen sink. With both hands she steadied herself on the Formica edge.

"This is different," she said without turning around. "How can we expect God to protect us from our own foolish decisions?"

There it was. Tossed out into the open like a bone for two dogs to fight over. It was his fault Paige was gone.

Nat didn't feel like fighting. His head still ached from a restless night's sleep, and his stomach was giving his breakfast toast a less than welcome reception. But arguments between man and wife rarely wait for a good day.

He was on his feet. "How many times do we have to go over this?" he asked, his voice rising. "Paige was trying to talk Travis into deserting! She was encouraging him to turn his back on his country and run away to Canada!"

"She was fearful for her brother's life," Allegra said, turning around and matching her husband's voice, tone for tone and pitch for pitch.

"She was aiding and abetting the enemy!" Nat shouted. "Can you imagine what that does to the morale of a young man who is about to go into combat? His own sister was putting doubts in his mind. In France you despised people for being collaborators."

"We're not in France, and this isn't World War II," Allegra countered. "The situation was different then. We'd been invaded. We were fighting for our existence, for our home country. Vietnam isn't anything like that. It's different."

"How is it different? We shipped soldiers to Europe to help our friends stop the spread of fascism. Now we're doing the same thing in Southeast Asia. This time we're helping our friends stop the spread of communism. So tell me, how is it different?"

"The United States hasn't declared war on Vietnam."

"War. Police action. It's a matter of semantics. We're sending soldiers into a foreign country to stop the spread of communism."

"I'll tell you what the difference is," Allegra said. "World War II united the States behind a common cause. This Vietnam conflict is tearing them apart! Worse yet, it has driven a wedge between a father and a daughter who love each another! Well I, for one, am not about to stand by idly and let that happen!"

Allegra folded her arms in an attempt to hold back her emotions and keep them from spilling over. It was a losing effort.

Though a passionate woman, Allegra was not one to weep readily, and never as a contrivance to get her way. When she wept it usually had something to do with family, in joy or in sorrow. While Nat was arguing politics, she was arguing family. He went to her and encircled her with his arms. He understood her concern now and berated himself for not seeing it earlier. How many times had he heard her say to the children, *Paige, Travis, there is nothing more important than God and family.*

She put him to shame. Two wars had deprived her of parents and family much of her life. During those early days she had always dreamed of belonging to a family like the Morgans. Now that she was a Morgan, she was their fiercest defender.

He buried his face in her hair. "You're right," he agreed softly. "I allowed my emotions to be swayed by politics and I overreacted. Forgive me?"

"You should be asking that of Paige," she replied. "She's the one who's been hurt."

Nat sighed. "You make a few more phone calls today around here," he said. "I'll stop by the university on my way to LA. Maybe she's there and the phone service isn't up yet."

Allegra wrapped her arms around his waist. She pulled him close to her. Nat felt a stirring inside of him and wished he had an hour or so to spend with her alone before heading north to Los Angeles.

Paige draped herself over the arms of one of the overstuffed chairs in the downstairs meeting area. She had lived there only three days and already she felt she knew everything about everyone. She scanned the downstairs meeting area. Nearly the entire population of the Shores Drive house was represented. Terri stood behind the couch flanked by two guys who didn't live at the house, one on each side. The girl was still in her two-piece bathing suit. She practically lived in it. While everyone was getting situated, her head bounced back and forth like a Ping-Pong ball as she carried on conversations with both guys.

The couple from the porch swing, who had decided to stay on at the house for a couple of weeks at least, were there. She sat on his lap at one end of the couch. Frank was there, the rather large guy who'd been playing the stereo when Paige had first arrived. And at least one of the two downstairs sleepers was there. Paige recognized one of them and thought she recognized the other, but she wasn't sure if it was the same guy.

The low din of a dozen different conversations was punctuated by silly pranks. Loudest was Terri's repeated squeal. The boys on each side of her had taken to poking her bare ribs. Someone threw a wadded-up piece of tin foil that plunked Frank on top of the head. He recovered it and promptly sent it back in the direction from which it came.

Allen and Del emerged from the kitchen to good-natured whistles and hoots. The guy from the porch reached around his girlfriend and clapped her hands for her. He looked from person to person for applause for his clever act.

Paige sat up as Del approached her. He perched himself on the arm of the chair. His clothes were wrinkled and odorous. He hadn't changed them in several days. Allen was neat and clean with every hair in place, looking very much like a television news anchorman. He took center stage in front of the stone-cold fireplace. Every eye was on him.

Paige grinned to herself and thought, *If the rest of these people only knew half of what I know.*

True, Allen was the good-looking one, the charismatic one, the one who stood in front of groups large and small and motivated them to action. The one who looked like the leader. But his every action was a precisely worded and choreographed script written and directed by Del Gilroy.

Just like in the movies, Paige mused. It was the actors and actresses who got all the applause, all the laurels, but in reality they were no better than their scriptwriters and directors. It was the writers who put the words in their mouths and the directors who told them how to stand and deliver them. So it was here. The witticisms, the oratory, the vision that Allen proclaimed, was not his. Every word he spoke, every idea he had, originated with Del. Allen was nothing more than a mouthpiece; Del was the genius.

Paige glanced up appreciatively at the man seated next to her on the arm of the chair. He wasn't much to look at. Smaller than her by a couple of inches, his nose had a prominent hook at the end, his beard was patchy and his hair was uncontrolled and wiry; add to that a face that was pockmarked with blemishes. He was definitely not the kind of man that readily attracted women.

Paige looked beyond his physical attributes to his creative and mental abilities, both of which were remarkable. The success of the student movement on campus was a result of Del's genius, plain and simple. Allen was nothing more than a carefully chosen element in the scheme of things, handpicked by Del to play the spokesperson for the movement. This too was a tribute to Del's genius. He knew that students would not follow him simply because of the way he looked. They needed an attractive, charismatic leader. He gave them one.

Allen cleared his throat and began addressing the group. He described the recent trip he and Del made to San Francisco and their meeting with Abbie Hoffman.

While Allen spoke, Del fidgeted on the arm of the chair. A couple of times Paige thought he was either going to fall or jump off the arm. She looked up at him. He was forming the words on his lips which, at that same instant, were being given life by Allen.

"Street drama!" Allen declared. "That's the key. Not just a demonstration, but a carefully choreographed demonstration that makes a statement. Something so outrageous, so unforgettable that the media can't resist reporting it."

Del nodded his head enthusiastically. He mouthed the words, *No more games.*

"No more games!" Allen proclaimed. "No more charades. The stupor of extravagance has paralyzed this country for far too long. No longer will America be able to sit at ease in Zion, half-drunk in a purple-haze funk. It's time for America to wake up."

"Wake up!" the group shouted back at him.

"It's time to organize!"

"Organize!"

"It's time to mobilize!"

"Mobilize!"

"It's time to stare them in the eyes!"

Laughter. Then, "Stare them in the eyes!"

"And say, Enough!"

"Enough!"

"I can't hear you!" Allen shouted. "It's time to say, Enough!"

"ENOUGH!"

"We're not going away!"

"WE'RE NOT GOING AWAY!"

"We're here to stay!"

"WE'RE HERE TO STAY!"

"Until things change, and change they will!" Allen was perspiring. It added a certain fervent glow to his oration. "Within a few short months we will enter a new year—1968. And this I promise you: 1968 will be a year of change."

Applause.

"It will be the year we blow America's mind."

Cheers.

"It will be the year that will forever be remembered in history."

More cheers.

Allen shouted, his face a righteous red, "For 1968 will be the year that America gets out of Vietnam once and for all!"

The room exploded with noise. Someone started a chant.

"NO MORE WAR! NO MORE WAR! NO MORE WAR! NO MORE WAR!"

It took awhile, but Allen silenced them with upraised hands. He continued, "It will be the year that Washington falls, and once more power will return to the people."

Everyone was on their feet cheering. Stomping. Shouting. Dancing. All except for Del. He remained perched on the edge of the chair arm, observing everything with a wry smile.

Allen shouted over them, "For 1968 is the year we will be heard and we will overcome!"

"WE WILL OVERCOME! WE WILL OVERCOME! WE WILL OVERCOME! WE WILL OVERCOME!"

For the next half hour the room was bedlam. Frank, the stereo player, cranked up the sound machine. Chords and vocals from the Grateful Dead reverberated off the walls, encouraging the revelers to take off their shoes and dance around the sun, to try on their wings and find out where it's at.

Paige and Del were the only ones not dancing. Del was deep in thought, and she didn't want to disturb him. And she was content to do so. Since the day she'd arrived at the house she'd never felt more at ease. At home. Anywhere.

All her fears had dissipated like the morning coastal fog. Despite the fact that there were no locks on the doors and people were coming and going at all hours of the day and night, she'd never felt more secure in her life. People respected each other's space here. If someone gave you bad vibes, you simply avoided that person and no one thought you the lesser for it. And, as for the sleeping arrangements, these fears too had been unfounded.

Del had been the perfect gentleman. He informed her outright that she was welcome to sleep in his bed with no expectations. He wrote at nights, oftentimes all night. He was content to curl up in the corner and sleep behind his makeshift desk. He told her bluntly that he was too busy being a revolutionary even to think about sex. And in spite of her encounter with The Suit, she knew Del well enough to take him at his word. All he asked in return was that she leave him alone when he was working.

With that understanding, Paige had secured for herself a place to live less than a mile from the university. What's more, she found new friends and a purpose far greater than her studies or herself. Reflecting back on the events that led her to Shores Drive, getting thrown out of her house was the best thing that ever could have happened to her.

※

Nat Morgan steered his cream-colored Pontiac Bonneville slowly down Shores Drive. Although he had no address, he was looking for a specific house—a two-story clapboard that served as residence for off-campus students.

Three days earlier he'd driven up from San Diego on the way to a meeting with his publisher in Los Angeles. True to his word, he'd stopped at the University of California at Rancho Diego searching for Paige. He found no one manning the guard station at the entrance when he arrived. The administration building was locked up; so were the dormitories. After wandering around for more than an hour, he concluded that Paige wasn't staying at the university as he and Allegra had hoped. Getting back onto the interstate, he went to his meeting.

A couple days passed. Then Allegra got a call from a woman at church. She'd overheard her daughter talking to Paige on the phone. Paige was indeed at the university, though not at a dormitory. She was staying in a house off campus, though the woman didn't hear which one.

It was enough information to send Nat back up to UCRD. As before, the campus was nearly deserted. He patrolled the streets hoping to find someone who could point him in the direction of known off-campus housing.

He was in luck. He spied two people walking in the distance. At first he thought it was two girls. From the back, both had nearly identical long blond hair and blue jeans. But as he got closer to them he realized one of them was a guy. The couple walked with a hand in each other's back pocket. Nat pulled up beside them and rolled down his window.

"Excuse me?"

The couple stopped and stared through the open window at him. From the front, there was no mistaking that one of them was a male. He had chiseled features and a blond goatee. He gave Nat's car the once-over, then leveled a distrustful glare at Nat himself.

"Can you point me in the direction of some of the off-campus houses?" Nat asked.

"You a landlord or something?" the goatee asked.

What a stupid question, Nat thought. A landlord would know where his own property was located. Nat chalked it up to just another example of the lack of education these kids were getting. Ignoring the comment, Nat said, "I'm looking for my daughter."

"Hey, that's your problem, man," the goatee spat. He led his girlfriend away from the car, but not without glancing over his shoulder a couple of times with a less-than-friendly expression.

Nat shook his head, disgusted at this generation's lack of respect for authority. Pressing down on the accelerator, he drove deeper into the campus. A short time later, he spied a group of guys shooting hoops on an outdoor basketball court.

This time, he decided to try a different approach.

"Hey guys, got a minute?"

Nat stepped from the car and reached for his wallet.

A scrawny kid well over six feet tall wearing nothing but a pair of gym shorts that were hanging so low the band of his under-wear was showing took a shot that banged off the rim. He then gave a disgusted look at Nat as though Nat were the reason his shot had missed.

Nat flashed his press pass.

"I'm lookin' for a story," he said.

Seven sweating guys gathered around him and examined the press pass.

"You really with *FLASH!* magazine?" the shortest of them asked.

Nat nodded. "I'm a photographer."

"Outasight! We're gonna be famous!" a tall redhead shouted.

Nat shook his head. "Sorry, fellas. I'm doing a story on cam-pus activities during the summer."

"What's wrong with us? We're an activity!" the redhead insisted.

Nat grinned. "Organized activity."

"Everythin's closed down," said the short one.

"Surely there's something going on," Nat said. "You know, football practice. Cross-country. Student meetings, that sort of thing. The kind of thing that would make a kid leave home and come to the university a week or two early."

They looked at him skeptically.

"Sounds pretty lame to me," Droopy Drawers said.

Nat shrugged. "Hey, considering some of the assignments I've been on, this is positively exciting."

"Football practices are in the morning and late afternoons at the field," the short one offered. "And cross-country runs in the morning."

Nat gave every indication that he was interested in this infor-mation. "And where do the athletes stay? The dorms are closed."

"Not all of them. One dorm stays open for the jocks."

That didn't help.

"What about the other people, the ones who aren't jocks. Let's say, those who are interested in rallies and protests and political things. Where would they stay?"

A chill descended over the group, the same one he'd felt come over the blond-haired couple.

Nat defended his question, "Hey guys, I'm just doing my job here."

Before leaving, Nat managed to get a general description of four houses that served as a dormitory of sorts for politically minded students. He'd visited the first one. No one there had heard of Paige. Now, he was driving to the second house on his list, the one on Shores Drive.

Finding the house was the easy part. Finding a parking place was difficult. All manner of working and broken vehicles littered the curbs. Nat had to park nearly a block away and walk to the house.

The steps leading to the open front door were badly in need of repair. Half of one step was missing completely. The pulsating beat of heavy rock music blasted through the door, making even the thought of knocking seem ridiculous.

Stepping inside, he was greeted by the odor of sweet smoke. He knew the smoke did not come from cigarettes. Nat spotted an overweight boy sitting on the floor between two speakers. The boy was rocking back and forth with his eyes closed, playing an invisible guitar. Nat tapped him on the top of the head. This startled the boy.

"I'm looking for Paige Morgan!" Nat shouted.

Still holding his invisible guitar, the boy glared up at him and said nothing.

"Paige Morgan!" Nat repeated.

Still the boy said nothing. But this time he pointed upstairs with his index finger. Then, closing his eyes, he resumed his playing.

Nat didn't know whether to be hopeful or not. He looked for the stairs.

He found them next to a closet door that stood open. A sleeping bag lay half-inside and half-outside the closet. It looked alive, almost like a fat green caterpillar. Only when Nat walked past it did he realize what was animating the caterpillar.

"Good Lord!" he said. He could barely hear his own words over the music.

The couple making love inside the bag was oblivious to his presence.

These people are animals! They have no shame at all!

Nat made his way up the stairs, not knowing what else to expect. The door to the first bedroom was open. After what he had just witnessed, he was hesitant to look inside, but how else was he going to find Paige?

He poked his head in. Three guys were seated on the floor Indian-style. They were passing a marijuana joint around the circle. Seeing Nat, one of them kicked the door shut with his foot.

Nat made his way toward the next open door, also a bedroom. He stopped and took a breath before poking his head inside. It was dark. In the far corner a young man sat behind an overturned dresser drawer that he was using for a desk.

"Excuse me," Nat said.

The boy behind the desk frowned, but didn't respond.

"Excuse me," Nat said again, taking one step into the room.

A streak of curses flowed out of the writer's mouth. He ordered Nat to get out. And Nat would have left, too, had he not recognized Paige's knapsack on the floor.

Shoving open the door, Nat went to the knapsack and picked it up. The kid in the corner leaped at him like a cougar. He snatched the knapsack from Nat's hands.

Nat grabbed it back. They struggled for possession.

"Let go, old man!" the boy demanded.

"This belongs to my daughter!" Nat answered.

This gave the boy pause, but he didn't let go. A glint appeared in his eyes and his lips formed a smirk. What he said next, he said with purpose. "It belongs to *my* girlfriend."

Nat released the knapsack.

He stared at the boy. The room. The unmade bed.

"Daddy!"

The cry came from the doorway.

Nat turned and saw Paige standing at the threshold.

"Daddy! What are you doing here?"

7

"Paige, pack your bags! You're coming home with me!"

The expression of surprise on Paige's face gave way to displeasure, then anger. She folded her arms defensively.

"What are you doing here?" she asked again.

"I'm here to take you home."

Paige strode across the room and reached for the knapsack. Both men released it. She clutched it to her chest and stepped back.

With Paige's appearance, Del's demeanor changed from hostile to amused. A thin grin spread across his lips as he watched father and daughter. It was as though they were performing a one-act play solely for his entertainment.

Nat was not amused. He took an instant dislike to the boy. The sooner he could get his daughter out of this immoral pot-house, the better.

"Pack your things," he said again. "I'll wait for you in the car. We can talk on the way home."

Paige stared at him. She hesitated. For an instant she was his little girl again. But only for an instant. Then her eyes hardened. Her jaw set. The obstinate adult Paige reasserted control.

"No," she said. "I'm staying here."

Nat leveled a finger of warning at her. "I'm not going to tell you again," he said. "Get your things. We're leaving."

"Excuse me, Mr. Hitler," Del interrupted. "Just what do you intend to do to her? Will she suddenly disappear to some work camp, never to be heard from again?"

"Del!" Paige scowled at him. "You're not helping."

Nat turned to the boy. "Stay out of this, son! This is not your concern!"

Through a smirk, Del replied, "Seems to me your little girl is telling you her life is no longer your concern … dad."

Nat took a step toward the boy with every intention of wiping the mocking smile off his face. And he would have done so had Paige not grabbed his arm.

"Daddy, don't!" she said.

Her intervention gave Nat the time he needed to regain control of himself.

"For the last time," Nat said to her, "pack your things."

"Daddy, listen to me," Paige pleaded. "I know Mom sent you to get me, and I know we have some things to work out between us, but I'm not going to go home with you. I mean, it doesn't make sense. Classes start in a week."

"So your plan is to stay here until classes begin?" he asked.

"Yes."

"And you see nothing wrong with shacking up with some guy until then?"

Paige couldn't have looked more shocked if he'd physically struck her. "I'm not shacking up with anyone!" she cried.

"Oh? What else would you call it when a girl moves in with a guy she isn't married to?"

"We're not sleeping together!"

With the image of the closet couple fresh in his mind, together with standing beside an unmade bed—the only bed in the room—

Nat found this impossible to believe. Apparently his face projected his thoughts.

"We're not!" Paige insisted.

"And what am I supposed to tell your mother? Paige is living in a house of pot and free love, sharing a bedroom with some anarchist, but don't worry, she's not doing anything wrong?"

"Revolutionary," Del corrected him from behind, "not anarchist." Nat grit his teeth and ignored the intrusion.

Paige's mouth hung open in dismay. "You don't believe me!" she said.

"How am I supposed to believe you?" Nat shouted. "You run away from home to a wreck of a house where two people are making love in a sleeping bag downstairs, three guys are smoking pot in another room, and I find you and some hippie sharing a room with a single bed!" He sputtered, searching for words, then threw up his hands in frustration. "I give up! I don't even know who you are anymore. Well, go ahead, turn your back on everything you've been taught. It's your life to ruin. But when it comes crashing down on top of you, don't come running back home!"

Paige was too overcome with tears to reply.

Del went to her. Rather clumsily he put his arm around her shoulders. He had to reach up to do so. While Paige buried her sorrow in her hands, he stood beside her and glared defiantly.

"Visiting hours are over, pop," Del declared.

The revulsion Nat felt for this boy was growing exponentially, so much so it frightened him. Never before in his life had he felt so strongly that he was about to lose control of himself. The sight of this scraggly-haired, barefooted, unkempt, filthy, smart-mouthed, smirking hippie with his arm around his daughter was just too much for him. All it would take to push him over the edge would be a single word. Biting his lower lip, he made his way toward the door.

"Come again soon," Del said. "It's been a blast."

Reason snapped. The angry animal inside him took over. Nat turned on Del, cocking a clenched fist.

"No, Daddy!" Paige screamed. She stepped between them.

Nat's fist hovered midair, quivering. For a long moment it hung there. Slowly it changed into an accusing finger that Nat shook at Del.

"I hope you're proud of yourself, son," he said, his voice shaking with forced restraint. "You've succeeded in ruining an innocent young girl."

"I've enlightened her," Del replied. "I've taken a naive product of the upper-middle-class suburbs and enlightened her."

"Why you ..." Clenched teeth bit off the end of Nat's sentence. "I know your kind. You're interested in only one thing—destruction. You despoil everything you touch!"

"You're right!" Del shouted over Paige's shoulder. "I do want to destroy things. I want to destroy inequality in this nation. I want to destroy rampant injustice. I want to destroy an established government that thinks nothing of sending its best young men to the slaughter in Southeast Asia. I want to destroy a decadent nation that protects its rich and oppresses its poor."

Nat shouted back. "You fashion yourself as a regular Robin Hood, don't you? Well you're not! You're nothing more than a pathetic coward hiding behind meaningless rhetoric. You attack things you don't understand. Worse yet, you do it while hiding behind the very freedoms your country affords you. Well let me tell you something, you're nothing more than a two-bit hoodlum who goes around setting trash cans on fire just to get attention."

A wry smile creased Del's face. He moved from behind Paige to face Nat directly. "That's what you'd like to think, isn't it? But there's a new revolution that is sweeping the land, and my name is going to figure prominently in its history."

"Right up there with Benedict Arnold," Nat said.

"More like Wendell Phillips," Del replied coolly. "Ever hear of Wendell Phillips, dad?"

"One of your left-wing communist buddies, no doubt," Nat replied.

The triumphant smile on Del's face made Nat feel uneasy. He was beginning to realize he'd been set up.

"If you knew your American history, pops, you'd know that Wendell Phillips was a passionate abolitionist who fought to do away with slavery in the United States. A worthy cause, wouldn't you agree?"

Nat said nothing. He was being baited and he knew it.

"To quote the good Mr. Phillips," Del continued, "'Revolutions are not made; they come. A revolution is as natural a growth as an oak.'"

Nat sneered. "Are you sure you're not quoting Lenin?"

"You should have paid attention in high-school history," Del chided. "How about this one? Can you identify the speaker of this quote? 'If by mere force of numbers a majority should deprive a minority of any clearly written constitutional right, it might, in a moral point of view, justify revolution—certainly would if such a right were a vital one.'"

Nat stared. He said nothing.

"Time's up, pops," Del teased. "Abraham Lincoln. One of the more communist-leaning presidents we've had over the years, don't you think? 'Justified revolution!' Imagine that!"

Paige stood off silently to one side. Her eyes were red and her cheeks stained with tear tracks.

"I'm not buying it," Nat said. "All your talk is nothing but a smoke screen to mask your cowardice while real men step up and serve their country like they have since day one. Real men like Paige's brother, Travis. But you ..." Nat sneered in disgust. "You and your kind not only undermine the efforts of these true patriots, but you attempt to cover your cowardice with riots and vandalism while spouting what amounts to nothing more than political mumbo jumbo."

Again Del smiled his superior smile. "Mumbo jumbo is it? How about the mumbo jumbo that was spouted by Thomas Jefferson when he said, 'I hold it, that a little rebellion, now and then, is a good thing, and as necessary in the political world as storms in the physical.'"

"Jefferson, eh?"

Del flashed a smile that said, *Checkmate.*

Nat took a step toward him. "Well let me ask you this, then. Once you have trashed this country, what are you going to replace it with?"

"A better system where everyone is equal," Del replied.

"A better system? Tell me about it. You see, Jefferson may have supported revolution, but he had something better in mind. Didn't he also say, 'When in the course of human events, it becomes necessary for one people to dissolve the political bands which have connected them with another ... that they should declare the causes which impel them to the separation. We hold these truths to be self-evident; that all men are created equal; that they are endowed by their creator with certain unalienable rights; that among these are life, liberty, and the pursuit of happiness.' So tell me, Mr. Revolutionary, what is your better idea? Quote to me your declaration of independence, the one you intend to use to replace this one."

Del sputtered. His eyes bounced side to side as he searched his mind for an adequate reply. Nat didn't allow him time.

"That's what I thought. You're no revolutionary. You have no grand idea for government. All you know is destruction. You're an anarchist. You're not Jefferson, you're Apollyon."

With one final glance at Paige, Nat left the room.

He felt no feeling of victory. He may have succeeded in scoring a verbal point against an obnoxious student, but in the only battle that counted for anything—the battle for Paige—he had lost decisively.

※

"I don't know why I'm doing this," Nat said.

Unsheathing an aluminum Christmas tree limb from its protective covering, he attached it to the metal pole, which served as the tree's trunk.

"Because it's Christmas, dear," Allegra said.

"I mean, what's the point? With Travis and Paige gone, I'm the only one who can see it."

"Then do it for yourself."

Allegra sat on the couch with her legs folded under her. She was knitting. Nat had glanced at her after his seeing comment. He hadn't meant to offend her, and she gave no sign of being offended. Those kinds of comments came up regularly from sighted people and Allegra never did take offense; though sometimes people stepped all over themselves to apologize once they realized what they'd said. Normally, Nat wouldn't have given it another thought, except this was Christmas, the first one with both kids gone, and for the last few days Allegra had been in an emotional state.

He finished placing the limbs on the tree and reached for the first box of ornaments. He sighed. Up until this year, this had always been a family night. Putting up the tree. Decorating it. Placing the manger under it. Reading the Christmas story from the Bible. Hot chocolate. A lot of laughter and silliness. Nat couldn't remember a time when Christmas had been this quiet.

"Isn't there a Bob Hope Christmas special on tonight?" he said.

"Would you like me to turn it on?"

"If you don't mind. We could use a little Christmas cheer, don't you think?"

Allegra didn't reply other than to set her knitting aside, get up from the couch, and turn on the television. Once the set warmed up, the sounds of laughter and music and Bob "Sponsored by Texaco" Hope's unique style of humor filled the room. Nat wasn't so keen on the special itself. It was the sound of voices and laughter he craved.

While Allegra returned to her knitting, Nat loaded the silvery aluminum tree branches with colorful ornaments. Some commercially made. Others made by the kids when they were in elementary school. There was an ugly purple and orange ornament Travis made from a section of egg carton when he was in the first grade. And a green and red velvet bell that Paige made. A smaller red bell lay atop a larger green bell. Nat lifted the red bell. Beneath it was a picture of Paige in the first or second grade, he couldn't remember which exactly. When the photographer told her to smile, she'd put everything she had into it. The result was a very prominent display of two missing front teeth.

"You're awfully quiet over there," Allegra said.

"Just reminiscing over some of the ornaments."

"Which ones?"

"Travis's purple and orange egg carton, and Paige's bell."

"The one with the picture?"

"Yeah."

"I thought she hid that one a couple of years ago. Didn't she threaten to throw it away?"

"That's right, she did."

"Where did you find it?"

"It was right here in the box."

Allegra smiled. "She must have put it back."

"Must have," Nat said. He lifted the red bell one more time before placing the ornament on the tree.

By the time the television comedian was wrapping up his program, Nat was putting the finishing touches on the tree. He knelt beside the light wheel and adjusted it so that it shone directly on the tree; then turned on the light. There was a soft whirring sound as the wheel began lighting the tree alternately red, blue, yellow, and green.

"Are you finished?" Allegra asked.

"All except the manger under the tree."

"You haven't opened the curtains."

"I don't think the neighbors want to see our tree."

"Certainly they do," Allegra insisted. "We get wonderful comments every year."

Nat didn't reply.

"If you don't open the curtains, I will."

"All right. If it means that much to you." Nat pulled the draw string and the living room curtains opened.

"Go out and see how it looks," Allegra said.

Nat started to object, then thought better of it. She would insist and he would end up doing it anyway, so why not get it over with?

Opening the front door, Nat stepped out of the house. A stiff breeze met him, coming off the ocean. He walked to the front curb and turned around. The tree shimmered in four colors, prominently displayed in the center of the window. He looked up and down the street. Roughly a third of the houses had some kind of exterior lighting or Christmas display.

"How does it look?" Allegra called. She was standing in the doorway, her arms folded to ward off the chill.

"Just like it did last year," Nat called back to her.

When he stepped back inside, Allegra rubbed his back and arms to help remove the chill.

"Show me the tree," she said.

Nat led her to the tree. Standing before it, she deftly raised her hands, her palms facing the tree. She moved her hands forward until they met the tips of the branches.

"I can feel that light," she said of the multicolor wheel.

"It puts off a lot of heat," Nat said.

"Where's Travis's ornament?" Allegra asked.

Nat guided her hand to it. She held it and traced its outline tenderly with her fingers.

"And Paige's bell?"

Nat moved her hand to the bell. Allegra stroked it, lifted the top red bell and felt the emulsion on the picture.

She began to weep.

Nat put his arm around her. He wanted to say something, but didn't know what. So he said nothing.

Allegra produced a tissue from her pocket and wiped her nose and eyes.

"I hate this tree," she said.

Maybe it was the way she said it, or maybe it was because it had taken him most of the evening to put it together, but for some reason her comment struck him as funny. He began to laugh.

"I thought you liked it," he said.

Allegra shook her head. "No, I've always hated it. You and the kids are the ones who like it."

"Well … what don't you like about it?"

"It's too artificial."

"It's modern."

"I hate it for that reason, too."

Again, he didn't know why, but the entire conversation struck him funny. He laughed again.

"Then why did you have me put it up?"

"Because it's Christmas."

"But you hate it."

"Yeah, I do."

Nat wiped laugh tears from his eyes. "Is it all Christmas trees you hate, or just this one?"

"Oh, I love Christmas trees," Allegra said. "I just hate this one."

"And why this one in particular?"

"Because there's no scent to it."

Nat stopped laughing. Of course! How selfish they had been. He and the kids had seen the new aluminum trees on display at a department store and fell in love with them just because they were shiny and new.

"Oh honey," he said. "I never stopped to consider—"

Allegra reached up and put her hand over his mouth. "You and the kids liked it," she said. "That's what was important."

The next day, while Allegra was out shopping with some church friends, Nat took down the aluminum tree and threw it away. He replaced it with a live tree and had it decorated before she returned home.

The look on Allegra's face when she stepped through the door and smelled the pine made the Christmas of 1967 an unforgettable one for him.

8

Travis looked out the window of the Braniff 727 charter jet at the inky black ocean below. The dinner trays had been collected and everyone's seat was in the upright position as they approached Guam to take on fuel.

They had crossed the international date line at about midnight. At that moment they entered tomorrow. Now, as they approached the largest of the islands in the Marianas chain, the plane banked left, then right. Outlying islands passed beneath them.

Travis watched as the flaps were extended. A loud thump and a grinding sound indicated that the landing gear was down. He looked at the scenery whisking by and couldn't help but imagine what the island must have looked like during World War II when the Japanese and Americans fought for control of it. Now he was heading toward another parcel of the earth's surface to do for it what a previous generation of Americans had done for this island.

There was a healthy jolt as the plane touched down. The fuselage shuddered as it slowed. At first, all Travis could see in the darkness was row after row of runway lights. Then the terminal came into view. Dozens of B-52s were lined up in front of it, wing tip to wing tip. The bombers were painted with camouflage paint, unlike the bright yellow Braniff charter that was transporting him and about a hundred other guys to Vietnam.

Travis was farther away from home than he'd ever been before. There was something about the distance that made him feel vulnerable. Nagging doubts began to enter his mind. It wasn't as though he'd never thought he might not return home, the thought had crossed his mind on several occasions—when he cleaned his room for the last time before leaving the house, when he was exposed to live ammunition during basic training, and whenever he heard grim stories in the barracks, tales of friends and relatives who made one-way trips to Vietnam. He'd thought about the possibility of dying all right. But this was the first time he'd *felt* he might never return home.

His mouth was dry and foul, and his hands were cold as soldiers began lining up to deplane. A snoozing soldier reclined next to him in the center seat, blocking his way to the aisle. When they boarded in Hawaii, the soldier had curled up as best he could and fallen asleep without so much as a word of introduction.

"Excuse me," Travis said to him.

There was no response. The soldiers standing in the aisle watched with humor Travis's attempt to wake the slumbering soldier.

"Excuse me," Travis said again, this time adding a nudge.

Still, the soldier didn't awaken.

Suddenly, a pillow hurtled through the air and hit the soldier in the face. He stirred to the laughter of the soldiers standing in line.

"Hey Riley, wake up!" The man who'd thrown the pillow, a pudgy redhead, was now shouting.

The slumbering soldier looked around with half-open eyes. "Are we at the war yet?" he asked.

"We're at Guam! Get up and let that guy out!"

Riley turned and looked at Travis sleepily.

Another pillow hit him on the side of the head.

"Come on, Riley, wake up!" the redhead shouted. In way of explanation, he added, "I've never seen a guy sleep so much as him, or as hard. Sometimes it would take three of us to wake him up at basic."

Undaunted by the pillows or the attention, the soldier named Riley straightened himself in his seat, crinkled his nose, and yawned luxuriously. In no hurry at all, and still half-asleep, he crawled over the empty aisle seat and made his way off the plane. With a nod of thanks to the redhead, Travis followed Riley.

He never knew what a glorious experience stretching one's legs could be. It had been twilight when they departed San Francisco and midnight when they landed in Hawaii to refuel. Travis looked at his watch. Now it was a little past 2:00 a.m.

A blast of hot air greeted him when he reached the doorway. Travis couldn't believe it. Two a.m. and as hot as a Southern California Santa Ana wind!

After the heat the next thing Travis noticed was the armed police encircling the soldiers and the high chain-link fence topped with barbed wire. He got the impression they were prisoners. Was the security to keep them away from the bombers? Or was it to discourage any of them from capriciously changing their minds and making a run for the dark jungle in the distance?

With his hands in his pockets, he ambled about the tarmac, avoiding the various pockets of soldiers that had formed. From the bits and pieces of conversation he overheard, the main topic of discussion seemed to be speculation on what Vietnam would be like. Travis didn't feel like talking, or listening, for that matter. The farther away from home they traveled, the more he withdrew into himself. For some reason he just preferred being alone with his thoughts.

There were two buildings available to them. Latrines and a liquor store. During basic one of the soldiers called liquor the great elixir of war. He said it was an American tradition just like apple pie, that Americans couldn't fight a war without it. They asked Travis if he drank. When he told them he didn't, they predicted he would before his tour of duty was over. If not drinking, then taking drugs.

Travis shrugged off their prediction. He'd always viewed alcohol as a crutch for people who weren't strong enough to face reality. Drugs were just stupid.

A gentle wind blew in off the ocean. It smelled of kerosene. When the signal was given, Travis boarded the plane again. He was thankful they were continuing on. He wasn't impressed with Guam.

The plane lumbered down the runway and soon they were back in the air, or as someone else put it, within striking distance of Vietnam. Travis closed his eyes and tried to get some sleep. Beside him, Riley was already snoring.

The next time I get off this plane, Travis thought to himself, *I'll be in Vietnam.*

He wondered why they had to fight a war that was so far away.

※

The change of engine tone woke him. Travis blinked open his eyes. They were landing. He looked outside the window. It was light.

Beneath them was a tangle of luscious green jungle. Over the radio intercom the captain announced they were about to land. But not in Vietnam. They were landing in Manila. He explained that the airfield they were scheduled to land at was being shelled. Consequently, they'd been diverted to the Philippines until the shelling stopped. There, they would also take on more fuel.

Travis groaned. It seemed as though he was never going to get to Vietnam. It wasn't that he was anxious to get into the war. He just knew that the sooner he got there, the sooner he'd be able to go home. The way things were shaping up, this was going to be one long tour of duty.

※

Not until noon did Travis get his first glimpse of Vietnam. From the air it was flat and gray-green. A grayish brown haze covered it like a blanket. Travis couldn't take his eyes off the landscape that stretched to the horizon. The sense of foreboding he'd experienced earlier returned. One thought kept coming to mind: He didn't want to die in such a colorless, dismal place.

Without warning, the plane's nose dipped downward radically. Their descent was rapid and steep. The fuselage began shuddering and wouldn't stop. Up and down the rows of seats, soldiers shouted and cursed. One guy, undoubtedly from Texas, let out an, "Eeeehaawwww!"

Looking out the window, Travis saw greater geographical detail rushing toward him. Gray veinlike estuaries. A land that was pockmarked with bomb craters, now filled with water. Plumes of black smoke, about a dozen of them, climbed skyward.

"It's to avoid antiaircraft fire from Saigon's suburbs," a voice from behind him said, explaining their rapid descent.

That made sense. Still, it didn't relieve Travis's anxiety. He thought, *Here we are, defenseless, in a flying banana. Why don't they just paint a target on us and announce our arrival over loudspeakers? With my luck we're gonna get killed before we even reach Vietnam!*

Moments later, the plane leveled off. Once more the wings gripped the air and held steady as it skimmed over rusted tangles of barbed wire and row after row of sandbags. Then, with a jolt, it touched down. Travis Morgan was in Vietnam.

It wasn't until he was off the plane that Travis fully realized how much the bright yellow bird that brought them over from the States stood out like a sore thumb. While all the other aircraft—fighters, bombers, transports and gunships—were camouflaged, the Braniff charter shouted, "Hey, everyone! The new guys have arrived!"

Like sheep being transferred from one pen to another, the new arrivals were herded from the plane to a waiting military bus. A sturdy iron mesh covered the windows. Again, Travis felt more like a prisoner than a soldier.

"The mesh is to keep kids and terrorists from lobbing fragmentation grenades onboard and wiping out an entire busload of us with one toss," someone said.

Travis wondered where the other soldier had picked up all these useful bits of information. Had he missed a Vietnam trivia class in basic somewhere?

The bus started up and roared off base. As it traveled through the outskirts of Saigon, Travis stared through the mesh at the motorbikes, pedicabs, and bicycles that jammed the streets. He stared at the brown-skinned populace and they stared back at him. Stories came to mind of children and the aged alike lobbing grenades at transports or suddenly producing guns of all sorts and shooting at Americans. Suddenly, everyone Travis saw looked suspicious. He felt edgy. The others on the bus were edgy, too. For the first time their lives were really in danger. And all they were doing was riding a bus! What kind of a country was this?

As if in answer to his question, Travis began noticing that machine-gun fire had marred the walls. So did splatter marks from rockets. Parts of the city they passed were nothing more than rubble. Broken, ragged walls, now useless, jutted out of mounds of debris. The results of the Tet offensive, no doubt. The recent attack on the American embassy had shaken the nation's confidence. And Travis could see why.

The heat inside the bus was oppressive, compounded by long hours logged on the flight over. Travis felt sick to his stomach.

He rode and suffered in silence, making no attempt even to learn the name of the guy sitting next to him. He and the others on the bus were replacements. After processing they would be divided up and sent to any number of locations to replace the dead and wounded. He'd probably never see the guy again. So why even bother to get to know him?

Upon reaching the processing center, each man was issued jungle fatigues with his medivac number stamped on them. The number was composed of the first four letters of his last name and the last four numbers of his service number. Travis's medivac number was MORG4907. Then they were given an orientation lecture during which the lecturer reminded them they were guests of the Vietnamese people. Funny. Travis didn't feel like a guest.

After mess they were assigned a bunk for the night, the best thing that happened to Travis all day. He was dog-tired and couldn't wait to get to sleep. However, to his chagrin, once his head hit the pillow, he found he couldn't sleep. First, because of the constant roar of convoy trucks and helicopters and jets. Then, because suddenly everything became quiet. Too quiet. So quiet, in fact, that he could hear the distant thump, thump, thump of artillery where the terrors of war awaited him.

The next morning Travis felt groggy. He'd slept little and what sleep he had was restless. He would have fared better staying awake all night. A thought came to him in the middle of the night and stuck with him now. Vietnam was like the flu, only a thousand times worse. It wasn't something you'd desire, but once you had it there was nothing you could do except endure it until it was over. This became his goal and motto: Endure it.

To do this, he determined it was best not to get close to anyone, or let anyone get close to him. That way, if they were killed, he wouldn't feel it as badly. He would keep to himself, do his duty, do whatever it took to survive, and go home and forget about it. In short, endure it like the flu. That was his plan.

He reaffirmed his plan as he and the others were herded into a huge Chinook helicopter. The two-rotor craft was cavernous, able to carry thirty or forty men. He walked up the cargo ramp and took a seat thinking, *Stay to yourself. Do your job. Go home.*

While the others loaded, he watched as other aircraft landed, took off, and refueled. Red clay dust covered everything. Mixed with spilled fuel, it ran down the sides of the aircraft, streaking their exteriors and looking like blood. Everything about this place spoke of pain and death.

The stench inside the Chinook was unbearable. Diesel fumes mixed with kerosene and gun smoke. Add to that the smell of stale urine and rancid latex from a rubber tree farm that bordered the base. Travis closed his eyes and repeated his newly created mantra to keep his mind off the offensive odors.

Stay to yourself. Do your job. Go home.

He felt his seat lift. The huge metal monster leaped into the air. Travis's queasy stomach complained. He glanced at those sitting opposite him. They looked as grim and green as he felt.

A half hour later the giant helicopter touched down, and Travis thought for sure they were being placed in the center of an attack, and still none of them had firearms. The entire transport ducked instinctively at the sounds.

A sergeant appeared at the rear cargo ramp and, with a superior grin, motioned for all of them to follow him. As Travis descended the cargo ramp and stepped onto the steel planking of the runway, he couldn't believe all the noise and confusion around him. A line of troop-carrying helicopters, "Hueys," was coming in to pick up infantrymen for an air assault. A few hundred yards away artillery batteries were firing salvos, but, as hard as it was to believe, their efforts were nearly drowned out by the noise of engines and turbines and the shouting of men nearby.

With wide eyes Travis took in all the action. *Stay to yourself. Do your job. Go home,* he repeated.

They were led to a row of sagging green tents pitched beneath some rubber trees. Beside each tent was a damp shelter made of sandbags and steel culvert halves, for use in case of mortar attacks. They were told to place their gear on a bunk.

Travis was the first to enter his tent. It was built on a wooden platform and housed a total of eight bunks, each with its mattress rolled up at the end. What he noticed next caused his heart to skip a beat. There were shrapnel holes everywhere. The tent and the wooden platform was riddled with them. Raw latex from the rubber trees overhead oozed through the holes in the tent. And when he unrolled his mattress, there were shrapnel holes in it too. Stuffing poked out of the holes.

Stay to yourself. Do your job. Go home, he thought.

Next they were led to the arms room where they were issued M-16 rifles, 14 magazines, and 250 rounds of ammunition along with the other equipment they would need—web gear, canteens, and so on.

Loaded down with all their gear, the replacements were then told they had the remainder of the afternoon to acclimate themselves. Following mess they would begin a five-day orientation course.

Travis was never so grateful for anything in his life. He remembered the long hours alone on the beach in La Jolla and how he'd taken them for granted. Now the promise of an unstructured afternoon was so welcomed, he nearly became emotional over it.

"Morgan! Drop and give me twenty!"

The shout came from behind him. With instincts born of training, he dropped his gear, fell to the ground, cranked out twenty pushups, then stood to attention.

Not until that moment did he see who had barked the order. The face he saw almost brought tears to his eyes.

"Keith!"

Keith Rawlins looked him up and down, then nodded approvingly. "Looks like the army has made a man of you."

"It's so good to see you!" Travis gushed.

Keith laughed. "You're not going to kiss me, are you?"

Travis laughed with him. But if the truth be told, he had to fight of an urge to hug the guy when he first recognized him. Seeing a familiar, friendly face was exactly the tonic he needed at the moment.

"Drop your gear in your tent and I'll give you a tour of the town," Keith said. "It's no Saigon, but it's quaint."

Travis was still so dumbstruck by his good fortune at running into Keith that he just stood there staring and smiling.

"What are you grinning at, you monkey?" Keith asked. "You look like a green recruit standing there like that."

"I *am* a new recruit," Travis said.

Keith smirked condescendingly. "Your uniform and fresh-scrubbed look broadcasts that fact; you don't have to act like one, too. Now stow your gear and let's get out of here."

The two strode side by side to the tent. As they walked, Travis shot a couple of glances at Paige's former boyfriend. He'd aged since Travis had seen him last, but the old Keith that Travis had worshipped as a boy could still be seen beneath the two-day beard growth and weathered skin.

"What are you doing here?" Travis asked.

"I got drafted, same as you."

Travis grinned. "No, I mean here right now."

Keith reflected his grin. "I'm your guardian angel."

"I don't understand."

"I'm your squad leader," Keith explained.

"Really?" Travis said. It was too much to hope for.

"Yep," Keith replied. "Requested you personally. Figured it was the least I could do for your parents. With me looking after you, your chances of survival just doubled."

Travis grinned, inside and out. Keith had always been confident. It was one of the things Travis admired about him.

"Speaking of your parents, how are they?" Keith asked. "Your Dad still with the *FLASH!* magazine?"

Travis nodded.

"Any chance of him getting a 'Nam assignment?"

"I don't think so. He's been with the magazine long enough he can pretty much write his own ticket. He prefers the political scene. Keeps him home."

"Always knew he was a wise man. Your mom doing all right?"

"Same as always."

"And Paige?"

Travis looked at Keith hoping to see a spark, some indication that he still had feelings for Paige. Along with everyone else he'd always hoped that Paige and Keith would someday get married. When they broke up, he was probably more disappointed than anyone.

"She's still at college," he said, still looking for some kind of romantic flicker in Keith's eyes.

"UCRD?"

"Yeah."

"She's not married or anything, is she?"

Travis grinned. That's exactly what he wanted to hear. "No, she's not married," he said.

He thought about mentioning the altercation between Paige and their father, the one that led to her getting tossed out of the house, but decided not to. He figured there would be plenty of time for that kind of stuff later. Right now, he simply wanted to enjoy being with Keith again.

After dropping off Travis's gear, the two of them made their way off base. As they walked past the guards, Keith leaned close to Travis's ear and said, "White Mice."

"Huh?"

"That's what we call them."

Travis looked over his shoulder at the guards. They were dressed in immaculate white uniforms, complete with white gloves.

"National police," Keith explained. "You'll see them all over the place. They take over guard duty only during the day. Nobody has any respect for them. At An Loc we used to watch the pilots play games with them. The pilots would land a little hot and head straight for them, jamming on the brakes at the last possible second. They wanted to see if they could make the White Mice run."

Keith laughed at his own story.

"Hey, around here you get your entertainment wherever you can," he said.

Just beyond the guard station a battery of local men were manning an array of pedicabs. Reaching into his pocket, Keith pulled out a wad of American bills and negotiated services with one of them.

"Come on," he said, hoping into the passenger seat. "It's cheap and it sure beats walking."

Travis joined him, not sure whether the thin brown boy behind them would be able to muster enough strength to transport two fully grown men. To his surprise, after a few hearty grunts the pedicab was moving at a steady pace.

It was still difficult for Travis to believe his good fortune. Here he was sitting next to Keith, going into town for a good time, leaving the army and the war and all his doubts behind him. Had it not been for the strange mode of transportation he could very well close his eyes and imagine that they were traveling down Torrey Pines Road on a Sunday afternoon.

Then Keith pulled out a cigarette and offered him one. Travis had never seen Keith smoke before. He didn't know what to say. He wondered what the people at church would say if they saw a cigarette dangling from Keith Rawlins' lips.

"No thanks," Travis said.

Keith grinned. "They didn't teach you that in basic?"

"Teach me what?"

"That all GIs smoke."

Travis grinned a half grin and looked away.

"You'll be smoking before your tour of duty is over. Trust me," Keith said, placing the pack back in his pocket.

The pedicab slowed as the road took an upward slope. The puffing sounds behind them grew more pronounced and labored. Travis wondered whether the load was too much for the driver. He glanced over at Keith to find him puffing leisurely on the cigarette, completely unconcerned with the driver's difficulty.

Ahead of them, atop the high ground, a walled city appeared. Travis thought it looked like a medieval fortress.

"Some rich French farmer built it," Keith told him. "It's the center of a huge rubber empire."

As they passed through the city gates, Travis noticed how thin the brick and stucco walls were. Yet the fact that the walls were still standing seemed to argue they were sufficient enough to keep the war out, at least until now.

The town opened up before them. Travis couldn't believe what he was seeing. It was as though they had passed through the gates of a French colonial theme park. The streets were cobblestone and lined with pastel-painted stucco buildings. Brightly painted shutters flanked the windows. Elegant balconies overlooked the streets.

In the center of town was a fountain around which ran a traffic circle jammed with motorbikes, bicycles, and pedicabs. White Mice stood impressively erect as they waved white-gloved hands to direct traffic. Apparently their presence was all show, much like London's palace guards, because the traffic ignored them completely.

"Over there!" Keith shouted to their driver.

The pedicab exited the circle and came to a halt in front of a sidewalk café. Keith climbed out. Travis followed close behind.

"I wait for you," the driver said.

His words hit Keith in the back. The older GI gave no indication he even heard them.

Travis stood between Keith and the driver, his head swiveling back and forth between them.

"Um, thank you," he said to the driver.

"I wait for you."

Again Travis looked at Keith and still saw only his back.

"Wait right here," he said.

He ran to catch up with Keith. "Um, the driver wants to know if he should stay."

Keith looked at Travis with an amused expression. "They all say that," he replied. "He can sit there all night for all I care. Don't give it another thought."

Travis looked back at the pedicab driver who hadn't moved.

"I'll be right back," he said. Running back to the driver, he said, "We won't need you anymore. There's no need to wait."

"I wait for you," the driver said again.

Travis shook his head. "We don't know how long we will be."

"I wait."

Did the driver not understand him? "No wait. No wait," Travis said, reducing his sentence for clarity.

"I wait," the driver insisted.

Travis looked at Keith who was sitting at an outdoor table leaning back in his chair. He was laughing.

Travis had to admit, he supposed his inability to communicate with the driver looked a little humorous.

He tried one more time, this time adding a shooing motion with his hands.

"We don't need you anymore."

"I wait," the driver insisted.

Travis shrugged and walked away. By the time he joined Keith, there were two bottles on the table. Their labels were identical: *Ba Mui Ba.*

"The local brew," Keith said, taking a swig. "It tastes like dishwater, but it's cheap."

Again thoughts of the church congregation came to Travis's mind. Not only did Keith Rawlins smoke, but he drank beer as well!

Travis took his seat and looked at the bottle in front of him. He made no effort to pick it up. "Do they have soft drinks?" he asked.

"Don't tell me you don't drink either," Keith laughed.

Unsure as to what to say, Travis shrugged.

"Are you sure you went to basic training?" Keith joked.

"Don't tell me," Travis said. "I suppose I'll be drinking before my tour is up."

"OK, I won't tell you," Keith replied. "But you will be."

Travis pushed the bottle of beer toward the center of the table. He leaned back in his chair, balancing himself on its back legs. Keith downed the first beer and reached for Travis's. For the first time in his life, Travis felt uncomfortable with Keith. There was something different about him that went beyond the smoking and the drinking.

"So what's it really like here?" Travis asked. Keith had always liked teaching him things. He hoped the question would bring out the old Keith.

The experienced GI swallowed and shook his head sadly from side to side. "Take the worst you've imagined it would be and double it," he said. "No, triple it. They haven't invented the words that can describe the terror you'll feel the first time you see the bear."

"Is that what they call it?" Travis mused, trying to make light of the warning. "During the Civil War they called it seeing the elephant."

Keith wasn't amused. He took another swig and said, "You learn that from your mom?"

Travis nodded. "She's the historian in our family. We had …"

"Yeah, I know," Keith cut him off. "You had relatives who fought in the Civil War. You've had relatives who've fought in every war. What's the matter with you Morgans? Can't you get along with anybody?"

Travis laughed. He thought it was a joke. But Keith wasn't laughing. He ordered another beer.

"Well, this ain't a war like any one your relatives have ever been in, that's for sure," he said. "First of all, there's no front here, only insertion points. We go in, fight and leave. Clearing an area is like putting your fist in a bucket of water. The instant you take it out, the water rushes right back in, covering all trace that you were ever there."

There was a bitter edge in his voice as he spoke. His speech was beginning to slur.

"You wanna know what it's like?" he yelled. "I'll tell you." He downed half a bottle of beer with a couple of gulps before continuing.

"We're a piece of meat out there. A piece of raw meat on a hook. The brass tosses us out there like steak to a lion. First, a platoon. Then, if the lion doesn't bite because it's too large a piece of meat, they toss out a squad, then a fire team. They keep doing this until the VC finally snap at the bait. Then, all hell breaks loose as they pour men and gunships and artillery into the area and pound the ever-lovin' daylights out of it. Sometimes we get 'em. Sometimes we don't. But you can count on one thing every time. The piece of meat has a big hunk taken out of it. Sometimes, all of it's gone. And in the end, it don't mean nothin'."

Travis regretted bringing up the topic. But it was too late now. He tried a different tact.

"How about if you show me the rest of the town?" Travis suggested good-naturedly.

"Great idea!" Keith said, suddenly joyful. He tossed a couple of bills onto the table. The two men stood; one unsteadily. To Travis's surprise, their pedicab driver was still waiting for them along with several others.

Travis started to climb into their pedicab. Keith grabbed him by the arm.

"Not that one," he said.

Turning to one of the driver's competitors, he negotiated a tour of the town. Their original driver took offense. Angry words were exchanged between drivers, but in the end Travis and Keith rode away with a different driver.

"Why did you do that?" Travis asked.

"Do what?"

"That guy who brought us all the way from the base was there waiting for us."

"Was he?" Keith said.

It was a lame question.

"You gotta keep these guys in their place," he explained. "You have to realize something. By day they're all smiles and they'll do just about anything for a buck. But at night they're the VC. They take to the jungle and will slit your throat without thinking twice about it."

It was a strange world Travis had fallen into, and the longer he was in it the less he liked it. After all, look what it had done to Keith.

A motorbike pulled up beside them on Travis's side and matched their speed. Travis glanced over and saw two attractive Vietnamese women, perhaps in their twenties, staring at him. The driver had a plump but charming, playful expression. The rider was thinner with black bangs and deep searching eyes.

"Hey, GI!" called the driver. "You want massage? Make love, good?"

Travis blushed. He looked away without responding.

"Not bad, eh?" Keith grinned. "Too bad it isn't this easy in the States."

The driver of the motorbike spoke again. "We give good massage, good make love, yes?"

"How much?" Keith asked.

"Keith!" Travis said. "What are you doing?" He turned to the girls. "No, we're not interested," he said.

At this the rider frowned.

"Don't pay attention to my friend," Keith said. "He's just shy. Probably his first time."

"You come with us, we take good care you," the driver said. "Not shy after we done." She really seemed to be enjoying this.

Literally caught in the middle of these negotiations, Travis had but a single wish, and that was that he could shrink until he disappeared. He wanted nothing to do with these girls. And he wanted to forget that Keith was even interested in taking them up on their offer.

"How much?" Keith repeated.

"Your first time, too?" the driver asked.

Keith shook his head and grinned at her wolfishly. "When we're done, you'll be offering to pay me!"

At this the rider with the bangs laughed.

"It really first time, him?" the driver asked skeptically.

Travis kept his eyes forward. He didn't even want to look at them. But he couldn't help but hear them.

"First time really," Keith said. Then, so that only Travis could hear, he said, "If it isn't, don't say anything."

"Twenty dollar you. Fifteen dollar for friend, his first time."

"See that, Morgan? I got you a discount!"

Travis straightened himself in the seat. "Let me out," he said.

"What?"

"I said, let me out. I don't want to have anything to do with this."

Keith looked at him, greatly disappointed. "Do you mean to tell me that in basic you didn't even ..."

Travis turned to the driver of the pedicab who, during the entire negotiation, kept pedaling and staring ahead as though two old friends had just hooked up and were discussing where they would meet for dinner. Travis spoke to him directly, "Stop this thing."

"Morgan!" Keith complained. "You're gonna upset the girls."

Travis ignored him. He repeated his command to the pedicab driver. "Stop this thing right now!"

The pedicab slowed and stopped. The girls on the motorbike stopped beside it. They eyed Travis suspiciously.

"Look, no offense to you ladies," he said. "But, I'm sorry, I can't do this."

"Fifteen dollar, massage, make love, two hours," the driver repeated.

Travis shook his head emphatically. "No. No massage. No make love."

"What is it with you, Morgan?" Keith bellowed. "This isn't Sunday school over here. So what's the matter? Are you afraid your mother is gonna find out?"

Travis didn't know what to say. He had looked up to Keith for as long as he could remember. Keith had always been his leader—in church, in high school, in Boy Scouts, in the youth group. But this was not the same Keith. This Keith had forgotten everything they'd been taught to believe. The sudden change confused Travis.

"Look, I just don't want to have anything to do with this, OK? I'm going back to the base."

"Come on, Morgan, be a man."

Travis shook his head. He felt lousy. Not for walking away from the girls, but for disappointing Keith.

Keith grabbed his arm and drew him close. His breath smelled of beer. He whispered, "You're embarrassing me."

"I'm not going with those girls," Travis insisted.

Keith glared at him. "You know I'm really disappointed in you, Travis," he said. "Some day you're gonna have to grow up."

He released his grip.

Jumping into the pedicab, Keith said to the girls on the motorbike, "Looks like it's just you and me, girls!"

The girl rider climbed off the back of the motorbike and sat next to him. He put his arm around her. With the girl on the motorbike leading the way, the pedicab carrying Keith and the other girl followed, leaving Travis standing alone.

Keith shouted at him over his shoulder, "It don't mean nothin', Morgan! It don't mean nothin'."

As the sun began to set and the shadows of the buildings stretched leisurely across the cobblestone streets, Travis wandered aimlessly with his hands thrust deep in his pockets. The good feeling that he'd been so carefully nurturing inside him all afternoon had fled, leaving behind an aching hollow spot.

He hailed a pedicab and negotiated a return ride to the base. The ride back, though downhill, seemed to take four times longer than the ride to town.

Later that evening, following mess, he barely heard a word of his first orientation lecture. He couldn't stop thinking about how quickly the afternoon had soured. And about Keith.

Was he expecting too much of people? It seemed like everyone he met predicted that the war would change him. Up until now, he'd ignored their predictions, concluding that they were hoping he would change merely to rationalize their own weaknesses and failings.

But Keith Rawlins had never been weak, and the war had changed him. If anyone could have held strong to his beliefs, Keith Rawlins could. So what chance did Travis have?

For the longest time that night Travis couldn't get to sleep on his shrapnel-riddled mattress. Then, just as he was finally dozing off:

KA-BOOM!

A horrendous explosion brought him and all the others in his tent sitting upright. The explosion was so near, he could feel its shock wave in his chest and sinus cavities. Some of the replacements were out of their bunks, heading for shelter.

"Go back to sleep!" shouted the sergeant at the end bunk. "It's only an eight-inch howitzer. Ours."

Travis could hear the shell splitting the night air with a sucking sound. Nearly a minute later he heard a distant explosion in the jungle.

Still shaking from the deafening sound, he lay back down. Twenty minutes passed, then:

KA-BOOM!

It soon became obvious to all that it took them about twenty minutes to reload the gun. For eighteen minutes Travis would lay in the dark, his limbs shaking. He would get two minutes of calm, then:

KA-BOOM!

Curled up on his bunk, Travis spent his first night in Vietnam listening to the bone-rattling repercussions of artillery, his mind swirling nauseously with images of Keith and the colonial French town, and the girls on the motorbike, and Guam, and their flight in on the Braniff charter, and visions of what it would really be like to see the bear or the elephant or whatever it was awaiting him in the jungle.

If he found any comfort at all, it came from repeating his mantra:

Stay to yourself. Do your job. Go home.

9

Paige was dead. She lay beneath a black shroud, one of nearly a hundred covered bodies that were strewn about Preston Plaza on the UCRD campus.

From the steps of the Student Center, Allen West shouted into a megaphone. His voice was uncharacteristically strained and shaky; he was near tears as he called attention to the scene stretched out before him.

A chant arose from the crowd of witnesses:

Hey! Hey! LBJ!
How many kids have you killed today?
Hey! Hey! LBJ!
How many kids have you killed today?

At the height of this drama, Paige's nose itched. Being dead, she knew better than to scratch it. But it was one of those itches that, the longer you ignore it, the more it itches. She tried to take her mind off the itch by listening to the sounds all around her.

It was only by chance that she was among the dead at all. To be realistic, Del had wanted all the dead to be males. But when a Studebaker full of male demonstrators broke down in Fullerton an hour before the demonstration, he made the decision to substitute females rather than reduce the dead count. Paige was one of the females who volunteered to die.

Pinning her hair up beneath a camouflage army cap, she had donned soldier's fatigues and, along with the others, mingled with the demonstrators. At the sound of gunfire—sound only played over the speakers, not actual gunfire—while the gathered demonstrators ducked and ran, she and the others fell to the ground. It was a powerful moment of street theater.

Then, according to Del's carefully choreographed script, undertakers appeared and covered each of the dead soldiers with a black shroud. Allen provided commentary, explaining that what they had just witnessed was an event taking place in cities and villages every day the entire length of Vietnam. The difference was that there the bullets were real and the dead were often innocent women and children.

Paige could feel the heat of the spring sun beating down on the cloth. Sunlight filtered through the cloth weave. From what she could hear, everything was going just as Del had said it would. She felt so proud of him.

Now if only her nose would stop itching.

The rally was assured a measure of success when the television camera crews arrived. Del had worked hard to get them there. He promised them a newsworthy demonstration. The police were there too, though they came uninvited. They came in force, but seemed content to watch from a distance.

When the sound of gunfire was played, the police dove behind cars and went for their weapons. Del had predicted they wouldn't fire and he was right. As the drama unfolded, it became clear to them that no shots were actually fired. They looked none-too-pleased about being drawn into the illusion, but there was little they could do. There was no law that said it was against the law to play sounds of gunfire.

The television camera crews reacted, too. Instinctively the cameramen crouched while continuing to record the action. Paige had seen the same concentration by her photographer father. Once his eye was pressed against the eyepiece, nothing could distract him. So, too, with the television cameramen. At the critical moment, they kicked into professional mode; ignoring their instincts, they focused on getting the shot. After the shroud was pulled over her head, Paige didn't see anything at all.

She heard feet shuffling nearby. Her nose itched more than ever. She crinkled it. The effort did nothing to relieve the itching. She waited, not knowing whose feet she was hearing. Demonstrators possibly. Maybe the news media. She hoped in their concentration to get a good camera angle of the plaza they didn't accidentally trip over her. That would be embarrassing.

In itching agony, she waited. Her every sense seemed focused on the itch. She clenched shut her eyes trying to fight back the urge to scratch it. Finally, she could stand it no longer. There were nearly a hundred dead scattered about Preston Plaza. What were the chances that anyone would see her scratching her nose?

As slowly and unobtrusively as she could manage, she pulled her hand up under the shroud. The itch was screaming now. Still, she didn't hurry. Her hand reached her hip, then atop her midriff, up her belly, across her chest, then—lifting slightly the shroud— it reached her nose and the itch.

She scratched it. Never had she known relief this pleasurable. Stifling a sigh, she rubbed her nose a second and third time for good measure. Then, just as slowly as it had crept up, she lowered her hand down the same path until it reached her side.

She held her breath, listening for any reaction. There was none. In the distance Allen was coming to the end of his prepared remarks. The chanting began again, accompanied by jeers for the administration, cries to end the war, and all manner of shouts and discontented voices. The spark Del had lit was now becoming a blaze.

Beneath her shroud Paige smiled. Del was a master. He had orchestrated everything to the tiniest detail, wound it up, and now it was running like a fine Swiss watch.

Allen's amplified voice gave the all-clear signal. He called upon the dead to rise and join their voices with the living in one united cry of humanity for a stop to the senseless war in Vietnam. As the shrouds were removed, Allen declared:

"Would that it were this easy to raise the fallen in the rice paddies of the Mekong Delta! But make no mistake. Those who fall in Vietnam, fall never to rise again! Death is forever in Vietnam! Fallen sons there will never see their country or girlfriends again! Fallen fathers there will never see their wives or children again! In Vietnam death is forever! Death is forever!"

With the other dead, Paige threw back the shroud that covered her. A small gasp escaped her lips, for there, inches from her face, was a television camera. Instinctively, she smiled. Then, realizing that Allen was shouting about death, she sobered, stood, and joined the other chanting demonstrators.

※

The walls of the house on Shores Drive reverberated to the music and screams and drunken revelry coming from within. Everyone was celebrating. Kegs flowed freely in nearly every room. Clouds of cigarette and marijuana smoke mingled against the ceiling. Everywhere people were dancing, jammed wall-to-wall. If they weren't dancing, they formed small pockets and talked, or sang, or passed a joint. If there was a common action among them, it was the frequent glance at the Coca-Cola clock on the wall. Had this been a fairy tale, one would have thought they were all Cinderella and this was a ball. But it wasn't midnight they were waiting for, but the five o'clock local news. They each were hoping to see themselves on television.

Paige sat with her former roommate on the couch. The console television—which would soon become the focal point of the entire house—was just a few feet in front of them in the corner next to the fireplace. At the moment, an antacid commercial was playing. An animated figure called Speedy was touting the benefits of the product. But while Speedy's lips moved, his message was being drowned out by the celebration.

"So where were you all afternoon?" Natalie shouted. Though she was inches away from Paige, she had to shout to be heard. "I thought you were going to meet me in the library."

"I was with Del," Paige shouted back. She smiled. "I've never seen him so excited. Or so talkative." She hesitated, lowered her eyes, and added, "Or so amorous."

Natalie's eyes lit up. She leaned forward and squared her shoulders, giving Paige her undivided attention. "Did you ..."

Paige blushed. "No!" she cried. "We talked ... and kissed. Well, we probably kissed more than we talked."

"And?"

Paige's blush deepened. "That's all," she insisted.

"Is Del a good kisser?"

Paige looked away, embarrassed. It wasn't the personal nature of the question that prompted the action, it was that Natalie was yelling it. She looked around her, certain that the entire room had heard the question. They hadn't. In fact, no one was paying them the slightest attention.

Her embarrassment was mostly real, but partly a put-on. The truth was that Del wasn't a particularly good kisser. Not that Paige was an expert on the matter, her experience largely limited to Keith Rawlins. But when it came to kissing, Del was awkward and self-conscious, and he had horrendous breath. Paige concluded he reserved all of his passion and excitement for his writing, for none of it was in his lips.

"Just as I thought," Natalie surmised, sitting back in her seat. "But you never know. Sometimes it's the least likely ones that make the best lovers."

"Del is very considerate," Paige said defensively. "It's just that he has a lot on his mind."

Natalie took a piece of gum from a small white vinyl purse. Unwrapping it, she lodged the end of the stick against her tongue and pressed, folding the gum like an accordion. After several chews, she said, "Honey, I don't mean to be the bearer of bad news, but I had that guy pegged the minute you told me you were sharing his room but not his bed. It just isn't normal. I mean, look at you. You're gorgeous. Any red-blooded American male would go insane from the temptation."

Paige frowned. She was content with her living arrangement with Del. Not once had he made any kind of sexual overture toward her. Not the slightest. Not even a hint. He was always busy writing or thinking. And the fact that he stayed on his side of the room made it easier for her to stay at the house, she reasoned. Had there been any complications, she would have had to move back into the dorm. She preferred the Shores Drive house. This was where all the action was.

Even so, Natalie's comment had struck a nerve. For though she enjoyed her largely platonic relationship with Del, there were nights when she lay in bed watching him write and wondered if there was something wrong with her. Shouldn't there be some kind of sexual tension between them? Yet there wasn't. Was she that unattractive to him?

Natalie reached over and touched Paige's arm reassuringly. "I'm sorry, honey," she said. "I didn't mean to upset you. It's just that if you're prospecting for marriage, I fear there are no diamonds in that mine. And I don't want to see you get hurt."

Paige smiled at her friend. "You didn't upset me," she said. "You're not telling me anything I haven't already thought about."

Natalie patted Paige's arm again. The two exchanged the kind of easy smile that passes between good friends.

Paige had met Natalie Archer her first day on campus and instantly liked her. They had been assigned to room together their freshman year and had gotten along so well they'd planned to be roommates again. But then Paige was kicked out of the house and arrived on campus a couple of weeks early and literally stumbled into the Shores Drive residence. And as much as she enjoyed rooming with Natalie, she enjoyed the freedom she had at Shores Drive. Still, she missed the daily interaction with Natalie.

A blonde-haired resident of Seattle, Natalie was genuine. There was an easiness about her that was nonthreatening. Paige had once heard Pastor Lamar describe one of the New Testament disciples—she couldn't remember which one—as being a man without guile. According to the pastor, the word *guile* meant snare or bait. That's the way Natalie was. She didn't befriend people to get something from them. She never had ulterior motives. She was warm—genuine and constant.

If it weren't for Natalie's congeniality, Paige doubted the two could be friends, simply because of the girl's other qualities. Natalie was brilliant, witty, and incredibly sexy. Her attraction, like her personality, was natural. She used little makeup, and she did not spend a lot of time working on her looks. She was quite simply one of God's female creations that couldn't help but attract all of his male creations. Every one of them, young and old, without exception.

Natalie, however, seemed oblivious to her universal appeal. Her focus was on a career. She aspired to be a defense attorney, and there was not a person on campus who doubted that she would make a good one. Her professors—who treated her like an equal—pointed out that she had everything going for her. They theorized that her combination of friendliness and good looks would disarm any and all opposition, while her wit and intelligence would tie them up in knots.

"The news is about to start!" Natalie said, pointing to the television. Sure enough, a montage of news clips flashed on the screen followed by pictures of the news team and concluding with a local station's channel number and call letters.

"Turn it up! Turn it up!"

When Natalie's cry for volume failed to prompt a quick enough response, she leaped from her seat and turned up the volume herself. Within moments there was a crush of humanity surrounding the television set. More than a hundred pairs of eyes jammed the room, straining to get a look at the console.

A crew-cut local anchorman appeared on the screen. Unsmiling. Focused. He held a sheaf of pages with both hands as he stared directly into the camera and read the top story. More casualties in Vietnam.

Boos and catcalls and profanities filled the room.

Paige looked around for Del. Where was he? He was going to miss the broadcast.

No sooner had she thought this when Del and Allen wedged their way through the crowd. Had it been any other duo, they would not have been let through.

Del plopped down on the couch beside Natalie. She shot him a glance and a smile. He didn't see it. In fact, she wasn't sure he knew he was sitting next to her. His attention was riveted on the television set.

Allen propped himself on the arm of the chair next to Natalie. He too was fixed on the glowing tube. He looked different to Paige. Allen was rarely a study in concentration. Like the anchorman, he was usually the focus of everyone's attention.

Looking at him, an odd thought struck Paige, one that brought a smile to her face. She looked down at Natalie. Why hadn't she seen it before? Natalie and Allen! The two even looked like a couple sitting next to each other. Both of them were attractive, standouts, successful. Paige grinned. A possible match?

After a moment's consideration, she dismissed the thought. Natalie was Allen's intellectual superior. She doubted a guy with an ego like Allen's would be able to handle that.

"Here it is!" Del shouted. "Everyone shut up!"

The room instantly grew still. From the back corner somewhere, an unknown voice mimicked the *Twilight Zone's* musical theme. He was soundly shushed by nearly half the room.

"And in related news," the anchor said, "here at home, a demonstration against the war was staged at the UCRD campus."

The picture on the screen switched from the studio to a shot of Preston Plaza. A cheer erupted, which angered Del because it prevented him from hearing the commentary. With a scowl he fell on his knees before the television and turned the volume knob as far as it would turn. The resulting sound was so loud the speakers couldn't handle it and the words emerged garbled.

Del cursed again. Without taking his eyes off the television for an instant, he shouted maniacally for quiet. Like echoes, his request was repeated around the room, accompanied by a half-dozen shushing sounds.

Paige blushed at Del's outburst, though it was typical Del. Explosive. Off color. And though she didn't want to fool herself into pretending he was something he was not, she wished he would be a little less blunt or crude at times.

Out of the corner of her eye, she saw Natalie looking at her, gauging her reaction to her boyfriend. Paige pretended not to notice.

Gunshot sounds came from the television speakers as a shot of the plaza filled the screen. The shot jiggled as the cameraman reacted to the sound, but only momentarily. He didn't fail to catch the reaction of students and the police. Then, all across the plaza, figures were seen falling to the ground, their arms and legs akimbo. Students standing nearby reacted with shock. Then, seeing no blood and realizing it was a demonstration, they applauded.

The undertakers appeared and covered the dead. A camera followed close behind one of them as person after person was covered. A male's heavily blemished face filled the screen; then it was gone, covered by a black cloth.

"That's me!" a voice shouted from the back of the room. "I'm famous!"

Sounds of congratulations came from his buddies, shushes from everybody else.

The anchor concluded the news story in a monotone voice, "And while there were no actual fatalities, the demonstration seems to have captured the spirit of discontent on the UCRD campus. While local authorities were reluctant to comment on today's demonstration, one police official, who wished to remain anonymous, told this reporter that while he did not condone the demonstration, no harm was done and no laws were broken. He categorized it as nothing more than a publicity-grabbing college prank, not unlike the swallowing of goldfish in the twenties. In other local news ..."

Del grunted loudly. He switched off the television with such vehemence Paige thought for sure he'd snapped off the knob.

"Prank?" Del screamed. "That's it? All our work tossed aside as nothing more than a college prank?" He looked for something to throw. Nothing was at hand. The room was so packed with bodies everything was either sat on or covered. So he clenched his fists and let out an animal-like howl.

Allen jumped to his side. "Hey, settle down, Del," he said soothingly. "You're gonna blow a gasket."

Del wasn't listening. His eyes bulged. His fists clenched. His face was beet red. He shook with rage.

"You know these local media are nothing but clowns," Allen said. "You've said so yourself."

With all the others in the room now watching Del as intently as they had been watching the television set, Allen looked to Paige for help.

A cold dread swept over her. She didn't know what to do. It had always been her practice to leave Del alone when he got like this. Sometimes it would take days for him to get over something.

"Hey, there's always the network," Allen said.

As suddenly as Del's rage had seized him, it began to subside. The word *network* worked on him like a sedative, though Paige had no idea why it would.

"Network?" she asked.

"Go ahead, Del," Allen insisted. "Tell them."

Del blinked several times. His eyes slowly crystallized with clear thought again. The room waited in silence for what was to come next.

"Allen's right," Del said, his voice raspy from shouting.

This admission itself brought raised eyebrows from some, including Natalie. Del rarely gave credit to Allen for anything he said or did.

"Just before this local yokel's broadcast began …"

His characterization of the anchorman prompted a few smiles and titters.

"… I received a phone call informing me that the national network has picked up the story. We're going to be on again at six o'clock."

Cheers erupted in the room. They were loud, too loud given the announcement. While it was indeed good news, the cries were more a release of tension than joy.

In short order the partying resumed. The network news was a good fifty minutes away.

※

"Paige! Paige Morgan!"

The shout somehow managed to cut through the party roar and reach her. Paige heard her name and looked around. People were dancing, talking, kissing, smoking, and drinking. No one was looking at her.

"Paige Morgan!"

There it was again!

She turned to Natalie. "Did you hear someone call my name?"

"Uh-huh."

Now both girls were craning their necks to locate the source of her name. Neither had any luck. Even the direction proved difficult to locate given the sound in the room.

Paige jumped up and stood on the couch. Now she could see above the crowd. She scanned the room.

"Paige! Phone!"

A guy she didn't know was holding up the receiver of the telephone. Apparently he knew her, for he held the receiver her direction.

"It's your mother!" he shouted.

Paige looked at her watch. Ten minutes to six. She didn't want to miss the national broadcast. For a moment she weighed the possibility of asking the guy with the phone to tell her mom she'd call back later. She dismissed the thought.

Climbing over the back of the couch, she wove her way through a tangle of gyrating bodies.

"Thanks," she said, taking the receiver.

"Don't mention it." He caught her eye and smiled, holding it longer than what would be considered cordial. Paige made a mental note to ask Natalie if she knew who he was.

"Hello?"

"Paige?"

"Mom?"

"Paige, what's all that noise?"

Her mother's voice was barely audible. Paige covered her exposed ear with the flat of her hand.

"It's a party, Mom. We were just on television."

"What, dear?"

Paige shouted the news again.

"It wasn't anything bad, was it?"

"No, Mom, it was good. A peaceful demonstration. And the networks are picking it up. It'll be on at six. You and Dad can watch it."

"It's almost six o'clock now."

"I know," Paige shouted, hoping her mother would get the hint. She did.

"I won't keep you long then," she said. "I just wanted to keep in touch with you."

Paige nodded. Her mother called her weekly just to keep in touch. During these telephonic visits Paige had kept track of her brother—whom she had written only occasionally while he was in boot camp. She also had learned that her father had been assigned by the magazine to cover Robert Kennedy's campaign. Best of all, though, her mother had recently confided in her that her father regretted deeply throwing her out of the house. Of course, this was satisfying news, but not as satisfying as if he had told her himself.

"I got a letter from your brother today," her mother said. "He arrived safely in Vietnam."

Now there's a contradiction if I've ever heard one, Paige thought. *My brother's arrived safely in hell.*

"And guess who his squad leader is?"

Paige was distracted by the way the noise was abating, also by the way people were gravitating toward the television.

"Who, Mom?"

"Keith Rawlins."

Instantly, Paige's attention was completely on her phone conversation.

"Did you hear me, dear?"

"Yes, Mother, I heard you."

"Isn't that great news? Keith can look after your brother while they're in Vietnam."

Or get killed together, Paige thought. She said, "That's great news, Mom."

Images of Keith played in her mind like a retroactive slide show. She and Keith holding hands at school. She and Keith on the beach. She and Keith riding side by side in his car. She and Keith kissing.

"That's what I thought," her mother said, "but your brother doesn't seem to be as excited about it as I thought he would be."

"How can you tell?"

"Oh, I don't know. Just the tone of the letter."

Paige shook her head. "You must be reading something into it," she said. "I imagine Travis is ecstatic hooking up with Keith that way."

"I'm sure you're right," her mother said, not sounding very convinced. "Maybe I'm …"

Waving arms caught Paige's attention. They were signaling to her that the newscast was about to begin. She looked at her watch. The big and little hands formed a straight vertical line.

"Mom, I gotta go!" Paige said hurriedly.

"Is it six o'clock already?"

"Yeah, and the newscast is starting. Bye. Love you!"

"And we love you, too, Paige, and …"

"Mom," Paige interrupted. "It's channel ten. Watch us."

"We will, dear."

"Bye, Mom!"

"Good-bye, de—"

Paige was already moving away from the phone while she hung up the receiver. She dashed across the now empty floor space, dove into the assembled crowd, worked her way to the couch, climbed over the back of it, and fell into her seat just as the commentator said his first words. They were about Vietnam.

Del looked over at her, none too pleased. "You almost missed it!" he said.

"I know. My mom called."

Del looked away, dismissing her explanation as irrelevant.

Their story wasn't aired until twenty-eight minutes past the hour. As the half-hour broadcast progressed, there was growing speculation that maybe the story had been cut. But then, as the familiar plaza scene appeared, as with the local broadcast, the initial hoots and shouts at seeing themselves on the television died out in a hail of shushes so that the commentary could be heard.

Paige thought the commentator's tone was light given the gravity of the subject. To her horror she knew why a moment later.

A picture of a black shroud filled the screen. A powerful image of death. Then, something beneath the shroud moved. It began near the knees and worked its way up the middle of the form, pausing near the face and wiggling back and forth; then, the movement worked back down the shroud to where it had originated.

"On the lighter side of the news, an antiwar demonstration at the University of California Rancho Diego campus was not without its humorous moments," said the commentator with a syrupy stage voice, "when an apparently less-than-dead fallen soldier had an itch."

No one in the room was laughing. It was as quiet as a morgue. Del was rigid—red-faced and rigid.

Paige closed her eyes, praying that the newsman would not identify the person beneath the shroud.

"Let's take a look at that again," the news anchor said, laughing. For the next thirty seconds, he and the coanchor joked as they followed a replay of the movement beneath the shroud. The anchor explained again he thought the person under the shroud had an itch. The coanchor disagreed; he guessed that the person beneath the shroud was a hungry student snacking on a cookie.

Del was on his feet. "Who was that?" he shouted. "Who was that?"

He looked from face to face. Few returned his gaze. No one confessed to being the moving shroud.

Paige cowered and prayed for an end to the broadcast. *Please just say good night and sign off. Please, please.*

She opened her eyes, startled. If it were possible, the room had grown quieter still. So quiet, in fact, she feared everyone had heard her silent plea.

"What do our viewers think at home?" the news anchor asked good-naturedly. "Itch or cookie?"

This can't be happening, Paige thought silently.

"Let's settle this question, once for all," the anchor suggested. "Continue rolling the clip."

The shroud again appeared on the screen.

Del took a step forward in angry anticipation.

A hand appeared from beneath the shroud, tossing it aside. The camera zoomed in. Paige's smiling face filled the screen.

Paige wished she could shrink into nonexistence.

"Well, there you have it," quipped the anchorman. "A coed with an itchy nose."

Del glared at the screen. He didn't move.

"Well, just because it's a coed doesn't mean she wasn't eating a cookie," argued the coanchor.

The residents and guest of Shores Drive began to filter out of the room with little discussion. They had expected to make a serious statement against the war and had instead provided comedy relief at the end of a broadcast—the spot usually reserved for stories like that of a female dog nursing a litter of kittens, or of a man walking on his hands attempting to break a Guinness world record.

On the television the view pulled back to show Paige standing and joining the rally.

"I'll tell you one thing," the anchorman said, "that's the prettiest soldier I've ever seen."

"They certainly didn't have soldiers like that when we were in the army, did they?" quipped the weatherman.

"It makes you wonder," said the anchorman, "if these demonstrators are hiring Hollywood models now. She's a knockout, isn't she?"

As the news anchorman said good night to the world and signed off, Natalie patted Paige on the arm. "Call me later if you need to talk," she whispered. Joining the others, she left.

Soon there was no one in the downstairs room on Shores Drive other than Paige sitting on the couch and Del standing like a statue in front of a television that was playing a dog food commercial.

10

"Del?" Paige had waited nearly fifteen minutes before speaking. She'd wanted to give Del as much time to cool off as he needed. But when the second edition of the local evening news broke for commercial and Del was still standing there, she decided to speak up. For all she knew, he wasn't even aware she was still in the room.

"Del, come sit down."

The statue didn't move. He gave no indication of having heard her. Other than the fact that he was standing there unaided, he gave no indication of being alive.

He was a strange one, there was no doubt about that. But while others feared or made fun of Del's eccentricities, Paige was attracted to them, at least some of them. Del was an individual. While everyone else lionized individuality, yet dressed and talked and acted like everyone in their particular group be it surfer or rebel or druggie, Del was his own person. He didn't try to be like anyone else; he didn't try to please anyone else; he didn't try to think like anyone else. Wasn't that the mark of true genius? Weren't all the great thinkers in history ridiculed by the smaller minds of their time? Weren't all the great thinkers and innovators of the world just a bit unstable? Didn't they gain their unique insight into things by daring to walk to the edge of sanctioned thought and taking one more step?

It was Del's uniqueness that attracted Paige to him. And it was his mood swings that most frightened her. Here was a man who knew meteoric highs and hellish lows. Paige concluded that this was the price he paid for his genius. She further concluded that her devotion to him could weather any storm. She saw this as her contribution to a new world order. While Del strafed the strato-sphere with his high and lofty ideas, she would be his anchor lest, like an errant balloon, he stray so high he was unable to find his way back to earth.

"What were you thinking?"

The statue spoke. He didn't turn, nor did he now give any evidence of having been the one to speak. But there were only the two of them in the room. It had to have been him.

"Del, I'm sorry. I didn't know the camera was there. My nose itched...."

"Your nose itched."

Paige giggled. It sounded trivial the way he said it. "It really was a bad itch, Del," she said. "You know ... the kind that, the more you try to ignore it, the more ..."

"Your nose itched?" Del thundered. He swung around. His face was as black as a thundercloud. "Your nose itched?"

His face was so distorted, he was barely recognizable. Paige shrank back into the couch as the storm of Del's wrath moved in and hovered over her.

"Boys are dying in Vietnam, their lifeblood staining the rice paddies red, and we try to make a simple, yet profound statement to this fact, one that will make the world sit up and take notice and possibly come to its senses and stop this insane violence, and all of it for naught! Why? Tell me why?"

"Because my nose itched," Paige whimpered.

"Because your nose itched! After years of hard work and strategizing and planning and organizing, we finally make the networks. But as what? Comedy relief!"

"Del, I'm sorry. I couldn't ..."

"All across America people are laughing at us! Not only us, but all demonstrators everywhere! With one film clip they have laughed us off, reduced us to nothing more than little kids wearing Halloween costumes. Nobody will take us seriously anymore! We're cute little girls hiding under blankets who come out smiling for the cameras!"

When Paige first saw the television spot, she didn't think she could feel any lower. She was wrong. She began to weep, not only because Del was screaming at her, but because he was right. She had single-handedly destroyed all of their efforts.

"I should have known better than to let women play a serious role in this," Del continued. "This is just a game for you, isn't it? What do you know of the terrors of war? While guys face the prospect of being butchered alive, all you girls have to do is wait for the whole ones to come back home so you can marry them. What was I thinking? You couldn't possibly know the terror of the prospect of what we're facing."

Paige sat up. She had felt every blow of his verbal bludgeoning and was willing to accept what was coming to her, but Del had just crossed the line. "That's not fair!" she shouted back.

"Oh, isn't it?" Del screamed at the top of his lungs. Apparently, he thought she was just supposed to sit there and take it, because her defense, as weak as it was, pushed him to the edge of self-control. "Isn't it? You didn't see any guys bouncing out from under their blankets like empty-headed coeds ready to cheer on their guys in the big game against Vietnam U!"

"I had an itch!" Paige screamed.

"Well your itch probably cost the lives of several platoons!"

Del hollered. "Because nobody will take us seriously again. Not the networks, not the people, and certainly not the idiots in Washington who have it in their power to stop the carnage!"

Paige trembled uncontrollably. Tears sprang with such force, she couldn't wipe them away fast enough. Rising from the couch, blinded by emotion, she stumbled toward the stairs with but a single thought—to flee. She didn't care where; she just had to get away.

At the foot of the stairs, she stopped, supporting herself on the railing. She couldn't leave without making an effort to make things right. If she left now, she wasn't sure Del would ever speak to her again. Drawing in a ragged breath, she said, "Del ... I'm sorry...."

"It's too late for that," he spat.

The floodgates of emotion were about to burst within her, and she knew she was about to lose control. With great effort she held them back for just a moment longer.

"Wh ... what can I do to make it up to you?" she asked.

"Get out."

His words were cold.

"Del ..."

"Get out!" he shouted.

"If I leave now ..."

"Get out! Get out! GET OUT! GET OUT!"

He was ranting uncontrollably, flailing his arms like a madman; shouting, howling, chanting all at the same time.

"GET OUT! GET OUT! GET OUT!"

The last measure of Paige's control failed. The floodgates opened. Pure emotion swept through her, blinded her, washed over her senses and reasoning and thought. She stumbled toward the front door of the house, down the steps, across the yard, into the street, not consciously aware that she had taken a single step.

She wasn't even aware that she was in the middle of the street until she found herself sprawled against the macadam surface. Her cheek pressed against the single yellow stripe. The palms of her hands scraped and bleeding. Her knees red and black and on fire.

Through her blurred vision she saw the lights of the women's dormitory.

※

"Paige! What happened to you?"

Natalie swung the door open wide. A look of motherly concern adorned her face. Paige wasn't exactly certain how she made it to the third floor of the women's dorm, but just the sight of Natalie's concerned face was a balm in itself.

"Did Del do this to you?" Natalie demanded.

Paige shook her head. "I fell."

Suspicion clouded Natalie's face as she helped Paige sit on the edge of her bed. Paige knew how it must look. She'd seen girls who'd been beaten by their boyfriends. Without exception, the girl defended the wretch with some lame excuse.

"Really," she insisted. "I know what it looks like, but I fell on the road."

With a series of sympathetic winces, Natalie examined Paige's hands and knees. She brushed dirt from her cheek.

"Did the road cause the redness in your eyes too?" Natalie asked with more than a touch of sarcasm in her voice. "You wait here. We keep a first-aid kit in the RA's room."

Natalie was gone for but a few minutes, during which time Paige shivered, but not because she was cold. On the way back from the resident assistant's room, Natalie had stopped at the restroom and grabbed a couple of paper towels that she'd run under water. Kneeling in front of Paige, she tenderly dabbed at the scrapes.

Paige pulled back instinctively at the pain. Natalie worked calmly and efficiently.

"Where did you learn to be such a good mother?" Paige asked, trying to lighten the mood.

A half grin formed on Natalie's face. "Instinct, I suppose. Does performing these motherly duties also give me the right to ask some motherly questions?"

"I told you. I fell in the street."

"And what were you doing before you fell?"

That was the odd part. Paige couldn't remember. It didn't take a genius to figure it out. She wept. She ran. She fell. But she could remember nothing between the time her dammed-up emotions broke loose and the moment she found herself laying with her cheek pressed against the street.

"Where were you going?" Natalie asked.

Paige shook her head. "Nowhere."

"Nowhere?"

"Just out."

Natalie shook her head. "Just out," she repeated.

If Paige hadn't felt so low, she would have laughed at the conversation. It was exactly the conversation she would have had if Natalie were her mother.

"Did Del Gilroy have anything to do with this?"

Paige didn't reply.

"That's what I thought."

"I told you, Del didn't do this to me," Paige insisted.

"But he was the cause behind it, wasn't he?"

Again, Paige held her tongue.

"Did he hit you?"

"No!" Paige said.

"But he yelled at you."

"Yes."

"What did he say?"

Paige shook her head. She stared at the floor. She felt Natalie's hand reach under her chin and lift it up. A cool, damp cloth brushed the dirt from her cheek.

"He blamed you for the news story, didn't he?"

Paige didn't respond.

"Typical male," Natalie said. "Things didn't turn out like he'd hoped, so he has to blame somebody. Anybody but himself."

"It wasn't his fault."

"It wasn't *your* fault," Natalie said.

"I was the only one who didn't act dead."

Natalie took a step back and stared at her in disbelief. "You *are* blaming yourself," she said.

Paige shrugged. "I shouldn't have moved."

Returning to her doctoring, Natalie said, "What am I going to do with you?"

Paige grinned. It felt good. Not only the grin, but being mothered by a friend. Although they were the same age, Natalie had always been the mature one. Paige thought of her as her big sister.

"You're not going to put me on restriction, are you, Mom?" Paige laughed.

"For what? You didn't do anything wrong. If I could, I'd forbid you from seeing Del Gilroy again."

The smile faded from Paige's lips.

Natalie had never approved of Del. It was the one tender point between them.

"Can I stay the night?" Paige asked, changing the conversation.

"You know you can."

Going to her dresser drawer, Natalie produced an oversized T-shirt with a picture of Snoopy sleeping on top of his dog house. Gingerly, Paige removed her blue jeans and top and slipped into it. The dorm room had two single beds. One had been reserved for

Paige until she decided to live at the house on Shores Drive. Her place had not been filled by another roommate, leaving Natalie alone in the room.

Still playing the role of mother, Natalie produced a sleeping bag from the closet. It would serve as Paige's bedding for the night. Paige slipped into it and watched as Natalie prepared herself for bed.

It was a procedure with which Paige was familiar, having shared a room with her for a year. *Methodical* was the word that always came to mind whenever she watched Natalie. Everything the girl did was done with purpose. Step by orderly step. Methodical.

She closed the books she'd been studying. One by one, but not before first marking her place. She stacked the books on top of her notebook and placed them on the corner of the desk, a pencil and pen stowed carefully to one side. Then she turned her attention to herself.

She undressed. Each piece of clothing was hung in a closet or folded. Even the clothes she put in the laundry basket to be washed were first folded, for what reason Paige could only guess. Donning an oversized T-shirt herself—this one with a large picture of Tweety Bird on it—Natalie opened a drawer and pulled out a toiletries kit. Excusing herself, she went to the bathroom halfway down the dormitory hallway.

Paige lay back on the bed and stared at the ceiling, knowing exactly what Natalie was doing and in what order. Face. Hair. Teeth. It had been that way every night for a year. Any other order and it wouldn't have been Natalie. Paige remembered when Natalie's orderliness used to bother her. Somehow, right now, it was a sense of comfort. It was as though Natalie restored a sense of order to a world in chaos.

But there was more to Natalie's orderliness than just a tidy room. It extended into everything she did. Her orderliness made her solid. Yet there was nothing stodgy about the girl. She was quick to laugh, got along with most people, could discuss any number of subjects intelligently, was liked by most everyone, and was as passionate as the next person on things that mattered, like opposition to the war. But in everything there was a balance, a sense of purpose.

She knew who she was and where she was going. Despite protests, boyfriends, and parties, she was determined to be a lawyer. Her goal was so real to her, at times she already acted like a lawyer. People thought of her as the soon-to-be lawyer. No one questioned that that was what she would be. Nations could rise and fall, administrations change, weather patterns vary, dynasties come and go, and Natalie would be a lawyer. It seemed preordained.

Solid. Orderly. Purposeful. Confident. That was Natalie. Paige wished she were more like her.

The door opened. Natalie stepped in. Her hair brushed to a sheen. Her face clean. Her breath with a hint of mint. She placed the toiletry kit back in the drawer and pulled down her covers. For a while neither girl spoke.

"Paige?"

"Yeah?"

"We're friends, aren't we?"

Paige propped herself up on an elbow. It hurt to do so. Though she hadn't scraped her elbows, they suffered mild abrasions from the fall, enough to smart.

"Of course we're friends," Paige said. "Closer than most. Almost sisters."

Natalie smiled at the thought. "Then we can be honest with each other."

Paige felt a chill pass through her. She knew where this conversation was going. Flopping back onto the bed, she said, "Please, Natalie, don't start."

"But what kind of a friend would I be if I didn't say something?" Natalie asked.

Paige stared at the ceiling.

"You're too good for him," Natalie said.

This brought a laugh from Paige. If anything, Del was too good for her. She was lucky that someone of his genius would give her a second look.

"Have you slept with him?" Natalie asked.

"Natalie!"

"Well, have you?"

"No."

"I'm not surprised."

Paige raised up again. "What do you mean by that?"

"I didn't mean that in a bad way," Natalie explained. "I think it's good you haven't slept with him. It would mean a lot more to you than it would to him."

"Now what does that mean?"

"Paige, it's obvious. The guy isn't interested in a relationship. All I meant was that if you'd slept with him, you'd be more emotionally attached to him than you are now. And if he'd slept with you, I doubt he'd even remember it."

Paige was hurt. "Now you're just being mean."

Natalie matched Paige's position. The expression on her face was one of sincere concern. "I don't mean to hurt you," she said. "Honestly, Paige, I'm saying this because I don't want you to get hurt. Del is not the kind of guy that settles down and gets married. He's wild. Untamed. Radical in every sense of the word. I don't doubt his passion for what he is doing, but I also can't see that passion being transferred over to anything else. He will never be more than a revolutionary, and I think you deserve someone who will at least treat you like you exist."

"You don't understand him like I do," Paige said. "I know better than anyone what he is like. And I'm not trying to change him to be something that he's not. I'm attracted to him for who he is, nothing more, nothing less."

"Do you love him?"

"I don't know. I think I do."

"Does he love you?"

Paige had asked herself this question a hundred times. "I think he loves me as much as he is capable at this time."

Natalie closed her eyes. For a long moment she said nothing. Then, "Did you hear what you just said?" She paused, though it was clear she wasn't expecting an answer. "I think you're exactly right in what you said. Only, I think you're fooling yourself if you think he will ever be able to love anyone with a genuine love. That's not mean, just an observation."

This wasn't a revelation for Paige. She'd pondered the thought before. In the end she'd concluded it didn't matter. If she could spend her days encouraging Del's genius and by doing so make the world a better place, wasn't that worth personal sacrifice? Would life be so terrible if Del never fulfilled her romantically? Wasn't there a greater good to consider here?

"Let me ask you this," Natalie continued. "How are your grades?"

This was a tender subject. Life at Shores Drive made studying difficult, not simply because of all the noise and activity, but because there always seemed to be something more important going on: strategy sessions, discussions about the future of America, the decadence of society, the need for radical reform, and helping Del get the newspaper printed and distributed. Consequently, Paige's attendance at class was sporadic at best. Her grades were poor. She kept promising herself that she'd find time to pull them up. But somehow, the time never materialized.

"And how about your painting? When was the last time you painted anything?" Natalie asked.

"There are more important things than painting," Paige said.

"Not for you," Natalie replied. "Don't you see? You're an artist—a talented one. You're letting your talent go to waste."

"For a greater cause!" Paige replied.

"That's Del's cause, not yours," Natalie replied. "Don't you see? The world is losing Paige Morgan. She's being swallowed up by events she cannot possibly change. You know me; I'm the first one to insist we have to speak out against injustice and atrocity and senseless killing. But not at the expense of our souls. If Del Gilroy or the Vietnam crisis diverts Paige Morgan from becoming who she was created to be, it has claimed one more victim, as surely as if you were shot in a rice paddy. And I, for one, would mourn the loss."

The lights in the dorm room were out long before Paige drifted off to sleep. The idea that she was indirectly a casualty of the Vietnam conflict was a disturbing thought indeed.

BAM! BAM! BAM! BAM!

"Paige! Are you in there?"

BAM! BAM! BAM! BAM!

"Paige!"

The hold sleep had on Paige was a strong one, but once it was broken, she bolted upright in bed. Glancing across the dark room, she saw Natalie in similar position.

"Oh, no," Natalie groaned.

From Natalie's reaction, Paige knew that she had recognized the identity of the door pounder just as she had.

BAM! BAM! BAM! BAM!

"Paige! Paige! Are you in there?"

Throwing back the cover of the sleeping bag, Paige glanced at the clock on Natalie's desk. It was ten minutes after four in the morning.

"Tell him to go away," Natalie said. Then, she sat up. "Better yet, let me."

Paige waved her off. "I'll talk to him."

Shuffling toward the door in the dark, she reached forward and felt the wall for the light switch. With a single click of the switch, the girls' eyes were assaulted by a harsh light.

BAM! BAM! BAM! BAM!

Paige unlocked the door and opened it a crack.

"Del! What are you doing? You'll wake the whole floor!"

He didn't seem to mind. His eyes were alive with excitement; his cheeks—patchy with beard—were spread in a huge grin.

"I have to talk with you!" he shouted. His voice echoed up and down the hallway.

Paige was confused, and her confusion was confounded by a head that was still groggy with sleep. The last she had seen Del he was screaming and ranting at her to get out of the house.

"Can't it wait until morning?" she asked.

"No, it can't! Please, Paige. I know I acted like a jerk and I'm sorry, but something good has come out of it, and I have to tell you about it."

A voice came from behind Paige. It was Natalie. "Del, go sleep it off," she said. "Leave Paige alone."

Del ignored her. Speaking to Paige he said, "I'm not on anything. And I haven't been drinking. I've been thinking. And—Paige—you've been my inspiration! Please come home so I can tell you about it."

There was no doubting that Del was ecstatic. Whatever it was that was exciting him was also animating his feet. He couldn't stand still.

"Please, Paige," Del pleaded.

Paige looked over her shoulder at Natalie. As expected, Natalie was shaking her head, advising her not to go with him.

"Give me a minute to get dressed," Paige said.

Del's grin grew even wider as she closed the door.

"Don't say it," Paige said with uplifted hand.

She walked to the chair next to her bed where her clothes were draped. She began to dress.

Natalie didn't speak. She slumped on the edge of her bed and watched Paige dress. Her disappointment was evident.

Paige knew there was nothing she could say that would adequately explain why she was going with Del. How could she explain something she didn't understand herself?

"Thanks for being here for me," Paige said, heading for the door.

"That's what friends are for," Natalie replied. She stood and gave Paige a hug.

When the door opened again, Del was standing in the middle of the hallway bouncing from one foot to the other. His hands were thrust deeply into his pockets. He was grinning like a little boy.

They walked the length of the dark hallway with only the light coming from Natalie's room to light their way, that and the green exit sign.

Leaving the building, they walked down three flights of exterior stairs, across the damp night grass, and into the street that led off campus before Del spoke.

"What you did today was terrific!" he said. "Had you not done what you did, I could have continued for years in the mistaken assumption that street drama could change things. But it won't. It can't. The very concept is flawed."

Paige looked at him. She could feel his excitement.

"Don't you see?" Del cried. "We're a product of an entertainment society. We use drama as an escape. And that's why it won't work."

He looked to Paige expectantly. "I'm not following," she said.

"It won't work, because we know it's drama. It's not real. John Wayne can mow down a legion of bad guys, but at the heart of it all, we know it's not real. We don't take it seriously. So, no matter how dramatic our drama, people will never take it seriously because they know it's not real. That's what you taught me, Paige. That's what you taught me."

He stopped her in the middle of the street, threw his arms around her and, before she knew what was happening, he kissed her. Hard. Passionately. Then, just as suddenly, he was walking again.

"It has to be real," he said. "Conflict. Pain. Suffering. They have to feel it. And they won't feel it unless it's real."

Paige wasn't listening. She stood in the center of the street, stunned—by the sudden change in Del, by the dramatic turn-around of events, and by the kiss.

What did it mean? And how could she explain the change in him other than that's the way he was? All at the same time she felt attracted to him, disgusted with him, and admiration for him. But while she felt all these things, she didn't know what to think.

11

I shall not seek, and I will not accept, the nomination of my party for another term as president.

—Lyndon B. Johnson

With these words, delivered during a national television address on March 31, 1968, the Democratic race for president became a free-for-all, much to the delight of student protesters across the country and around the world. By voluntarily stepping aside, President Johnson cleared the way for alternative voices in his party. Younger voices—voices that called for an end to the war in Vietnam.

Earlier in the primaries, antiwar candidate Senator Eugene McCarthy of Minnesota had polled 42 percent of the New Hampshire vote over against 48 percent for the yet unannounced candidate and incumbent Johnson. Soon afterward Senator Robert Kennedy, also a major critic of U.S. involvement in Vietnam, announced his candidacy. When Johnson announced he would not run, Kennedy quickly became the frontrunner.

Nat Morgan couldn't have been happier. While he was a firm believer in backing the president's policies in Vietnam for as long as our troops were needed to stop the spread of communism, he was disturbed by the way the Vietnam conflict was tearing the country—and his family—apart. While McCarthy was too liberal for him, Kennedy seemed to be a candidate able to bridge the gap between young and old. As far as Nat was concerned, he was the nation's best chance for reconciliation and healing. The polls seemed to agree with him. Kennedy's campaign took off quickly and gained momentum with each state primary.

The younger brother of slain president John F. Kennedy rode the nostalgic wave of popular sentiment for a family that had been likened to *Camelot*, a popular Broadway musical based on King Arthur and his beautiful queen, Guinevere.

The Kennedys were a family acquainted with tragedy. Joe Jr., the oldest of the Kennedy brothers, had been killed in battle during World War II. The next oldest, John Fitzgerald, entered office as a senator, then as president on a heroic campaign that highlighted his wartime role as commander of a PT boat, for which he was awarded Navy and Marine Corps medals as well as a Purple Heart. His *Profiles in Courage* was awarded a Pulitzer Prize in biography in 1957. He was youthful, energetic, photogenic, and—together with his beautiful wife, Jackie—raised the White House to a higher cultural level.

Then came the gunshots in Dallas on November 22, 1963. Camelot came crashing down. The early bulletins that came from Dallas that day stunned the nation. Nearly five years later people could still vividly remember where they were and what they were doing when they first heard the news of John Kennedy's assassination. And now, brother Bobby, the third of the four Kennedy brothers, was taking a run at the White House. The nation seemed eager for a revival of Camelot, especially when the charging white knight also promised them an end to the nightmare of Vietnam.

Nat had been assigned to cover the Kennedy campaign shortly after the New York senator announced his candidacy. In quick succession Kennedy won major primaries in Indiana and Nebraska. And on primary election day in California, shortly before the Democratic National Convention would meet in

Chicago, he was leading in a tight race against McCarthy. A win in California would almost assure him his party's nomination.

JUNE 5, 12:00 a.m.

Nat rubbed his eyes and looked at his watch. It had been a long day. Waiting was always the hardest. Following a whirlwind campaign tour of California, Nat found himself in the Ambassador Hotel in downtown Los Angeles. Although he knew it would probably be after midnight before the final tally was announced, he'd hoped for something of a miracle. With home only a two-hour drive away, he was counting on an early victory so that he could hit the road and spend the night in his own bed.

He looked at his watch again. No such luck. Even if Kennedy were to make an appearance soon, Nat probably wouldn't make it home until after 3:00 a.m. So now, the question was—stay in LA for the night and go home in the morning, or drive home tonight? Was he awake enough to do that?

The question itself made him yawn. There was a stirring near the podium. He gripped his camera and readied himself to take the shot. Then, when he saw who it was, he lowered his camera.

Milton Berle, the television comedian, stood behind the microphone. He announced that Robert Kennedy would make an appearance soon. "At the moment, he's kinda tied up," quipped the comedian. He paused, then added, "I oughta know, I'm the one who tied him up."

The room—crammed with people from wall to wall—erupted with laughter. Greater laughter than the joke deserved.

12:03 a.m.

An entourage made its way to the podium. Robert Kennedy was among them. Nat could barely see the top of his head. Once again he readied the camera for the shot.

Ordinarily, Nat was part of the entourage. *FLASH!* magazine was a prestigious and popular pictorial publication. Free publicity for any candidate. Even a family as wealthy as the Kennedys couldn't afford to buy the kind of exposure Nat gave a candidate with his pictures. For this particular announcement, though, Nat wanted a straight-on shot of the candidate, from the point of view of the voters and campaign workers. Afterward he would rejoin the entourage and get some behind-the-scenes shots.

All around him was bedlam. People shouted and waved banners and tooted horns and threw streamers and confetti. They were anticipating good news—a victory speech.

Bobby Kennedy took his place behind a podium, the words AMBASSADOR HOTEL featured prominently on the front. He waved at the cheering crowds. They responded with more noise and chants. After a time he managed to calm them down enough to be heard.

The Democratic candidate made it official. Election polls were now projecting him as the winner of the California primary.

The place erupted.

Nat framed the scene in his camera's viewfinder. The senator was in the center of the frame. His wife, Ethyl, was behind him to the right. Filling the sides and bottom of the frame were jubilant hands and arms. Nat expertly composed his shot. He threw the arms slightly out of focus, thus making the figure in the center of the exposure stand out.

CLICK.

The picture would probably make the cover of next month's magazine. Nat took several more pictures as Bobby Kennedy addressed his supporters.

The candidate said he wanted to thank his dog, Freckles, who had been much maligned during the campaign.

Laughter filled the room.

He also wanted to thank—not necessarily in order of importance—his wife, Ethyl, for standing beside him during the difficult days of the campaign. He thanked all of his supporters in California and credited them with the win.

Kennedy was tired. Nat could see it. The man's weariness was evident as Nat focused on his face.

"And now it's on to Chicago and let's win there!" Kennedy shouted. He waved one last wave and turned to leave.

Nat glanced at his watch. *I knew I liked this guy for a reason,* he said to himself. *Probably the shortest political speech during the entire campaign. I might just get home tonight after all.*

12:15 a.m.

Slinging his camera over his shoulder, Nat pressed through the crowd toward the podium and the retreating senator. He noticed there had been some confusion just as the senator stepped down from the podium. While Kennedy's entourage turned right, the senator turned left to exit the room through the kitchen, the same way he'd come in. The men who acted as his point guards called after him. He either ignored them or didn't hear them, forging his own trail out of the ballroom.

Now why would he do that? Nat wondered. He was usually one of the people walking ahead of Kennedy. It gave him constant opportunities to swing around and photograph the candidate.

Ahead of him, Kennedy disappeared into the crowd. Nat pushed and squeezed and shoved his way behind him. After a few moments he regained sight of the candidate. He could clearly see the back of his head. Remembering how tired Kennedy looked from a distance, Nat wanted to get in front of him to take a close-up, sort of a war-weary candidate at the end of a hard-fought-battle type of shot.

He pushed harder, hoping to get past Kennedy before he exited the kitchen.

BLAM!

A shot rang out. There was no mistaking it. It was a gunshot.

BLAM! BLAM! BLAM! BLAM! BLAM! BLAM! BLAM!

There was a moment of stunned silence. An instant when everyone knew exactly what had happened yet hoped against hope that they were wrong; an instant when a single thought was shared by everyone who was jammed in that crowded kitchen space.

Oh no! Not again!

With instincts born of battlefield photography, Nat raised his camera and began shooting. The senator, once again in the center of his viewfinder, threw his hands into the air, turned slowly and spiraled to the floor.

Just beyond him, Nat saw the man with the gun. Dark. Young. Angry. People were shouting, pointing at him.

"He's still got the gun!"

"Get the gun! Get the gun!"

George Plimpton, a writer, and Rosy Grier, a professional football star, wrestled with the gunman. It wasn't an easy task subduing him. Though small, he was wiry. Grier managed to wedge his finger behind the trigger to keep the gunman from firing again while Plimpton found himself staring straight down the smoking barrel.

The gunman shouted, "Don't hurt me! Don't hurt me!"

A television newsman standing nearby shouted, "Hold him! Hold him! We don't want another Oswald!"

With the gunman under control, attention turned to the wounded.

"Get a doctor!"

"Get an ambulance!"

Behind him, Nat could hear someone crying over the public address system, asking if there was a doctor in the house.

Bobby Kennedy was sprawled face up on the floor. A hotel waiter kneeled behind him, supporting his head. A growing pool of blood stained the kitchen tile. The senator's eyes were opened, but unfocused. His hand moved slightly.

Nat looked away. He's seen enough wounds during the war to know this one was not good.

12:30 a.m.

An ambulance arrived. Senator Kennedy was lifted onto a gurney. The number of people pressing around them made it difficult for the attendants to do their work.

12:43 a.m.

The senator was loaded into the ambulance. Ethyl, his wife, climbed in after him. Nat could heard her muttering, "Please God, say it isn't so."

※

A weary Nat Morgan drove to the hospital and took up vigil with a growing number of reporters, officials, and spectators.

As the sun rose, he leaned against the hospital wall. As strange as it seemed, he couldn't get images out of his head that had them all back on the campaign trail in a couple of weeks. He knew better. He'd seen the wound.

At first, reports were given hourly. Then, when several reports had nothing to add, they were given less frequently. The senator had undergone surgery. It was too early to tell how much damage—should he survive—his brain had sustained. It was still strictly a matter of survival.

JUNE 5, 12:00 noon

Nearly twelve hours had passed since the shooting. Nat was hungry. Tired. And cold, even though it was midday. He knew he should leave. There was nothing he could do here. He was a photographer, not a reporter. Still, he couldn't bring himself to go home. He'd signed on to cover Senator Kennedy's campaign for the duration, and that's exactly what he was going to do.

JUNE 5, 11:00 p.m.

The senator was still alive, but all hope was gone. A succession of people was ushered to his bedside, his children, his brother, Edward. Even Jackie Kennedy, JFK's widow, had flown in from the East Coast to be with the family.

It was just a matter of time now. Bobby Kennedy was as good as dead. Still, Nat could not bring himself to leave.

JUNE 6, 1968, 1:44 a.m.

Senator Robert Kennedy was pronounced dead.

Nat wept openly. Not so much because he'd grown close to the man; he'd only known him for a couple of months. And not merely from release because it had been a long vigil and he was tired.

Nat was weeping for his country. What kind of monsters had they become? At what point had everyone concluded that violence was the answer to everything?

They'd killed JFK.

They'd killed Martin Luther King Jr.

And now they'd killed Bobby Kennedy.

It didn't make sense. Nothing made sense anymore.

And for the first time in his life, Nat Morgan was ashamed he was an American.

12

The rotors of the Huey thwacked overhead. The air was already humid, and the sun wasn't up yet. It was going to be a hot one today.

Travis settled into the canvas seat and situated his gear. The scent of kerosene was dizzying. The screaming of the turbine engines drowned out most attempts at communication. Suddenly, just as the last man of his squad scrambled onboard, the sound of the turbines grew even louder. The deck swayed and lifted beneath Travis's feet. Looking out the large double doors, the ground fell away.

Travis took a deep breath. It burned his lungs and left a rancid taste in his mouth. His first mission in Vietnam. On-the-job training, as Keith called it.

As the Huey ascended, the air got cooler. A thin reddish-orange streak lined the horizon, separating a silhouetted jungle from the night sky.

"Enjoy the ride," Keith had told him before they loaded up. "It's the only good part of the day."

Travis glanced out the doors. As the sky grew lighter and the landscape became visible, dense jungle, small villages and farms, and serpentine rivers whizzed beneath them. As they continued on,

the landscape changed. The forests were shell-pocked; the farm-
lands abandoned; and the villages burned out. The war had touched
this part of the land, leaving behind its destructive footprint.

Travis sat back. The air that rushed beneath the rotors was
sweeter now, cleansing the interior of the chopper of its kerosene
odor. He risked another breath. This one was better. It calmed him.
And even though it was a fleeting experience, he welcomed it.

No sooner had he completed his orientation than Keith
showed up again. Nothing was said about their less than cordial
parting when Keith got angry with him for refusing the services of
a local prostitute. He was the old Keith again. Friendly. Confident.
Acting like a big brother. Had he forgotten about their day on the
town already?

Travis hadn't. And he couldn't help but feel that Keith's smile
and friendliness were not all genuine.

In the chopper Keith sat in the doorway, his feet dangling out.
Sitting beside him was Lem Tischler, their radio man. Keith had
made hasty introductions moments before they boarded the
Huey. Travis had learned then that Lem was a Jewish accountant
from Phoenix, Arizona.

Thinking back on the introductions, Travis felt uneasy. It was
the way his new squad buddies looked at him. There was no sense
of welcome in their eyes. More like suspicion and fear. As though
he were more dangerous to them than the VC.

"This is the new guy," Keith had said to them. When each man
passed him by and looked at him as though he was the grim
reaper, Travis began to wonder what Keith had told them about
him. It was after the introductions that Keith explained.

"Don't take it personally," he said. "But they don't trust you."

"Why?"

"You're the new guy."

"Yeah, so?"

"The majority of new guys who come in get killed within a week or so by doing something stupid. Usually a couple of the squad members are killed too. Sometimes the entire squad is wiped out. That's why they don't trust new guys."

Travis still caught them looking at him suspiciously. Sizing him up. Once, when he looked up, he locked eyes with Earl Gower, a Texan from College Station and the squad's machine gunner. Travis nodded and smiled at him, hoping to convey a sense of confidence. Gower shook his head and rolled his eyes in disgust. From then on, whenever Travis caught anyone looking at him, he just looked back. No smile. No nod. Nothing. After a moment they'd look away.

Seated next to Travis was Ernie Osgood, from Oakland, California. The guy looked like a stick figure in fatigues. He couldn't have weighed more than a hundred and twenty pounds. He was frail and the nervous type; always fidgeting, his eyes staring at the deck at nothing, constantly moving back and forth.

Beside him was Rupert Selig from Cherry Hill, New Jersey. He was their explosives expert. The guy acted as though he were half dead. His gaze was dark and hollow. His handshake was limp. When he walked, he shuffled his feet. Had he always been like that? Travis wondered if such a man could be counted on when the firing began.

Then there was Uriah Platt, a mechanic from Petal, Mississippi, the squad's only black man and blues singer. And finally, Rafferty "Rafe" Blair, a tall, stringing fellow, who provided the squad with an alternative form of music. Before he was drafted, Rafe was a country-western singer from Great Falls, Montana.

The pitch of the turbine engines changed. The chopper began to sink. Inside, the men sat up, adjusted their gear, and peered toward the open doors.

The ground rose up to meet them. There was a definite thump as the skids hit the landing zone and everyone began piling out. Travis followed Selig out the door, jumping into tall elephant grass. He spotted Keith up ahead. Crouching beneath the thwacking rotors, he ran after his squad leader.

He felt as though he was running through liquid air. The moisture rising from the grass combined with the stifling heat of early morning—it was probably ninety degrees already—combined to make a sticky, wet, sauna environment.

The squad gathered around their leader at the edge of the clearing. Just beyond them were woodlands composed of small trees, a foot or less in diameter and fifty to seventy-five feet tall. At first, nothing was said. They waited as the remaining choppers unloaded and, without so much as a farewell, took to the sky.

Travis was grateful that his first insertion was an easy one. He had been warned that a typical VC tactic was to hide at the edge of the landing zones under cover of the woods and, just as the choppers touched ground, when they were most vulnerable, to open up with machine-gun fire.

"Listen up!" Keith said. "We're on our own today. Our mission is to check out a village a couple of kilometers away. Tonight we'll do the ambush thing, and then we'll join up with the rest of the platoon at midday tomorrow. Intelligence reports the plantations on the north side of the village are heavily mined, so let's be careful. Everyone got it? Let's move out."

There was a rustle of gear as guns and ammo packs and supplies were lifted and situated. Platt took the point with Selig close behind him. Rafe stuffed a piece of chewing tobacco into his cheek, then set off singing, "Hi ho, hi ho, it's off to work we go."

"Keep a lid on it, Blair," Keith said.

Travis fell in line. Someone gripped him by the arm. Gower, the beefy Texan.

"Don't get us killed, rookie," he muttered.

From the tone of it, it was more a threat than a warning or request.

Travis started to say something, but then decided that there was nothing he could say that wouldn't come off sounding stupid. So he said nothing, yanked his arm free, and took off into the woods. This was one of the guys he would have to work with most closely.

Machine guns were the heart of the platoon because they barked the loudest. Each gunner had an assistant gunner whose job it was to feed ammunition to the fire-spitting beast. This was Platt, the mechanic from Mississippi. Then there was the ammo bearer, the third man of the crew, who carried four hundred more belted rounds in addition to his own weapon and ammo. This was Travis. Eventually, with experience, he would work his way up to being assistant gunner, then gunner.

So this is Vietnam, Travis thought. He'd heard about it, been trained for it, and now he was here. Beyond the relative safety of the airport, the cities, and the bases, he was in the jungle. On patrol. The enemy could be meters away. There was something surreal about it. Nothing anyone had said had actually trained him for this moment. And all of a sudden, even he didn't trust himself.

What was he doing here anyway? He was a lifeguard. His place was in Southern California, not some Southeast Asian jungle. He knew tides and water safety and lifeguard rescue procedures. What did he know of Vietnam and their civil war and their people and their culture, much less about jungle warfare and bamboo booby traps and underground tunnels and rice paddies and firefights and bombing runs? If there was anyone out of place, it was he.

He thought of La Jolla Shores and the daily routine; of plunging into the waves just to cool off; of the refreshing tingle of the salt against his skin as he climbed out of the surf; of the warmth of the Southern California sun, nothing like the muggy wet heat he was experiencing here.

He thought of his parents. His mom. Gentle. Wise. Always happy. He wondered what she would think of her son if she knew he was plodding through a killing zone looking for people to kill before they killed him. He thought of his father. Stern. Professional. A man who'd photographed the world. He wondered how his experience in the army compared to Vietnam. He thought about Paige. He liked his sister, always had. For siblings, they'd been unusually close. And though he didn't share her radical political leanings, he knew that she felt strongly about them. He respected her for that. He only wished she and their father would learn to get along. It was the one thorn in an otherwise happy family.

The dense brushy undergrowth of the jungle brought his attention back to the present. Much of the undergrowth was big greasy-leaved shrubs. Not this stuff, however. These were tough, thorny vines, crotch level, that ripped away at cloth and flesh. "Wait-a-minute vines" they'd been dubbed for their delaying nuisance. Travis worked his way through them, occasionally feeling their bite.

The whacking sound of chopper blades could be heard overhead. There was the crackle of a loudspeaker, then a voice in a language he didn't understand. He knew from orientation that a message was being broadcast to a nearby Vietnamese village, possibly the one they were heading toward. The message blared for about fifteen minutes, then was gone to the sound of retreating chopper blades.

All was quiet again, except for the rustle of bushes as Travis's squad traversed the dense underbrush. After a few more minutes they wound their way down to a stream. It became their watery road. Travis sloshed through the stream behind the rest of his squad. He heard a rooster crowing.

Ahead, Keith raised his fist. As one man the squad dove for cover. Eyes were wide. Alert. Heads pivoted in every direction. Fingers massaged weapons, eager to point and fire.

Travis lay at water's edge as still as he could. He searched the vegetation. Nothing but green and patches of blue sky. The only sound was the trickling of the stream.

Then, another cock crowing.

This agitated the squad. Eyes darted every direction. Heads jerked this way and that.

Rafe was closest to Travis. He inched even closer, then whispered. "VC. They're shadowing us."

"The rooster crows?" Travis whispered so low he could barely hear his own voice.

Rafe nodded, then turned his attention again to the bushes.

They probably waited only five minutes or so, but it seemed like half the day to Travis. At any moment he expected the bushes to spit deadly fire at them. He wondered how many soldiers were killed on their very first patrol. How embarrassing.

Keith raised his hand again, signaling the squad to move out. While Travis was no coward, he let the others step into the middle of the stream first. Then, when there was no fire, he joined them.

He trudged upstream. Half of one side of him was wet from lying in the water. He was scared. His heart pounded from the exhilaration and the unknown. Though not a single round had been fired, he felt as though he'd just emerged from the most dangerous moment of his life.

Lord, what am I doing here? he thought.

The village was nothing more than a few huts and a pitiful piece of farmland. The only visible inhabitants were three old women, an old man, one middle-aged woman, and three infants, only two of which wore any clothing.

The squad approached cautiously from the west, avoiding the northern side, which intelligence had warned them about. When they arrived, the people came out of the huts and met them with stony silence. Keith motioned for the buildings to be searched. He pointed directly at Travis, then to one of the huts. Travis got the idea.

With his rifle at the ready, Travis approached the hut. The casualness of the villagers suggested that there was nothing dangerous nearby. But Travis wasn't taking any chances. He was determined not to get killed on his first patrol.

Standing to one side of the doorway, he paused, readied his rifle, then lowered his head and charged inside. His initial reaction was fear. As bright as it was outside, it was just as dark inside. He couldn't see a thing! If someone were hiding inside, someone who was armed, he was a sitting duck!

How do you make your eyes adjust faster? He swung the barrel of his rifle back and forth menacingly until he could see something. Then, after what seemed like two eternities, his eyes adjusted.

There was no one in the hut.

Straw mats were laid out on the floor. The smoking remains of a small fire burned near the center of the room. The people who lived here were incredibly poor. Travis wondered how people could exist this way.

He heard a noise behind him. He swung around. Two children had followed him. They stared up at him with dark, hungry eyes. Travis smiled at them. The expression on their faces didn't change. They stared at him with wide-eyed wonder.

Turning his attention back to the room, Travis examined the fire. Nothing suspicious there. With the muzzle of his gun he over-turned first one straw mat, then another, and another. Beneath the third mat he found a handful of bullets. Reaching down, he scooped them up and left the hut to make his report.

"Find anything, Morgan?" Keith asked.

Travis held out the ammunition. Keith took one bullet and examined it. "AK-47," he said.

Holding the bullets in the palm of his hand, Keith shoved them at the elderly man.

"Where did you get these?" he demanded.

The old man began chattering excitedly at the sight of the bullets. Keith could make out none of it.

"Lem! Get over here," he said.

Tischler sauntered over to them.

"What's he saying?"

The accountant from Phoenix listened, wrinkled his nose, and listened some more. He spoke a few Vietnamese words, then listened again.

Turning to Keith, he said, "The man claims some VC guerrillas came through here three nights ago. They left the ammo behind by mistake."

Keith shook his head. He wasn't buying it.

"Ask the old man if that woman is a communist." He pointed to the middle-aged woman.

"No, no, no, no!" replied the old man shaking his head from side to side. "Go USA!"

Keith approached the woman directly. "Are you a communist sympathizer? Do you help the North Vietnamese? Give them information?"

"No, no, no! No spy! No spy!"

Keith looked at her directly. "Yes you are! You help the VC!"

The woman kept insisting she didn't.

"Platt! Come here!" Keith said.

The black man approached.

"Guard her," Keith said to him. "We're taking her in. Headquarters wants to question her."

Platt nodded. Without any emotion he led her away from the village to the protests of the elderly and the wailing of the children.

Finding nothing else in the village, the squad wandered off. About an hour later they were at the edge of a designated landing zone. Tischler placed a call to base informing them of their prisoner.

Everyone dropped their loads and then collapsed beside them.

"What do we do now?" Travis asked.

Rafe answered, "We wait for them to come get Mary Poppins of the North," he said. "Headquarters wants to ask her a few questions."

Travis unloaded himself and dropped to the ground. He sighed contentedly to get off his feet.

"Do you think she's VC?" he asked Rafe.

Rafe pulled out a pack of cigarettes. He lit one. "Chances are good she helps 'em," he said. "Sometimes they do it willingly; sometimes they don't have a choice."

"What do you mean?"

Leaning his head back, Rafe let loose with a long stream of smoke. He looked at Travis. "You don't smoke? What's the matter with you?"

"Just don't like the taste," Travis said.

Rafe laughed. "Taste has little to do with it. You'll start smoking before your tour's up. Everyone does."

"That's what people keep telling me," Travis replied. He glanced around at the other members of the squad. He was the only one not smoking.

"Anyway," Rafe said, "when the VC come into a village for the first time, they take the village leader and tie him to a stake. Then, they disembowel him in front of everyone in the village. While the man is dying, they say, 'This is what happens to anyone we think is not on our side. So, are you on our side or not?'"

"Some recruitment program," Travis said.

"It's effective," Rafe replied.

Travis reclined. He put his hands behind his head and closed his eyes. The sun beat against his clothes, making them warm, but doing little to make him comfortable. He began to drop off. As he did, he thought of the little children at the village. He wondered if the elderly villagers would be able to take care of them.

The faces of the little ones kept flashing before him in his mind. They were dirty. They were Vietnamese. They were just little kids.

The squad spent much of the afternoon waiting for the chopper to pick up their prisoner. When it did, they moved out. After walking for two hours without incident, they stopped and ate. Then they moved on again until it was dark.

They set up their ambush on a trail they believed was used to transport supplies, then took up positions on both sides of it. Gower set up the machine gun and aimed it at the trail. Platt positioned himself beside the gun. Travis was on the same side as Platt and behind him, ready to hand him belt after belt of ammo whenever it was needed.

Once in position no one said a word. No one smoked. No one dozed. They waited. Waited for some unsuspecting VC to choose the wrong road to transport his goods.

The jungle, which had been muggy and hot during the day, grew chilly and cold with amazing speed after the sun went down. Travis had to crane his neck to look past Platt and see the road, but then that wasn't his job. His job was to make sure the machine gunner didn't run out of ammo.

Still, he couldn't get his mind off what they were doing. A chill sent a tingle through his body every time he thought about it.

It wasn't an unusual reaction. As a child, whenever he played hide and seek, the act of hiding always affected him the same way. He felt a chill. To his chagrin he also usually felt the urge to use the bathroom. What was it about hiding that affected him that way?

As he lay deep in the elephant grass, he began having other feelings too, ones he didn't enjoy. These were also associated with his childhood and Saturday afternoons.

When he was growing up, Saturday afternoons meant the movies. One of the movie houses not far from where he lived had a promotional agreement with one particular cola company. Six bottle caps would get a person into the matinee. So all week long Travis would scan the ground when he walked looking for bottle caps. Most weeks, thanks to a small mom-and-pop grocery store located near a high school, he found six or more of the bottle caps he needed.

Saturday matinees meant one thing: old black-and-white cowboy movies. So every Saturday, Travis saw a cowboy movie at the local theater. He knew all of them—Gene Autry, Roy Rogers, The Cisco Kid.

This was something he and Keith shared years later. Keith knew all the old cowboy movies, too. And when Travis was in high school, the movies he'd seen as a kid at the theater houses were now shown on television on Saturday afternoons. On more than one occasion, Keith would beg Paige, who wanted to go out, to wait until the end of a cowboy movie.

The thing that made Travis think about that now was the code of the West that he had grown up with. In the cowboy movies the good guys always told the truth, they always did what was right,

and they always fought fair. The bad guys fought dirty. They bushwhacked people and shot people in the back. This was how you
knew who was a good guy and who was a bad guy; other than the
fact that the good guys always wore white and the bad guys
always wore black.

It was the idea of bushwhacking that Travis couldn't get out
of his mind. Bushwhacking. Ambushing. What was the difference? Here he was, lying in wait to kill some unsuspecting people.
To kill them before they even knew what hit them. There would
be nothing fair about it.

It just didn't seem very American.

Hours passed and no one came down the path. Keith signaled
the squad and they moved to a different location and set up again.
Then, when no one appeared on that road, they moved again.

Travis glanced at his watch. It took him a couple of tries to
read it by moonlight, but he finally managed it. Most of the night
was gone. It would be light in thirty to forty minutes. He had managed to survive his first full day in Vietnam.

A crackling sound was heard.

Travis tensed. So did Platt. His leg jerked noticeably. Craning to
see around the Mississippi native, Travis peered through the foliage
that concealed them. On the road there was a line of men pushing
bicycles loaded with goods, at least a dozen of them. Except for the
single crack, they walked noiselessly, peering with wide eyes into
the foliage and trees that bordered both sides of the path.

They never had a chance.

The jungle came alive with machine-gun and rifle fire.
After a night of total silence, the noise was ear-splitting.
Adding to the sound of the guns was Texan Earl Gower. As fire
shot from the muzzle of the machine gun, spraying everything
and everyone on the path with metallic death, he let out a
long, "Eeeeeeeeehaaaaaawwwwwwww!"

Travis passed the ammo belts. Platt fed the fire-spitting dragon. Gower worked the gun up and down the path.

On the path men spun as the bullets hit them. Packs of supplies exploded when hit. Bicycles pitched to one side or the other. The men who once pushed them fell on top of them, jerking with each bullet strike.

As suddenly as it began, it was over. This time, there was no return fire. No reinforcements were called for. None were needed. The ambush had been a complete surprise. The VC never had time to react, let alone fire back.

Keith bounded out of the bushes, jubilant.

"Yes! Yes!" he shouted, hoisting his gun over his head.

The rest of the squad joined him with whoops and shouts of celebration.

Travis was the only one who wasn't celebrating. Keith took notice.

"Count the bodies, Morgan," he said.

"What?"

"Count the bodies for my report!" Keith glared at him, not appreciating the fact that he'd had to give the order twice.

Travis walked up and down the path, counting the number of dead without trying to look too closely at them. Still, he couldn't escape noticing their open, startled eyes; gaping mouths; broken and bloodied limbs; and bullet-riddled torsos.

Welcome to the war, Mr. Morgan, he thought.

He made his report to Keith. "We bushwhacked thirteen of them," he said.

The celebration started again, led by Keith. If he caught the reference, he didn't show it.

※

Morning light sliced through the trees as the squad made its way back to the landing zone where they would be picked up.

They were none too quiet about it as they walked, which made what happened all that much more curious.

They passed a small opening next to the river. There, three VC were cleaning their clothes and washing themselves. They didn't hear the squad coming. They were caught completely by surprise.

The moment Travis saw their faces, he knew he would never forget them. Surprise. Shock. Fear. For these men, one moment they were casually relaxing. The next, they were staring death in the face.

Keith was the first to open up on them.

Once again the jungle was alive with gunfire. Small geysers erupted in the water. Bullets ripped away flesh. Bones exploded. Both the river and the bank grew red with blood.

"A bonus!" Keith shouted. "Life is good! Add three more to the count, Morgan!"

Travis turned away from the scene. Slumping against a tree, he wretched until he felt his insides were coming out.

13

The platoon's assignment was tantamount to a death sentence. Everyone knew it. Come morning, Travis's squad would be one of the first out of the choppers in a hot landing zone. Whole platoons had nearly been wiped out in similar offensives. A funereal pall covered the tent that sheltered Travis and his squad as they contemplated their fate just hours before the insertion.

Keith was on a top bunk taking long pulls on a reefer. The sweet smell of marijuana smoke billowed over him. Beneath him on the lower bunk, Earl Gower cradled a bottle of whiskey that he shared with Rafe on the lower bunk next to him. Ernie Osgood sat cross-legged atop a bunk nursing a can of beer and playing solitaire. Lem Tischler was curled into a fetal position with his back to the group. Selig, the explosives guy, was outside wandering around somewhere. Travis could hear his occasional cough through the thin fabric wall.

"How come Platt got so lucky?" Rafe asked, his speech blurred from the alcohol.

"Yeah, that's what I want to know!" the beefy Gower shouted much too loud. "What kind of a guy deserts his squad like that?"

"He didn't desert us," Keith said. "If you had R&R comin', you would have taken it, too."

"Bet he's shacked up with some babe in one of them Hong Kong hotels right about now," Rafe said.

Travis reclined on his lower bunk on his side, supporting his head with his hand. His Bible lay in front of him. It was opened to Deuteronomy. Why, he didn't know. He'd been flipping through it, looking for an encouraging word of some kind. All he'd found so far was an instruction not to rebuke an older man harshly, a disturbing passage about a valley of dry bones, a proverb that equated an honest answer with a kiss on the lips, the distribution of land to the tribes of Israel, and a list of marriage violations.

"At least it wasn't the new guy who got us killed," Gower shouted. He raised his whiskey bottle in salute to Travis. "Way to go, new guy!" he said.

Travis had been with the squad for a month now. Gower still referred to him as the new guy.

"The name's Morgan," Travis said.

Gower nodded in a way that acknowledged Travis's right to have a name. "All right," he said. "Way to go, Morgan!"

Keith looked down on Travis and grinned. Even after a month, their relationship was still strained. Keith couldn't light up a reefer or take a drink without first looking at Travis, as though he were the eyes of the church back home. And Travis couldn't open his Bible without receiving some kind of verbal hit from Keith. One of his favorites was, "Them Jebusites aren't gonna help you out here, Morgan."

Travis tried not to let the jibes get to him. Though, in truth, they were taking their toll. First, because they were coming from Keith, but more importantly because he feared Keith was right. He had found little comfort in his Bible since arriving in Vietnam. His prayers also seemed a waste of time. These things that were important to him at home seemed foreign in Vietnam. From all appearances, God had nothing to do with this place.

God made sense in church when the pastor preached about him, and when men and women in dresses and suits gathered in groups to pray to him, and when the family gathered around the table to ask him to bless their food. In the States, Travis could feel God's presence. Not here. It was as though God missed the plane and never arrived in Vietnam.

Travis had never felt so alone, so abandoned in his life. Though he had no desire to smoke, or drink, or take drugs, he was beginning to understand why the others did. There was a hole in him, an emptiness that wouldn't go away. Something was eating away at his insides, and he couldn't stop it. When he first saw Rupert Selig and shook his limp hand, he couldn't understand how a man could be so empty of life. The man looked like the walking dead.

Travis understood now. Unless something stopped the cancer of loneliness he felt inside, he would be just like Selig by the end of his tour. That is, if he wasn't killed first.

On his first day in Vietnam, Keith had said to him, "It don't mean nothin'." That pretty well summarized everything over here. It didn't mean nothin'. And it scared him.

He closed his eyes. *Lord, if you can hear me, I need you now more than I've ever needed you. I'm scared. I'm scared of dying. I'm scared of living. I don't like what I'm becoming, but I can't seem to help myself. Please, if you're here, help me. Help me.*

He opened his eyes to see Keith staring at him. For the longest time their eyes locked. Keith knew what he was doing. To Travis's horror, he also knew the result.

There was no change. The prayer didn't go through. God's lines were down. On the night before the biggest fight of his life, Travis felt more alone, more empty, than he'd ever felt in his life.

Lying back on his pillow, Keith took another drag on the reefer and stared blankly at the top of the canvas tent.

The sky was gray and threatening. The ceiling was low. Travis shivered as the cold air rushed through the Huey's double doors. The turbine whined overhead, accompanied by the all-too-familiar thwacking sound of the chopper blades.

Strange how the sound means different things at different times, Travis thought. When they were waiting to be picked up and lifted out of the madness, it was the most welcome sound on earth. When they were en route to a hot landing zone, it was the beat of a death clock, ticking off the last few moments of life.

Inside the Huey there was less than normal chatter. Expressions were grim. Each in his own way had come to accept their fate.

Travis wondered what it would feel like to be ripped apart by bullets. He only hoped that one would strike his heart or head so that the deed would be done quickly with a minimum of suffering. The last thing he wanted to do was lie bleeding in a rice paddy, staring at the Vietnamese clouds, moving in and out of painful consciousness, waiting for the life to drain out of him.

The chopper began its descent. The sinking feeling he felt in the pit of his stomach was more than just an altitude thing. He closed his eyes in one last desperate attempt to reach God before they reached the landing zone.

Behind closed eyes he saw only darkness. He felt no comforting presence. His awareness was limited to the stench of kerosene as the chopper slowed and the wind no longer cleansed the air as efficiently.

With an ironic shake of his head, Travis concluded that he'd find out if there indeed was a God and a heaven in the next few minutes. For, if there was, he expected to be there shortly.

"Let's go!" Keith shouted as he jumped out the door.

Heavy gunfire could be heard outside.

Travis followed closely behind Gower. The two of them were the machine-gun team for this mission. With Platt in Hong Kong, Travis was not only carrying the ammo, he would feed the gun, doing both his and Platt's job.

Gower jumped out the door. At that point Travis saw that the chopper's skids were a few feet from the ground. A watery marsh lay just below. As soon as Gower splashed out of his way, Travis jumped.

For a moment he hung in space. Completely vulnerable. Exposed. Unable to defend himself. At the same time he could hear bullets whizzing by him. Beneath him miniature water geysers appeared everywhere the bullets hit. Thousands of them. It was the longest moment of his life. With that concentration of fire, he knew he didn't have a chance.

SPLASH!

He hit the water and ducked down, surprised that he wasn't riddled with bullets. It was then he realized the hits on the watery surface were made mostly by raindrops. He ran after Gower, following the backside of his machine-gun partner closely.

An armada of Huey choppers was all around them. Men fell from the open doors with such regularity that Travis was reminded of a string of pearls.

Bordering the rice paddy in the distance was a thick jungle. It was from here the bullets came. It was also the direction in which they were running, right into the hail of gunfire.

Travis could see one VC straddling a limb high in a tree. He was easy to spot because he wore a white shirt. Either the guy didn't have time to change, or he had a death wish, for he was an easy target. Travis kept an eye on him as he ran. The man chose his targets carefully. He seemed in no hurry at all, almost as though he were shooting ducks at a carnival gallery. Travis wished he could stop long enough to pick the guy off, but he had to keep running.

Somebody, however, found time to get a few rounds off. All of a sudden, the trunk of the tree in which the VC was perched exploded in splinters, the limb upon which he was sitting cracked, and the white-shirted sniper fell from the tree.

Several cheers went up around them. Travis hadn't been the only one with his eye on the sniper. Then, the cheers stopped as the white shirt appeared at the base of the tree. An instant later, he was escaping into the jungle.

Travis spied Keith hunkered against the base of a tree on the edge of the jungle. He was signaling to the rest of the squad. Travis and Gower were a hundred yards distant.

Just then Travis heard what sounded like a wasp, but only for an instant. The darn thing bit his ear. He grabbed his ear with his hand. It was wet. Sticky wet. Pulling his hand away, he saw blood. He'd been shot!

Holding his ear, he ran for the cover of the trees. Geysers erupted around his feet. Not rain. These were larger. He had fifty yards to go.

His heart alternated between seizing and racing. His throat was raw from the exertion. His clothing was soaked, pulling him down, like a magnet it seemed, water pulling to water. Twenty-five yards to go.

Keith and Rafe and Lem were urging them on.

Travis concentrated on pulling one wet boot after the other out of the mud. He urged his legs to pump faster. He was almost there. It would be embarrassing to get this far only to get killed.

He could hear the voices of his squad now, above the sound of the choppers and the rain and the gunfire.

Gower stumbled in front of him. He splashed wildly, trying to keep from falling. The effort slowed them considerably. Travis reached out to try to steady the large Texan. It was no use. Like a sick water buffalo, the machine gunner listed, then fell to his side, creating a wave of water when he hit.

They were just a few yards from cover. But they were no longer moving. A phrase popped into Travis's head that described their condition. *They were dead in the water.*

Travis could no longer hear shouts of encouragement as he reached down to help Gower up. The large, clumsy machine gunner splashed violently as he struggled to his feet. Between both of them, the Texan managed to right himself. They started again for the trees.

As they did, Travis could see why the shouting stopped. To the man those who had reached safety had turned toward the trees and were unleashing their own barrage of fire. Tree trunks and limbs and leaves flew in every direction.

With a few final lunges Gower and Travis arrived at their goal, collapsing from the effort it took to get there. On their heels were Osgood and Selig.

The entire squad had made it safely.

They looked at one another and laughed like fools. Even Selig showed signs of life in his eyes as they celebrated their good fortune.

Keith examined Travis's ear. It was burning something fierce. The squad leader pronounced it a minor wound, though he predicted that Travis would go through life with a nick in his ear. But with that being the extent of their casualties, they considered themselves the luckiest squad in the platoon.

Travis looked back at the rice paddy as the last of the choppers lifted off and swung back around toward base. Not every squad was as lucky. Dozens upon dozens of soldiers lay facedown in the water; their backs, rears, and heels were all that broke the surface.

"All right, let's move out!" Keith said. "We've been lucky to this point. Let's hope our luck keeps holding out."

Crouching low, he led the squad into the jungle.

They pushed through the heavy wet foliage for two hours before Keith told them to establish a defensive position. They had met surprisingly light resistance along the way. There was occasional fire. The squad would hit the ground. Then, before they could return fire, the shooting would stop. Twice, Travis caught sight of the fleeing VC. Both times it was the same man. The one wearing the white shirt.

While Keith and Lem radioed in their position, Travis grabbed a shovel and began digging. In the last month he must have done this at least a hundred times. They dug a single hole for each group of three men. Usually, that meant Gower, Platt, and him. This time, however, it was just him and Gower. The hole was shoulder-deep with firing ports angled right and left. Once this was completed, they settled in, checking their equipment and familiarizing themselves with their immediate surroundings.

The rain started coming down harder. Travis was soaked to the bone. For the first two weeks of his tour he tried using a rain poncho to keep dry. Between the heat and nonbreathing material of the poncho, he got just as wet from his own sweat. He decided that no covering at all was better.

"What are we supposed to do?" Gower asked.

"Hold this position," Keith replied.

"Why?"

Keith gave him a look deserving of a dumb question. "They told us to hole up here and so we'll hole up here. That's all I know right now."

"Just askin'," Gower muttered.

It wasn't until late afternoon, when Lem established routine contact, that they were given further information. Keith gathered them together.

"We can expect company tonight," he said. "A lot of company. We're to hold out as long as we can."

"That doesn't sound too encouraging," Selig said. It hadn't taken long following the insertion for his eyes to return to their usual hollow look. During the entire time they set up their defensive position and he set up the claymore mines around their perimeter, he hadn't said a single word. But then, this was usual for him.

Travis had assisted him with the mines once. The explosives were green plastic rectangles that contained a layer of explosive covered by a layer of ball bearings. On the top of the casing there were raised, bold letters that said: "This Side Towards Enemy." The instruction did little to instill confidence in Travis for the level of expertise the army required for the men handling these mines.

Darkness moved in suddenly like a black fog. With it came the initial sounds of battle. The whump, whump, whump of mortars were followed by the ripping of leaves and cracking of tree limbs. Earthshaking explosions erupted in the distance. The enemy was coming. The mortars were meant to stop as many of them as possible before they reached the perimeter of troops.

Travis felt his adrenaline level rise. There was a time when the feeling frightened him. Now he welcomed it, depended on it. It sharpened his senses.

A thousand points of fire blazed through the trees, each one an enemy weapon. Travis had never seen so many of them at once. There were too many. They would never be able to hold out against that many VC.

Beside him the machine gun came to life, spitting back fire for fire. Gower sprayed the deadly lead evenly from side to side, not aiming at anything in particular. The goal was to mow them down, line by advancing line.

Travis concentrated on feeding the deadly beast. There had to be no lag in the rate of fire. Their only hope was to pour it on so thick nothing in front of them would have a chance of ever reaching them.

Round after round flowed through the gun. Still the opposing fire didn't let up. Several bullets whizzed by Travis's head, much too close for comfort. His bandaged ear began to throb.

"Selig, get down! What are you doing?"

The voice was Keith's. Travis glanced that direction to see what was happening. By the time he looked up, Selig had already climbed above the ridge of the foxhole. He carried no weapon.

Behind him, Keith was scrambling up the side of the hole, reaching up, trying to grab Selig by the back of his pants before he got too far.

Selig straightened himself. He took two, then three hesitant steps. His arms were raised slowly at his side as though to embrace death.

He didn't have to wait long.

The first bullet staggered him. The second spun him around. Three more rounds hit simultaneously. His back exploded. The force lifted him off his feet and threw him back into the foxhole. It looked as though he was taking a swan dive into a swimming pool.

Keith's cursing could be heard above the din of the firefight. There was no use checking Selig for signs of life. The squad leader resumed firing into the darkness.

Normally, when Gower fired the machine gun, he added his voice to it in a strange duet to which the squad had grown accustomed. For some reason, tonight Gower was silent. As Travis loaded the next clip, he glanced at the Texan. Gower was perspiring heavily. His jaw was set. There was fear in his eyes.

Travis wouldn't have guessed it possible, but the fire from the trees increased. It reminded him of the first rainstorm he experienced in Vietnam, about a week after his arrival. The skies opened and it started pouring, harder than Travis had ever seen before. Then, just when he thought it couldn't rain any harder, the heavens dumped sheets of water down on him.

That's the way it was now. Only it wasn't water that came like sheets, it was bullets. Travis ducked behind the lip of the foxhole. All around him, death and destruction ripped the planet apart. Trees trunks were exploding. Limbs were falling. The earth was erupting.

"Uhh!"

Gower was hit. He slumped to the bottom of the pit. Worse yet, the machine gun was silent.

Travis looked at Gower. Blood splattered the right side of his face. It looked as though some wild animal had taken a huge bite out of his neck and shoulder.

"Get that machine gun going!"

The voice was Keith's. He was yelling at Travis.

"The gun! We need the gun!" he shouted, pointing frantically at the silent weapon.

Stepping over Gower, careful not to get their legs entangled, Travis got behind the machine gun. He reached toward it.

The gun exploded, hit by round after round of ammunition. It was thrust back at him, knocking him off balance, back into Gower.

Travis and the gun fell unceremoniously on the wounded man, who let out a howl. The storm of lead continued over-head. Without the machine gun, there was little they could do to stop it.

BOOM!

Smoke and dirt exploded a dozen yards away.

Grenades!

BOOM! BOOM! BOOM!

The earth shook all around them. The sound was deafening.

Dirt and mud rained down. Lead flew inches over their heads, imbedding in the back wall of the hole.

Travis sunk deeper into the hole. Defenseless, he held onto the now unconscious Gower. The Texan was so big Travis couldn't wrap his arms around him completely.

They had minutes before their position would be overrun. Travis glanced over at the other foxholes. He was too low. He couldn't see them. All he could see was exploding foliage and dirt and mud shooting up.

He buried his head against the Texan's arm. The noise, the destruction, the death, the waste, the darkness, all came down upon him in that hole. Panic rose inside him. He screamed, but could barely hear any noise coming from his own mouth.

In fear, his boots clawed at the dirt, trying to get lower, thinking lower might save them. If they could just dig deep enough the bullets couldn't reach them. They would be safe.

It was an irrational thought. But rational thought had nothing to do with their situation. All that was left was irrational hope and an irrational clawing at the dirt.

A movement caught his eyes. Something flew overhead and landed inside the foxhole.

A grenade!

It was over. Travis knew it now. His parents would get one of those letters. "On behalf of the president of the United States, we regret to inform you ..."

Suddenly, exactly where his boots had been clawing, the earth gave way. It started slowly at first; then, like a giant mouth, it gaped open. Travis felt the earth give way beneath him. He took Gower with him, clutching to the big Texan. One moment they were in the foxhole, the next they were falling, slipping, sliding, deep into who knew where.

The next instant, there was an explosion.

And just as suddenly as the hole opened, it closed.

It was pitch dark. Travis and Gower slid farther, then began tumbling and tumbling, until finally, they stopped.

Gower was completely limp. Travis was dazed.

It was dark and cold and dank. And all Travis knew was that he was alive and that he was somewhere in the middle of the earth.

14

Allegra Morgan had just finished lunch when she felt it. In all of her life she had never felt anything like it. She shivered, then got up to walk around, but the feeling would not go away. Panic began to rise within her. She fought it back with will power.

If she cried out, no one would hear her. She was home alone. Nat was at work.

She wondered if she was coming down with something. No, it wasn't any kind of physical pain she'd felt. But if it wasn't physical, what was it? Emotional? Spiritual?

Spiritual. Something had disturbed her spirit.

Disturbed, no it was far deeper than that. Chilled. Shocked. Maybe a combination of both.

She didn't know what to do. She could still feel the after-effects, which were almost as disturbing as the initial feeling. She rubbed her chest to see if that helped. It didn't.

Going to the phone, she dialed. She did so with the ease of a sighted person.

Three rings. Four.

"Please be home," Allegra muttered.

"Hello?" came the voice at the other end of the line. It was female.

"Mother?"

"Allegra? Is that you? Are you all right?"

Allegra grinned. Already she felt better. Laura Morgan was more of a mother to her than a mother-in-law.

"I think so," Allegra said. "Why do you ask?"

"Something in your voice. It's just not right. Are you sure everything's all right with you, dear?"

Allegra took a deep breath. "No, I'm not sure. Would it be possible for you to come over here?"

"Allegra, dear, what's the matter?"

"I don't know. I just need someone to talk to and Nat's in LA."

"Certainly, dear. I'll be right over. Can I bring you anything?"

"No, Mom, I just need you."

There was a slight pause, then, "I'm on my way, dear."

Allegra hung up the receiver. She was relieved knowing that Nat's mother was on her way, but not so relieved that the feeling inside her chest didn't bother her.

It was nearly an hour before Allegra heard a soft knock on the door. She answered it without opening the door.

"Yes?"

"It's me, dear."

Allegra recognized Laura Morgan's voice. She immediately opened the door. Though she couldn't see her mother-in-law's face, she could feel the woman's concern.

"You look a little drawn, dear. Let's sit down," Laura said.

The two women went arm in arm to the couch where they sat down. Allegra felt a little foolish now. While the feeling had not gone away completely, it wasn't nearly as strong as it once was.

"I'm not sure if it's anything," she began.

"Of course, it's something," Laura interrupted. "If it wasn't, you wouldn't have called me. Tell me exactly what happened."

Allegra took a deep breath. It would be so much easier if she could look into Laura's eyes while they talked.

"I had just finished lunch when, all of a sudden, I got this feeling."

"Feeling?"

Allegra nodded. "In my chest."

"It's not your heart, is it?"

"No, it's nothing like that. That's the strange thing about it. That's also what makes it so difficult to describe."

"Do your best, dear."

Allegra reached out her hands. They were quickly intercepted and covered by Laura's own. The physical touch calmed her.

"This is going to sound crazy," Allegra continued, "but the feeling that I got in my chest was a chilling one. Like a cold finger reached inside me and touched me."

"That sounds dreadful!"

Allegra agreed that it was. "I'm still feeling the aftereffects," she said. "Almost as though I'm having to thaw out."

"What do you think caused it?"

"I don't ..."

When she began the sentence, Allegra truly had no idea what could have caused the feeling. But then, as she began to speak the words, she had a hunch; more than a hunch, really, because all of a sudden, it was crystal clear. She knew exactly what had caused the feeling!

"Travis!" she cried.

Travis shivered so hard, his jaw ached. Overhead, somewhere on the topside of the world, the battle still raged. He could hear the muted sounds of gunfire and grenades.

The worst thing right now was his imagination. All he knew was that the earth had swallowed him and he was safe for the moment. But where was he? All those children's stories from when he was a kid didn't help. Was he in an animal's lair? What would it do when it found him and how could he protect himself against it?

Gower was still unconscious, which was probably a good thing. When Travis lay real still, he could hear Gower breathing. He wanted to move and explore. Then again, he felt safest if he just lay there and did nothing.

After an hour or so—just a guess—it sounded like things on the surface were slowing down. He didn't know if that was good or not. Had their position been overrun? Or had they succeeded in holding it? From the way things were just before he left so abruptly, it was hard to be optimistic. He tried not to think too much about it, because when he did, the only images that came to mind were those of the entire squad wiped out.

Overhead everything grew quiet. Then silent. In the silence and in the dark, Travis began to feel very much alone. The need to know where he was grew stronger with each passing minute.

He needed a light of some kind. But he knew he didn't have one. What about Gower?

Travis began to rifle systematically through Gower's pockets. It was weird to feel inside a man's pockets, but the need to know their situation overshadowed the discomfort.

"What have we here?" Travis whispered.

In his hands he had what felt like a book of matches. His fingers explored the item. A cover flipped up. Yep. Those were matches all right.

He lifted Gower off of him and scooted away a short distance. Not knowing what to expect once the match was lit, he thought it best to have a measure of mobility.

Pulling one match from the pack, he closed the cover and felt for the striking strip. He struck the tip of the match against the strip. There was a momentary spark, a slight one. Then, nothing. He struck again. Another spark. This one smaller. Then, nothing. He tried a third time. Nothing.

Oh no! he thought. *The matches are wet!*

Tossing that match aside, he tried another. The result was the same.

He tried a third one. After the first strike there was nothing. After the second strike the head of the match sputtered.

Come on! Come on!

The sputtering gave birth to a tiny flame that came to life. At the tip of Travis's fingers a tiny light danced happily.

Holding up the match, Travis got his first glimpse of his surroundings. What he saw made his jaw drop open.

※

"Are you sure it's Travis?" Laura asked. "How do you know?"

Allegra shook her head. "I can't explain it. I just know."

Laura hesitated, then said, "What do you think the feeling means?" Another hesitation. "He's not dead, is he?"

Tears rose into Allegra's eyes. "I don't know," she replied. "I just feel that he's all alone, abandoned, in the dark."

"Doesn't he have that other boy with him? What's his name? The boy that used to go out with Paige."

"Keith Rawlins."

"Yes, that's the one. Aren't the two of them together?"

"They're in the same platoon."

It was a grasping at straws, and now that the information was out, it was seen as such.

"Oh, Mother," Allegra said. "You went through this during the Second World War. You had four children involved with the war. How did you handle it?"

"Not very well, I'm afraid," Laura said wryly.

Allegra smiled. It was hard for her to imagine her mother-in-law ever being out of control. Nat had inherited her calmness.

"You know what it was like during the First World War," Laura said, "though you were only a child."

"But, for me, being on the front lines was a far sight easier than having children in the war and not being able to do anything except wait to hear from them. How did you manage to keep your sanity?"

"I almost didn't." There was no levity in her voice this time.

"What did you do?"

"I got down on my knees," Laura said. "I spent a long time praying and reading God's Word. And not until I accepted the fact that God had given my children to me in the first place, and that he would have to watch over them and bring them back to me, did I find any measure of peace."

"You had to let go of them."

"And trust God."

Allegra nodded. "That's not an easy thing for a mother to do."

"I have found that trusting God is seldom an easy thing to do," Laura said.

Allegra felt her hands being squeezed. The next thing she heard was her mother-in-law praying.

"Dear God in heaven, comfort this mother who is so concerned for her son. She wants so much to help him right now. For some reason his anguish has reached halfway around the world and touched her. Yet, wanting to help, we find ourselves powerless to do anything. So, we turn to you, dear Lord. You know where Travis is right now. You know his needs. You know his heart. Please, Lord, cast your protective hands around him. In Jesus' name we pray. Amen."

Allegra leaned forward and hugged her mother-in-law.

The tunnel in which Travis found himself was big enough to drive a truck through. It was full of equipment. American equipment. Boots. Fatigues. Cots. Ponchos. Helmets. All of it stolen. The VC had more supplies here than Travis's squad had back at camp.

The flame burned his fingers. Travis dropped the match and instantly was engulfed in darkness again. He managed to light another match.

Extraordinary!

Again, the match went out.

Travis could hear Gower moaning. He was coming around. Dropping to his knees, he inched his way toward the injured machine gunner. He felt his way forward with his hands.

The instant he touched Gower, the man came alive. He grabbed Travis's arm and twisted and clawed and punched.

"Gower! It's me! Travis!"

The man was fighting too frantically to hear. Travis was getting pummeled in the dark. He tried to push away, but couldn't. He took a fist to the face, a knee to the gut; his arm was just about to come out of its socket.

"Gower!"

The flailing continued.

"Gower! Stop! It's me!"

A hand rammed him in the jaw.

Unless he did something to neutralize the machine gunner, Travis was going to be knocked senseless. He had no choice but to do what he did. It was like being in the water rescuing a drowning swimmer. Sometimes, for their own safety, they had to be neutralized. Travis struck in the direction of the man's wound.

His first blow landed squarely on Gower's wounded shoulder. A howl echoed in the cave, but the clawing and fighting continued.

Travis landed a second blow, then a third.

The man stopped fighting.

"Gower! Listen to me! It's me, Travis Morgan! Stop fighting!"

"Morgan?" The voice was weak, pained.

"Yeah."

"I can't see you."

"It's too dark to see anything."

"Morgan?"

"Yeah?"

"Are we in hell?"

Travis couldn't help but smile. If hell was anyplace around here, it was a few meters above ground.

"No, we're not in hell. We fell through a hole in the earth. We're safe for now."

"What about the others?"

"I don't know."

There was a moment of silence, then: "How do you know we're safe?"

"Let me show you. I'm going to light a match. It's going to be bright."

It took him several attempts, but Travis finally managed to light a match. The look on Gower's face when he saw where they were was almost comical.

"Where'd they get all this stuff?" he asked.

"Beats me."

"And how did you say we got in here?"

Travis described to him the action above ground just before they were swallowed up.

"Hey Morgan? You're all right."

"Why do you say that?"

"You stayed with me when I was wounded, didn't you? You pulled me down here with you, didn't you?"

"I guess so."

"You saved my life. I won't forget it."

"Well, we're still not out of danger," Travis said. "We have to figure out how to get out of here. And then we have to figure out which side of the war we're on."

15

Paige and Natalie were still giggling over the secretary's initial response when, earlier in the day, they had led twenty-five students into the academic dean's outer office. The secretary—a middle-aged woman with horn-rimmed glasses and wide hips—surmised immediately what was happening.

"Oh no you don't!" she had said.

"Oh yes we do!" Natalie had replied.

She and Paige sat down on the carpet with their backs against the secretary's desk. The other students filed in behind them and sat wherever they could find room.

The secretary buzzed the dean on the telephone intercom. "You'd better get out here," she'd said.

Moments later the dean's office door opened. A bald-headed, bespectacled man in a gray suit took one look at his crowded reception area and said, "Oh no you don't!"

Taking their cue from Natalie, in unison, the students replied, "Oh yes we do!"

Natalie had leaned over and whispered to Paige, "Not very original, is he?"

"What do you expect from an academic?" Paige had replied.

The sit-in began at three o'clock Friday afternoon when a

force of nearly two hundred students descended upon the administrative offices of the UCRD with the intent of occupying the buildings in protest of the Vietnam War.

Del had appointed Paige and Natalie captains of the academic dean's office while he and Allen led the group that occupied the president's office. The spillover crowd was told to plant themselves wherever there was room.

Within the hour the police had arrived and read the students the riot act: "This is an unlawful assembly. You must disperse. Desist and disperse to your several homes or lawful employments."

That was the official version. Throughout the evening and well into the morning came promises, then threats, then angry outbursts, then more threats, and finally a deadline. According to the police, the students had until 3:00 a.m. to vacate the premises voluntarily, or they would be removed by force.

"Have any more reinforcements arrived?" Natalie asked.

Paige stood at the second-story window and looked down at the assembled police force. Red lights flashed steadily just as they had all night.

"I don't see any more than were out there an hour ago," Paige reported.

"Any troops?"

"Do you really think they'll call out troops?"

"We can only hope," Natalie replied.

"What?"

"I'm not kidding!" Natalie declared. "Have you seen some of those guys' pictures in the magazines? They're gorgeous! There was this one National Guard guy who was at the Berkeley protest. In the picture a scrawny, bare-chested, scraggly student stood opposite him and was placing a daisy in the guy's gun barrel. Why is it the other side has all the good-looking guys? Paige, let me tell you, when I saw that Adonis standing like a statue with just a hint of dimples in his cheeks, my first thought was, 'I'd lay down arms in a second for that guy! And anything else he wanted!'"

"Natalie!" Paige squealed.

Natalie laughed. She said, "You wouldn't react like that if you'd seen him!"

Paige never expected the sit-in to be this much fun. For some reason she'd thought they'd all sit solemnly and stare at one another for hours or something. This was almost like a coed overnight party. But then, half the fun was Natalie. It had always been that way. And as much as she loved living at Shores Drive, she missed rooming with Natalie.

"I think the police are going to miss their deadline," Natalie said, looking out the window for herself.

Paige checked her watch. "They already have." It was five minutes after three in the morning. "Let's go check in with Del," she said.

The two coeds stepped over and around bodies that were sprawled, scrunched, cramped, and squeezed into every square inch of the academic dean's office. Some were reading or study-ing, others were sleeping, or talking, or necking. Some were listening to the radio or playing chess or cards. The sound of a guitar and singing came from the stairwell. Food bags and wrappers and boxes were scattered everywhere. Every hour on the hour, the protesters gathered around radios to see if any further developments would be reported. Most of the night the story was the same: The building had been overrun by students who refused to come out; the police were weighing their options.

Excusing themselves and stepping over the guitar player in the stairwell, Paige and Natalie worked their way up one flight of steps to the third floor. In the hallway everyone was gathered around a flat box. Someone had ordered a pizza and managed to get it delivered.

In the president's office, Allen stood at the window with a pair of binoculars in his hand. His features were scored with nervous lines. Del was slumped in a chair nearby. He appeared to be sleeping.

"Just wanted to report in," Paige whispered. "Anything we should know about?"

Del stirred and sat up. "I'm not asleep," he said.

"Then how do you explain the snoring?" Natalie asked.

Del ignored her.

For some reason Natalie loved to poke fun at Del. The more serious he became, the sillier she got.

"It's three o'clock," Paige said. "Any instructions?"

Del moved to the window and looked out. As he did, Allen reported, "No change."

"We sit until they move us," Del said. He scratched the scruffy growth he called a beard.

"Have you had anything to eat?" Paige asked him.

"Generals don't eat," he said, looking out the window again.

"What about wimpy potheads, do they eat?" Natalie asked.

Allen smiled at her retort.

"Natalie!" Paige said.

"Let her have her fun," Del said. "Someday when she's pregnant with her fourth brat she'll be telling everybody how she once was part of Del Gilroy's revolutionary army."

Natalie opened her mouth to reply. Paige shoved her out of the room.

"Why do you do that?" Paige asked.

"Do what?"

"You know what! Why are you always picking on Del?"

"You don't want to hear it, so don't make me say it."

"Go ahead. Say it."

Natalie looked sadly at Paige. "I'm sorry, but I don't like your boyfriend. He takes himself too seriously. Besides, I'm not sure he's firing on all cylinders."

Natalie's comments stung. Paige pretended she wasn't hurt by them. Apparently she didn't do a very good job.

"See?" Natalie said. "That's why I didn't want to tell you! But now that we're on the subject, when are you going to dump Del?"

"Dump him? Why?"

"You deserve better!"

Paige shook her head. "I'm lucky to have him."

"He doesn't deserve you."

The conversation died as they went downstairs. They stepped over the guitar player in silence; he paused in his strumming as they did so. Back in the hallway neither girl picked up the conversation.

At 3:30 a.m. another deadline was announced via police bullhorn. The students crowded around windows to see and hear for themselves. According to the police chief, they were being granted a three-hour extension. The deadline was now 6:00 a.m. If the students didn't vacate the building by then, they would be forcibly removed, arrested, and charged with trespassing.

Following the announcement the protesters wandered away from the windows quietly and returned to whatever they were doing before. One of the guys yawned, stretched, and said, "Three more hours of sleep. Outasight!"

His comment pretty much summed up what the rest of the protesters were feeling. It was late. Dark. They were tired. And, away from the windows, any threat was quickly forgotten.

"Think I'll get some sleep, too," Natalie said. "Wake me up for the six a.m. extension."

The late hours and relaxed atmosphere also were working on Paige. While Natalie curled up next to a wall, Paige sat beside her, leaned against the wall, and closed her eyes. Soon she was dozing.

❊

She awoke a little less than two hours later. Lifting her arm, she glanced at her watch.

4:55 a.m.

Blinking hard to clear her vision, she surveyed the room. Two guys who had been playing chess all night long were still hunched over the board. There were a couple of hushed conversations that could be heard as well as the echoing sound of the guitar in the stairwell. Everyone else was sleeping.

A part of Paige wanted her to close her eyes and go back to sleep; another part of her didn't want to. That side of her feared she would continue on with the dream she'd just been dreaming.

She was home again. In her room. Refusing to go to church again. Her father was furious. He left and came back a short time later with his camera. He began taking pictures of her. When she asked why, he told her that he was going to place her picture in prominent places in the church so that everyone could see what a heathen she had become. Not only had she turned her back on Keith, a good Christian man, but now she was turning her back on her family, the church, and God. He wondered aloud whether or not she had ever believed in God.

The camera's strobe light flashed in her eyes as he took picture after picture.

Paige defended herself. She said she didn't love Keith, but that she loved her family, her church, and God—though, in her dream she didn't feel any love or devotion for God. This disturbed her.

Suddenly, her father was no longer taking pictures. The camera in his hands turned into some kind of rifle. He was shooting at her! She was hit several times. Always in the leg. It surprised her, though, that the bullets didn't seem to hurt. Hit after hit, all in the upper part of her leg, and all she could think was how surprised she was that the bullets didn't hurt.

She awoke to Natalie's foot poking her in the leg. Natalie herself was dreaming. Her leg was jerking and her foot was bumping Paige.

Stretching, Paige got up and ambled around to get the kinks out. She concluded that the only thing that would make this sit-in any better would be if she could sleep in her own bed.

She wandered to the window and looked out. Everything below was peaceful, just as it had been before. Police lights flashed red consistently. There was little movement at all around the cars. She wondered if the police officers had also found places where they could catch a few winks.

Suddenly, something caught her eye. A dark shadow between the buildings seemed to move. She stared hard in that direction and waited. Nothing. Her imagination? Then it moved again. And again. And again. The shadows took on shapes. The shapes of crouching men carrying guns.

Did Del and Allen see what she was seeing?

She turned and ran toward the hallway, stopping only long enough to wake Natalie.

"I think they're coming!" Paige cried.

A groggy Natalie stared at her through sleep-filled eyes. "Who's coming?"

"The army, the National Guard—I don't know, but they've got guns! I'm going to tell Del."

Natalie struggled to her feet. They were a little wobbly. "I'm coming with you," she said.

The two of them vaulted over the guitar player in the stair-well, not giving him time to stop playing, let alone make any kind of move to get out of their way.

The third floor resembled the second. Most people were sleeping. A few were holding hushed conversations. One or two were reading or playing some kind of card game.

Paige and Natalie ran into the president's outer office, stepping gingerly, but quickly over bodies sprawled out all over the place. They burst through the door into the president's office. Del was asleep in a guest chair. Allen sat in the president's desk chair. A pair of binoculars rested on his stomach. His head lolled to one side.

"Del! Get up!" Paige called.

"Allen!" Natalie shouted.

The two men started, looking around wildly.

Paige pointed excitedly. "Out the window! Look out the window!"

Allen swung around and lifted the binoculars. "Trouble," he said. "Big trouble."

Del ran to the window. Paige was right behind him. She looked over his shoulder. What she saw caused her heart to jump, then take off running like a frightened hare.

The shadows she'd seen weren't shadows anymore. They were pouring from between the building. Hundreds of them. All National Guard.

They didn't stop at the police cruisers, but kept coming.

"They're storming the building," Del said.

"Brilliant observation, general," Natalie snapped. "Any orders?"

Del whirled around. "Get back to your posts," he said. "Wake everyone up along the way. Tell them we have visitors. Remind them this is a sit-in. None of us has legs. Anyone leaving this building had better be carried out."

Paige nodded. She turned to go, then looked back at Del hoping to catch his eye or hear a word of assurance or comfort. All she saw was the back of his head. He'd turned his attention to the approaching guard.

Sounding the alarm, Paige and Natalie worked their way back toward the stairwell. Taking the steps two or three at a time, Paige called out to the guitar player, "It's showtime. The National Guard are on their way."

He paused in his playing and looked up. "Bummer," he said. He rose without haste and started following them downstairs.

"You have friends on the second floor?" Paige asked.

The guitar player shook his head. "I know a way out of here," he said. "Can't afford to get arrested again. My dad would have a fit."

"A big boy like you worries about Daddy?" Natalie asked.

"It would be my third arrest this month. The old man can only take so much."

"How are you going to get out of here?" Natalie asked.

Still moving unhurriedly, the guitar player said, "The janitor's room in the basement. It has a window ground level; it faces the back of the building."

"You've done this before, haven't you?" Natalie asked.

The guitar player grinned slightly and shrugged.

"Good luck," Natalie called to him as they parted ways, him to continue down the stairs, the women to the second floor. Once there Natalie grabbed Paige's arm.

"I can't get arrested," she said.

"What? This is a fine time to think of that!"

"I thought of it before. Even reconciled myself to it. But now that the time is at hand, I can't bring myself to get arrested."

"Why not?"

"Might hurt my chances in law school."

Paige hadn't thought of that.

"Come with me," Natalie said.

"Where are you going?"

"I'm gonna follow that guitar player."

Paige hesitated. "I'd feel bad skipping out on Del."

"So you'll allow yourself to get arrested? What will your father say?" Paige didn't want to think about her father; she still couldn't shake the image in her head of her father shooting her.

"Come with me!" Natalie pleaded.

Paige looked down the hallway. There were more than enough people to get arrested. They really didn't need two more.

"All right," she said. "Let's go."

Plunging down the stairwell as fast as they could run, Paige heard a pounding followed by a door giving way on the ground floor.

"Faster! They're coming!" she said.

She caught a glimpse of a door flying open and green National Guardsmen pouring in.

They spotted her!

"Ohhhhhh! Faster, Natalie. Faster!"

They reached the basement. Paige looked behind her, watching the stairwell door swing closed. It moved slowly, too slowly for her taste. She expected it to burst open any second.

It didn't.

Halfway down the basement hallway, she glanced over her shoulder again. The door remained closed. Good.

"Where's the janitor's room?" Natalie shouted. The words no sooner cleared her mouth when she saw it. "Oh, here it is!"

Someone had jimmied the door open. It stood ajar. As Paige and Natalie rushed in, a pair of feet scrambled out the small horizontal window. Then they were gone. They assumed the feet had belonged to the guitar player.

There was a desk beneath the window. Natalie jumped on top and wedged herself into the window. With a few kicks she was out.

Shouts echoed down the hall.

"Natalie! Hurry! Someone's coming!"

The shouts grew louder.

Standing on the desk, Paige ducked into the window and jumped. From the other side Natalie caught her by the shoulders and pulled. A few wiggles and kicks and Paige was out, though she half expected a guardsman to grab her feet and pull her back inside at any moment.

They found themselves on the back side of the administrative building. A large bluff rose up immediately in front of them. It ran the length of the building. They were in an alley with dirt on one side and a building on the other side.

Grabbing Paige's hand, Natalie led the way. They came to the end of the building. Natalie peeked around the corner.

"Clear!" she said.

Within moments they'd cleared the buildings and were hiding behind some large bushes. They watched as a three-pronged assault team attacked the building.

"What time do you have?" Natalie whispered.

Glancing at her watch, Paige answered, "A little after five o'clock."

"You just can't trust the establishment," Natalie groaned. "What happened to the six o'clock deadline?"

"They set us up. Wanted us to get comfortable."

"Well, we certainly obliged."

Emerging from a similar basement window on the side of the administration building, Paige recognized Del and Allen. The two men scrambled out of the window, looked side to side, then sprinted for cover.

"What was Del saying earlier? None of us has legs? If anybody leaves this place they'll have to be carried out?"

Paige was speechless.

"Some general," Natalie said sarcastically.

At the moment—weary and frightened—Paige was inclined to agree.

16

"What are you doing here?"

Del swung around, surprised to see Paige and Natalie closing in from behind.

"Seems to me," Natalie said, "we're the ones who should be asking that question. What happened to, 'None of us has legs,' and, 'If anybody leaves this place they'll have to be carried out'? Your legs seem to be working just fine."

While Del and Natalie were squaring off, Paige took a glance at Allen. He seemed nervous. Preoccupied. All the time the other two were fighting, he was looking at the ground in thought.

"In a war there are generals and soldiers," Del shouted. "I'm the general."

"Who's deserting his troops," Natalie added.

Del glared at Natalie a moment longer, then let the argument drop. He turned to Paige. He said, "You should be in the building. Why did you leave?"

Paige shot a look at Natalie and thought it best not to say anything about her desire not to be arrested. The information would only serve to fuel their fight.

She said, "We saw another guy crawling out of the basement window. It seemed the best thing to do at the time."

"You would have been safer in there," Del replied. "You should have trusted me. But now that you're here, come along."

He turned on his heel and strode purposefully away. Allen, still preoccupied, absently fell in stride with him.

Natalie held her ground.

Paige stood between Del and her. "Where are we going?" she called out to Del.

He turned, saw she wasn't following, and stopped. He looked perturbed that she wasn't right behind him. Then, rolling his eyes in resignation, he said, "The battle isn't over. The sit-in is only the first strike."

Paige turned to Natalie. "Are you coming?"

Natalie folded her arms. "I'm not sure."

"Who invited her?" Del asked.

"I did!" Paige replied.

"We don't need her."

"I need her! You're going to go off and do your general stuff and leave me all alone. I'm not saying that to complain. That's the way it should be. But I need somebody to be with me."

Del was clearly dissatisfied, but he was also in a hurry. "All right," he said. "She can come."

A wry smile graced Natalie's face. "Oh joy! I have permission from the general himself!"

Del and Allen walked away.

"Please come," Paige pleaded.

"Do you have any idea what that warped little brain of his has cooked up this time?" Natalie asked.

Paige ignored the dig at Del. "He doesn't confide in me," she said. "He likes to analyze it afterward with me. What he was hoping to do. What went right. What went wrong. That sort of thing."

"So you have no idea what he's up to?"

"No."

"That scares me."

Paige moved beside Natalie and gently took her arm. "Whatever happens, if it looks like police are going to start arresting people again, we'll get out of there. Agreed?"

With pursed lips, Natalie thought it over. "Agreed," she said.

≥

They followed Del and Allen to the Shores Drive residence.

"Who are all these people?" Natalie asked.

"I have no idea," Paige replied.

Cars and motorcycles of every description were parked everywhere, doubled up on the street, on lawns, and sidewalks. A stream of people could be seen coming in and out of the house. Many of them, unfamiliar with the house's peculiarities, stumbled on the broken front step.

Del and Allen mounted the porch. Whoever these people were, they seemed to recognize the two men, for the crowd gathered around the front porch. For a few moments Del whispered into Allen's ear, his hand seeming to divide the crowd before them in the same way he would cut a pie into three pieces. Allen nodded several times, then straightened himself to address the crowd.

"Thank you for coming," Allen said. His voice was strong and clear. He had a good voice for this sort of thing. It carried well and could be understood from a good distance away.

Del stood slightly behind him and to the rear, his arms folded. He seemed pleased at the way things were going.

"As we speak," Allen continued, "the pigs are arresting our fellow protesters at the academic building. The media has been alerted and should be arriving shortly."

There was an uneasy rumbling through the crowd when Allen mentioned the arrests.

"It's time to show the establishment what we think of their heavy-handed tactics. Who do they think they are? What makes them think they have the right to arbitrarily change the Constitution of the United States?"

The crowd stirred in angry protest.

"What makes them think they have the right to ignore the Bill of Rights?"

A louder stirring, this time with a few angry shouts thrown in.

"Are we going to sit idly by while they illegally carry away our friends who are merely exercising their right to assemble peacefully?"

"No!" the crowd shouted.

"Are we going to stand here and do nothing while they take away our right to free speech?"

"No!"

"Are we going to stand idly by and do nothing while our friends and fellow students have their personal rights stripped from them?"

"No!"

"The time for talking is over!" Allen shouted at the top of his voice.

The Shores Drive crowd cheered him.

"Talk is cheap!" Allen called again.

Another cheer.

"Then let's go there now and let them know how we feel. It's time we stand up for our rights and put down a heavy-handed establishment that wants to treat us like so many children!"

The crowd was waving things and cheering.

"We're not children anymore!"

A cheer.

"We have rights!"

A cheer.

"And we're willing to fight for our rights!"

A cheer.

"We must speak out with one voice!" Allen proclaimed. "Let our people go! Let our people go!"

The crowd took up the chant.

"Let our people go! Let our people go! Let our people go!" They were working themselves into a frenzy.

Allen motioned for a third of them to move toward the administration building under siege. They began to move out. After a few moments he motioned for the second third of the crowd to move out. They did.

After another ten minutes he released the last third of the group. Maybe it was all in Paige's mind, but this last group looked tougher than the first two. They had also armed themselves with rocks and bats and two-by-fours, and most anything else that could be thrown or swung.

Del moved just in front of this third group. Passing Paige and Natalie, he grinned. "Come on!" he said. "You don't want to miss the fun."

Allen, as usual, was right beside him. Despite the rousing cheers the spokesman had been able to elicit, he looked fearful and worried.

"Who are all these people?" Paige asked Del.

"Concerned citizens, just like us."

"Where did they come from? I don't recognize any of them."

"From around," Del said. "UCLA, USC, UCSD. We even have a group that came down from Berkeley. They wanted to see how the whole thing played out."

"What whole thing?" Natalie asked.

At first it didn't look as though Del was going to answer her. Then, he said, "It was Paige who inspired the whole thing."

Natalie and Paige shared a surprised look that seemed to please Del.

"Remember that last debacle? The shroud demonstration? The one where Paige made the national news?"

Paige flushed. It wasn't her favorite memory.

"This effort was born of that disaster!" Del said excitedly. "Remember? That was our first attempt at street theater. Only we did it all wrong! Last time we staged a play and invited the media and the cops to attend." He shook his head pathetically and muttered, "I can't believe how naive we were then." He turned to Paige. His eyes were alive with excitement. "This time is different. This time we not only invite the media and the cops, we make them players in the drama." He laughed. "Let's see them make fun of that."

※

By the time the four of them reached the front lawn of the administration building, the first wave of protesters were already at work, jeering, taunting, harassing, heckling the police as they carried one sit-in protester after another from the building.

The National Guard had formed a perimeter around the police effort, a human fence armed with rifles, to protect them while they carried out their arrests. Van after van was filled with limp protesters.

The second wave from the Shores Drive assembly was just arriving. The National Guard responded by pulling more men into position to keep back the crowd.

"This is where we leave you," Del said.

"Got general stuff to do?" Natalie asked sarcastically.

Del ignored her. To Paige, he said, "Watch from a distance. In fact, right here is just fine."

"We're big girls now," Natalie said. "We can take care of ourselves, thank you very much."

Del started to respond to her, then didn't. To Paige he said, "I'm serious. This could get ugly. You already disobeyed me once today by leaving the building. Don't do it again."

While Paige disliked the fact that Del was treating her like a child, Natalie bristled visibly.

"Listen here, Comrade Lenin, where do you get off giving us orders?"

But Del wasn't listening. With a nod of his head to Allen, the two of them began jogging toward the far side of the administration building.

"The nerve of that guy!" Natalie cried. "How can you stand there and just take that kind of abuse?"

"He's really not that bad," Paige replied. "You seem to have a knack for bringing out the worst in him."

Natalie grinned. "I do, don't I?"

Paige tried to suppress a laugh. She couldn't.

"Come on, let's get a closer look," Natalie said. "Maybe my National Guardsman is here. You know, the one with the dimples."

"Leave it to you to find romance in a protest," Paige said. Her comment was born of truth. She had never known anyone like Natalie who could benefit from any situation. She was the kind of person who, if her car broke down on the freeway, would have a highway patrolman and mechanic both stop to help her. Then, as luck would have it, by the time the mechanic got her car to the shop he would have offered to fix the thing for free, and Natalie would have a date lined up with him that Friday. And he would be gorgeous.

Paige didn't know why Natalie was so afraid of getting arrested. Chances are, she'd marry the arresting officer, and the judge who heard her case would probably give her a personal recommendation to law school.

"Come on, Paige! Don't dawdle. This is a protest, remember? We're supposed to be taking this thing seriously!"

"Del told us not to get too close."

"All the more reason to do it. Come on!"

Natalie led the way onto the large grassy expanse in front of the administrative offices. Paige followed after her.

With the arrival of the third group of protesters, the National Guard was clearly outnumbered; still their line held tight. Behind them the students from the sit-in were methodically being removed from the building. Most of them hung like a sack of laundry between two, sometimes three, police officers. Of course there were those who shouted all the way from the building to the police van.

"Get our troops out of Vietnam!"

"Sieg Heil, Sieg Heil!"

"Ho Ho Ho Chi Minh!"

Some of the more musical sang, "This land is your land, this land is my land...."

Then there were those who fought. They wriggled. They kicked. They twisted and turned. These were the ones who were given special attention.

Paige looked beyond the line of guardsmen and saw three policemen with nightsticks pummeling one of the protesters mercilessly. He attempted to fend off the blows with his arms. He rolled over. They kicked him in the ribs. He tried to get up. They knocked him down and beat him harder. Finally, he lay still and offered no resistance. Whether he was conscious or not, alive or not, Paige couldn't tell. Still the police kicked him. Hit him. Then, finally, they picked him up, tossed him into a van, and went back for another protester.

Paige felt her anger rising. The beaten boy had been no threat to the police. He was unarmed. There were three of them, and only one of him. What kind of a threat did he pose to them? What had he done to deserve that kind of beating?

"Stop it! Stop it!"

Paige found herself shouting with the other protesters.

"He didn't do anything!"

The crush of humanity behind her pushed her dangerously close to the guard perimeter. She was face-to-face with a pock-marked boy wearing a riot helmet. He was frightened. Turning his rifle sideways he pushed her back.

Paige felt someone grabbing her arm, pulling her back. It was Natalie.

"Whoa, Tiger!" she said. "First you get an introduction, then you dance with the young man."

"Did you see what the police did to that guy? They beat him senseless. And for no reason."

Out of the corner of her eye, she caught sight of a projectile, little more than a gray blur to her. To the pock-faced guardsman it was something more tangible.

With a loud THWACK, the rock hit his face shield, staggering him. A volley of rocks followed the first one.

Suddenly, everyone became agitated. Guardsmen. Police. Protesters. The image that came to Paige's mind was that of a beehive.

"Let's get out of here!" Natalie shouted.

Paige agreed. They pushed and wove their way through the shouting, angry, fist-waving crowd. Pushed this way and that. Stumbling. Running into people's chests. Pushing off. Being pushed. Staying low, Paige followed Natalie's blonde hair through the crowd until finally, they broke into the clear.

Both of them were panting from the exertion. Paige also found herself shaking. There was a moment in there when she began to panic. Never before had she understood the force of a human crowd like she did now. Had she fallen to the ground, she likely would have been trampled to death, and there was noth-ing she would have been able to do to stop it. The force of humanity was too strong for her. For a few moments she'd been at their mercy, a helpless cork in a sea of arms and shoulders and hands and chests.

As they backed away, they could see the two tides battle for position. A man's voice, amplified by a bullhorn, could be heard over the din of confrontation.

"This is an unlawful assembly. Disperse immediately! Anyone attempting to interfere with this police action will be arrested."

The announcement was answered by a hail of rocks, hitting protesters and guardsmen alike.

"Are you all right?" Natalie asked.

"A little shaken, but yeah, I think I'm all right." Paige took a good look at Natalie. She had a couple of scrapes on the temple near her right eye. Her hair was disheveled, which was quite unusual. Natalie's hair was never disheveled.

"While you were in there," Natalie asked, "up close to the guardsmen, did you happen to see one with dimples?"

BOOM!

Before Paige could laugh, a huge explosion rocked the entire scene. A fireball, followed by a billowing tower of black smoke, rose from a parked car. The sound and sight of the explosion caused everything and everybody to stop what they were doing, but only for a second.

Under orders the guardsmen began marching forward, pushing the protesters back. Pelted by rocks, they pressed ahead. The tactic worked. The protesters began to disperse. The guardsmen stopped and retreated to their original position.

Given the explosion and the advancing guards, the protesters were pretty much scattered over the lawn while, behind them, the evacuation of the administration building continued.

It stayed this way for a while. The guard seemed satisfied that they held their line. The protesters were beginning to thin out, scattered every which way. Television cameramen wandered here and there, but seemed mostly content to stay behind the guard line and photograph the arrests of the sit-ins.

Then the protesters seemed to get a second wind. While they kept their distance from the guards, the number of rocks seemed to escalate. Bottles were added to the mix as well.

Again the protesters were warned to disperse or be arrested.

"I don't know about you, but I've seen enough," Natalie said. "Have to give him credit for this one."

"Who?"

"Del."

"You're giving Del credit?"

Natalie grinned at Paige's response. "Well, he's right on one thing. The press won't be able to laugh this one off."

The words no sooner escaped her lips when …

BAM! BAM!

"Were those gunshots?" Paige asked.

BAM! BAM! BAM! BAM!

Panic broke out on the green. Protesters screamed and ran. Some fell to the grass. The guardsmen ducked, then dropped to one knee. They raised their rifles to return fire.

BAM! BAM! BAM! BAM! BAM! BAM!

The first volley cut through the crowd of protesters. People dropped all around Paige.

BAM! BAM! BAM! BAM! BAM! BAM!

"Natalie! Let's get out of here!" Paige screamed.

Natalie didn't answer.

"Natalie?"

The girl lay on the grass. She didn't move.

"Natalie!"

17

Travis reclined against the damp dirt wall. All around him the cave was pitch-black. He could raise his hand inches from his face and see nothing. He and Gower had one match left and Travis wasn't sure it would even light. For every three matches that lit, one didn't.

"What time is it?"

Gower's voice, which came out of the darkness, was faint. As far as Travis could tell, the machine gunner had lost a lot of blood. The huge Texan was so weak, he could barely raise his own head.

Working in the dark and lighting matches only when absolutely necessary, Travis had examined Gower's wound. He'd opened one of the crates in the cave and used the fatigues inside as blankets. He'd also built the Texan a little room by moving the crates around—this, in an attempt to contain Gower's body heat. These efforts alone had used four matches.

"I don't know what time it is," Travis said. In truth he didn't know what day it was. Without any natural change in dark and light, he'd become time disoriented. While he checked his watch with the lighting of every match, he and Gower had been buried so long the watch might inform Travis that it was 3:20, but he

didn't know if that was a.m. or p.m., nor did he know how many
3:20s had passed since they fell into the cave.

"Have you found a way out yet?" Gower asked.

"Not yet."

"How long have I been asleep?"

Travis didn't know that Gower had been asleep. Was the
Texan slipping in and out of consciousness?

"Not long," Travis replied.

For some time now Travis had been working up his courage
to strike the last match. If the match even lit, he had the length of
its burn to find a way out of the cave. For as large as the cave was,
he originally thought finding the opening would be easy. And it
might have been if they had plenty of light, but they didn't. And
Travis had yet to find a way out.

"I'm c-c-cold," Gower said.

The Texan had enough fatigues piled on him to suffocate a
smaller man.

"Relax. I'll have you out of here soon," Travis said, attempting to bolster Gower's hope. "I think I may have seen something
with the last match. I'm just resting up a bit until I dig us out of
here."

"G-g-good," Gower replied.

It was a lie. Wanting to give a dying man hope, Travis had lied.
After he'd said it, it disturbed Travis. Not that he'd lied, but
because lying came so easily given the circumstances.

An image came to Travis's mind, an image based on something he'd learned in church years ago. Everything about the
image fit their situation. The image was of Sheol, the realm of
the dead, and Travis concluded that's exactly where they were
at the moment. Neither dead nor alive, they lived in the realm of
darkness as shades, suspended between earth and hell, neither
world claiming them.

Travis had stalled long enough. It was time to light the final match. As he had done each time before, he listened first for noises coming from above.

After the first hours of constant gunfire and mortars and thumps and shouts, it had been relatively quiet. But relatively quiet didn't mean that the danger had passed. The first night—at least he assumed it was night—he heard voices. He couldn't make out what the voices were saying; not because the dirt separating him from them muffled the sound, but because the voices were Vietnamese. The casualness of the voices and occasional laughter convinced Travis that his squad's position had been overrun. He wondered if there were any survivors other than Gower and himself.

After awhile the voices left. Having taken care of Gower, Travis began searching for a way out. Then the voices returned. They stayed for a long time. The longer they stayed, the more Travis's fear grew.

Did the voices know about the cave? What if the earth began to crumble and an opening suddenly appeared? He had his rifle, which he kept with him at all times. But their position was hardly defensible, at least not for very long. One grenade dropped down a hole could wipe them out. Of course some of the supplies would be damaged. A thought struck him. He found it oddly humorous. Would the enemy think twice about killing him, not wanting to damage a few crates of ponchos?

Travis was stalling. He knew it. He was afraid to light the last match. He was afraid the length of the burn wouldn't be sufficient time to find a way out. After all, how many had he burned already? Six? Seven? What made him think he could be success-ful with just one more?

"Gower?"

No response.

"Gower!"

Still no response.

The Texan was probably unconscious. Just as well. If he witnessed the burning of the last match and Travis didn't succeed in finding a way out, the discouragement might cause him to give up hope. Just like Travis figured he would probably do.

Travis reached in his pocket for the matchbook. Finding it, he pushed off from the wall and stood. He'd been working his way around the circumference of the cave from right to left. This was as far as he'd gotten when the last match burned his fingers.

Travis paused before striking the final match. It seemed appropriate to pray first. But what for exactly? That the match would light? Most certainly that should be part of the prayer. That he would find an opening? He'd been praying for that since they fell into the cave. Should he pray that God would extend the burning of the match beyond its natural life, giving him time to find a way out?

Why shouldn't he? God made the sun stand still in the heavens to save the Israelite army, didn't he? Was extending the life of a match for two soldiers asking too much?

Travis didn't close his eyes to pray. He just prayed.

"Lord, this is it. Help us get out of here."

Opening the matchbook cover with burned fingers, he felt for the remaining match. He ripped it out. The words, "Close Cover Before Striking," came to mind. He'd done this all the other times to protect the remaining matches from accidentally catching on fire. But with no remaining matches to catch on fire …

A thought struck him. A wondrous thought! Why hadn't he thought of it until now?

Naturally, he'd already looked for other things to burn. He'd tried to start splinters from the crates on fire. He'd tried burning fatigues and anything else he could lay his hands on in the cave. Each effort was unsuccessful. But there was one thing he hadn't thought of. The matchbook cover itself. Burning the matchbook cover would double the life of the flame.

To a person chilled to the bone, consigned to death, buried beneath the enemy with a dying man, this realization was not only an answer to prayer, it was akin to a miracle. Travis felt tears well up in his eyes.

His heart pounding, Travis struck the match. There was a spark, then nothing save the smell of sulfur. His heart rose into this throat. *This couldn't be happening. The match had to light. It had to!*

With trembling fingers, he struck the match again. There was a lesser spark.

Please God. Please!

He struck the match a third time. This time there was no spark at all.

Travis slumped against the dank wall. He trembled. The cold? Fear? Anger? All three? He didn't know. Nor did he care. All he knew was that he was trembling and couldn't stop. Hope drained from him as surely as if he had sprung a leak.

He didn't know what caused him to try again. Desperation, probably. Of the matches that lit, none of them lit after a third failure. But what other course did he have? If this didn't work he would be reduced to rubbing splinter pieces of wood together, either that or spend his days rooting around in the dark like some kind of mole.

Pushing off the wall, he stood confidently with his feet slightly apart as though to will the match to light. With one bold stroke, he swiped the match.

Nothing.

Not even a spark.

Oh, Lord ...

He struck it again.

A spark.

A fizzle.

Sputtering ... sputtering ... sputtering ...

Then ... a flame! Travis had fire!

He wanted to whoop, to jump up, to do something to celebrate, but time was precious. With renewed hope, he moved toward the dirt wall and examined it up high for an opening to the upper world.

The flame moved steadily down the length of the match.

Holding the match high, he examined cracks, explored crevices with his free hand, pulled at rocks. There was no opening here. He moved to his left, exploring, gouging, clawing.

His flame-sensitive fingers felt the fire's nearness. With previous matches, Travis had let them burn all the way down until they singed the tips of his fingers. But he couldn't take the chance with this one that it might burn out. Holding the edge of the matchbook close to the flame, he held his breath as he waited for it to catch on fire.

The match light dimmed as though it was an effort for it to share its flame with something else. Then, the matchbook caught on. A larger flame leaped upward, casting a much larger sphere of light. Travis continued his search.

"Find an opening yet?"

Gower was awake again. There wasn't time to talk.

"I'm close," Travis said curtly.

For whatever reason, Gower didn't reply. Maybe he heard the urgency in Travis's voice. Or maybe he slipped back into unconsciousness. Whatever the reason, Travis counted it a blessing. It allowed him to concentrate fully on the task at hand.

The matchbook was flaming heartily now. Nearly half of it was consumed by the fire. For all the increased light, the result of Travis's search was the same. He could find no opening.

There was a time when he'd considered digging randomly upward. He'd even gone so far as to take a piece of jagged crate wood and attack a portion of the roof. It was easy digging. There were no rocks. Only red dirt. And with each jab, dirt fell. It fell too fast. Worse, it began falling without an encouragement from Travis. He found himself pushing against it, not unlike applying pressure to a bleeding wound. It took him several minutes to heal the growing rupture.

It was at that point that Travis realized how fragile their cave was. One good mortar could collapse the entire thing upon itself. One good poke could do the same. If there was no other way out, it might be worth the risk, collapsing the entire cave upon itself. But it wasn't Travis's first choice.

The flame flickered. It was in the early stages of dying. Travis worked faster. His fingertips were raw and sensitive. Ignoring the pain, he jabbed at the earth with them as though they were a steel trowel.

The light was fading.

Travis moved left. Exploring. Digging.

The death of the flame was rapid. It collapsed into a thin blue line, then reddish embers, then it was gone.

Travis stood in the dark.

There was no more light.

He wanted to weep, to curse God for building up his hope only to leave him empty-handed. For Travis thought for sure that the lighting of the last match was a sign from God that they were going to get out of the cave, that he would find an entrance. But the light had died and with it, his hope that they would ever get out of the cave alive.

He tossed what little was left of the matchbook aside. There was nothing left to do but keep searching in the dark.

"Find it?" Gower called to him.

Do I tell him? Travis wondered. *Should I lie again to protect him, or should I tell him the truth and get it over with? If he dies, he dies. That's the way things are here in Vietnam. It doesn't mean a thing.*

His hands felt something other than dirt. It felt like bamboo. Poles. Side by side. It wasn't a natural formation.

An opening?

He felt again. More bamboo. Before he found dirt again, his fingers had traveled nearly two and half feet.

"Morgan?" There was an edge of panic in Gower's voice.

Travis kept exploring the bamboo.

"Morgan? Morgan!"

"I'm here."

"What are you doing?"

"Trying to get us out of here."

"Did you find the opening?"

Travis was able to get a grip on the bamboo. He pulled. It was firm. No way was it going to give way.

"Morgan? Why aren't you answering me?"

If it can't be pulled down, how about …?

"Morgan! Answer me! Do you hear me? Answer me!"

Gouging the toes of his boots into the dirt wall for leverage, Travis pushed on the bamboo. It creaked. It was heavy. He pushed again.

It moved!

"Mooorrrgaaaaannn!"

The bamboo lifted in one piece. He'd found the entrance to the cave!

A sliver of gray light slipped past the edges. It was raining above. Water trickled in through the opening. Fresh air poured through the cracks too. Travis had never smelled anything so sweet.

Excitement nearly ambushed his better judgment. He wanted desperately to shout to Gower that he'd found a way out. But then he remembered where he was: inches from the surface, probably the surface of enemy territory. Caution overcame his excitement.

Travis lowered the bamboo cover back into place.

"Mooorrrgaaaaannn!"

"Shut up, Gower!" Travis insisted in a restrained shout.

"Where were you? What were you doing?"

Travis felt his way toward the voice. "Shut up!" he said again. "I've found a way out."

"Eeeeeeha …"

"Shut up!" Travis cut him off. "Do you want this place crawling with VC?"

Gower's cry fell quickly silent. In a hushed voice he said, "How are we going to get out of here?"

"I don't know. I haven't thought that far ahead yet."

Gower was silent.

"It daylight above and it's raining. Maybe we should wait until it's dark."

"The VC move at night," Gower said.

He was right. Travis knew that. Why did he have to be reminded?

"I guess the only thing we can do is take our chances," Travis said. "I'll stick my head out and see what's out there."

Travis took his rifle off his shoulder. "Here," he said, "I'm handing you my rifle—butt first."

He extended the weapon into the dark, felt something hit it, then grab it.

"If I get my head shot off," Travis said, "I'm afraid you're on your own." It had sounded funny when he thought of it. Now it didn't sound so funny. Apparently Gower didn't think so either, because he didn't laugh.

"You're not going to leave me, are you, Morgan?"

Travis was surprised that Gower would even think such a thing. "Of course not!" he replied.

"Promise me you won't leave me."

"Knock it off, Gower."

"I mean it! Promise me!"

"I promise."

There was a moment of silence in the dark. Gower seemed to be weighing the sincerity of Travis's promise. Finally, he said, "OK."

"I'm going now," Travis announced.

A heavy sigh came from the dark. Then, "Be careful."

Travis felt his way back to the side of the cave. Following it with his hands, he made his way to where he could see a streak of gray light.

This is it, he thought.

Finding the footholds he'd dug in the side, he crept silently upward. He pushed gently, slowly, on the bamboo covering. Just a crack at first. He paused and looked out.

There was a trail a short distance away, then dense foliage and trees. He saw no movement.

He listened hard. There was the soft patter of rain on the ground and leaves and the top of the bamboo covering. He could hear no movement, no voices.

Slowly, he pushed the cover open farther. It creaked from the effort. He stopped, waiting for a reaction. There was none. Pushing again, he lifted the cover and shoved it to one side.

Rain splattered his face. It felt good. Fresh air filled his lungs. It felt even better than the rain.

Travis gripped the sides of the opening and pulled himself upward. He didn't get far before he felt the cold steel of the deadly end of a rifle against the back of his neck.

Allegra shivered.

"Are you all right dear?" Nat asked. The shiver was so pronounced, it had taken his eye away from the newspaper article. He watched as Allegra rubbed the back of her neck.

The two of them were sitting in the den of their La Jolla home. Whenever Nat thought of home he thought of this room. This was the homiest part of home for him. There was no place on earth where he felt more comfortable.

It had been a quiet evening. Allegra had fixed a simple dinner of eggs and corned beef hash. Following the evening news, they had switched off the television. Allegra had placed Mahler's *10th Symphony* on the stereo while he settled into his overstuffed recliner and she retreated to her work area.

Allegra had introduced him to classical music. Through her persistent tutelage—for he was an unwilling student at first—he found a depth and passion in this music he never knew existed. It was just one of the ways this remarkable woman had changed his life.

"Are you sure you're all right?" Nat asked.

Allegra stopped rubbing her neck and lowered her hand rather self-consciously. "It was nothing," she said. "A sudden chill of some kind."

"You're not coming down with something, are you?"

Allegra smiled at his concern. "No, Mother," she said with mocking sweetness, "I'm not coming down with anything. Really, it's nothing."

Nat didn't return immediately to his newspaper. His eyes remained fixed on the woman in the corner. He watched as she resumed her knitting. Nimble fingers counted the knitted rows.

Allegra seemed to stop aging ten years ago. After all these years she still had the power to move him in every way a man could be moved.

"You can stop staring at me now," she said with a smile.

"Sorry."

Nat still had to remind himself on occasion she was blind. She knew he was still looking at her because she hadn't heard the newspaper rustle in his hands. And she couldn't be fooled. She knew the difference between a fake rustle and a real one. How, God and she only knew.

With one last glance Nat returned to his newspaper.

Mahler's somber strains filled the room. This particular symphony had been left incomplete at the composer's death and remained that way until an English Mahler expert discovered some of the composer's sketches that were complete enough to finish the work. Allegra had told him that just as she was placing the LP on the stereo. She dispensed these bits of information in bite-sized pieces in ways that made each listening unique and enjoyable.

Allegra shivered again. Her knitting dropped into her lap. Nat was out of his chair and kneeling by her side in an instant.

"What is it?" he asked.

Her hand was on the back of her neck again. Her brow furrowed in concern.

"I don't know," she said. "Just a cold shiver."

"Should I call the doctor?"

She thought a moment. The furrows on her forehead eased. "No," she said. "I feel fine." Apparently sensing his disbelief, she reached out to him. Her hand reached out and held his. "Really, Nat, it's gone now. I feel fine."

Nat stood, still holding her hand. He was still concerned.

The telephone jangled loudly, startling them. They both laughed at their mutual fright. Allegra reached for the phone and answered it.

At her workstation everything was easily within her reach.

Skeins of yarn lay neatly side by side. For each project Allegra would have Nat or a friend lay out the colors. After that nothing more was needed. An electric typewriter sat in the corner. On it, Allegra typed letters to friends and relatives mostly.

"Hello?" She listened for a moment. The furrows on her brow returned. "Yes, I'll wait." Covering the mouthpiece, she said to Nat, "Long distance."

For years long distance calls, like telegraphs, were associated with bad news. Now, with long distance rates becoming more affordable, this wasn't always the case, though Nat still felt a twinge of panic whenever he heard the operator use the words.

They waited in silence for the connection to be completed. Nat's eyes wandered to Allegra's typing area. She'd been doing a lot of typing lately. Nearly every day this week when he'd come home he'd found her typing. And she always finished the moment he came in, covering the typewriter without removing the paper.

Nat glanced at a stack of pages that was about a quarter of a ream thick. The top page was turned upside down, but it lay somewhat askew, allowing him to see some of the words on the page beneath it.

Abigail held an exhibit of her work on the upper end of Queen Street in New York. Admittance was two shillings.

"Hello?" Allegra's face lit brightly with surprise. "It's Travis!" she cried.

At the sound of his son's name, Nat's senses were instantly focused on the one-sided phone conversation. He tried to read his wife's face as she listened. The good news was that Travis was alive, but until he heard otherwise, Nat's was a guarded optimism. He could be calling from a hospital.

Allegra covered the mouthpiece of the phone. "He's all right," she whispered.

A wave of relief swept over Nat.

"Oh, Travis, that must have been frightening!" Allegra said. "And the other soldier, he's going to make it?"

Nat fidgeted. Then he remembered the phone in the kitchen, an extension of this line.

"Hello? Hello?"

Allegra listened a moment, then hung up.

"We lost the connection," she said. "It was a bad one to begin with."

"Well?"

Allegra sat back in her chair. "Apparently, we're going to be receiving official notice that our son is missing in action."

"An administrative error?"

"No, he *was* missing in action for a couple of days."

"Oh?"

"Seems he and another soldier fell into one of those underground caves the North Vietnamese have dug. It took them awhile to find their way out, which, according to Travis, actually saved their lives. Seems the enemy held the ground overhead the entire time they were in the cave. Travis poked his head out of the ground just as a U.S. squad was passing by."

"Was he injured?"

"No. The other soldier was shot in the shoulder, but he'll be all right."

"What about the rest of his squad?"

"Travis said the fighting was the heaviest he'd seen since being there, but somehow the squad managed to survive for the most part. There was one death. Travis didn't go into the details."

"And so Keith's all right?"

Allegra nodded. "Keith was with him when he called. He was going to give me a message to relay to his parents, but we were cut off."

"At least they're both OK," Nat said. "We can thank God for that."

"You didn't get to talk to him," Allegra said, dismayed at the thought.

Nat didn't mind. The news that his son was still alive and not wounded was enough for him. He said, "Travis got to talk to his momma. There's not a better tonic in all the world for a soldier."

18

They were in Colorado somewhere. That's all Paige knew. Allen had steered the Volkswagen van into a gas station on Platte Avenue to get gas and directions. While Natalie and Paige pumped the gas, Del and Allen talked to the attendant.

"How's your leg?" Paige asked. "Is it still throbbing?"

Natalie examined her wrapped leg, which a National Guardman's bullet had injured during the sit-in. Both entry and exit wounds were clean. No damage had been done to the bone. She got around with the use of a cane for now.

"It burns now and then," she said. "I think the aspirin helped stop the throbbing."

When the bullets starting flying and Natalie went down, Paige thought for sure she was dead. The emotional blow she received while bending over the still form of her friend was a powerful one. This wasn't a game they were playing. This was just as much a war as the one that was being fought in Vietnam. And while the doctor predicted a full recovery for Natalie, Paige was certain she would never fully recover from what she had seen that day.

Eight students were wounded during the sit-in confrontation. Two died. The guitar player in the stairwell was one of them. Like

Paige and Natalie, once out of the building he didn't have the good sense to stay away.

The strangest part about the whole thing was Del's reaction afterward. Of course the incident made national headlines. Del was even interviewed. The crowd at Shores Drive erupted in celebration as Del denounced the deaths of the students, the deaths of young boys in Vietnam, and the death of free speech in America.

That night, when he and Paige were alone together, inexplicably, Del became amorous. He was all over Paige. Kissing. Groping. Fondling. Pulling at clothing.

Paige had rebuffed his advances. There were any number of reasons to do so. First, the deaths of the students depressed her. Second, while Natalie's wound had not been serious, still Paige worried about her. And third, it wasn't the time or place to allow Del to make love to her. She felt like Del was using lovemaking as the crowning trophy of his day.

Of course Del became furious. He cajoled. When that didn't work, he tried to force the issue. When she pushed him away, he got angry. In tears Paige fled the room and slept that night on the downstairs couch. Neither of them had spoken to each other about the incident since.

When the Volkswagen could hold no more gasoline, Paige checked the numbers on the pump. Twelve gallons at twenty-five cents a gallon.

"You get back in the van," she said to Natalie. "I'll pay the cashier."

As it turned out, the cashier and the attendant were one in the same person. The discussion was animated when she arrived. Del and Allen were arguing over the best way to reach Chicago. They stopped when Paige showed up. All three of them looked at her.

"Oh ... um, we pumped twelve gallons," she said in way of general announcement. To the attendant, she said, "It was three dollars even." She handed him three wadded up one-dollar bills that had been stuffed in her blue jeans pocket.

Allen turned toward the van. "It does us no good to argue about where we should have turned. We're here, and we want to get to Chicago."

"Fine," Del said sarcastically. "Only next time just drive, don't think. You're not very good at it, you know."

Paige slipped her arm into Del's, hoping to calm him down. He jerked his arm free.

"Del! What's the matter?" Paige asked.

Backing away, he held up both hands in the form of surrender. "Nothing, all right? Everything's fine. Just as it should be."

"Where are you going?"

"To powder my nose!" He looked at her mockingly; his voice dripped with sarcasm.

He was in one of his moods. Paige hated it when he was in one of his moods.

Del got a key—attached to a large piece of wood—from the attendant and walked around the corner of the building to the men's restroom.

Allen and Paige exchanged glances. The first few steps back to the Volkswagen were taken in silence. Then, Allen said, "Can I ask you something without you getting angry?"

Paige looked up at him. Worry lines marked his attractive face. It was the same expression he'd worn the morning of the sit-in massacre, and the same one he'd carried around with him ever since.

"Sure," Paige replied. "What do you want to know?"

"Why do you stay with him?"

Allen wasn't trying to be funny. He was serious.

Paige shrugged. "I'm lucky to have him. I often ask myself a similar question. I wonder why he stays with me."

"You're kidding, right?" Allen said, ready to laugh.

When Paige didn't break into a grin, Allen's smile died of lone-liness. In all seriousness he said, "Any guy would be lucky to have you. You're too good for Del."

Paige bristled. "I don't see how that's any of your business."

They were almost to the van. Allen slowed his pace, obviously wanting to tell her something without it being overheard.

"You're right," Allen said. "It's just that … well …" His thoughts were having a difficult time forming into the right words. "I wouldn't want anything to happen to you, or to hurt you."

Paige smiled at Allen's struggle for words. The two of them rarely talked; they hardly knew each other. Their only point of familiar contact was Del.

"That's sweet, Allen. Really, it is. But you needn't worry."

"But I do worry." The look on his face convinced her of his sincerity. He glanced beyond her in the direction of the men's restroom. With a crooked finger he signaled her to draw closer.

Paige stepped toward him, curious as to what he had to say. Allen bent low and whispered in her ear.

A small cry escaped her lips.

The next thing she knew, Del and the three of them were climbing back into the van. Allen behind the wheel, Del in the front passenger seat, and Paige with Natalie in the back with their bedrolls.

"Well?" Natalie asked. "Did anyone find out where we are?"

Paige barely heard the question. She stared blankly out the window, though her eyes focused on nothing beyond the glass.

When nobody answered her, Natalie nudged Paige. "Is it one of those towns like in *Wild Wild West* that nobody's supposed to know about? A town where everyone is under the spell of a genius gone mad who plans to destroy the world?"

"Huh?" Paige said.

"The town!" Natalie repeated. "Did you find out where we are?"

"Oh that. Yeah."

"Well, are you going to tell me?"

"Oh. Um. Colorado Springs."

Natalie slumped back in her seat. "Pity," she said. "I was so hoping to run into James T. West."

※

The rocking rhythm of the van on the open highway had put her to sleep. That same rocking woke her up. *Why did sound work like that?* Paige wondered. It was the same with the stereo in her room. She loved to stack a few LPs on the spindle and listen to music as she went to sleep. However, she found that if she stacked more than three LPs, the music that soothed her to sleep later woke her in a rather annoying way.

Lifting her head, Paige looked around. It was dark. Allen was behind the wheel again. Del had taken a turn after dinner and drove until midnight. Allen agreed to drive through the night. The girls would take their turn come morning.

Del was slumped in the front passenger's seat. Natalie was asleep with her head against the window pane. Paige leaned forward and touched Allen's shoulder.

"How are you doing?"

Allen looked at her in the rearview mirror. He nodded. "I'm fine," he said.

They had the road all to themselves. There were no lights to be seen in either direction; nor were there any lights on either side of the road. Nothing but flat uninhabited land. The Volkswagen's engine droned monotonously.

Paige settled back. As she did, Natalie awoke. She took a deep breath, stretched her wounded leg with a wince, looked around, then settled back against the seat. She pulled the sleeping bag she was using as a cover all the way up to her neck. Her eyes remained open. She stared at Paige.

"What?" Paige asked.

At first Natalie didn't say anything.

"Why are you staring at me?"

Allen looked at them in his rearview mirror, then turned his attention back to the road.

Natalie scooted closer to Paige. She whispered, "What did Allen tell you at the gas station?"

Paige looked down at her leg and pretended to brush something off her jeans. "He didn't tell me anything," Paige said.

"Liar."

Paige looked at her friend but said nothing.

"You've been sullen ever since we left Colorado Springs," Natalie said. She glanced at the rearview mirror. Allen's gaze was straight ahead on the road. "You've hardly said two words. Whatever he told you disturbed you."

Paige rubbed tired eyes with her hands. Allen's words had indeed disturbed her. Shook her to her very core. She didn't want to believe him. But the longer she thought about what he'd told her, the more she knew he was telling the truth. She understood now why Allen was acting the way he was. And now, apparently, she was acting the same way.

"I can't tell you," Paige said.

"You can't tell me now, or you can't ever tell me?" Natalie asked.

"I don't know."

Natalie looked at her, disturbed by her answer. "You know you can tell me anything, don't you?" she said. "That's what friends are for."

A pang stabbed Paige's heart. Tears came to her eyes. She knew these were not idle words. Natalie was a strong, caring person who befriended people for life. But as badly as Paige wanted to talk to someone about this, she couldn't do it at the moment. She felt she had to figure out what she was going to do with the information first.

Paige reached out and took Natalie's hand. "I don't deserve a friend like you," she said.

"Oh honey," Natalie said, "you deserve the best this world has to offer." She paused. "And it just so happens that that's what you've got in me."

They both laughed.

Natalie squeezed Paige's hand. "Whenever you're ready, I'll be here," she said.

"Thank you," Paige whispered.

With a reassuring smile, Natalie turned over and settled against the seat. Soon she was asleep.

Sleep didn't come to Paige the rest of the night. She stared out into the darkness. In the distance she could see occasional farmhouse lights. Then, after a time, the sky in front of the van began to take on a rosy glow. Another day was dawning.

But it was dawning in a different world than Paige had been living in just a day earlier. That world had died when Allen whispered his news into her ear.

19

"Chicago will give us a chance to play with the big boys, to show them what we've got."

These were the words that initiated the trip to the Democratic National Convention. Del spoke them. By "the big boys" he meant Abbie Hoffman, Jerry Rubin, and Tom Hayden. For weeks leading up to the convention, Del had plastered his room walls with event posters:

DEMONSTRATE
to show our opposition to
the Vietnam War
Assemble in front of the
major delegates at the
Conrad Hilton Hotel
Pick Congress Hotel
Palmer House
August 25th at 2:00 p.m.

And,

Confront the Warmakers!
Chicago, August 25–29, 1968

And,

Student Mobilization Committee
to end the war in Vietnam!

He devoured underground newspapers featuring articles like, "Pigs Outfoxed: First Round Won," "Know Your Enemy," and "Don't Get Busted Twice."

He studied and memorized maps of Lincoln Park on Lake Shore Drive, which the yippies planned to turn into a gathering area called Drop City, complete with subdivisions: Music Area, Grub Town, Future City, and Free City. The park had a stage, an open-air theater, parking, a beach on the other side of Lake Shore Drive, a ball field, a pond beside which would meet the Church of the Free Spirit, and a zoo within walking distance. There were even plans for a communications center and makeshift hospital.

According to Del the yippie plan was to stage a Festival of Life at the park. It was billed as a multimedia experience with everything free. Performers might include Bob Dylan, the Animals, the Beatles, Janis Ian, the Smothers Brothers, the Who, Jefferson Airplane, and the Monkees. There would be free microphones, mimeos, underground newspapers, teach-ins on film, and underground media that would promote living free, guerrilla theater, and how to avoid the draft. If all went as planned, Chicago would be the protest event of the year.

It was this media description of Chicago that attracted Paige, but she didn't want to travel across the heart of the country alone with Del and Allen. With the school year finished, the house on Shores Drive emptied out for the most part. Paige had chosen to stay on at Shores Drive rather than return home, a decision that was not endorsed by her father. Father and daughter had not spoken to each other since.

Natalie had taken a summer job in Rancho Diego to earn money for the next semester. And although she said it was against her better judgment, she allowed Paige to talk her into using one of the spare rooms at Shores Drive. That way she could save money by not having to rent an apartment on her own.

Now, just a few weeks before school was to start again, Paige convinced Natalie to join them on the trip to Chicago, arguing that she needed at least some time off during the summer. Natalie agreed to go, against her doctor's wishes.

Even though it had been months since the shooting, the leg still gave her trouble, and her physician feared that too much walking would aggravate it, possibly even give her a permanent limp. Natalie chose to go anyway. She reasoned she and Paige would be planted in front of the music grandstand for the majority of their stay; she'd take it easy on her leg.

Del, unlike the girls, wasn't going for the music. There was another agenda in Chicago that attracted him. While the Festival of Life was meant to appeal to masses of demonstrators, the primary yippie plan was to block traffic, throw blood, burn money, mill about, mess up the draft, and bottom up the revolution. Promoters re-dubbed the Democratic National Convention, the Convention of Death. Their pledge was: "Chicago is LBJ's stage, and we're going to steal it."

Paige and Natalie sat in front of the band shell at Grant Park across from the Conrad Hilton and a host of television cameras. At the moment the band shell was empty.

Three days ago they had arrived at Lincoln Park, but at night police drove everyone out. So much for Future City. For some reason the authorities let the demonstrators spend the night at Grant Park, so that's where the foursome settled.

For Paige it was just as well. While Lincoln Park attracted mostly yippies and hippies and college students, the Grant Park crowd was more clean-cut. There were yippies and hippies, but there were also older demonstrators, McCarthy volunteers, and a growing number of Kennedy delegates who were there to support a peace plank of the Democratic platform. Even so, the mood was ugly and demonstrators of all types walked around

with rocks and bottles and huge chunks of concrete and bal-
loons filled with urine to throw at police, and Viet Cong and red
flags to wave.

Natalie moaned loudly beside Paige. Squinting through sun-
glasses, she scanned their surroundings. "We've been here three
days, and I've yet to see a Beatle, an Animal, or a Monkee," she
quipped.

Paige laughed. None of the music that had been promised was
at either park. Absolutely none. For the girls the whole experience had been a boring disappointment. They did little but wait in
the park while Del and Allen went chasing after Hoffman or some
other prominent yippie. Then, every few hours, the guys would
return with news and rush off again. Actually, Del rushed; Allen
straggled reluctantly along behind him.

Del seemed to be feeding on the mounting tension wherever he could find it: among the Democratic delegates,
between the demonstration leadership and the city authorities, and between protesters and police. Skirmishes erupted
every night in the parks and on the streets. Each night was
worse than the previous night. Del thrived on it; Allen was
looking drawn and tired, and the girls managed to keep out of
harm's way, at least so far.

Natalie straightened her leg to stretch it. She'd been favoring
it all day. Whenever Paige inquired about it, Natalie would grin
and say, "Don't worry about me. I'll live."

It was midafternoon. The last report they had received from
the guys was that the convention delegates were going to hear
final arguments for the peace plank at 1:00 p.m. The plank had
already been rejected by the platform committee. If the delegates
voted it down, their action would mostly certainly spark more
protests in the streets.

"Natalie?"

"Yeah?"

"Remember that day at the Colorado gas station when Allen told me something and you asked about it but I told you I couldn't tell you then?"

Natalie grinned at the breathless sentence. "Yeah."

"I think I should tell you."

"I already know."

"Allen told you too?"

"No. It's all over campus. Everybody knows."

Paige said nothing. She was confused.

"The car," Natalie said. "The one that exploded on campus that day. Del did it. He set the charge." Natalie gave a sheepish grin and shrug as if to say, *Sorry to spoil your news.*

Paige stared at the ground. She found it difficult to look her friend in the eyes. "That's part of it," she said.

"Part of it?"

"Yeah."

Paige worked up her courage and glanced up. All trace of levity was gone from Natalie's face.

"Paige … you're scaring me," Natalie said. "You look as though you've seen Satan himself."

"I may be sharing a room with him," Paige replied.

"What has Del done? Has he hurt you?"

The emotion that started as a small ball of pain in the pit of Paige's stomach rose within her like the tide. She had hoped she would be able to get through this without experiencing again the whirlwind of feelings she'd felt over the past few days.

"It's not me he's hurt," Paige whispered. "But you."

A questioning frown framed Natalie's face. "Me? What are you saying?"

"It was Del who hurt you and all the others who got shot that day."

Natalie was shaking her head. "I'm still not following you. You're saying Del shot me?"

"Not exactly. But he's the reason you were shot."

Natalie waited for more.

Paige wiped away the first tears that came. Others followed. "After Del and Allen left us, they snuck over to the side of the administration building and hid in some bushes. There, they watched Del's demonstration plan unfold. But what he didn't tell anyone was that he had one more act in his little drama that would insure that the event made it on the evening national news."

Paige found it difficult to go on. Natalie waited for her.

"He wanted casualties," Paige said. She began to cry openly. "He knew that if there were casualties, the news would be picked up nationwide. Deaths were even better."

"Del said that?"

Paige nodded. "At least according to Allen. But the way Del's been behaving ..."

"... it's easy to believe," Natalie finished her sentence for her.

Paige continued: "Del had a starter pistol. It was he who fired the first shots, knowing that the National Guard would assume they were being fired upon and knowing that they would probably shoot back."

Natalie was stunned. "That little weasel," she said.

Paige reached out to her friend. "Natalie, I'm so sorry ..."

"Sorry? For what? You didn't do anything."

"I talked you into coming to Chicago."

"Oh, that. You didn't know."

"Still, I feel bad that ..."

Natalie leaned toward her, looked her in the eyes and said, "Paige, you didn't know!"

"I should have known something was wrong by the way Allen has been acting. Del, too, for that matter."

"I've noticed that about Del," Natalie said. "In fact I find it hard to realize that we've all been so blind to it until now."

"The night of the shootings?"

"Yeah."

"He wanted to make love."

Natalie screwed up her face. "That's sick! You didn't, did you?"

"Of course not."

"Have you and Del ever …"

"No," Paige said. She realized how fortunate she was now that they had never made love. There were times she'd been tempted. Now even the thought sent a chill through her.

"Lord knows how many times I've tried to warn you about him," Natalie said.

"I know," Paige replied. "So did Allen."

"So, what are we going to do?"

"What *can* we do?"

Natalie stared off into the distance in thought. "Well, our first item of business is to get back home as soon as possible. Do you have any money?"

"Just a few bucks, why?"

"That's all I have, too, which rules out bus tickets. I suppose we could hitchhike."

The image of a Cadillac, a salesman, and groping hands flashed in Paige's mind. She shook her head. Besides, that would be the worst thing for Natalie's leg.

"What other choices do we have?" Natalie asked.

Paige thought for a moment, then said, "This whole thing is just about over. How about if we just ride it out? Besides, there are three of us, if we include Allen, and only one of Del. Let's just keep our heads, get through this thing, and go home."

Natalie pursed her lips in thought, then said, "Three of us and only one of Del. Why don't the three of us go home now and leave Del behind? After all it's Allen's van."

Paige laughed. Natalie was kidding. At least she thought she was.

"All right," Natalie agreed, "we'll stay. Under one condition."

"What's that?"

"You have to promise me that when we get back to Rancho Diego you'll move out of Shores Drive and leave Del."

Paige started to answer. Natalie cut her off.

"Furthermore, you have to promise to be my roommate this semester. I've missed you."

Once again Paige's emotions began to rise. However, these were good feelings. She leaned toward her friend. The two of them hugged.

"I don't know what I'd do without you," Paige said. "It's a deal."

Slightly self-conscious, the two women parted. Both of them dabbed their eyes. Already Paige was feeling better. She no longer held any secrets from Natalie; their relationship was stronger than ever; she had a plan to leave Del—something she knew she would have to do ever since Colorado Springs; and a part of her future had already fallen into place. She and Natalie would be roommates again. Now the only thing separating them from a brighter future was a couple thousand miles of American heartland. All they needed to do was stay out of trouble, load up into the van, and hope the thing would make it all the way back to California.

Staying out of harm's way would be the toughest assignment though. The number of people in Grant Park was increasing. More and more of them were carrying rocks and bottles. The mood was already turning ugly.

"There's Allen and Del," Natalie said. She pointed across the park.

Paige spotted them. She stood and waved an arm to get their attention. Allen spied her first. The guys ran toward her. Even from a distance, Paige could see that they both were angry.

Del arrived first; Allen was close behind.

"Two things," he said without first trying to catch his breath. "First, the pigs arrested Abbie Hoffman this morning."

"What for?" Paige asked.

Allen replied, "He had an obscenity printed on his forehead. They charged him with disorderly conduct and resisting arrest."

Natalie: "That's all? They arrested him for that?" Her leg was stiff, and she struggled to get to her feet. Paige reached down and helped her up.

Del: "They want to keep him from the rally and convention march tonight." His face was nearly purple with rage, or lack of oxygen, or both.

Allen: "The second thing—"

Del cut him off: "The second thing is that the convention delegates just voted down the peace plank."

Allen: "By a vote of 1,567 to 1,041."

Del swore.

Allen: "We heard a part of the debate from the lobby. Some congressman named Hayes said that the peace plank was a sop to radicals, and that it would substitute beards for brains and license for liberty. He said radicals want pot instead of patriotism, sideburns instead of solutions, that we would substitute riots for reason."

Del shouted: "He got that right at least!"

Paige glanced around them. News of the peace plank's defeat was spreading quickly through the park. She could feel the anger all around her.

"So what happens now?" she asked.

Del looked her in the eye. "I'll tell you what happens now— we're at war!"

There was a glint of joy in Del's eyes that caused Paige to shiver.

20

Nat Morgan hated political conventions. They were little more than a gathering of the politically self-important, who wore silly buttons and hats, who bellowed instead of talked, and who said and did things at the convention they never would say or do back home. Photo opportunities were limited to men standing behind podiums giving speeches, delegates standing belly-to-belly jawing, or slumped in their chairs on the convention floor asleep, and the predictable balloon drop when everyone pretended they were not hurt by the rancor and animosity of the past few days and that they were now of one accord.

The only reason Nat had agreed to this assignment was to cover Bobby Kennedy. Following the senator's assassination, Nat tried to get out of it. His boss wouldn't let him. Nat was told he had to see the political assignment at least through the convention, possibly through to the national election in November.

He stood in the aisle of the convention floor. The delegates had just been dismissed for dinner. It had been an interesting afternoon—that is, if you think arguing and squabbling and name-calling are interesting. There was one bright moment when Pierre Salinger entered into the debate for the peace plank. He called on his ex-boss' name saying, "If Senator Robert

Kennedy were alive he would be on this platform speaking for the minority."

But now the convention hall was silent. Nat thought about going back to his hotel and propping up his feet for a while and then ordering room service. He had heard rumors of riots and illegal marches through the Chicago streets, so he knew he'd be working. If the previous nights were any indication, it would be another wild one. At least there would be something worth getting on film.

Before going back to his hotel, Nat decided to wander over to Grant Park. He thought he might be able to get some indication as to where the action was going to be tonight.

Paige estimated there must be between ten and fifteen thousand people in the park. Police had already surrounded the band shell on three sides. A small group of officers, most of them black, were handing out leaflets warning the protesters that they would be arrested if they attempted to march. A few hundred yards away, National Guardsmen were visible on the rooftop of a museum.

In the band shell a variety of speakers began to address the crowd. Del would announce them to the three standing with him. David Dellinger acted as a master of ceremonies of sorts. Jerry Rubin spoke. Then Carl Oglesby, the ex-Students for a Democratic Society president.

Just as Carl began to speak, a teenage boy climbed the flagpole on the south side of the band shell. He began to lower the American flag. Immediately police pushed their way through the crowd and surrounded the flagpole. They managed to pull him down and then proceeded to beat him with their clubs. The officers, in turn, were pelted with food, rocks, and other debris.

While the police managed to drag off the teenager, another

group of young men took down the flag. In its place they raised a red T-shirt. Once again police officers pushed through the crowd. This time, however, the perpetrators managed to run away. The police chased after them.

The crowd in front of the bandstand was on its feet, everyone straining to see what was happening. From the back of the crowd a chant originated: "Sit down, sit down, sit down, sit down!"

Dellinger took the microphone. He did his best to calm the crowd and stop the rock and bottle throwing and get on with the speeches. Another man appeared on the platform and tried to take the microphone away from him.

"That's Tom Hayden," Del told them.

Hayden was furious. Eventually, he gained control of the microphone. He began by shouting into it that his friend, Rennie Davis, had just been hospitalized with a split head, compliments of the police.

"This city and the military machinery it has aimed at us won't permit us to protest," he shouted. "Therefore, we must move out of this park in groups throughout the city and turn this excited, overheated military machine against itself! Let us make sure that if blood is going to flow, let it flow all over this city. If gas is going to be used, let that gas come down all over Chicago and not just all over us in the park. That if the police are going to run wild, let them run wild all over this city and not over us. If we are going to be disrupted and violated, let this whole stinking city be disrupted and violated. Don't get trapped in some kind of organized march that can be surrounded. Begin to find your way out of here. I'll see you in the streets!"

"We'd better get out of here," Allen said.

Paige and Natalie agreed.

"What's the matter, Allen? Chicken? Afraid you'll get arrested?" Del mocked.

"Take a good look around you, Del!" Allen shouted. "What person in his right mind would stand here and wait for the rocks and bullets to really start flying?"

He was right. The National Guard was moving in armed with M-1 rifles, grenade launchers, gas dispensers, bayonets, and .30 caliber machine guns. Protesters were breaking up cement park benches to use as weapons.

"We're going with Allen," Paige said to Del. Natalie stood beside her to show they were in agreement.

Del's face grew black with rage. "Go! Run! Save yourselves. Forsake the cause! Get out of here!"

Even with everything going on all around them, Del's tantrum drew the attention of the immediate crowd. If you asked her to explain it, Paige wouldn't be able to. But she hated to leave him like this. In spite of all that she had come to learn—and fear—about him, she found it difficult just to abandon him.

Natalie took her by the arm. "Come on," she urged.

Paige looked at Del. To Natalie, she said, "No, you go. We'll catch up with you."

※

Nat arrived at Grant Park just in time to see the police hauling a teenager down from the flagpole. He reached into his bag and grabbed a telephoto lens. The exchange of lens was done as easily and quickly as a person buttoning his shirt. It required no thought; his eyes were kept on the drama unfolding in front of him.

Lifting the camera to his eye, he took a light reading and made the appropriate speed and aperture adjustments. Through the viewfinder he saw the protester's grip give way.

CLICK!

He captured the protester falling back into the outstretched arms of the police, the boy's hand outstretched toward the flagpole.

CLICK!

The next picture was of the boy on the ground, surrounded by police with angry, distorted faces, police batons raised high; the boy was protecting himself with an upraised forearm. You could see his face. He was afraid.

CLICK!

Nat caught some other young men raising a red T-shirt up the flagpole in defiance of the police arrest of the teenager.

CLICK!

This one was a wide-angle shot of the crowd, the bandstand, and the National Guardsmen surrounding them on three sides.

Nat moved into position to see the speakers on the platform. He heard Tom Hayden telling about his friend's arrest and urging the crowd to meet him on the streets. Nat didn't take a picture of the speaker. He had too many pictures of speakers already.

A nearby crash caught his attention. He turned to see four young men standing over a busted park bench. From the looks of it, they had just lifted it and smashed it to the ground. It was nothing more than rubble now. They were picking up pieces of it and stuffing the smaller chunks in their pockets. The larger chunks they handed out or stacked in piles.

CLICK!

Nat took a picture of it. He moved to get another angle. One of the men looked up at him, startled at first, as though he expected to see a baton-wielding policeman or a National Guard bayonet thrust at his face. Nat thought the expression captured the fear of the moment.

But there was no click of the shutter. Just as he was about to press the shutter release, something in the background of the picture caught his eye.

Paige? No, it couldn't be!

He lowered the camera and searched the crowd. People were milling everywhere, some listening to the band shell speaker, others taking inventory of their weapons, still others pointing to the guard lines on one of the three sides, and still others working their way toward the only unguarded side of the park. There were hundreds of people in his line of vision. Thousands. But no Paige.

Raising the camera to his eye, he scanned the crowd again, this time with the aid of the telephoto lens. Every kind of person imaginable appeared in the viewfinder—clean-cut delegate types, long-haired hippies, both male and female. There were people of every race, angry people, laughing people, couples making out.

But no sign of Paige.

He lowered his camera. Just as he did, he thought he caught a glimpse of her. He looked again. He saw the back of a redhead of similar build as Paige. The head bobbed slightly as she walked.

"Come on! Turn around. Turn around!" Nat muttered.

As though she heard him, the woman in his viewfinder looked over her shoulder.

Paige!

There was no mistaking her.

Nat lowered the camera and pushed his way through the crowd calling his daughter's name.

"I don't want you here," Del said to Paige. "Go. Get out of here."

"I'm not going to leave you alone," Paige said. "We can catch up with Allen and Natalie later."

Del looked at her with disgust. "I don't need you!" he shouted. "I don't need anybody! Don't you know who I am yet? You've been with me all this time and still you have no clue? I am revolution-incarnate. I am the future of America. If need be, I will single-handedly reduce this country to rubble and, out of the ashes, raise a country people can be proud of. Mark my words, tonight is the beginning of the end for America as we know it."

Natalie was pulling on Paige's arm. "Come on, dear, let's get out of here."

"To the streets! To the streets!" Del shouted. He was prancing about with balled fists stretched over his head. "To the streets! We'll take this war to the streets!"

Paige felt helpless. Even though she had resolved in her mind that she and Del had no future together, she found it difficult to walk away from the man she had admired and supported and championed for over a year.

Reluctantly, she let herself be pulled away. Arm in arm with Natalie, they worked their way through the crowd, following close behind Allen. However, Paige couldn't resist one last look over her shoulder at Del.

He was jumping and shouting at the top of his lungs. "To the streets! To the streets!" With the din of thousands of people surrounding her, she could barely make out what he was saying.

※

It seemed as though the tide of humanity in the park was against him. The harder Nat attempted to push his way past, around, and over people, the more they seemed to get in his way. In fact they seemed to sense that he had a mission, a purpose. And these people were against anyone who was trying to accomplish anything positive. This was a negative force. A destructive power. They knew nothing of building, only of destroying that which was built.

He lost sight over her. The crowd simply swallowed her up. Still he pushed and shoved and squeezed his way in the direction he last saw her. But after fifteen minutes of struggle with not so much as a flash of her image in the crowd, he gave up.

※

"Do you remember where the van is parked?" Allen asked. He had stopped on the sidewalk about a hundred feet from a downtown intersection.

Paige and Natalie exchanged glances. "Yes," Natalie replied. "If we get separated, I'll meet you there."

"We won't get separated," Natalie said.

Allen shrugged his shoulders. "Hopefully not," he said. "But on a night like this, you never know."

Darkness was falling. It came quickly to the downtown area with the shadows of towering buildings hastening its arrival. As if to illustrate Allen's warning, a scuffle broke out in the intersection.

The center of the scuffle was a mobile television camera truck. The camera's bright lights attracted demonstrators to it like moths to a bare light bulb. People waved signs and chanted epithets. And where there were television cameras and demonstrators, the police were sure to follow.

Some of the demonstrators taunted the policemen. They threw garbage and rocks and signs and bottles at the officers. Reinforcements were called. Protesters were ordered to leave the streets. Some began to do so.

"Stay on the sidewalks," Allen said. "If you stay on the sidewalks, they'll leave you alone."

Hugging the buildings, Allen attempted to lead them around the corner of the intersection. Paige and Natalie held hands and followed close behind him. A couple of times a policeman looked at them, then, seeing they weren't participating in the protest, let them pass.

It amazed Paige how quickly the protest grew. People came from nowhere. Police, too. One of the police officers was shouting orders to his men using a bullhorn. He alternately urged his men to hold their line steady and ordered the protesters to disperse.

Paige saw an officer fall. Then another. The fallen police were set upon mercilessly by the protesters who punched and kicked them or threw rocks and caustic sprays of their own. In response

the other policemen rushed to their fellow officers' aid, screaming curses, using their clubs, fists, knees, and Mace, anything to
move the protesters back so that the bloodied officers could be
rescued.

"We have to cross the street," Allen shouted.

Paige's heart nearly fainted at the thought.

"Is there any other way?" Natalie shouted.

Allen shrugged. "Not that I know of."

Paige looked at her friend. She'd never seen Natalie scared
before. Not even on the day she was shot by the National Guard.
But the fear in her friend's eyes was unmistakable. It made Paige
want to cry. The only reason Natalie was here was because Paige
had talked her into it. If anything happened to Natalie while she
was here, it would forever be on Paige's conscience.

Allen stepped tentatively into the street, attempting to gauge
the flow of the fighting. Arriving demonstrators ran past them to
join the fight. The entire street was chaos. Approaching sirens
could be heard above the thumping sounds of clubs against flesh,
the cracking sound of rocks against helmets, the shouts and
curses from both sides, and the screams and cries of the
wounded.

Cautiously, Allen, Natalie, and Paige inched their way across
the street.

With frightening speed the tide of the battle changed. A bulge
of protesters shoved back a weak point in the police line. One of
the officers was shoved into Allen. The two men sprawled onto
the downtown Chicago pavement. The policeman's helmet came
off and bounced as crazily as a football.

The man beneath the helmet had gray hair and a matching
mustache. A good-sized paunch was folded over his belt. Blue
eyes were wide with fright. He struggled to overcome the round-
ness of his midsection and get to his feet. Allen did the same. He

was a bit woozy since he took the full weight of the officer when he hit.

Allen raised both hands, possibly to show the officer that he was no threat. But the officer was in a vulnerable position and the look in his eyes indicated he felt very threatened. He reached for his belt, grabbed a can of Mace, and sprayed Allen in the face.

"Aaaaaaauuuuuuuugh!" Allen screamed. He rolled about blindly, attempting to get up, attempting to see. In the attempt he grabbed the officer by the front of the shirt and managed to stand.

By now, help was arriving. Another policeman came up from behind Allen and cracked him in the back of the head. Allen fell to his knees. Another blow and another crack. He was facedown on the pavement.

His voice was faint, but the words were clear. "Go, go!" he said over and over.

For the second time that day Natalie had to be the strong one. Paige wanted to go to Allen, to help him. Natalie pulled her away.

A policeman saw them. He started after them.

"Come on!" Natalie shouted.

The policeman was closing, his club held high.

"Run, Paige, run!"

Paige needed no more convincing. The two girls ran down the street, not knowing exactly where they were running, only that they were running away from the policeman who was pursuing them.

"Here!" Natalie called. She pulled Paige into a building through glass double doors. It was a discount store with every-thing from toys to dish towels and a lunch counter. The two girls ran through the aisles. Paige looked back. The policeman was still there. He was closing.

Natalie was limping badly. Starting out, she was in the lead, but Paige had passed her and was now the one in front. Their hands still clasped, Paige was pulling her along. It made running that much more difficult. And it slowed them down.

They burst through the glass doors and found themselves on the other side of the city block. Paige shook her head. If they'd only known about this store earlier, this whole thing could have been avoided.

On the sidewalk Paige looked up one side of the street and down the other. Which way to go? She also glanced behind them. The policeman was nearly to the doors.

Natalie was out of breath. There were tears on her cheeks. Running was hurting her more than she let on.

A honking sound caught Paige's attention. It was a persistent honk. A familiar one. It was the sound of a Volkswagen van.

Lumbering up the street was Allen's van. But how?

The van pulled to a stop. Doors flew open.

Del was sitting behind the wheel.

"Get your rear in gear!" he shouted. "The cavalry has arrived."

Putting her arm around Natalie's waist, Paige fairly threw her into the van. She followed, and with a tinny roar that was familiar to all Volkswagen owners, the van lurched off, leaving a cursing policeman behind standing in the middle of the street.

21

"Keep it quiet! Come on, everybody, hold it down, we can't hear!"

A man Paige guessed to be in his late twenties, dressed in a gray suit with a striped blue tie, squatted beside the hotel room's console television. He adjusted the volume knob with one hand, in the other was a champagne glass that spilled with every move of his arm.

Walter Cronkite, news anchorman for CBS, appeared on the screen. In reality the anchorman was only blocks away at the convention center where the balloting for the Democratic presidential nominee would take place later that night. Cronkite began the broadcast by describing the clash between demonstrators and police on the Chicago streets. Videotaped shots of the police clubbing and kicking and Macing demonstrators played out on the screen.

Paige and Natalie watched from a distance. Natalie sat in a low-back hotel chair with her foot propped up on the bed. Paige sat on the floor in front of her. Del was at the wet bar getting himself a drink.

"I don't feel comfortable being here," Natalie whispered. "People keep looking at us."

After parking the van on the street, Del had led them to the fourth floor of the hotel. The door was open when they arrived. They were met by Rick Masterson—the man in the gray suit squatting beside the television—who recognized Del and called him by name. Del introduced the host of the party as one of McGovern's biggest financial backers. Paige had a hard time envisioning the twenty-something man in the gray suit as a wealthy political backer. Except for the suit, he could easily be a grad student at UCRD.

"Hey! Everyone be quiet!" Masterson shouted. "I want to hear this."

The room fell quiet. Paige positioned herself so that she could see half of the television screen between two standing people. She saw Walter Cronkite ask Chicago's mayor for a response to the violence on the streets outside the convention hall.

Mayor Richard Daley's round, heavy-jowled face took center screen. He said:

"It is unfortunate and we can't say it, that the television industry didn't have the information I had two weeks ago. These reports of intelligence on my desk that certain people planned to assassinate the three candidates for the presidency. Certain people planned to assassinate many of the leaders, including myself, and with all of these talks of assassination and it happening in our city, I didn't want what happened in Dallas or what happened in California to happen in Chicago. So I took the necessary precautions. No mayor wants to call the National Guard. In the interest of the preservation of the law and order for our people, and I don't mean law and order in itself in the brutal way, I mean law and order with justice—that I would call up the National Guard."

Catcalls, curses, and moans filled the hotel suite. None were louder than Del's.

"Look at Cronkite's face," the gray-suited host shouted. "Even he doesn't believe Daley!"

On the television the mayor went on to commend his police force and to attack the "terrorists" and outside agitators who'd attempted to disrupt his city and convention.

While the twenty or thirty people in the hotel suite jabbered among themselves excitedly about Daley, the violence in the streets, and the upcoming convention vote, Paige turned to Natalie.

"Let's get out of here," she said.

"Back out on the streets? Where will we go?"

Natalie's voice was uncharacteristically weak. She looked ashen. Tired.

"Your leg's hurting, isn't it?"

Natalie nodded. With obvious effort she was holding back tears.

Paige searched the room for Del. Surrounded by a guy and two women—all well-dressed—he was describing and heatedly denouncing the police tactics in the parks and on the streets. Words like "police state," "fascism," and "people's revolution" were tossed about with abandon. He was in his element.

For the first time Paige saw him clearly. His was a world of ideas and rhetoric. He was not a man of action. Not a leader. Society was torn apart and rebuilt in his head, neatly, painlessly—at least for him. All the suffering came at someone else's expense. His idea of society-changing conflict was to hide in the bushes and fire blanks at the National Guard and watch as other people died in the retaliatory response. He was nothing more than a little boy playing with army figures. Only in his world, real people were the figures. Real people like Natalie.

Paige couldn't believe she'd almost lost Natalie just because she couldn't see Del for what he really was. Natalie had tried to warn her. She just wouldn't listen.

She thought of poor Allen. Bleeding. Bruised. By now he'd probably been shoved into a bus and was on his way to jail. She understood now his recent sullen attitude. He'd once believed in Del, too.

She glanced over her shoulder at Natalie. Her friend's head was slumped awkwardly against the low back of the chair. Her eyes were closed.

"Drink?"

Paige turned to see Del hovering over her. He had drinks in both hands. One was extended to her. In the amber liquid floated a couple of ice cubes.

"You know I don't drink, Del," she said.

"Your loss." He downed the drink with two gulps. "I brought one for Natalie, too. Just like her to sleep away an opportunity." He downed the second drink.

Natalie wasn't asleep after all. She said, "And it's just like you, you little weasel, to offer drinks to two women who don't drink. Why don't you grow up, Del?"

Her verbal blow registered on the face of the diminutive man with the scraggly black beard.

"If you were a real man, you'd bring us a couple of sodas," Natalie answered.

With a sour look on his face, Del started to go.

Natalie wasn't finished with him. "And by the way, Don Quixote, how did you reach the van before us?"

A sly grin spread across Del's face. "I moved the van," he said.

Natalie nearly came out of her chair. "And you didn't tell us? You let us run a gauntlet through riot-filled streets?"

"Hey, I came after you, didn't I?"

"Tell that to Allen!" Natalie shouted.

Her voice was loud enough to quiet the room. Everyone turned their direction and stared.

"Just go get us the sodas," Natalie said, as though she dismissing a cocktail waiter.

Del, red-faced and fuming, stomped away.

"All right, everybody, here it is!"

Their gray-suited host was again calling for quiet and stooping over to adjust the television set's volume. All eyes turned to the screen.

"Who is that?" Paige asked of the man standing behind the convention podium.

Natalie shot her a look of disappointment. "Connecticut Senator Abraham Ribicoff. He's the one who's going to place George McGovern's name in nomination for president."

Paige tried not to take the rebuke personally. Her political awareness had been limited to Vietnam and events Del had staged at UCRD.

After a few introductory remarks, Senator Ribicoff addressed the scene taking place outside the convention hall. He shouted, "With George McGovern we wouldn't have Gestapo tactics on the streets of Chicago!"

The hotel suite erupted with shouts and cheers. This went on for the remainder of the nomination speech.

For the rest of the evening, while the slate of Democratic nominees was completed, including Humphrey and McCarthy, among others, Natalie and Paige kept to themselves. As the balloting started, fewer and fewer of Masterson's invited guests looked their direction.

"A peace offering," Del said.

He held out two sodas, first to Paige, then to Natalie.

"Thank you, Del," Paige said.

"It took you long enough," Natalie said.

"Do you always have to be down my throat?" Del asked Natalie.

Natalie sipped her drink, and then replied, "Yes, yes, I do. I don't like you, Del. I don't like the way you've virtually enslaved Paige. And I don't like the chicken way you practice politics."

Anger was threatening Del's forced geniality.

"Why is it that you talk of confronting established authority, but you never actually do it? Can you answer me that, Del? Can you tell me why you would organize a sit-in and then duck out a back window?"

Del raised a finger with which to defend himself. "I already …"

Natalie wasn't listening. "Can you tell me how you can talk hundreds of demonstrators into standing up against the National Guard while you go hide in the bushes?"

Del's jaw clenched.

"Or possibly you can tell me how you can live with yourself, knowing that you are personally responsible for sparking National Guardsmen gunfire that resulted in two deaths and eight others wounded while you sat cowering behind rhododendrons?"

Del recovered, but was still clearly disquieted. "Allen!" he said with a threatening tone.

"Yes, Allen," Natalie said. "Another of your victims. And it's about time he ratted on you. Now we know who the real rat is. And, believe me, when we get back to California, everybody's going to know!"

Somewhat winded, Natalie took another sip of her soda.

Paige, sitting between Natalie and the standing Del, didn't exactly know what to make of the whole thing. She expected Del to explode with anger. And he nearly did. But then, like a summer storm, the anger passed.

His smile was unsettling.

"Do your best," he said. "I have plenty of others who are willing to follow me unconditionally. Let's just consider the drinks a token of apology.

"A very small token," Natalie replied.

Del left them alone. He joined the others who were watching as the Missouri delegate was casting that state's votes.

Natalie sipped her drink.

"All that was bottled up inside you?" Paige asked.

"Not anymore," Natalie grinned.

"One question."

"Yeah?"

"Del has the van, right?"

"Right."

"So how are we going to get back to California?"

Natalie waved off her concern. "It's Allen's van. Tomorrow, we'll bail him out of jail. Then, the question may very well be— how does *Del* get back to California?"

※

Paige didn't like the way Del kept looking at them. As the balloting continued on the convention floor, the McGovern supporters found little to cheer about. When the final tally was taken, Vice President Hubert Humphrey of Minnesota breezed to a first-ballot victory with 1,760 delegate votes compared to 601 for McCarthy and 146 for McGovern.

All the while Del sat in a chair next to the bar and grinned at them like Alice's Cheshire cat. He seemed little interested in the events on the convention floor.

Behind her, Natalie moaned. Her eyes were closed, her head lolled side to side. She looked like she was having a bad dream.

"Natalie?"

The moaning continued.

"Natalie!"

Natalie's head rose unsteadily and bobbed about. Her eyes were half closed. She wore a silly, dazed grin.

Across the room Del laughed out loud.

Getting on her knees, Paige examined her friend. A growing

fear knotted her stomach. Natalie's eyes were dilated. Her arms stretched leisurely, but lifelessly over the arms of the chair. An empty soda cup lay on the carpeted floor.

Paige turned on Del. "You put something in her drink, didn't you?" she said. "Didn't you?"

Del's eyes were lit with mischief. He nodded.

Paige was on her feet now, hovering over her friend.

"Natalie! Natalie! Can you hear me?"

"'Course I can hear you, silly!" Natalie said dreamily. "You're screaming in my ear." Something about Paige's ear seemed to fascinate her. Natalie added, "You scream in such wonderful colors!"

Del howled.

Paige was livid. "What did you give her, Del?" she demanded.

For the second time that night, the three from California captured the room's attention. Masterson, whose mood had become increasingly surly all night long with every vote cast for Humphrey, demanded to know what was going on.

Paige spoke first. "Del slipped acid into my friend's drink."

"What?" Masterson yelled.

Del gave him a boys-will-be-boys shrug.

"You brought LSD into my suite? You little …"

"WEASEL!!!" Natalie jumped up and finished the sentence for him with a sing-song voice and a pirouette.

"Get out!" Masterson demanded. "All of you! Get out!"

Paige went to Natalie. She put her arm around her friend's waist and guided her toward the door. No one in the room was paying attention to Hubert Humphrey's acceptance speech on the television.

"Go on, get out!" Masterson said, giving Del a shove toward the door as he walked by.

Del turned and bowed slightly. "It's been a wonderful evening," he said with heavy sarcasm. "Give my regards to McGovern."

"Get out!" Masterson shouted as he slammed shut the door.

As Paige helped Natalie down the corridor toward the elevator, Natalie started singing: "One pill makes you larger, and another makes you small ..."

A couple of doors opened. Hotel patrons stuck their heads out to see who it was that was making such a racket.

Without any help from Del, Paige got Natalie to an elevator. The doors opened and the two of them stepped in. Del slipped in behind them just before the doors closed.

"Push the lobby button," Paige said.

"What? Are you talking to me?" Del asked.

"Push the lobby button, Del!" Paige shouted.

He did. The elevator car gave a slight lurch and began its descent.

"I'm never going to forgive you for this," Paige said. She was so angry, she was crying. She didn't care.

Natalie clung to her as they passed the third floor. Before they got to the second, she had turned her head and saw Del. Growling like a tigress, she leaped at him, knocking him to the ground. She growled and roared and clawed at him, scratching his face.

"Get off me!" he shouted. "Paige help! Get her off me!"

Although she felt Del was getting only what he deserved, she reached down and, with great effort, managed to pull Natalie off of him.

The elevator dinged and the doors slid open.

Natalie was still going after Del. It was all Paige could do to keep her from scratching out his eyes.

"Help me get her to the van," Paige said.

Del recoiled. "I'm not getting near her!"

"Help me!" Paige shouted. "You did this to her in the first place."

"She deserved it after the things she said about me," Del said.

The girls looked like two drunks staggering across the polished lobby floor. They were attracting the attention of guests and employees alike. Paige tried not to notice. It was all she could do to keep Natalie's knees from buckling and pulling them both down.

With unflagging effort, Paige managed to push Natalie through two sets of glass doors and into the street. The August night air was still warm. In the distance she could hear sirens rising above the sounds of the riots.

"We'll wait here," Paige said to Del. "Go get the van. Bring it around here."

"The van," Del repeated.

"Yeah, the van. Get it and bring it around here. That's easier than trying to take Natalie to the van.

"Oh, yeah," Del said. "Well, OK, I'll go get the van and bring it around front."

They had parked on the street nearly two blocks away and felt lucky they could even find a place as close to the convention center as they were.

"Right. I'll be right back," Del said. Reaching into his pocket, he produced a set of keys, jingled them, then disappeared around the stone corner of the hotel building.

Natalie's knees became unsteady. Paige found it next to impossible to hold her up any longer. "Come on, Natalie, let's rest over here."

She led her friend to the curb, hoping to get Natalie to sit down. Natalie refused.

"Let's find another party!" Natalie yelled at the top of her lungs. "We need another paaaarrrrrty!"

Pressing down on top of Natalie's shoulders, Paige managed to get her to sit down. They waited for thirty minutes. Del didn't return.

"It's just around the block," Paige complained. "What could be keeping him?"

Fifteen more minutes passed. Natalie was getting harder to control. She wanted to dance and sing. For ten minutes she tried to convince Paige she could fly.

Paige let out a frustrated grunt. "Come on," she said, pulling Natalie to her feet. "Let's go find that ..."

"WEASEL!!!" Natalie sang. "Weasel, weasel, weasel, weasel, weasel, weasel, weasel."

With the singing Natalie in tow, Paige half walked, half ran the two blocks to where they had left the van. Fortunately, the streets were quiet. They passed about a half-dozen well-dressed types who stared at them wide-eyed and crossed the street so as not to get too close to them.

When they reached the place where they'd left the van, it was gone.

"That weasel!" Paige said.

"Weasel, weasel, weasel, weasel, weasel, weasel!" Natalie sang.

Paige stood on the sidewalk next to the vacant parking place with one hand holding her drugged friend, and the other waving helplessly in the air. Allen was in jail and Del had deserted them. Between them they could probably scrape together twenty bucks.

Paige didn't know what to do or where to go. The park was a riot zone. They didn't have enough money for a hotel. And she didn't know anyone in Chicago.

"Fly away, fly away, high away," Natalie intoned. She moved her arms airily like a fairy princess.

"Natalie, I need you," Paige wept. "I need you, and you're off in never-never land."

With a quickness that startled Paige, Natalie broke free. She ran down the middle of the street, her arms stretched out as though in flight.

"I'm Tinkerbell!" she shouted.

"Natalie! Stop! Come back!"

Paige ran after her. Even with a wounded leg, Natalie was fast. There was no limp as she ran. Paige concluded that the drug was masking the pain.

"Natalie!"

Natalie disappeared around a corner. Paige followed. They ran the length of a block. Another corner and Natalie disappeared until Paige could reach the corner.

Rioting noises grew louder. Shouts. Bullhorn warnings. Screams. Curses.

"I'm Tinkerbell!" Natalie said again, flying down the street. She ran toward Michigan Avenue.

Paige's lungs burned from running, her legs were heavy. She couldn't go much farther. She had to reach Natalie soon.

Natalie flew down the street effortlessly, dancing, springing upward as she ran.

A feeling of dread engulfed Paige, a horrible, dark, premonition that something terrible was happening. It felt like she was being possessed by shadows, and she couldn't free herself.

"Natalie! Please, dear. Listen to me. Stop. Come back! Come back!" Her voice was hoarse and raspy. She could barely hear herself; how did she expect Natalie to hear her?

Natalie reached Michigan Avenue and disappeared around another corner. Paige stumbled to get to the corner. She fell against it, depending on the building to hold her up; without it, she would not be able to stand.

Upon turning the corner, she looked for Natalie and saw a war zone.

Everywhere police and demonstrators clashed; garbage cans were ablaze; clouds of tear gas billowed here and there; rocks flew like missiles; police batons slashed the air furiously and landed with sickening thuds on skulls and backs and arms and legs.

Reporters stood around taking notes and snapping pictures. Whack! A policeman cracked one newsman across his head. He fell to his knees; his camera clattered to the ground; his white shirt was stained with blood.

Like a fairy princess Natalie floated in and out and around the many confrontations. No one paid any attention to her; she floated among them unhindered, as though she were invisible.

"Natalie! Natalie!" The rational Paige knew that the pandemonium of battle swallowed up the sound of her voice before it reached Natalie, but she had to try.

Paige clung to the sides of the building. She had to rescue Natalie, but she was afraid. The scene before her was nothing like she imagined she would ever see on an American street—Saigon maybe, but not America. Arms and legs flailed in anger; lights flashed and glinted off police face shields; heads and faces and shirts were bloodied. But the worst of it was the sounds. The shouts and grunts and whacks and screams and cursing and wailing.

And in the midst of it all, Natalie floated untouched like a butterfly.

Pushing off from the building, Paige waded into the battle, zigzagging around the pockets of confrontation. She passed a demonstrator as he hurled a piece of concrete that hit a policeman square in the throat. While the cop clutched his throat and wheezed to catch his breath, two of his buddies charged the attacker, beating him to the ground, kicking him, pummeling him with their nightsticks.

Paige was tossed this way and that by the tide of the battle, but she managed to keep Natalie in sight.

"Oh no," Paige said as she saw what was attracting Natalie. The National Guard had formed a line of defense. Their rifles were set and extended; their bayonets flashed in the dark.

"Natalie! Come back here! Natalie!"

The bouncing fairy didn't hear her.

Paige pushed and shoved and ducked to reach Natalie. She was managing to close in. Natalie had stopped. With fighting going on all around her, Paige managed to keep her balance. She was nearly within arm's reach of Natalie. So close.

Natalie stood a few feet from the front line of the National Guard. Her arms waved over her head as she danced in place.

"Natalie!" Paige cried.

Suddenly, the crowd compacted, pushing people tightly together, police officers and demonstrators alike. There seemed to be no outside force doing this, it just happened. Paige was closed in. She couldn't advance, she couldn't retreat. At best she tried to ride the tide without getting knocked to the ground.

There was a thin line of space separating the demonstrators and the guardsmen. Natalie had found it. What's more, she seemed to think of it as a stage. Her stage.

She sang and waved her arms overhead and flirted with the National Guard. Opposite her one of the guardsmen seemed briefly amused by it all. Behind his clear face shield Paige could see bright, eager eyes, and prominent dimples.

For an instant everything seemed to stand still as this beautiful young lady swayed before a soldier with his weapon drawn. Natalie smiled sweetly. She was a little girl again. Innocent. Playful. The guardsman smiled back at her. In a different time and setting, they looked the perfect couple. A camera flashed.

There was a sudden surge; Paige didn't see it coming—there was no way she could; it hit the crowd like a wave crashing upon a beach; only the wave was people and the beach was the National Guard with weapons drawn.

Paige had experienced moments in life when time slows. This was such a moment. Paige saw what was happening, but she was helpless to do anything about it. The crowd surged, lifting Natalie from her feet, dashing her against the National Guard like waves against a rocky shore.

"Natalie! No!"

A bayonet protruded from Natalie's back.

"Please, Lord, no!"

The guardsman's face was one of shock. Horror.

"No, God, no!"

Paige reached out over the crowd, frantically stretching for her friend. If she could reach her, touch her, be there for her, it could be like the administration lawn again; Natalie would roll over and be all right. But Paige's arms were inadequate to the task. She reached, but felt only air.

The guardsman dropped his weapon and grabbed Natalie by the shoulders. Slowly, he lowered her to the ground. He was weeping.

Paige tried to shove her way to them. She pushed. The human wall was solid. She pushed and shoved and pleaded. The wall grew arms, and a nightstick, and a face—a face that belonged to a policeman.

With a vicelike grip he grabbed Paige by the arm. She shouted for him to let her go. Her friend was hurt. The policeman was deaf to her cries. He pulled her away from Natalie. Paige struggled. The officer nearly lifted her off her feet. She was hauled to a bus and shoved up the steps, down the aisle, into a seat.

Within moments of seeing Natalie impaled on the bayonet of a National Guardsman, Paige was whisked away to jail.

※

"Hello, Mom?"

"Paige? Is that you?"

The sound of her mother's voice had a solid sense of reality about it in the midst of the surreal events of Chicago.

"Oh, Mom …" Paige began to weep uncontrollably. It took her awhile before she could control herself to talk.

"Paige? What's wrong? Where are you?"

"I'm in Chicago."

"Chicago?"

"I've been arrested. I'm in jail."

"Dear Lord! Whatever for?"

"Disorderly conduct."

"Oh, Paige!"

"Can you send me some money for bail? And some money to get home? The people I came with ..." She broke down again.

"Paige, honey, your father's in Chicago."

"He is?"

"He's covering the convention. Let me give you his hotel phone number."

"I'm allowed only one call, Mother."

"Of course. Well, then, I'll call him and have him come get you."

"Thank you, Mom."

"Paige, are you all right? I've been listening to the news."

Paige wept into a handkerchief.

"Paige? Paige, dear?"

"No, Mother, I'm not all right. Natalie is dead."

"Oh, dear God ..."

"I want to come home, Mother. I want to come home."

"Of course, dear. We'll get you home. We'll get you home as soon as we can."

22

"Hey, buddy. Hear they're releasing you today."

Travis looked up from his bed. Keith strolled in casually, his cap folded in his hands. He'd been a regular visitor for the three days Travis had spent in the hospital, twice a day, in fact. And it was the old Keith who visited, not the Vietnam Keith. For Travis it was almost like old times.

"Yeah. They're taking off the bandages today." He lifted up both hands, heavily wrapped in gauze.

"Fingers doing better?"

Travis nodded. "They're sensitive as all get-out right now. The doctor said between the deep cuts from the digging and the burns I'll probably lose some feeling in them, but not enough to keep me from doing anything."

Keith pulled up a chair and sat beside the bed. "I see you still got your night-light." He nodded to the lamp on a stand beside Travis's bed. No other bed in the ward had one.

With a glance at the light Travis grinned. "Went all night without it last night."

Since his return Travis had trouble with dark places. His first night back when he awoke in the middle of the night, he became disoriented and confused. Anxiety washed over him like a cold bath. He began sweating. His fingers burned like fire. He thought someone had thrown him back into the cave and buried him again. He started screaming.

"All night?" Keith said. "Good for you."

The comment was without sarcasm. That would have been the Vietnam Keith. The old Keith understood. He knew a friend's fear wasn't something to joke about.

"How's Gower doing?" Travis asked.

Keith's face lit up. "He's going home! The doctors sewed the tendons together in his neck, but they're shipping him home for rehab. They say he'll regain about 80 percent of the use of his arm. Of course they're still talking about the fact that if it weren't for you, he'd be dead."

Travis shrugged. "You do what you can to survive."

"Well, you certainly surprised me," Keith said. "I knew you were a good kid and all, but I didn't know you had it in you to pull off something like that. Everybody's still talking about it."

Travis tried to take the news modestly, but in truth, it felt good to hear that the other soldiers in the platoon respected him— especially Keith.

"Oh! I almost forgot," Keith exclaimed. "We got word back from the fly boys. With the coordinates you gave them, they plastered that entire area. The VC won't be using that cave and its supplies anytime soon."

Travis grinned. The news just kept getting better.

The two men sat in silence.

"Platt's back from Hong Kong," Keith said after awhile.

"Yeah? Did he have a good time?"

Keith laughed. "To put it mildly. I'll let him tell you about it himself."

Travis nodded.

Silence again. Keith fiddled with his cap and stared into the distance. Travis occupied himself by looking at the folds of his blanket.

Keith cleared his throat. "Um, when you talked to your parents on the phone …"

"Yeah?"

"Did they say anything about Paige? How she's doing, that sort of thing?"

Travis grinned a controlled grin. It didn't begin to reveal the rising joy he felt inside. He'd always felt that God had created Keith and Paige for each other. The happiest days of his life were when they were together.

"They said she was still at UCRD, protesting and stuff. She was on the news one night," he said excitedly. Sobering, he added, "She was there that day of the shooting, too."

Keith looked at him with concern.

"She didn't get hurt," Travis said quickly. "A friend of hers did, though. Right next to her. Got shot in the leg."

"Yeah, I read about that one," Keith said. "Glad Paige didn't get hurt."

Silence rose between them as Travis temporarily ran out of things to say. Then, he thought of something.

"I can get her address for you, if you don't have it."

Keith looked up and grinned.

"That would be great, kid."

"Sure! I'll write for it …" he looked at his hands, "well, as soon as I can. Maybe I can get a chaplain to help me or something."

"That'll be great, Travis. Thanks a lot."

While Keith looked pleased at the prospect of reestablishing ties with Paige, it was Travis who was the most excited.

"Tell you what," Keith said, standing. "You get out of here when?"

"About 1400 hours, just as soon as they rebandage my hands."

Keith nodded, "All right. I'll come back for you at 1430 hours and we'll go into town. How does that sound?"

Scenes of their first trip to town together flashed in Travis's mind. He and Keith were beginning to get along together again, and Travis didn't want a couple hours of R&R to mess that up. On the other hand, wasn't that what friends did together?

"OK," Travis said with guarded enthusiasm.

❊

With new bandages on his hands, Travis could use his fingers for the first time in days. Each finger was wrapped individually this time instead of the entire hand.

Just as he promised, Keith showed up at 1430 hours and the two of them headed for town. Whatever reservations Travis had about the outing dissolved quickly. It was a weekend in La Jolla all over again, except of course, without Paige.

They laughed and joked the entire way into town. Never once did Keith smoke or even ask Travis if he minded if he smoked. When they stopped for drinks at a café, both men ordered soft drinks. Keith promised Travis a great French restaurant for dinner, and he didn't disappoint. The food was outstanding, the atmosphere calm with subtle lighting, and a string chamber group played softly in the background.

That night back on base was even better. The guys of the squad welcomed Travis like he was a conquering hero. They sat around together all night long, talking and swapping stories about home. Platt and Travis were the focal point most of the time; Platt telling about his R&R exploits, and Travis describing in detail his harrowing experience with Gower. He did it in detail because if he left out the slightest thing, they asked him.

The only solemn moment of the evening was when someone mentioned Selig.

"I could tell it was comin'," Keith said. "We all could. He got that faraway look in his eyes. Emotions dried up like a prune. He shuffled his feet. When guys get like that, they're lookin' for a way to die. No way you can stop them."

Everyone expressed regret at losing Earl Gower, though they were glad he was going home early. Even twitching, fidgeting Ernie Osgood seemed to relax and have a good time that night. For Travis it was the first night he felt he was actually part of the squad. He was no longer an outsider. He was one of them, a battle-hardened veteran.

"Wonder what new kid we'll get to replace Gower?" Rafe said. "Sure hope he isn't so green that he does something stupid that gets us all killed."

Travis found himself agreeing with Rafe.

23

The next three insertions went like clockwork. The squad acted like a single entity. They thought, moved, fought, and rested as one. Together they knew they would survive. Their single-mindedness gave them an advantage over the enemy. Where one man might be weak, together they were strong. For Travis this was family, these men were his brothers, and he wasn't alone in his desire that nothing be done to mess this situation up. Headquarters, however, didn't see things his way. They sent the squad two new guys.

With rotors thwacking overhead and the roar of turbine in his ears, Travis studied the new arrivals. They looked like high-school kids. The redhead kept fumbling awkwardly with his gear. The kid with the shaved head looked like a marine, but he moved like he had webbed feet; his huge boots slapped the pavement when he walked.

In turn each of the new guys glanced up and saw him looking at them. They didn't maintain eye contact very long. They pretended something needed their attention for an excuse to look away.

Travis disliked the new guys and he didn't even know them. They represented a random element that had been injected into the group, an unproved variable. Their very presence changed the chemistry of the squad. Now Travis knew how the others felt when he first arrived. But understanding didn't take the fear away that these guys engendered. He hoped they didn't do anything stupid that would get them all killed.

The whine of the turbine deepened; the chopper began its descent. Once its skids hit the ground, the squad scrambled out like they had a hundred times before. The new guys stuck close by, their eyes as wide as saucers, their shirts soaked with nervous perspiration.

They were lucky. There was no opposing gunfire at the landing zone. Like a pride of lions on the prowl, the squad trampled through the elephant grass. Their assignment was to scout north. If they found resistance, they were to order air strikes. At night they were to set an ambush.

Travis pushed through the grass that was heavy with moisture. It had rained hard seven days straight. Everything was dripping wet. It made moving slower. Already, Travis's boots and socks and pants were wet. It was getting so that he couldn't remember what dry feet felt like.

The day went without incident. Down the stream, up the bank, along the path, through one village, then another, there was no sign of the VC. Highly unusual.

They had pushed through enough bushes that they were soaked from head to foot. It might as well be raining. The good news was that the sun was peeking past a scattering of clouds. The bad news was that in the jungle, things didn't dry. They steamed. It felt like they were in a sauna.

For much of the day they had walked the base of a mountain, and for that reason when sundown came, it came quickly. Assessing the terrain as he had done so many times before, Keith directed them where to set the ambush. While the day was uneventful, the night promised to be different. Intelligence reports put a large number of VC in the area.

Travis helped set up the machine gun that Platt now manned. He had graduated to that position now that Gower was gone. Travis, in turn, now fed the beast during a fight. The new guy with the red hair carried the ammo and handed it to Travis.

"Hey Travis, got a sec?"

Keith motioned to him. He flicked a cigarette at a large mound. An anthill. Travis had never seen anthills like this before—three to four feet high. Travis wondered if Keith flicked the cigarette away because of him, or because it was getting dark. Lately, Keith didn't smoke whenever Travis was around. Neither did he drink. Travis took this as a sign of respect for his beliefs, the beliefs they had once shared.

Travis grabbed his rifle and followed the squad leader about a hundred yards distant when Keith turned around. He was all smiles. He reached into his left breast pocket and pulled out an envelope.

"Got a letter from my parents," he said. "Paige is back home."

Travis thought for a moment. "That makes sense. The fall semester at UCRD doesn't begin until the last week in September."

"That's not why she's home."

"Oh?" Travis sensed that Keith had news about his sister. It seemed to him odd that Keith would hear about it first from his parents while Travis hadn't heard anything about it from his own parents.

"She was in Chicago during the Democratic Convention and all those riots."

"She was? What was she doing there? Wait, she was protesting, of course. Paige has been big into protesting against Vietnam."

In the fading light, Keith referred to the letter. "According to my parents, she went there with two guys and a gal from UCRD."

Suddenly, an awful thought swept over Travis. "She didn't get hurt, did she?" he asked.

"No, but she did get jailed."

"Jailed?" Travis shouted the word so loud it echoed in the trees and against the rocks. "*My* sister?"

Keith laughed. "That's something to rib her about, isn't it? Your dad had to bail her out. He was in Chicago taking pictures of the convention and all the riot stuff."

Travis smiled. He found it difficult—amusing, but difficult—to imagine his sister in jail.

"She's moved back home," Keith continued. "My mother says she attended church one Sunday."

Wow, things have changed, Travis thought, *considering the blow-up on the last Sunday I was home. Man, that seems like a lifetime ago.*

Keith broke into his thoughts. Still referring to the letter, he said, "And that friend of hers? The one that got shot in the leg at UCRD? She was killed in the riots. I tell you what, it seems to me that girl had some kind of black mark against her."

"Does the letter say how Paige is doing? Is she all right? My mom said last time she talked to her she seemed kinda depressed, but I guess you would expect that considering …"

"Cap'n Rawlins?"

Lem Tischler, the radio man, was walking toward them, carrying the radio on his back. He said, "You gotta come here and see what this new guy is doing."

Keith rolled his eyes in disgust. "Can't it wait?" he asked.

"No sir, I'm afraid …"

Without warning, the jungle came alive with rifle fire. Sheets of lead poured out of the trees. Tischler was hit. He spun around and hit the ground, his radio flying a few feet away.

Platt and the others returned the fire. It was a pitiful response, like spitting into a Vietnam cloudburst. The response was further lessened by the fact that Travis wasn't beside the machine gun feeding it. The weapon sputtered and fell silent while the red-headed new guy fumbled with the ammo belts. For a moment the gun came alive again, but not for long.

The force of the barrage threw Keith and Travis over a ledge where the road fell away and descended to the river. They tumbled and slid, skidding to a stop about a dozen feet from the precipice.

"You OK?" Keith shouted, himself a bit dazed.

"I think so," Travis said. He spied his rifle that had landed several feet away and scrambled to get it. Thinking the VC might come over the ridge any second, he took aim at the road.

No one appeared. But if the sound of gunfire was any indication, the squad was getting the life kicked out of them. Keith began climbing up the ridge. Travis followed close behind him. They hesitated, then raised their heads to take a look.

The squad was pinned down, returning fire as best they could. Lem lay close by. He was rocking back and forth, moaning.

"We've got to get the radio to call for reinforcements!" Keith shouted. "Cover me!"

He began to climb over the ridge. Travis pulled him back.

"What are you doing?" Keith shouted.

"I'll get it!" Travis said. "You cover me!"

He handed Keith his rifle. Keith looked into his eyes, then nodded.

"OK!" he shouted. "On three."

Travis readied himself.

Keith began the count. "One … two …"

Travis dug his toes into the soft ground.

"Three!"

Keith raised up and laid down a steady fire into the jungle. Travis vaulted over the ledge and, crouching as low as he could crouch while still running, he sprinted toward the radio.

Bullets impacted the earth at his feet. They whizzed by his ears.

He reached the radio and grabbed it. Tischler moaned. Travis paused and reached over to see how badly Lem had been hit.

PING!

A bullet hit the radio, knocking it from his hand. Their lifeline hit the dirt road and skidded out of reach.

"Travis! Get back here!" Keith shouted.

Travis lunged for the radio. Then, taking three giant steps, he dove for the ridge. He came up short. Hitting the ground, he rolled over the ledge, the radio banging against his chest and arms as he tumbled.

"That was stupid, Morgan!" Keith shouted. "I thought you were a goner! First you get the radio so we can call for reinforcements. Then we can think about getting Tischler!"

Keith was right. But it went against Travis's nature to leave Tischler behind. Travis had been trained to save lives; it didn't matter to him if they were in the water or in a fire storm.

Keith slipped down from the ridge and grabbed the radio. A moment later he'd made contact. He called for reinforcements and air strikes.

KABOOM!

The earth shuddered. The VC were lobbing mortars. Geysers of dirt erupted in front of them.

Travis took his rifle and his place on the ridge. He fired into the jungle at anything that moved. Bark and leaves went flying, but little else. A smoky cloud of gunpowder hung heavily over the squad's location.

KABOOM!

Again the earth shook. Dirt rained down on Travis's helmet and back. Behind him, Keith was screaming into the radio.

KABOOM!

This one was close. Too close. This time the ground did more than shake, it lifted Travis with it.

"Reinforcements are on their way!" Keith shouted. "We have to hold out for just a few minutes."

He began climbing over the ridge. Travis grabbed his arm.

"Where do you think you're going now?" he shouted.

Keith looked at him angrily, glaring at the hold Travis had on him. He released it.

"I'm going to my squad. You got a problem with that?"

KABOOM!

Travis never had a chance to answer. The mortar explosion lifted the two men off the ground and tossed them down the hill like they were a couple of rag dolls. The tumbling didn't stop until they splashed into the river.

The river couldn't have been more than four feet deep, but the current was swift and Travis found it difficult to get a foothold on the bottom. Keith's flailing arms indicated he was having difficulty, too. The river swept them farther and farther away from their squad.

Still not touching bottom, Travis managed to right himself and get his bearings. He swam to Keith, who was splashing and sputtering and swallowing a lot of water.

Travis grabbed him and, placing his arm across Keith's chest, attempted to calm him. At first Keith struggled. Then, when he realized who it was who had him, he relaxed.

It was hard to determine just how far downriver they'd floated, but when Travis looked up at the road, he saw men in uniform double-timing it to where their squad was still pinned down. At the same time, a couple of fighter planes screeched overhead.

Seconds later the thumping sound of bombs carpeting the jungle could be heard in the distance.

Travis yelled to the soldiers for help. At first, startled by the sound of a human voice coming from the river, guns were trained on them. Then the squad's leader sent a couple of men down to fish them out of the water.

On the banks of the river, Keith and Travis fought to catch their breath.

"My men," Keith said. "We've got to help them."

Nobody tried to stop him as he scrambled to his feet. As always Travis was close at his heels.

Travis estimated that it took them three minutes to get back to the squad. Three minutes. Long enough to wipe out a squad of soldiers.

The firefight dissipated once the air strikes began. The VC ran away. This was not uncommon. It was typical for them to melt into the jungle at the first sign of serious firepower. One moment they were there, the next they were gone, able to jump out at you another day.

Keith and Travis were the first ones to arrive at the place where the squad had set up their ambush. The entire area was devastated. Bodies lay scattered everywhere. Not one of them showed any signs of life.

Travis was numb, as though a part of him had just been amputated. From the look on Keith's face, he felt the same.

As the reinforcements plunged into the jungle, pushing any remaining VC back even more, Keith and Travis walked among the dead.

The jungle was silent now, all except for the sound of Keith's voice as he stood over the lifeless form of Ernie Osgood.

"Did you know he had a twin sister back in Oakland, California?"

Travis shook his head. "No, I didn't."

As he stood over Ernie's body, he noticed something. With all the blood and mess from multiple wounds, he almost missed it. He glanced at the others in the squad. Doing so confirmed what he'd feared.

"What? What do you see?" Keith asked.

"They're all facedown," Travis said. "And look here." He pointed to the back of Osgood's head.

Keith looked to where Travis was pointing and cursed. Then he looked at the others. "All of them?"

"Looks that way."

Without exception each man had been shot in the back of the head. The VC had come through and systematically shot them. They executed those who might have only been wounded.

Travis began shaking uncontrollably. He had to sit down to keep from falling down.

"Rafe Blair," Keith said, standing over the Montana resident. "Won't ever hear him sing those horrible cowboy songs again."

Keith walked over to the silent machine gun.

"Uriah Platt. He was gonna open up his own garage when he got back to Petal, Mississippi. Petal. What kind of name is that for a town?"

"Keith, don't do this to yourself."

"Did you ever catch the name of the redheaded new guy?"

"Martin, Marvin, Melvin ... I heard it once, but wasn't paying attention," Travis said.

Keith gazed down sadly at the new guy. His red curly hair rustled slightly in the breeze. "His first mission," Keith said. Looking over at the big-footed new guy, he said, "His, too. Wonder what they were doing that had Tischler in an uproar."

The accountant from Phoenix lay where he had fallen. He

was no longer rocking back and forth. He was now facedown in the dirt. Keith wandered over to him.

"He was the first one to respect me as squad leader," Keith said. "He told the others that regardless of the past this was my squad, and if they followed me I'd get them through this hell. Looks like you were wrong, Lem."

"Keith, there was nothing you could do ..."

"I know that!" Keith shouted at him. He straightened himself suddenly. His jaw was tight as he looked over the killing field. His voice had a hard edge to it when he spoke. "All this ..." he said, waving his hand over the scene. "It don't mean nothin'."

Keith and Travis rode the Huey back to the base. Travis was exhausted from carrying the dead back to the landing zone. He knew Keith must be, too. The entire trip back, Keith said nothing. He stared out the window at the passing scenery. Travis stared at the corpses that were piled on top of one another inside the chopper, their boots sticking out in a jumbled array. This morning they were talking and laughing and joking together. One unit, one mind. Now the absence of human voice made for an eerie silence despite the loud whine of the turbine engine overhead.

The next day Keith was given the assignment to write letters to the parents of the dead men in his squad. Travis watched as he made several attempts to write. His hands shook so badly, he couldn't even hold the pen.

"Morgan, you're good with words," Keith said. "Write these letters for me, otherwise they'll never get done."

"Naw, Keith, I think it will mean a lot more to the parents coming from ..."

"JUST DO IT, OK?" Keith shouted.

The room echoed with the sound of his voice.

"Sorry, man," he apologized. "Just do it for me, OK?"

"Sure, Keith," Travis said.

While Travis wrote the letters, Keith sat across from him and stared at nothing in particular. At the end of each letter, Travis looked up from his task and each time Keith's eyes were a little emptier.

"Keith, you've got to take it easy on yourself," Travis said.

Keith didn't respond. Travis wasn't sure he'd been heard. He said, "Keith ..."

"Morgan, just shut up," he said. "I'm fine. I know how to deal with this kind of thing. I'm a survivor."

Travis nodded. He let it drop.

"You want to know my secret?" Keith asked.

"What's that?"

Keith lit a cigarette. He was in no hurry about it. After taking a long drag on it, he waved his arm casually. "See all of this? It don't mean nothin'."

Travis sat there helplessly as Paige's high-school boyfriend continued staring off at nothing in particular. He couldn't help but notice how Keith's eyes were looking more and more like Selig's just before he died.

24

Each day Keith Rawlins grew more and more unresponsive. In the field, he was as sharp as ever, determined to exact retribution on the VC for the death of his squad. He was methodical. Efficient. Cold. He never spoke to anyone unless it was a matter of business. And when they weren't in the field, he stayed to himself and never spoke to anyone at all.

Travis tried to get him some kind of help. He spoke to their commanding officer who examined Keith's record and liked what he saw. "Son, never mess with a star player," he was told. "Just hand him the ball and let him run."

When the CO refused to help, Travis spoke to the chaplain who expressed proper concern and agreed to talk to Keith. But a conversation takes at least two people and, for all the good it did, the chaplain might just as well have spent the afternoon talking to himself.

"Morgan, get off my back," Keith ordered. "I'm not your mission field. This is a war zone, not a feel-good Sunday-school class. We're here to kill the enemy. And I'm going to kill as many of them as I can before my time is up. If you have a problem with that, tough. Just stay out of my way."

So Travis backed off. He decided the best thing he could do

for Keith was to give him space. In time he would come around and be himself again. Then, an idea hit him, one that just might help bring the old Keith back.

He pulled out some stationery, found a book to use as a desk, propped himself up in his bed, and began to write:

Dear Paige,

Will wonders never cease? Your little brother is actually writing you a letter, so you know it must be serious. If you could find it in your heart to write to Keith, he could sure use a letter from a friend right about now ...

The insertion went without incident. Whereas Keith and Travis were used to working with a more or less independent squad, they were now part of a larger platoon. The sky was filled with Hueys flying in formation, dropping to the landing zone in an impressive array as hundreds upon hundreds of soldiers poured out of their bellies.

Travis found it hard adjusting to a group this size. There were too many names and faces. He could hardly remember anyone's name from mission to mission. However, the new situation seemed custom-fit for Keith. He didn't try to learn any names, saw no reason for it. They were here to kill VC, not socialize, he said.

On this particular mission, the major in charge divided them into squads. Their assignment was to check out designated villages that, according to intelligence reports, were VC friendly. They were to confiscate any arms they might find and question suspected sympathizers. Those who were confirmed as spies were to be brought back to the landing zone where they would be flown to base for further questioning.

The major placed Keith in charge of one of the squads. Travis was placed in the squad with him.

Travis had mixed feelings about this. On the one hand, giving Keith a squad of men might be exactly what the doctor ordered;

on the other hand, he wasn't so sure Keith was mentally competent to lead a squad.

"Let's move out!" Keith shouted. His squad followed him.

It took them the better part of the day to reach the village. To do so, they had to wade through one rice paddy after another while the farmers and their families glared at them. Walking through the paddies destroyed the crops, but the footpaths that separated the paddies were often laced with landmines. The squad willingly exchanged possible death by explosion for angry glares any day.

Travis's boots were heavy as they climbed out of the paddy and onto a road. He'd been fighting a foot fungus, and his toes alternately burned and itched. They were driving him crazy.

The village came into sight. Less than a dozen dwellings. Thatched roofs. Small vegetable and herb gardens here and there. A couple of chickens chased each other around one of the huts. At the sight of the approaching soldiers, some of the village adults came out to meet them. All were women with the exception of one male who looked to be a hundred and twenty years old.

"Spread out!" Keith shouted. "Search the huts. Watch out for the gardens, there may be mines. Bring anything you find back here to me."

Travis started toward one of the dwellings.

"Morgan! You stay with me," Keith ordered.

Doing as ordered, Travis moved to Keith's side and stood there. When Keith moved, he moved; when Keith stopped, he stopped.

Keith motioned to one of the women. "Mama-san! Come here." He waved her forward.

For a moment hard eyes stared back at him. It wasn't that she didn't understand, it was a stare of defiance. She walked toward him, her eyes fixed on his every step of the way.

"Where are the men of the village?" Keith asked.

"In field. Work."

"Really? I think they're in the jungle killing my men."

"No. In field. Work."

"This is a VC village. Everyone knows that."

"We no VC."

"Then where are your men?" Keith shouted.

The woman didn't so much as blink. "In fields. Work," she said.

Keith struck her with the back of his hand. The blow knocked her to the ground. She scrambled to her feet and looked him in the eye as though nothing had happened.

"Men in fields. Work," she said.

A couple of men returned from searching the village. They were holding two AK-47s, the standard rifle used by the Viet Cong.

"Aha!" Keith gloated. "Evidence A and B! What do you say to that, Mama-san?"

She was unfazed. "Men in field. Work," she said.

The elderly man stepped forward. His eyes were wide with fear. "We no enemy! We no enemy!" he pleaded.

Keith pushed him aside.

Three more members of the squad returned. In their hands they carried parts of dismantled mines. Keith took the parts from the soldiers and showed them to the woman.

She looked at them, then up at him. "Men in field. Wor—"

A closed-fisted blow from Keith cut short her words. He stood over her, shaking the parts in her face. He was livid. His face was purple as he shouted, "Is this what they're planting, Mama-san? Is it? Are your men planting mines to kill my men?"

He stood up and threw the parts at her. They hit her in her forearms, which she'd raised to protect her face.

BLAM!

A shot rang out.

BLAM! BLAM!

A soldier standing next to Keith crumpled to the ground. Everyone else ducked low.

"It's from that hut over there!" Keith shouted, pointing.

The muzzle of a rifle poked out of the doorway.

The next instant the hut was riddled with bullets as nearly everyone in the squad peppered it with gunfire. The enemy rifle clattered to the ground. Beside it fell a young Vietnamese woman who couldn't have been more than twenty years old.

When the gunfire stopped, everyone raised up slowly, ready to hit the deck if the shooting started again.

While a couple of squad members charged the hut, Keith turned to the fallen soldier. He knelt beside him. The boy was dead.

"What was his name?" Keith asked.

"O'Malley," one of the soldiers answered.

"Where was he from?"

"Iowa. Coon Rapids, Iowa."

For nearly a minute Keith bent over the soldier, his head hung low. He placed a trembling hand on the fallen soldier's chest, in the same way the president-elect places his hand on the Bible and takes the oath of office.

All the members of the squad gathered around him and waited. Many of them were touched by the scene, especially since Keith didn't even know the boy's name.

Slowly, Keith stood. He pointed to the sniper. "Bring her here," he said.

The two soldiers standing closest to her grabbed the dead girl by the arms and dragged her out into the open. With the villagers looking on, Keith stood over her, drew his service revolver, and shot the dead girl three times in the head.

When the ringing of the shots died out, he said to the dead girl, "That's for O'Malley, Osgood, and Lem."

The villagers clustered together in shock and fear. Some of the women wept. But not the woman he had questioned. She stood with clenched fists and glared at him, hatred in her eyes.

The villagers weren't the only ones in shock. The squad stood around with their arms hanging limp by their sides and their mouths hanging open.

Keith sauntered up to the Vietnamese woman. "Care to change your answer? This village is friendly to the VC, isn't it?" he shouted.

She stared back at him, unafraid. "Men in field. Work," she said defiantly.

For a long moment Keith exchanged glares with her. Then he burst out laughing.

"You'd kill me if you could, wouldn't you?" he asked her.

This time the woman did not respond with her standard answer.

"Yeah, that's what I thought," Keith said. "But I'm not going to give you a chance."

He turned and motioned to one of the soldiers, a tall thin young man with a pointed chin.

What happened next would be burned into Travis's memory forever. It would haunt him night and day for the rest of his life.

Without a word Keith grabbed the astonished soldier's automatic weapon, turned and began firing, spraying the villagers with bullets. Like wheat before a sickle, they fell with a single pass of the weapon. However, Keith didn't stop there. He made a second pass, then a third.

Calmly, as though he had just performed a routine maintenance operation, he handed the weapon back to the dumbfounded soldier. Then, drawing his pistol again, he stood over the stubborn old woman and pumped two more bullets into her.

"That's for Rafe and Platt, Mama-san," he said to her unhearing ears as he reloaded his pistol. He began to turn away, then turned back as though he'd forgotten to tell her something. "Oh, and when your men return from the fields where they're working, give 'em my regards."

Travis couldn't believe what'd he'd just witnessed. The whole thing was unreal, like something out of a movie, and the women on the ground and the old man were merely actors that would stand up and dust themselves off as soon as the director yelled, "Cut!"

But there was no director. And the blood and wounds that were already beginning to attract flies were real.

"What have you done, Keith?" Travis said.

"Oh, this?" Keith waved his hand over the bodies. "It don't mean nothin'. Haven't you learned that yet, Morgan?"

"But Keith, a bunch of women?"

"I've heard enough from you, Morgan."

"But how can you ..."

Keith turned on him like a wild man. "Shut up! Shut up! Shut up! Shut up!" he screamed. Pulling away, he calmed himself, adjusted his helmet, and said, "And that's an order."

Turning to the rest of the squad, he shouted, "Let's clean this mess up! Drag the bodies into the huts and burn them. Burn everything! I want this place completely leveled! Let's wipe this VC village off the face of the earth!"

Suddenly, a woman darted out from one of the huts. She ran away from the squad toward the jungle.

BLAM!

Keith shot her in the back with his revolver.

The woman fell to her knees.

BLAM!

Hit again, her head flew backward from the impact. Then, she fell to the ground and didn't move.

Keith shouted, "No survivors! This village never existed! Got it?"

Travis had never seen such a demonstration of pure hatred. And from the looks on the faces of the other members of the squad, neither had they.

He walked over to the fallen woman. Keith was right behind him. As they stood side by side looking down at her, her body moved.

Keith pointed his pistol at her.

"No!" Travis shouted. "Look!"

He bent down. The woman was dead. There was something beneath her that had moved her.

Travis turned the woman over. An infant was wrapped against her chest. A fussing sound gave way to howling.

Keith pointed his revolver at the infant.

Travis shoved it away. "What are you doing?" he shouted.

Calmly, Keith replied, "I'm ridding ourselves of a future VC." He brought the gun back on target.

"No!" Travis shouted. He shoved Keith's arm aside and moved his own body over the baby's to protect it.

"Morgan, get out of my way!"

"You're not going to kill a baby!"

"Get out of my way!"

"If you're going to shoot the baby, you're going to have to shoot me first!" Travis demanded.

Keith shook his head. "All right, then, have it your way." He brought the revolver to bear on the back of Travis's neck.

Launching himself into Keith's legs, Travis bowled Keith over. Within seconds he was back over the mother, removing the cloth that bound her baby to her.

He stood, cradling the baby in his arms. As he did, he found himself looking down the barrel of his squad leader's service revolver.

"Put the baby down, Morgan."

"I'm not going to let you kill this baby, Keith."

"Put it down."

"No."

"I'll shoot you along with it! Now put it down."

Travis stood his ground.

"PUT THE BABY DOWN!"

Looking Keith in the eyes, Travis shook his head no.

"I'M GIVING YOU A DIRECT ORDER! PUT THE BABY DOWN!"

"You're just going to have to shoot me," Travis said. "But how are you going to explain my death to HQ? What are you going to say to Paige? My parents? Our church?"

Members of the squad had gathered around the drama forming a human amphitheater. "Get back to work!" Keith shouted. "I told you to burn this village!"

There was a moment of hesitation on the part of some of them, but one by one they followed his order. Using anything they could get their hands on—rocks, tree limbs, bamboo—or when those weren't readily available, feet and heels or just their arms—they pushed and tore and ripped the village apart. Then they set the rubble on fire.

"What's it gonna be, Morgan? Are you willing to give your life for this VC kid? Be smart. We wipe crud like him from the bottom of our feet every day. He's not worth it."

Travis listened while the infant squirmed in his arms. "I'm not going to let you kill him, Keith. And I don't think you'll kill me, either. We've been together too long. We've had too many good times. You'd never be able to look yourself in the mirror again."

"I can't do that now," Keith scoffed. "Put the baby down."

"I know you're hurting over the deaths of our friends, but you can't let something like that totally impair your judgment. Give it time. You'll get over it."

"I don't want to get over it," Keith said. "Thoughts of revenge are what keep me going. Now put the baby down."

Travis shook his head. "No, Keith. I'm not going to put the baby down."

Keith fingered his pistol. "Then run," he said.

"What?"

"You heard me. Run!"

"So you can shoot me in the back?"

"I'll give you to the count of ten. One ..."

Travis stood his ground.

"... two ... three ... four ..."

If he ran, where would he run to?

"... five ... six ... seven ..."

And if somehow he managed to get back on base without getting shot by one side or the other, it would just be his word against Keith's. He doubted the other members of the squad would attack their leader to protect someone they didn't even know."

"... eight ..."

Keith was going to pull the trigger. Travis could see it in his eyes. He'd probably come up with an explanation he could sell to HQ.

"... nine ..."

This was unreal. Keith wouldn't shoot him.

"... ten!"

Time stopped. Travis and Keith were suspended between the ticks of the clock. Scene after scene of the past flashed in rapid succession in Travis's mind: Keith and him watching black-and-white cowboy movies on Saturday mornings ...

Keith's hand gripped and re-gripped the revolver.

... sitting at the beach around the campfire with the youth group, with Keith playing the guitar and leading the singing ...

His eyes were hardened and hollow.

... riding in the back seat of Keith's convertible watching his sister and Keith as they sat close to each other and whispered into each other's ears things they didn't want him to hear ...

His lips were dry; pressed tightly together in determination.

... throwing the football with Keith in the park and going out for ice cream afterward ...

Keith took a breath and held it.

Travis ran. Not away, but toward the barrel of the gun.

BLAM!

The revolver discharged next to his ear. It resounded like a cannon. But because he wanted to live, he lowered his head and kept charging.

Travis literally ran over him, sending Keith sprawling backward. The revolver flew from his hand.

His legs churning like pistons, Travis looked for some kind of shelter, something to duck behind. Keith wouldn't be down forever.

He spied a thick patch of bamboo on the side of the road. Not wanting to give away his intentions too soon, he ran straight forward and waited until he was parallel to the back of the bamboo patch.

Planting his foot, he pushed off it to his left.

BLAM!

Bamboo splinters flew. But Travis wasn't hit. The infant in his arms was wailing. Travis knew exactly how the little one felt. He wanted to cry, too. The man he'd idolized all his life was trying to kill him.

He could hear Keith's voice in the distance, yelling at the other soldiers to go after him and bring him back. The ringing in his ear from the first shot turned out to be a blessing. After hearing the man he loved like a brother label him a traitor and a deserter, the sound of Keith's voice dissipated quickly, and he could hear him no more.

25

Paige tried not to think about how much she hated life. It only depressed her more.

She reclined on her bed, alone in her room. That's where she spent most of her time. The stereo in the corner was quiet. The music that used to speak to her spoke to her no longer. Her art easel was pushed to one side. Canvases of unfinished paintings were stacked here and there, a still life, a landscape, an attempt at modern art. She doubted she would ever finish any of them.

A physics book lay open in front of her. She was supposed to be studying. She didn't want to do that, either. And not just because it was physics, though if she thought about it, she would wonder why an art major had to study physics to begin with.

There was simply nothing in La Jolla worth getting excited over. She was attending a commuter college, so she breezed into and out of classes without ever getting to know the people in them. She went to church with her parents on Sunday, an easy concession to make for a disillusioned protester. But there was nothing for her there, either. Her College and Career Bible Study class had nearly evaporated once school started, and all the students returned to their various colleges and universities scattered across the country. Those who remained behind either weren't attending college, or didn't have the grades to get into a decent one. And while the teachers of the class attempted to involve her, she couldn't see that they had anything to offer. So she put in her time and endured the sermon that followed and went home with her parents and then to her room—her four-walled universe.

There was a tapping sound on her door.

"Paige?" It was her mother.

"Yeah?"

The door swung gently open. "Are you OK, dear?"

Paige rolled over on her bed. "Yeah," she said unenthusiastically.

"May I come in?"

"Sure."

"Is it safe?"

These three words were code words in the Morgan house. Mother navigated just fine in an orderly room, but a room with things frequently strewn about could be at times hazardous. And while Mother had learned to move cautiously to avoid roller skates or tubes of paint or tennis rackets on the floor, they had devised a code to let her know what to expect. By answering "yes" to the code, "Is it safe?" meant that the floor was relatively free of clutter.

"Just a sec," Paige said. She slipped off the bed and moved some canvases out of the way. While she was up, she got her mother a high-backed wooden chair from her desk. She told her mother about the chair.

"Thank you, dear." Her mother felt for the chair, then, instead of sitting in it, turned it around and straddled it. She lay folded arms on the back of the chair and her chin on her arms. "You've been awfully quiet of late," her mother said. "Anything troubling you?"

Paige flopped back onto the bed. Her physics book bounced, losing her place. She didn't care.

"Everything's fine, Mom, it's just quieter around here without Travis. Not like it used to be."

Allegra grinned. "The two of you could get loud at times, I'll grant you that. Still, I'm not convinced you're feeling as well as you claim to be."

It was Paige's turn to grin. She had never been able to hide her emotions from her mother. What made her think she could now?

"You're still hurting badly over Natalie's death, aren't you?"

The rapidity with which her emotions rose within her made Paige angry. That's why she didn't think about these things. Thinking about them only brought back the pain.

"You know, dear, the hurt is part of the healing process. You can only pretend the pain doesn't exist for so long. It will always be there until you deal with it."

It was next to impossible for Paige even to admit to herself that Natalie was gone. Her mind kept telling her that they were still on summer break and come fall the two of them would be reunited on campus.

But it was fall now. And classes had begun at UCRD without her and without Natalie.

"Oh Mother, I miss her so much!"

"I know you do, dear."

"She knew exactly what she wanted out of life. She was the strongest person I've ever known. She was a good friend and fun to be with. She deserved better, Mother, she really did."

"And you blame yourself for her death because you talked her into going to Chicago."

Paige's silence was her way of agreeing with the statement.

"Her death wasn't your fault."

"The only reason she was there was because of me. And then the things we went for—the music—never happened. It was such a waste, Mother."

"But it was Del who put the drug in her drink. There was no way you could have prevented that."

"It's not just Natalie. It's my entire life. Look at me! I have nothing. I'm going nowhere. I have no friends. If I were to disappear off the face of the earth at this moment, the only two people in the world who would even care are you and Dad, and sometimes I'm not sure he'd care."

"I'll let that last statement pass without comment. We'll just chalk it up to anger and frustration talking. You know very well your father loves you."

"So then, why can't we get along? We never had any problem before."

"Well, now that you're older, you look at things from a different perspective. And sometimes both of you let your differences of opinion overshadow the deeper love you have for each other."

"I guess that's true," Paige said. "At least that was when I had an opinion."

Allegra was slow in responding. When she did, she said, "I'm not sure you ever had an opinion."

Paige wasn't sure how to take that. Her mother's statement offended her and puzzled her at the same time. "And just what do you mean by that?"

"Ever since you went away to college, you've not had an opinion about anything."

"How can you say that? Do you know how hard it was for me not to go to church that one Sunday? And what about all the rallies I've attended? How can you say I don't have an opinion?"

"Because in every single instance you just cited, you weren't expressing your opinion. You were expressing Del's opinion."

There was enough truth in her mother's statement that it made Paige think for a moment.

"Let me ask you this. Whose idea was it for you to stand up to your father and refuse to go to church with us? Was it something you thought of yourself?"

"Del pointed out the hypocrisy of it all," Paige admitted.

"And why were you at those rallies? Were you there because you had to be or because ..."

"... because Del was there." The truth was beginning to dawn and Paige didn't like what it revealed.

"Why did you go away to UCRD?"

"Because I began to realize that I had no life of my own. Everything I did, I did because of Keith."

"That's right," Allegra said. She waited for Paige to make the connection herself.

"And I promptly went up to UCRD and did the exact same thing. I was attracted to Del's passion. But it was *his* passion and not my own."

Her mother nodded. "And what is it that attracted you to Natalie?"

"She was her own person! She knew who she was and what she wanted out of life and she wasn't afraid to go after it."

Allegra smiled. "And what do *you* want out of life, Paige? What are *you* passionate about?"

"I don't know. I honestly don't know."

Paige walked along the beach at sunset. After her talk with her mother, she grew restless. It disturbed her that she had no idea what she wanted out of life, and that for most of her life all she had done was ride piggyback on other people's dreams.

She carried her shoes so that she could splash her feet in the water. The roar of the waves made her think of Travis. The beach was his home. She wondered where he was right now. What he was doing.

"Paige? Paige Morgan? Is that you?"

A familiar face—or more correctly—a familiar body was walking toward her.

"Terri! What are you doing here? Why aren't you at UCRD? Haven't classes started?"

Terri Tucker was wearing a bikini like she always did. Paige couldn't ever remember seeing her in anything else.

Terri shrugged. "I let them start without me. I never was much interested in school. Only went there for the parties. I guess my dad figured that out after two years. So he cut my funds. How about you?"

Paige shrugged. How much should she say? "Well, I just didn't feel that I should go back there again ..."

"Yeah, after that whole Chicago mess," Terri said.

Paige lowered her gaze.

It suddenly dawned on Terri. "You live here, don't you? That day you hitchhiked up and that salesman was climbing all over you, you said you lived down here."

Paige pointed to the residence on the side of the hill. "Yeah, just up there."

"Wow!" Terri said, staring at the houses. She never was one to have a large vocabulary.

"So what are you doing here?" Paige asked.

"Oh! Here!" She handed Paige what looked like a dollar bill folded over. A cheap counterfeit to be sure.

Paige looked at it, unsure what to do with it.

"Open it up!" Terri squealed.

Paige did so. In bold green letters, it read: "Don't be deceived." Scripture verses followed. It was a religious tract.

"Isn't that neat?" Terri said. "I'm a Christian now and we're out witnessing. We live in a Christian house in Pacific Beach, right over ..."

"Yeah, I know where Pacific Beach is. Hey, that's great, Terri. I'm happy for you."

For some reason Paige found the whole idea of this bikini-clad blonde finding religion rather amusing, though she did her best to hide it.

"This is how we usually do it," she said.

She crumpled up the tract and tossed it on the ground. At a glance it looked like a dollar bill. Who wouldn't stoop down to pick it up?

Terri snatched it up. "But we can't use it that way on the beach because they're very strict about litter laws, so we just hand them out here."

"That's great, Terri. I'm so glad we ran into each other. And I'm really happy about your newfound faith and everything, but I've got to be going."

"Oh you can't go yet!" Terri said. "Allen will want to see you."

"Allen? Allen's here?"

He appeared behind Terri, walking toward them wearing trunks and a muscle shirt. He was grinning from ear to ear.

"Paige? Is that really you?"

The last time she had seen Allen he was slumped on a Chicago street being beaten and kicked by Chicago's finest. She remembered the way he'd looked on that trip, so tired and drained when he told her how Del had manipulated the shooting, and how he did his best to shepherd them safely to the van Del had moved.

How different he looked now. Tanned, confident, happy.

He stood in front of her. "Man, it's good to see you, Paige! I've been praying that we'd meet up again."

Paige never was able to explain it, whether it was emotion, or release, or God-ordained. But the next thing she knew, she had her arms around Allen's neck and was holding onto him for all she was worth.

26

"It has to be a duplicate!" Nat said.

"Months apart?" Allegra replied.

"Well, you know how the army is. If it's worth making a mistake once, it's worth making it twice."

A telegram lay between them on the kitchen table informing them that their son, Travis Morgan, had been reported missing in action.

"The last time he called us and warned us to expect the telegram," Allegra said.

"Maybe he doesn't know about this one. Maybe this is just a bureaucratic mix-up."

"How do you mean?"

"Well, suppose instructions to send the first telegram got buried under piles of paper on someone's desk." Nat said. "Now, months later, it's unburied. If the date on it is smudged or missing, they may think it's a current order and issue it again."

"That's a lot of supposing."

"Believe me, that's a mild scenario compared to some of the mix-ups the army's been involved with."

Allegra turned her wedding ring over and over on her finger nervously. "How can we know for sure?"

"I can do some checking tomorrow. Make a few calls. See if we can get this thing cleared up."

"And if Travis *is* missing in action?"

Nat reached across the table and took his wife by the hands. He said, "Let's not cross that bridge until we come to it."

※

All the next day Nat was given the bureaucratic two-step as he was transferred from one desk to another. Twice he lost the phone connection and had to start all over again. After the first time, he wrote down his journey through the phone maze by linking boxes together on a piece of paper. Each box had in it the name of the person he talked to, their phone number or extension number, their rank and title, what they said, and why they thought the next person in the chain would be able to help.

It was all for naught. In the end the message he was given was that if the army had sent the telegram, it must be true.

※

Two nights later the phone rang. Allegra answered it.

"Hello?"

"Hello? Mrs. Morgan?"

"Yes, this is she."

"This is Keith Rawlins."

A cold shiver went up Allegra's spine. She covered the mouthpiece of the phone.

"Nat! Nat!"

"What is it?" Nat came into the kitchen with newspaper in hand.

"Get on the extension! It's Keith Rawlins."

Nat moved quickly back into the living room.

"I'm sorry for the delay, Keith. I wanted my husband to get on the other phone."

"Sure," Keith said.

332   J A C K   C A V A N A U G H

The other extension clicked to life. "Hello? Keith?"

"Hello, Mr. Morgan."

"Where are you calling from, son?" Nat asked. "You're still in Vietnam, aren't you?"

"Actually, I'm calling from Hong Kong, sir."

"Hong Kong?"

"Yeah. I had a little R&R saved up."

"I see. When do you come home?"

"My tour is up in about a month," Keith said. "Anyway, the reason I'm calling you ..."

"Yes," said Allegra, "we don't want to waste your money."

"... my parents said it would be a good idea if I did."

This is it, thought Allegra. *Why else would he be calling if he didn't have word about Travis?*

"It's about Travis," Keith said.

"Yeah, we got another one of those MIA telegrams," Nat said. "Please tell me it's some army mix-up."

"I wish I could, sir, but I'm afraid it's not."

Allegra closed her eyes as the impact of the news hit her.

"Are you still there?" Keith asked.

"We're still here," Nat replied. "Tell us what happened."

"Well, sir, it's sort of a real mystery. We were out on a regular patrol, and we were checking out this village. I was the squad leader, so I gave the assignments and everyone searched the huts for weapons and anything that might indicate the villagers were aiding the Viet Cong.

"Anyway, we did that and when we reassembled, Travis didn't return. Then, just as we started looking for him, a firefight broke out and the squad went diving for the bushes. As a result, there were heavy casualties among the villagers. And afterward, we looked again for Travis, but still couldn't find him. Like I said, sir, a real mystery."

"So you left him there?" Nat said.

"Believe me, sir, I didn't want to leave him behind. We had no choice. If we're not at our designated LZs, that's landing zones, at the designated time, then we could be left behind ourselves."

"I understand."

"I want you to know that I would have done anything to save Travis, sir. He's like a little brother to me. But what can you do when someone just disappears?"

"Don't blame yourself, Keith," Nat said.

"There's one other thing," Keith said.

"What's that?"

"It really doesn't look good for Travis, sir. You know, being out there alone."

"Thanks for the warning, Keith. And you have a good time in Hong Kong."

"Will do, sir. Good-bye."

"Good-bye, Keith," Nat said.

Allegra didn't say good-bye. She just hung up the phone.

Nat walked into the kitchen. Allegra hadn't moved away from the phone on the wall. He put his arms around her.

"Well, at least now we know." He squeezed her tightly.

"He's lying."

"What?"

"Everything Keith told us is a lie."

Nat stepped back and looked at his wife. She was amazingly perceptive in these things and not given to hysterics or wild accusations.

"You're sure? This isn't just a mother grasping at straws, is it?"

"I tell you, Nat, the boy is lying."

"So you think Travis is not missing in action?"

"I don't know what to think. I only know that every part of his story is untrue. So now, the question is, what *is* the truth?"

Nat thought a moment. "I'll go up to LA tomorrow. Maybe I can pull a few strings and get the real story. Heaven knows, doing it by telephone is a long and circuitous route to the truth."

Allegra moved toward him. He opened his arms and allowed her to step in. They held each other tight.

"And if you can't find out anything?"

Nat sighed. "Then I march into my boss with a story idea and convince him to send me to Vietnam. Somebody has to go looking for our son."

27

"Welcome to the Catacombs."

Allen held the door open for Paige and Terri. They walked into an orderly, clean, quiet living room on Bayard Avenue, Pacific Beach, that looked like any one of the residential houses on the street. Only this one was a Jesus commune. In the corner of the room was a long-haired guy wearing shorts, sandals, and a T-shirt with "You have a lot to live; Jesus has a lot to give" printed on it. He was sitting in a chair beside a lamp reading a pocket-size New Testament.

"Do you mind if we sit over here and talk?" Allen asked him. "We don't want to disturb you."

"Peace, brother."

Allen took that as an assent. He motioned for the girls to join him on the sofa.

"I'm gonna go upstairs and throw something else on," Terri said. "Be back in a minute." She ducked into a hallway and could be heard bounding up a set of stairs.

Paige sat on the sofa. Allen joined her.

"Tell me about Chicago," he said. "What happened after we got separated?"

"You mean you don't know?" Paige said. "Didn't you hook up with Del again?"

Allen shook his head. "I haven't seen Del since that day in the park when we left him."

"What about your van?"

Allen chuckled. "I haven't seen it, either."

"Then ..."

"How did I get home?" He stuck out his thumb to indicate he'd hitchhiked. "What about you?" he asked. "Surely you hooked up with Del again."

Paige told him the whole story. How Del had saved them, but only by stealing the van. How he spiked Natalie's drink and then deserted them. The news of Natalie's death shook him.

"Oh, Paige, I'm so sorry," Allen said. "I'm afraid I let you and Natalie down terribly."

"Let us down? What more could you do? The last we saw you, you were getting the stuffing knocked out of you."

"I should never have taken you to Chicago with that lunatic," Allen said. "My head was messed up. I just wasn't thinking straight."

Terri bounced into the room wearing an extra large white T-shirt over her swimsuit. It came down to her knees. She sat next to Allen on the sofa, close enough to him to give Paige the impression the two of them might be going together.

"What are we talking about?" she asked.

Allen told her about Natalie's death in Chicago. She too expressed a heartfelt loss.

"You and Natalie were best friends, weren't you?" Terri asked.

Paige nodded, tears welling up in her eyes. She got angry with herself. How long was it going to take before she could talk about Natalie without crying?

Allen reached out and placed his hand on hers. He left it there. It was warm, comforting and assuring. Paige glanced at Terri. She didn't seem to mind. When Paige finally succeeded in composing herself, he lifted his hand.

"How did you manage to get home?" he asked.

Paige described how she, too, had been arrested and jailed. And how her father happened to be in Chicago on assignment.

"God was watching over you," Terri said.

"I suppose so," Paige said, still taken aback with religious talk coming out of Terri's mouth.

"So tell me about this place," Paige said. "It reminds me of Shores Drive, only quieter."

Allen smiled. He shook his head. "This is nothing like that. Shores Drive was an attempt to establish a human community based on the value of persons, rather than on what that person did or could produce. But it had a fatal flaw which doomed it to failure."

"A fatal flaw?" Paige asked.

"It's missing love," Terri said, pleased that she knew the answer.

"Not a human love," Allen explained, "but a love that comes from God, the kind of love that we can't produce. It comes from him and flows through us to one another."

Paige smiled. "You've changed, Allen. You're more confident than I've ever seen you before."

"That's because I'm no longer Del Gilroy's parrot. I've found something worth living and dying for."

A passion. Allen had found his own passion. So there was hope for Paige after all.

"And when did all this happen?" Paige asked.

"In a Chicago jail cell. It was there I finally came to myself and turned my life over to Jesus Christ. Before that I'd had people witnessing to me and praying for me—here's one of them right here." He put his arm around Terri and gave her a hug.

Terri the UCRD party girl? The girl who had her arms around a different guy every day? This Terri had become the equivalent of a twentieth-century John the Baptist?

"… but it took the trip to Chicago to finally bring me to the end of my rope. I gave my life to God in a Chicago jail cell."

The front door opened and a couple walked in, arm in arm. They were smiling and carrying Bibles.

"Tonight's Bible study!" Terri said. "I almost forgot." She jumped up and ran up the stairs.

Paige stood. "I really should be going," she said.

"Please stay," Allen said, standing with her.

"I don't want to intrude."

"No intrusion. We have people coming and going all the time. You're more than welcome."

"Well, I don't know …"

Terri appeared again with a Bible. "You're not leaving us, are you, Paige? Please stay."

Three more people walked into the room. Each of them was carrying a Bible.

Paige wanted to stay; she wanted to talk to Allen some more. But she wasn't sure she wanted to sit through a church service just for a few more minutes with him.

"We snatched you off the beach," Allen said. "Someone's expecting you, aren't they?"

"Oh, just my parents."

"You could call them and tell them where you are," Allen offered.

"It's Allen's turn to lead the Bible study tonight," Terri said.

Now that might be something worth staying for, Paige thought. *Allen West turned preacher.*

"OK, I'll stay," she said.

"The phone's in here," Terri said. She guided Paige through a short hallway into the kitchen. The place was spotless, nothing like the kitchen at the house on Shores Drive.

Paige made her phone call with Terri standing beside her. When she was finished, Terry took her by the hand and led her back into the living room like a little girl taking her friend to Sunday school.

Several more had arrived in the short time Paige was on the phone. Some wore leather with fringe, some wore long hair, others short; there were hippies, surfers, and even a couple who looked like they'd stepped out of the television program *Leave It to Beaver.*

Allen sat in an overstuffed chair with an open Bible in his lap. He was looking a bit nervous. Terri led Paige across the room. They had to step over and around several people to get there. She sat at Allen's feet and pulled Paige down to the floor with her.

The door opened and six more people came in. There must have been twenty-five or more in the small living room. Those who came late stood against the walls.

"Let's begin tonight's study with prayer," Allen said. He bowed his head. Everyone else in the room followed his example. "Lord, for your Word, we thank you. As we open it tonight, use it as manna to feed your wandering people in the same way you did so long ago in the wilderness. Amen."

A chorus of amens echoed his. Every face in the room looked at Allen expectantly. Paige couldn't help notice how different these people were from the people at Shores Drive. They looked the same, but that's where any similarity ended. There was an intensity of purpose among them, a quiet earnestness. These people were serious about what they were doing.

A casual glance around the room revealed Bibles that were dog-eared and worn to the point of being floppy. These were Bibles that were read—functional Bibles, not the pristine Bibles with fresh covers and gold edges so often seen at her own church.

"I covet your prayers," Allen began. "I've been an elder for a short time, and when it comes to leading Bible study, I still feel inadequate."

"Trust Jesus, brother," one man said.

"Guide him, Holy Spirit," said another.

"After much prayer," Allen continued, "God has led me to a passage that has come to mean an awful lot to me in my walk with Jesus. I've often wondered why God allows bad things to happen to his people. I mean, after all, if God loves us, and if he's all-powerful, then why does he let his own people go through bad times? Why does he let them suffer? Well, I found something in Second Corinthians that has really opened my eyes. The passage is Second Corinthians, chapter one, beginning with verse three."

As Allen lifted his Bible to read, everyone in the room opened their own Bibles and examined the text with him. Terri shared her Bible with Paige, pointing to the verse with her finger.

Paige thanked her with a smile.

Allen read aloud:

> Blessed be God, even the Father of our Lord Jesus Christ, the Father of mercies, and the God of all comfort; who comforteth us in all our tribulation, that we may be able to comfort them which are in any trouble, by the comfort wherewith we ourselves are comforted of God. For as the sufferings of Christ abound in us, so our consolation also aboundeth by Christ. And whether we be afflicted, it is for your consolation and salvation, which is effectual in the enduring of the same sufferings which we also suffer: or whether we be comforted, it is for your consolation and salvation.

"What has helped me most in these verses is the promise that when we do suffer, God does not abandon us like so many friends on the street. You know how it is. On the street if you have money, you have friends."

There was a mix of laughs and amens.

"If you have drugs, you have friends."

Some more amens.

"But get down on your luck, or get strung out, and nobody wants to have anything to do with you. God's not like that. It's when we're strung out that God is there for us. Just like it says here, he comforts us in our tribulations."

"Praise Jesus!"

"Amen!"

"Now that's good news. But you know how it is. We're not content for God to mother us, to say to us, 'There, there, don't cry. It'll be all right.' We want to know why bad things are happening to us, especially if we've gotten our lives straight and turned them over to Jesus and the bad times just keep rollin' on. Well, here's the answer."

Allen referred to his Bible. He read:

"That we may be able to comfort them which are in any trouble, and farther down, *whether we be afflicted, it is for your consolation and salvation."*

He looked up. "I found my reason!" he said. "If I'm suffering, it's for you. My suffering helps me to help you. And let me tell you, if I can help you by going through a little pain, I'll gladly do it."

Paige thought of Allen in Chicago, how he took the blows of the policemen, giving her and Natalie time to get away. His pain had rescued them.

"And think of the bad trips you've had, the withdrawal pains of coming off drugs. God can use your pain to help others. You can sit down with hippies in the park and say, 'I know what you're going through. I've been there. I know how you feel. And I also know where you're heading. Let me tell you about Jesus. He can help you get your life straight.' You can do that, man, because you've been there. You've suffered. And they'll listen to you. What chance do you think some suit from a downtown high-rise would have with that hippie or drug user? Can't you see? Your suffering can be used to help others!"

A long-haired guy with leather fringe on his coat sleeves raised his hand. "In theory that sounds good. But how do we know this really works? I mean, I took a class on marriage at UCSD, and it was taught by a guy who had never been married in his life. I mean to tell you, he had some pretty strange teachings, and those who were married in the class kept telling him he didn't know what he was talking about. How do we know the guy who wrote this knows what he's talking about?"

A ripple of laughter crossed the room.

Allen raised his hand. "It's a legitimate question," he said. Addressing the questioner directly, he said, "This is a letter written to a church in Corinth, Greece, by the apostle Paul. A little later in the letter, he gives his qualifications to write about such things."

Flipping the pages of his Bible, Allen found the place he was looking for.

"Here it is. Look at chapter eleven, verse twenty-three." He read:

> Are they ministers of Christ? (I speak as a fool) I am more; in labours more abundant, in stripes above measure, in prisons more frequent, in deaths oft. Of the Jews five times received I forty stripes save one. Thrice was I beaten with rods, once was I stoned, thrice I suffered shipwreck, a night and a day I have been in the deep; in journeyings often, in perils of waters, in perils of robbers, in perils by mine own countrymen, in perils by the heathen, in perils in the city, in perils in the wilderness, in perils in the sea, in perils among false brethren; in weariness and painfulness, in watchings often, in hunger and thirst, in fastings often, in cold and nakedness. Beside those things that are without, that which cometh upon me daily, the care of all the churches. Who is weak, and I am not weak? Who is offended, and I burn not?

Allen looked up. "Does that answer your question?"

"Far out, man," came the reply.

And so it went for two hours as Allen led them to examine verses in the Bible and fielded their questions. It was an honest give-and-take as together they searched for answers, trusting that they would find everything they needed in the Bible. Paige had sat through many Sunday-school lessons and sermons before, but never had she seen people as fascinated with the Bible as these people were.

Following the Bible study they had Communion.

The atmosphere was solemn as each person was encouraged to pray individually. Soft mutterings could be heard all over the room.

Paige bowed her head and tried to focus her thoughts on God, but they kept coming back to the startling change in Terri and Allen. She peeked at them through slits of open eyes. Terri was serene and seemed comfortable in prayer. Allen looked at times like he was wrestling.

She also wondered what the relationship was between them. They seemed close, and at times acted like a couple. But then again, they could just be friends. Even close friends at that.

Paige wondered why she wanted to know. She'd never been attracted to Allen before. In Chicago, when he helped them in their ill-fated search for the van, she gained a measure of respect for him. Before that he had only been Del's mouthpiece, his puppet. She'd seen him with a succession of girls, but nothing ever seemed to be serious or to last with any of them. She tried to remember if she'd ever seen him with Terri before, but couldn't remember them being together.

One of the other elders in the commune—the man who had been reading the New Testament when she first arrived—blessed the elements of Communion. The entire ceremony was different from the way Communion was served in Paige's church. First a basket of broken saltine crackers was passed around. A person took the basket, prayed for the person to the right, then placed a cracker in that person's mouth and said, "This is the body of

Christ broken for you," or something similar. The same thing was done with a common cup of grape juice as it was passed from person to person.

Although she was supposed to be praying, Paige couldn't help but watch as Terri served the cracker and the cup to Allen. She looked for some kind of spark between them, something to indicate a hint of romance. What she saw was a genuine love. Not romantic, but that didn't mean romance wasn't an underlying factor.

Then Allen took the basket of crackers and turned toward her. His eyes and voice were soft, warm, brimming with love. Taking a piece of cracker, he held it out to Paige.

As she had seen others do, she opened her mouth. Tenderly, Allen placed the cracker on her tongue. In a rich, soft male tone, he said, "Jesus loves you, Paige. This is his body, broken for you."

As Paige had watched the basket make its way around the room, she had anticipated this moment. She expected to feel nervousness, since only one person at a time in the room received Communion. But she also anticipated feeling some kind of spark between her and Allen. Ever since the beach, she felt like something was developing between them. It might turn out to be nothing, but the possibility was there.

What she felt when Allen gave her the cracker was unlike anything she'd anticipated. She felt Allen's presence, but she felt another presence, too. It was a spiritual moment, unlike any she'd ever had before. It was as though, for an instant, their souls touched and were anointed with a warm, liquid love.

Allen offered her the cup. "Jesus showed you how much he loves you, Paige, by shedding his blood on the cross for you," he said.

As she sipped from the cup, her eyes looked over the rim and met his. Together they floated in a sea of God's love.

Singing followed the Communion service. And although they had broken up the Bible study occasionally with song, the singing now was with deeper emotion. Occasionally, two or three would get up and go to another part of the house to pray. Others lifted their arms and swayed back and forth in adoration as they sang.

No one watched the clock, and it surprised Paige that it was 1:30 a.m. before the Bible study began to break up.

Allen and Terri drove her home. The three of them sat in the front seat, Terri in the middle.

"You're always welcome at the Catacombs," Terri said as Paige climbed out of the car.

"I had a great time," Paige replied. "Thank you for including me."

"Stop by anytime, Paige," Allen said. "I can't begin to tell you how great it was to see you again."

Allen put the car in reverse and pulled out of the Morgan driveway and headed down the street.

In the posh La Jolla suburb at 2:00 a.m., as the car pulled away, Paige could hear Terri shouting, "And remember, Jesus loves yoooooouuuuuuuuuuu!"

28

I thought you were smarter than this," her father said.

"Haven't you learned your lesson?"

Grabbing shirts from his dresser drawer and pants from the closet, he tossed them angrily into a travel bag. Paige stood in the bedroom doorway, her arms folded defensively. Allegra sat on the edge of the double bed.

"All you're doing is trading one drug house for another!"

"The Catacombs is not a drug house! That's one of their strictest rules. No drugs are allowed, period. If anyone tries to bring them or alcohol in, they're asked to leave."

"Of course that's what they're going to tell you," her father said. "If word gets out otherwise, the police would be camped on their doorstep. But, don't forget, I saw what was really going on at that Shores Drive place."

"The Catacombs is nothing like Shores Drive," Paige insisted. "If you would just come and see for yourself, you wouldn't be saying these things."

"Well, that's convenient, isn't it? Seeing that my flight leaves in less than an hour." He zipped up his bag and took one glance around to see if he'd forgotten anything. Convinced he had everything he needed, he slung his camera bag over his shoulder and snatched up his luggage.

"Tell you what," he said. "Delay moving into that place until I get back and then I'll look into it. But I have to tell you, I've heard some strange stories at the *FLASH!* about those religious communes. And I mean strange."

"How long will you be gone? Weeks? Months?" Paige asked.

"Possibly. I don't know."

"I can't wait that long," Paige said. "I wish you would just trust me in this. The people who live there are good people. Spiritual people. When I'm around them, I want to be more like them."

"Sounds like a cult," her father said. "They use peer pressure to get you to join. Then, once you're in, you can't leave. They control you."

Paige sighed. It was useless. She wasn't going to convince him, and he wasn't going to dissuade her. It had been this way between them for years now.

"Have a nice trip, Dad. And I hope you find Travis."

"What about the commune?"

"I'm moving in."

Her father let out an exasperated groan. To Allegra he said, "Will you please talk some sense into your daughter?"

Allegra seemed completely unfazed by the argument.

"I don't know," she said, "from what Paige has told me, it sounds refreshing."

"Great! I'll probably find that you've both moved into the place when I get back."

"If you do, stop by and see us," Allegra said. "I'll put in a good word for you. Maybe they'll let you join."

A horn honked in the driveway.

"That's my taxi," Nat said. He went over to his wife and embraced her without putting down the luggage.

"Please find Travis for me," Allegra whispered.

"I'll do everything I can," Nat replied. To Paige as he walked past her, he said, "Take care of your mother."

"I will," Paige replied. "And trust me on this, Dad. After all, I'm old enough to make my own decisions."

"Seems I've heard that before," Nat said as he raced down the hallway and out the door.

The Catacombs had fifteen residents when Paige moved in: ten men and five women. Allen was one of three elders who made the decisions for the house. Her orientation was left to Terri. Simply put, she said, "We have one rule that is above every other rule in this house. Love others as you want to be loved. It's easier to say than it is to do," she confessed, "especially when you consider that there are fifteen—oops, make that sixteen with you … people living here and only one bathroom."

Their day began about 10:00 a.m. with prayer and Bible study. The remainder of the morning was spent cleaning the house. The elders divided the household duties. For the most part the women did the cooking, sewing, and inside cleaning; the men did the yard work, made repairs, and sometimes held jobs that brought in needed cash.

The furniture was secondhand, and the walls showed signs of needing paint, but the place was clean and relatively comfortable.

The afternoons were spent witnessing on the streets, at shopping centers, or on the beach. This was done daily by the men; the women occasionally joined them. And they always went with a male escort. The women also helped out by caring for children and volunteering to help at local rest homes.

The evenings were spent doing a variety of things: more street witnessing, Bible studies, prayer meetings, neighborhood ministries in private homes, and sometimes coffee shops. Evening events always tended to run late into the night or next morning.

Paige roomed with Terri and another girl named Cindy who used to walk the streets of Pacific Beach to afford her drug habit. That was, until Terri followed her into a bar one night and led her to the Lord.

While the residents of the Catacombs did everything to make Paige feel welcome, it took awhile for her to feel comfortable in the house. It seemed to her that everyone else was so much more spiritual than she was.

She had visited the Catacombs almost daily for two weeks before making the decision to join them. Though she didn't admit as much to her father, it was strictly an emotional decision. She felt happy there.

For the first few days at the house she was disappointed that she didn't get to see Allen more. Then, when it was announced that the women would accompany the men to Balboa Park to hand out tracts, she began working up her courage to ask Allen if she could go with him. The idea of a casual stroll with Allen through the historic arched walkways and gardens, or walking in the sunshine across the grassy expanse with a eucalyptus tree canopy, seemed like a perfect way to spend an afternoon. But it wasn't meant to be.

To her chagrin she learned that the elders did the pairing, and she was placed with the largest man in the house. There was no mistaking why he went by the nickname Moose. Over six feet tall, he was built like a professional wrestler.

When Moose and Paige were dropped off at the Organ Pavilion in the park, they began to wander around and hand out tracts that read "God's Speed Doesn't Kill."

"How well do you know Allen?" Moose asked.

"I've known him for a couple of years. We met at UCRD. He and my former boyfriend organized several demonstrations up there. How about you? How long have you known him?"

Moose looked down at the sidewalk while he figured it out. "I guess about eight weeks now."

"And how long have you lived in the Catacombs?"

He did some figuring again. "Six weeks."

A Japanese couple pushing a stroller came toward them, heading the other direction, tourists, most likely. A 35 mm camera dangled around the man's neck. Moose handed him a tract and said, "Jesus loves you."

Both the man and the woman smiled and bowed as he accepted the tract. Both parties kept walking.

Paige couldn't help herself. She looked over her shoulder. She had to see the couple's reaction. The man was holding the tract open as his wife put her head against his to get a look at it. The man was pointing to something in the tract. He was either reading or explaining it to her in Japanese.

"I wish we had Japanese tracts," Moose said. Then he wondered aloud, "I wonder how long it would take me to learn Japanese."

The image of Moose sitting in a Japanese class struck Paige as amusing, though she stifled any humorous response. On the other hand, it was one of the sweetest, least selfish things she'd ever heard. It reminded her of Allen's Bible study. Moose was willing to suffer the pain of learning Japanese—for she could not imagine him picking it up easily—that others might benefit. People he'd never even met before.

"What did you do before you joined the commune?" Paige asked.

"I was a bouncer at The Pelican Club on Mission Boulevard. Ever been there?"

"No," Paige said.

"Sure? It's a popular spot."

Paige grinned. "I'm sure I would have remembered it if I'd been there."

Moose nodded. "It's really just a hole-in-the-wall bar," he said. "I'm surprised the city hasn't already shut it down with all the drugs that go in and out of that place. But it's a happenin' place."

"So where did you and Allen meet?"

"At the bar."

"Really?"

Moose nodded. "Want to hear the story? It's a good one."

Paige smiled. "Sure."

"Well …" Moose began, clearly pleased that Paige consented to hear his story, "… Allen and some other guys from the house used to park themselves in front of the bar and hand out tracts. It really cut into business, and that used to tick off the owner. The owner would go out there and curse at Allen and shove him and spill beer on him, anything to get him to go away. But Allen kept coming back. The owner even called the cops on him one night. But the cops couldn't do anything since Allen stayed on the public sidewalk.

"So anyway, the owner was mad as—well, let's just say he was mad as anything. So he called me into his back room one night and offered me a hundred bucks to discourage Allen from coming back again. You know, discreet like."

"You beat Allen up?" Paige asked.

"It's not something I'm proud of," Moose said. "Anyway, me and this other guy took Allen into an alley and roughed him up pretty good. And just as we were finishing the job, the cops cruised by and shined their light on us. Well, we were busted."

"And that's how you and Allen met?"

"There's more," Moose said. "I haven't told you the good part yet. Next day we were sittin' in jail and this cop comes and tells us that someone has posted bail for us. I figure it's the owner of the bar. Wrong! Guess who it was?"

"Allen?"

"Yep. Can you believe that? Right after we roughed up the guy! Well, you know, you never hear of guys doin' things like that. It hit me real hard."

"I imagine it would."

"Anyway, we're walkin' out of the police station and he shows me this tract. I take it and we sit down right there on the steps of the police station and he tells me that it wasn't him lovin' me, but Jesus lovin' me through him. Can you beat that? So I prayed the prayer right there on those steps. How many other people do you know who were saved on the steps of the police station?"

"Not many," Paige said.

❖

"The other elders have asked me to talk to you," Allen said.

"Have I done something wrong?"

It was late afternoon on a Friday. Allen had pulled Paige out of the kitchen where she'd been cutting lettuce and vegetables for the evening meal. They sat opposite one another on the sofa.

Allen laughed softly. "Of course you haven't done anything wrong," he said. "Everyone is pleased with the way you have fit in so quickly. You do your work. You are kind to others. And you seem to want to be here."

"But …"

"But, we don't know why you're here," Allen said. "And, if we're reading you correctly, you don't know why you're here, either."

How could they have known that? Was it so obvious?

"Isn't it enough just to want to be here?" Paige asked.

"Wanting to be here is a wonderful first step, Paige. But it's not a final destination. You have to move beyond that. You see, God has given each of us gifts and talents to use in service to him. It's our gifts that give us purpose."

Purpose, direction, a passion for something—hadn't she just had this conversation with her mother a few weeks ago?

"Paige, I recognize the signs because I was just like you. My identity was always tied up with someone or something else. You know what it was like at Shores Drive. I was nothing more than Del Gilroy's alter ego. It was his dream that we followed. I was just along for the ride.

"And, I have to confess, at least at first I enjoyed it. It gave me a high being in front of thousands of people, getting them excited, telling them what to do and then seeing them do it, having my picture in the newspapers, looking like a leader with a cause. But I had no cause other than to do what Del told me to do. In a way it was almost like demon possession. I wasn't in control of my body or brain. Del was. Instead of selling my soul to the devil, I sold it to Del. And look where it got me—a Chicago jail."

Allen wasn't telling her anything she didn't already know. But she found it fascinating that he knew what was happening when it was happening. She'd written him off as a mindless dupe. Come to find out, he wasn't mindless.

"And you were just like me, Paige," he said. "You're a chameleon. You change yourself to blend in with whoever you're with. When you were with Del, you adopted Del's passions. When you were with Natalie, you were like Natalie. And our fear is that being here, you will simply do what you've always done and blend in."

"Is that so bad?" Paige asked.

Allen smiled warmly. "Not bad, just wrong."

Her emotions began to rise. With all her might, she fought them back. She didn't want to cry. Not here, not now. Everything was going so well.

"Paige, I know this hurts …"

So much for hiding my emotions, she thought.

"… but it's a necessary step for you. God has something won- derful in store for you. But only you can find out what that is. You're a strong woman, Paige. God wants to use that strength for good."

The tears came. "I—I don't know where to begin," she said. "I'm not even sure I know who Paige Morgan is."

"The important thing is that God knows who you are. More importantly, he loves who you are. He'll help you find yourself, Paige, if you'll only let him."

"I want to let him," Paige said. "But where do I start looking?"

"Let me ask you this: Have you ever given your heart com- pletely to Jesus?"

Paige nodded. "I think so. When I was little. At our church. At least I think I gave my heart to him as much as I was able at the time."

"Were you baptized?"

"Yes."

Allen smiled. "That's good. One of God's greatest promises is that he will complete the work he started in you years ago."

"Well, it's not been *that* many years ago," Paige laughed.

Allen reached for a Bible on the end table next to the sofa. Paige recognized it as his Bible. Apparently, he'd placed it there in preparation for their talk. He flipped the pages of the Bible until he found the place he was looking for.

"Start here," he said. "Read these verses …" he pointed to them with his finger, "… and ask yourself these questions. Ask them as if God is speaking directly to you."

Paige took the Bible and looked at the verses. Allen stood.

"You're going to leave me?"

"It's something you have to do for yourself, Paige. I may be leaving you, but you're not alone."

Paige took his statement to mean that God would be with her.

"The elders are up in my room praying for you. I'm going up there right now to join them."

"They're praying for me? Right now?"

Allen smiled. "This conversation is far too important to have without undergirding it with prayer," he said. "And Terri is up in your room. She's praying for you, too."

"Terri's praying for me?"

Paige was overwhelmed. So many people pulling for her at one time, wanting for her the very thing she wanted for herself— to find some direction in her life.

Allen left her and went upstairs.

Paige looked down at the open Bible in her lap. She read the first verse Allen pointed to:

> Jesus said to Simon Peter, "Simon son of John, do you truly love me more than these?" "Yes, Lord," he said, "You know that I love you." Jesus said, "Feed my lambs."

"All right," Paige muttered, "ask the questions as though God is speaking to you directly. OK. Paige Morgan, do you truly love me more than these?"

She looked up.

"Do I love God? Sure I do." She looked down and read: "Feed my lambs. Feed my lambs?"

She went on to the next verse.

> Again Jesus said, "Simon son of John, do you truly love me?" He answered, "Yes, Lord, You know that I love you." Jesus said, "Take care of my sheep."

"Again?" Paige said aloud. "All right ... Paige Morgan, do you truly love me? Why would he ask me a second time, unless he thought I didn't mean it the first time? OK, Lord, I love you. All right?"

> Take care of my sheep.

"Take care of my sheep?"

She moved on to the next verse. When she saw it, she said, "Not again!"

> The third time he said to him, "Simon son of John, do you love me?" Peter was hurt because Jesus asked him the third time, "Do you love me?" He said, "Lord, you know all things; you know that I love you." Jesus said, "Feed my sheep."

"This is getting a little ridiculous. Three times the same question; three times the same answer. All right, God, if that's what you want. 'Paige Morgan, do you love me?'"

While the question was asked glibly, this time the answer was not immediately forthcoming, glibly or not.

"Paige Morgan, do you love me? Do you love me?"

"Yes, Lord."

"Do you?

"Yes."

"Do you?"

"Yes! Yes! Yes! What must I do to convince you?"

"Feed my sheep."

"What?"

"Feed my sheep."

"Lord, I don't understand."

"Feed my sheep."

"Sheep ... sheep. Sheep have a shepherd. A shepherd looks after the sheep. Cares for them. That's the shepherd's job. Feed my sheep. My sheep. God is the shepherd. They're his sheep. God wants me to feed them. But isn't that the shepherd's job? But he wants me to do it. He wants me to do his work, the work of the shepherd. To take care of his sheep ... sheep ... because they can't take care of themselves! Jesus wants me to take care of those who can't take care of themselves!

"But God, how can I? I can't even take care of myself!"

"Do you love me?"

"Yes, Lord, you know I do."

"Do you love me?"

"Yes, but—"

"Do you love me?"

Paige was weeping freely now. "I get it, God. I get it."

※

She ascended the stairs and went straight to her room. There she found Terri clad in blue jeans and a T-shirt. She was kneeling beside her bed. Praying and weeping. In the short interval that Paige stood in the doorway unnoticed, she heard Terri utter her name several times.

Paige announced her presence by shuffling her feet.

Terri looked up, expectantly.

"I'm supposed to feed his sheep," Paige said.

A wide grin broke out on Terri's face as she jumped up from beside the bed and ran with open arms to Paige.

As they hugged, Paige said, "This is the second time you've saved me."

Terri pulled away just enough to look Paige in the eyes. She was puzzled.

"The first time," Paige explained, "was in the UCRD parking lot when you lit into that salesman who was mauling me. The second time was on the beach, the night you brought me here."

Terri grinned. She took quick swipes at the tears on her cheeks. "Well, I'll admit that I beat the daylights out of that masher," she said. "But it was Jesus who saved you a second time."

"Through you, Terri. He did it through you. And I will be forever grateful."

29

Keith Rawlins was surprised to see him. Shocked was more like it.

"Mr. Morgan! What are you doing here?"

He hurriedly put out his cigarette and tried to slide a pint of whiskey under his bunk before Nat saw it.

"The magazine sent me here to do a story on MIAs. They figured I would do a good job since I have a vested interest in the subject."

Keith straightened his fatigues and extended his hand. Nat shook it. The boy's hand was surprisingly chilled considering it was a sweltering day.

"I'm sure sorry about what happened to Travis," Keith said. "You know, I feel responsible. I mean, you and everyone at the church were sorta counting on me to look after him and all that … I mean, after the way Paige and I dated and the way we were almost family … 'cause, you know, I always considered Travis my little brother, and you're supposed to take care of little brothers. It's expected of you."

"I understand you're short," Nat said.

"Yes, sir, I go home in a week. And, to tell you the truth, sir, it's coming none too soon. I just want to get out of this place and go home."

"I know the feeling," Nat said.

"Yes, you would, sir. You being in the war … the big one, and all that."

Nat extended his hand. Keith glanced at it questioningly at first, but shook it nonetheless. His hand was colder than the first handshake.

"Well, I'll not keep you," Nat said. "Just thought I'd stop by since I was in the area. Say hello to your parents for me when you get home. Can't say for sure when I'll be home, but when I get there, I'm sure I'll see you at church."

"Um … yes, sir. You can count on that."

Nat turned and began to walk away.

"Uh … sir? Mr. Morgan?"

"Yes?"

"You know, I just had a thought. Um, maybe I can pull some strings and, you know, sort of be your guide while you're here. Show you the village where we lost Travis, that sort of thing."

"Thanks, but no thanks," Nat said. "You're short, and this may take longer than a week. I'll get someone else from the squad."

"I really don't mind doing it, sir. We might even be able to wrap things up in a week's time if I help you."

Nat turned and walked away. He waved. Over his shoulder, he said, "Thanks anyway, but I wouldn't know how to face your parents if anything were to happen to you the last week you were here. You just get home safely, OK?"

He quickened his pace to indicate to Keith that the conversation was concluded.

The chopper blades thwacked loudly overhead, making it difficult to talk.

"Down there, sir!"

Nat leaned out the doors and looked at the village below. The harness across his chest tightened with his weight. Beside him, also strapped in, was a corporal who was a member of Keith's squad the day Travis was reported missing. It was he who pointed out the village. Beside him was the chopper's gunner, ready to defend the craft should the VC decide to take potshots at them. While the helicopters often flew low and slow, hovering over jungle area was decidedly more dangerous. This was evident by the way the gunner's eyes shifted nervously as he squinted at the jungle below, looking for any sign of trouble.

Nat had little trouble talking his editor into giving him the assignment. In fact he jumped at the angle: A father and veteran of World War II goes on a personal search for his son who is MIA in Vietnam.

"Are you sure that's the village?" Nat shouted.

"Positive, sir!" the corporal shouted back.

Below them was an active Vietnamese village with close to a dozen huts. People could be seen working in the gardens, milking goats, going about their daily chores. Children chased the chickens in the open area. At the sound of the chopper, they all stopped what they were doing and looked up. Mothers rushed to their children and pulled them inside the huts.

CLICK! CLICK!

Nat took several pictures of the village.

CLICK!

He leaned back inside the chopper and shouted to the copilot, "What are our coordinates?"

The copilot checked his instruments and charts. He shouted their present position back to Nat.

Reaching inside his camera bag, Nat pulled out a notepad. He wrote down the coordinates the copilot had just given him.

Then he leaned close to the corporal again. "You'll have to forgive me," he shouted. "I'm a father who's trying to find his lost son. So I need to ask you one more time. You're positive this is the village where Travis disappeared?"

The corporal nodded. "Positive, sir!" he shouted.

Nat flipped the page of his notebook, which flapped erratically in the wind of the chopper blades. "Then tell me soldier, how do you account for this?"

Nat showed him the page. On it was written a set of coordinates.

"What are those?" the corporal asked.

"These are the coordinates to which your squad was sent on the day my son vanished."

The corporal shook his head. "Where did you get those, sir?"

"HQ."

"You must have written them down wrong, sir."

"No, this is what they gave me. We could have the pilot radio back and doublecheck."

"Sir, after the mission, our squad leader reported back to the platoon leader the coordinates of the village so that a rescue could be launched to find your son. If you'll check the record—"

"I already checked that record, son," Nat said.

"And the coordinates?"

"They match exactly the coordinates the copilot just gave me."

The corporal nodded as though vindicated.

"But you weren't sent to those coordinates," Nat said. He held up his pad. "These are the coordinates you were sent to. Are you telling me that your squad mistakenly went to the wrong village?"

The corporal's eyes widened nervously. "Sir, if you'll read our squad leader's report—"

"I've already done that, son," Nat said. "It said nothing of going to the wrong village."

"Sir, I'm sure that—"

Nat stopped listening. Turning to the copilot, he handed him the page from his notepad. "Take us there," he shouted.

The copilot gave him a thumbs-up sign. Within seconds, the deck of the chopper tilted radically as the pilot changed course.

Nat closed his eyes and groaned, thinking for sure he'd just left his stomach back at the village below. *Now I know why the army uses young men,* he moaned.

N

"Mum-mum-mum-mum-mum ..."

Travis rocked back and forth, uttering the nonsense sound over and over. It was the only comfort he had.

It was dark. Pitch dark. And damp. And cold. All the elements of which his nightmares were made. But it was the nightmare that had saved him and the baby. He'd had to choose, nightmare or death. Sometimes he wondered if he'd made the right choice.

Knowing that he couldn't outrun his pursuers carrying a baby, he had to find a way to disappear. That was when the ground called to him. It didn't open up and swallow him as it did before, but his experience living underground seemed to have taught him how to communicate with it, or it with him. Things weren't very clear to him right now.

All he knew was that he saw the opening in the ground. It was his only hope of survival. He'd shuddered at the very thought of going underground again. Chills swept over him. He began to babble incoherently, so strongly did he not want to go into the ground again.

"Mum-mum-mum-mum-mum ..."

He did it to save the baby. He'd looked over his shoulder. No one was in his line of sight. He saw the hole and skidded toward it like he was sliding into second base, all the while holding the infant against his chest. Then—despite the chills, despite the anxiety, despite the fact that his chest and throat were constricting—he slithered down the hole like a snake.

It was dark.

Miraculously, the baby didn't cry.

And the others didn't see the hole.

They ran right by it.

Travis and the infant had been living in the ground ever since.

"Mum-mum-mum-mum-mum ..."

He didn't know whether it was safer to come out during the day or at night. U.S. squads roamed the jungle by day; the VC by night. Whether to be shot as a deserter or an enemy made little difference. Shot was shot. Dead was dead.

"Mum-mum-mum-mum-mum ..."

He raided the villages for food. Vegetables from the gardens mainly. He stole a goat from one village and tied it up nearby to provide milk for the baby. When it disappeared, he stole another.

"Mum-mum-mum-mum-mum ..."

This cave was not nearly as large as the one that had entombed Gower and him. Nor did this one have any supplies in it. It wasn't even large enough for him to straighten himself. He was curled up like a baby whenever he was in the cave, which was most of the time.

"Mum-mum-mum-mum-mum ..."

He lived in constant fear. Fear of the dark inside the cave. Fear of being shot or captured outside the cave. Fear that when he left the cave to get food and milk that he would be killed and that the baby would die alone in the cold dark underground room; fear that when he was in the cave with the baby, the infant would cry at the wrong time, when the VC were walking past, and that someone would lob a grenade in with them, or stick the muzzle of an AK-47 or an M-16 into the hole and start blasting away.

But his greatest fear was that he would escape detection altogether and that the war would end and that he and this little infant would live and die in the jungle and no one would ever find them and that no one would ever mourn their deaths when they both grew old and died.

"Mum-mum-mum-mum-mum ..."

Travis felt for the baby. She was sleeping now. He could sense rhythmic breathing simply by placing a hand on the baby's chest. When she woke up, she'd be hungry. He grabbed a shallow bowl he'd stolen and which he'd used to feed the baby. He would tilt the milk until it was just at the edge, then place the edge against the baby's lips. She took it from there.

As he had done hundreds of times before, Travis moved toward the opening, slowly, listening, moving, listening, moving, until finally he poked his head out. Every time he did this, he fully expected it to be whacked off. But it wasn't. Not this time at least. His head swiveled every which way. He could see no one. Nothing stirred.

Cautiously, he crawled out of the cave. The goat was tied up about a hundred yards distant, with enough jungle between it and them that he figured it would take an entire platoon three or four days to find them should they put two and two together and conclude that someone was living nearby.

He was halfway to the goat when he heard the chopper blades. The chopper came in fast and low.

On stiff legs, cold and cramped from the cave, Travis sprinted for the hole. He had to disappear. Quickly.

He could see the chopper through the trees. The muzzle of the machine gun in the door stuck out like a bee's stinger.

Travis's legs and back screamed with pain. They began to cramp up on him. He continued running.

The chopper kept coming.

Had they found him?

He dived for the hole and overshot it. Scrambling on his hands and knees, he crawled inside. His sudden movement startled the baby. She screamed at the top of her lungs. Travis hoped the thwacking of the chopper's blades and the roar of its engine were sufficient to cover the sound.

Unless it inserted a squad and then took off. Then they'd hear the baby for sure.

He held the baby in his arms and rocked back and forth and listened to the chopper overhead.

"Mum-mum-mum-mum-mum …"

"Did you see that?" Nat shouted.

"See what?" the corporal shouted back.

"Down there!" He pointed to a thin patch of trees. "I thought I saw something move." To the gunner: "Did you see it?"

The gunner shook his head. But his attention was focused there now. Squinting eyes were zeroed in on that area. So was the machine gun's sights.

"I guess it was nothing," Nat said.

At his direction the chopper hovered over a clearing that was black and charred. "These are the coordinates?" Nat shouted.

The copilot gave him a thumbs-up sign.

Like before, Nat leaned out the door and shot several pictures. "Set it down!" Nat shouted.

"Sorry, can't do that, sir," the copilot shouted back.

"I've been given authority to do whatever is needed to complete my assignment," he shouted back.

The copilot relayed this to the pilot. The two of them engaged in an animated discussion that Nat couldn't hear.

Finally, the copilot shouted, "It wouldn't be advisable, sir."

Nat looked out the door. He turned back to the copilot. Motioning with his index finger, Nat shouted, "Set it down!"

The copilot looked hard at him. Clearly he didn't want to relay this to the pilot. The corporal's eyes were wide as saucers. The gunner was no longer squinting. He too was wide-eyed.

With no verbal response from the copilot, the chopper began to descend. The gunner's head was on a swivel. He was looking as many different directions as quickly as he could. The gun was ready. So was he.

When the skids hit the ground, Nat released the catches on his harness. He punched the corporal in the side. "You're with me!" he shouted.

Before anyone could stop him, Nat jumped out of the chopper. He ran a short distance in a crouched position until he was no longer under the blades. The corporal was right behind him, clearly an unwilling tagalong.

Nat sifted around the burned areas. From the patterns on the ground, it was clear these had once been huts. Moreover, with just the tip of his shoe, he overturned utensils and bowls and other household items.

He walked a distance to the edge of the burn area. He pulled up short and closed his eyes. What he saw turned his stomach.

Human remains stuck out of the ground. Arms. Legs. Apparently, they'd been uncovered by wild animals, for they were chewed.

Nat took pictures.

Beside him, the corporal stared in horror. His face was pale.

Nat turned on him. "Care to revise your story, corporal?"

Inside the cave Travis heard the chopper land. He apologized to the wailing baby for not doing a better job protecting her from harm.

He waited and stared at the hole leading to the upper world, knowing that any moment death would poke its head in and claim them both.

Then, the whine of the chopper's engines grew louder. It took off and, after a time, could be heard no more.

He waited.

Death didn't arrive as scheduled.

The jungle grew dark. The cave even darker.

"Mum-mum-mum-mum-mum ..."

※

The real story came out. The corporal who had accompanied Nat Morgan led a host of eager witnesses. Keith Rawlins was arrested and charged with war crimes.

"I want to go back there!" Nat shouted. "My son is out there someplace!"

The major who sat behind the desk was reluctant to let him go. He feared that evidence might be disturbed, as well as the additional danger to Nat and the chopper crew. He rubbed his bald freckled forehead in contemplation.

"If he's still alive, he's probably nowhere near there," the major objected.

"But I saw something move, just before we set down," Nat argued.

"Probably an animal. Worse yet, a VC. It's too risky."

"What if I promise we won't set the chopper down this time? We'll just fly around the area. Check it out. If nothing's there, we'll come straight back."

The major was shaking his head. But he didn't say no. That's when Nat knew he'd convinced him.

The next morning Nat climbed aboard the Huey chopper. It was the same one he'd had before, with the same crew.

The copilot turned from his preflight checklist long enough to say, "You're not going to have us set down in the middle of Hanoi, are you, sir?"

※

It was a rare day. The sun was bright and warm. It poured through the opening of the hole like liquid spring. Travis knew the pull such a sunny day has on lizards and snakes, making them leave the safety of their hiding places to sun themselves on rocks, for he felt it himself.

Just for a few minutes, he told himself. *The baby needs it; I need it.*

Still, a holiday in the jungle would not be taken without caution. He went through his usual routine to make sure the area was clear, and he lifted the baby out of the hole and placed her on the earth side of the rim. Then he crawled out after her.

With the infant in his arms, he leaned against a tree, feeling the glorious warmth of the sun from both sides—from the sun itself, and from the tree that had been warmed by its rays.

He stretched his cramped legs. And for the first time in weeks, he was able to work the cramps out, thanks to the combination of sun and exercise. The baby, too, enjoyed the sun and the air. She was fascinated by the movement of the leaves overhead, moving with the breeze, playing hide-and-seek with the sunlight.

The chopper came in low and fast, just like before only more quickly this time. It caught him off guard. The things were so loud, why hadn't he heard it sooner? He had no other explanation than he'd not been paying attention. The sun had lulled his senses, and may very well have been the death of them both.

It swooped down on him, between him and the hole; it was as though it knew exactly which way to approach, like a predator lying in wait until its victim is just out of reach of safety.

He began running. Down the small dirt path that he'd followed during his foraging excursions.

The chopper followed.

Sliding down a ravine, he splashed across a stream and up the other side. The chopper passed overhead. He looked up and saw its stinger protruding from the side.

His only hope was a field of tall elephant grass on the other side of the stream. If he could get there, he could possibly escape the blasted thing. Entire platoons could hide in a field of elephant grass if the field was large enough. And this was a large field. It would be like looking for a needle in a haystack.

With his lungs bursting from the exertion and his joints burning and threatening to quit on him, he renewed his effort. He had to make it to the grass.

Then his luck changed. For some reason the chopper rose up and away. They had a chance!

"Someone's looking over us, little one," he said.

Clearing the far side of the ravine, Travis stumbled downhill a short distance and ran into the elephant grass. He glanced over his shoulder. The chopper had yet to clear the trees. They couldn't see him!

He took a sharp right turn, ran a dozen feet or so, and fell into the grass. It was high enough to cover them completely. And the field was large. Very large. He'd done it! Let them search all they wanted. They'd never find him now.

Clutching the infant against his chest, Travis said, "We did it!"

The roar of the chopper cleared the trees. Travis huffed and puffed, but inside he was breathing easy. All he had to do now was to wait for the crew to get low on fuel. Out here in the open, he could hear a chopper miles away. He'd know when they were gone, and then, he'd return to the hole.

The chopper hovered nearby.

It would do them no good.

The sound of the thwacking blades got louder and louder.

Travis was unconcerned.

Louder still. He could feel the wind from the blades.

The wind from the blades!

Travis's heart leaped into his throat. He looked up. The wind from the blades was combing through the grass, parting it as cleanly as God parted the Red Sea.

The wind rose. The grasses parted. The infant in his arms began screaming.

He was helpless. Caught. Travis found himself looking up at the huge metal monster overhead. His captors looked down at him. The pilot. The gunner who operated the stinger. And one other man who was leaning out the open doors.

No, it can't be! Travis thought.

※

From above Nat looked down. There, with elephant grass swirling all around him like an exotic underwater scene, was his son, curled up in a fetal position, protecting a Vietnamese baby.

"I found him, Allegra," Nat said. "I found our son."

30

It was the first time in ages they would all be together. Allegra had set out the family china and crystal, normally reserved for Christmas dinner and anniversaries. But reunions were special occasions, too. Especially this one.

Church had been anything but worshipful this morning, which had soured the mood of Travis's homecoming; and Paige hadn't helped by telling her father she was too busy doing the Lord's work at a rest home to attend church with the family on Travis's first Sunday back. But at least she agreed to join them for Sunday dinner. Allegra expected to hear her come through the door any minute now.

She'd fixed the traditional Sunday dinner for the family, hoping that would spark a bit of nostalgia. Actually it was one of two Sunday dinners. The Morgan tradition alternated between pot roast and meat loaf. What they didn't have one Sunday, they had the next. This being a special occasion, Allegra had opted for the pot roast.

Allegra filled four glass tumblers with ice cubes. She poured tea in each glass, using her index finger held over the edge of the glass as a guide to know when the glass was full.

Nat breezed into the kitchen. "Can you help me with the gravy, dear?" Allegra asked him.

She heard muttering, then a drawer open and metal utensils clanging against each other. Good. She could put up with the muttering as long as he fixed the gravy.

"Where's Travis?" she asked.

"In his room."

"He's not changing out of his suit, is he? Not until after dinner. I want this dinner to be special."

"You told him three times on the way home from church. He's a grown man now. I'm sure he got the hint."

Allegra laughed. "Sorry, dear. Once a mother, always a mother, I guess. You still have your suit on, don't you?"

Nat didn't reply.

"Nat?"

"What?"

"You still have your suit on, don't you?"

"Of course I do. I follow orders with the best of them."

She heard him stirring the gravy on top of the stove. She felt the dial on the timer. The roast would be done in five minutes. What was keeping Paige?

Nat was muttering again. If Allegra was any judge of her husband's moods, she knew he was going to spout any moment now.

"Can you believe Abner and Elsie? Of all the nerve! You think you know people … in my wildest dreams, I never imagined they would turn on us that way."

"Honey, the Rawlinses are hurt. They're just defending their son."

"By attacking my son!" Nat declared. "Keith Rawlins is being court-martialed for what he did in that village. He's reaping the consequences of his actions, nothing more. If anything, we should be angry with *them!* It was their son who shot at our son and drove him into the jungle! But no, they accuse Travis of turning on Keith and blame him for ruining their son's record!"

"Calm down, Nat."

"Calm down? How can I when half the church believes what they're saying?"

"I doubt if half the church shares their belief."

"Enough do. How can they be so blind to the facts?"

"They like Keith. They've loved and supported him for years. It's hard for them to believe the changes that can come over a person in a place like Vietnam. And they don't want to admit that one of their choicest young men became corrupted."

"Well, you would have at least thought that Pastor Lamar would have set the record straight from the pulpit."

"I sympathize with our pastor. He's in a difficult position. How do you love and support two church families who are at odds with each other without making one or both of them angry?"

"You do it by siding with the truth, that's how," Nat said. "And how come you're so calm about this? He's your son, too. Where's that motherly protective instinct? Aren't you angry about what happened at church today?"

"I choose not to be angry today," Allegra said with a smile. "I want today to be a festive reunion for our family. I'll be angry tomorrow."

She heard Nat laugh. From the sound of the laugh, he was coming closer. The next moment she felt his arms encircle her waist. "You've always been the calm, cool, and collected one, haven't you?"

"Watch it, mister. Don't start something you don't have time to finish."

The front door opened and closed. A second later Paige came into the kitchen.

"Hello, Mom, Dad."

"Paige, didn't your mother tell you to wear your Sunday clothes?"

"These are my Sunday clothes," Paige said.

"She's wearing a blouse and vest with blue jeans," Nat said.

Disappointment crept into Allegra's mind. She pushed it aside. "I'm sure she looks lovely," she said. "It's just good to have all the children home." She stuck out her arms. A moment later she felt Paige's arms around her as the two women hugged.

"Where's that brother of mine?" Paige said.

"Here I am."

His voice was deep. Allegra had yet to get used to it.

"My, my, my, look at you!" Paige declared.

From Paige's reaction Allegra wondered if Travis had changed into his dress uniform for the occasion.

Nat burst her bubble when he whispered to her, "Three times, huh? He's wearing trunks, a T-shirt, and is barefooted."

The disappointment she had shoved aside came back and brought its twin. They stayed a little longer than the first time, but again, Allegra pushed them aside. She was not going to let a little thing like clothes ruin this meal.

"Oh, it's good to see you!" Paige said.

From the sound of Paige's voice, she was giving her brother a good squeeze.

Allegra had never been bitter about her blindness. But there were a few times in life when she felt cheated. Those times usually involved the children. She never got to see their first step. She never got to see the expressions on their faces when they opened their Christmas gifts. And she would never get to look her children in the eyes and tell them how much she loved them. And she would have given almost anything at this moment to be able to see brother and sister hugging.

"Is that pot roast I smell?" Paige said. "Now I know it's Sunday and I'm at home. Brings back memories, doesn't it, Travis?"

"Yes," he said flatly.

"Listen up," Allegra said. "If everyone lends a hand, we can have this show on the road in no time. Travis, you get the glasses of tea. Nat, you carve the roast. I'll get the vegetables. And Paige, there are some dinner rolls warming in the oven."

Allegra luxuriated in the sound of drawers opening, ice cubes clinking in the glasses, and the oven door banging shut. Most days, recently, the only sounds in the kitchen were the ones she made. This was a kitchen symphony. It meant her family was home.

She had been planning this dinner since the day Nat called her and told her that Travis had been found. This gathering was to be more than a meal. She planned it to be a part of three centuries of Morgan tradition.

As everyone took their places at the table, she walked by a side table and felt for the Morgan family Bible. It was still where she'd put it. This was the Bible Drew Morgan brought with him from England when he landed on the shores of the New World in 1630. Having established himself in the land, it was his desire that there would never be a generation of Morgans who did not know Jesus Christ as Savior. To see to this, he began a tradition based upon this very Bible.

In the front cover he wrote his name and a Bible reference that had particular meaning in his life. For Drew Morgan it was Zechariah 4:6.

> This is the word of the Lord ... "Not by might, nor by power, but by my spirit," saith the LORD of hosts.

Following his name was his son's name, and his son's name after that. Allegra knew them by heart:

> Christopher Morgan, 1654, Matthew 28:19
>
> Philip Morgan, 1729, Philippians 2:3–4
>
> Jared Morgan, 1741, John 15:13

Jacob Morgan, Esau's brother, 1786, 1 John 2:10

Seth Morgan, 1804, 2 Timothy 2:15

Jeremiah Morgan, 1833, Hebrews 4:1

Benjamin McKenna Morgan, 1865, Romans 8:28

Jesse Morgan, 1892, Genesis 50:20

Johnny Morgan, 1918, Mark 10:43–45

Nathaniel Morgan, 1945, Matthew 24:12–13

Ten generations of Morgans were represented with this Bible. The book itself had been lost for a time and found among the Narragansett Indians; it had crossed the heart of the country in the days of the pioneers; and it had flown over Hitler's Germany in a B-52 bomber where it intercepted a shard of flak that would have otherwise killed Nat's brother, Walt. It embodied a spiritual tradition upon which this family was built, and Allegra was going to use this reunion to remind them of their rich heritage.

"Nat, will you please ask the blessing?" Allegra asked.

There was a moment of silence, after which Nat began, "Our precious Lord and Father, for this bounty you have placed before us, we are grateful. Bless it—"

The doorbell rang.

Nat paused.

"We can answer the door after the prayer," Allegra said.

Nat continued. "Bless it and our family according to thy will. And, on this occasion—"

The bell rang again. This time the pause was momentary.

"… on this occasion we wish to express our gratitude for thy loving-kindness in reuniting our family. In Jesus' name we pray. Amen."

The doorbell rang again.

"I'll get it," Paige said. She was up and out of her seat.

"Tell whoever it is that we're eating," Allegra called to her.

The dishes clanked as Nat helped himself to the pot roast. But everyone's ears were tuned in the direction of the door.

"Del! What are you doing here?"

Nat put the platter of roast down without taking any.

They could hear the sound of two voices mumbling but couldn't make out what was being said. A few moments later Paige returned to the table. She did not take her seat.

"Del's at the door," she said. "He says he needs to talk to me. I invited him to join us, but he can't."

"Good," Nat said.

"I'm terribly sorry, but he's just passing through town and he doesn't have long. Mom, Dad, I feel I have to talk to him. I'll explain why later. But please excuse me. Travis, it's so good to see you. We'll talk later, OK?"

She hurried out of the room. A moment later the family heard the door shut.

At the head of the table Nat let out a frustrated grunt.

The telephone rang.

"I'll get it," he said.

Pushing his chair back, he left the table. His voice could be heard answering the phone.

"Hello? Ed! Thanks for returning my call, but I'm afraid it's not a good time … uh-huh … uh-huh … is there any way I can reach you there? … No, I understand. Hold on a minute."

Nat returned to the table but did not sit down.

"Honey, it's my editor. He's getting back to me on that story idea, and he's flying to Martha's Vineyard in about ten minutes. Actually he's calling me from the airport. Sorry, but I've got to take this call. I'll pick it up in the study."

He left the room.

Allegra sighed.

"Looks like it's just you and me, son. You've been awfully quiet."

Her comment was greeted by silence, then, "Sorry, Mom, I just can't do this. I can't explain it, but I've got to get out of here. I'm going to the beach to try to clear my head."

There was the scrape of a chair and the sound of the front door closing again, and Allegra sat all alone.

She tried not to cry, but her tears were determined to make an appearance.

31

It wasn't working.

The waves. The sound of the gulls. The feel of the sand under-foot. The sky blue canopy overhead. The sound of people having fun. The setting sun.

It don't mean nothin'.

The magic wasn't there. It used to be that Travis wanted to live on the beach. He felt a part of it, and it of him, like he had salt-water in his veins and sand was a natural covering.

Give it time.

But time was running out. The sun was setting. It would be dark soon. Dark.

He could feel the panic begin to rise. It was foolish of him to have walked to the beach and stayed this late. It would be dark soon. And dark meant hearing Gower's moans; it meant listening for approaching death, trapped alive in a grave, curled up for days in a fetal position.

"Mum-mum-mum-mum-mum."

Stop it!

Travis got up. Stretched as casually as he could. If the beach had been synonymous to life for Travis, sunsets had been the equivalent of nirvana. There was no better place or time to be.

Travis drank in the brilliant orange glow as the sun dipped into the liquid blue horizon. He felt the onshore breeze kiss his flesh with salt.

And he felt nothing.

It don't mean nothin'.

What really meant something was that the sky overhead was darkening. Black was swallowing up blue in huge gulps. It would be dark in ten minutes, and he was a good half hour from home.

Turning his back to the beach, he began to walk. "I can do this. I can do this," he told himself over and over.

He passed a bank of pay phones.

Maybe I should call. Dad could be here in just a few minutes. But what would I tell him? Dad, your grown son is afraid of the dark? No ... terrified, unnerved, devastated. Dad, you know your son who you're so proud of? The one who survived the horrors of Vietnam? Did you know that when the lights go out, he comes unglued? So what do you think of him now? Huh? What do you think of your hero son now?

Travis passed by the phones and kept walking.

I wonder if they make night-lights in the shape of a Purple Heart.

The darker it got, the faster Travis walked. Then he ran. In the distance he saw his salvation—a gas station. A well-lit gas station. He ran toward the light as the darkness closed in behind him.

He sprinted under the huge white metal canopy that covered the pumps. He was winded and had to rest his hands on his knees to catch his breath. He was in the light. Everything would be fine.

"Can I help you, sir?"

The attendant, a boy who couldn't have been older than sixteen or seventeen, stood wiping black grease from his hands with a shop rag.

"Um, no, I'm just meeting someone here in a little while. You don't mind if I wait here, do you?"

The attendant grinned. "No crime against that, sir."

While the boy went back to work, Travis stood around with his arms folded, looking up and down the street as if he really were expecting someone. In reality he was checking the edges of the light, making sure that the darkness couldn't reach him where he hid.

His parents, of course, would start to worry about him; would probably even go looking for him. While he felt bad about the anguish he would cause them, he couldn't bring himself to go back to that life. Church was bad enough. Everybody was whispering, blaming him and his father for Keith's court-martial. But the thing that drove him out of the house was the Bible.

He'd forgotten all about it until he saw it sitting out near the dinner table. The Morgan hall of heroes. Generation after generation of them. Every one of them heroic.

He remembered his last church service before leaving for boot camp. The Morgans were well represented. Grandfather Johnny, a World War I ace; father, a famous World War II battlefield photographer. And him. He was outclassed.

Another image from the past came to his mind. He was a little boy, sitting on his mother's lap. She would tell him that someday his name would be added to the Morgan family Bible, right below his father's name. They would have a ceremony and everything.

A ceremony. They planned on doing it today. Why else would the Bible be sitting out? Travis couldn't let them. He didn't deserve to have his name listed with his ancestors. He was no hero. His name would only dishonor the list.

Poor Dad. He had no other son to give the Bible to.

An hour passed. The teenage attendant returned. "Did they forget you?"

Travis laughed nonchalantly. "They tend to run a little on the late side," he said.

"You could call them. We have a pay phone in the—"

"Naw. Why waste a dime? They'll be here."

Another hour passed. The boy returned. He looked at Travis suspiciously.

"You know," Travis said, "maybe they did stand me up. I guess I'll be on my way, since it's pretty clear they forgot me."

How could he tell this kid he was terrified of the dark?

"Yep, guess I'll mosey along, pardner." Travis laughed at his cowboy imitation.

The boy stared at him and wiped the grease from his hands.

As much as he hated the thought of it, he walked to the edge of the light. Like a mighty dragon hidden deep in the back of the cave, darkness awaited him to step into its realm.

Travis looked back at the station. The boy was still looking at him. Travis turned and stepped into the dark like any normal human being would do.

Only he wasn't a normal human being. He might just as well have stepped on a live electrical wire or into a cobra's cage. The fear started in his foot, the one that took the first step, and worked its way up his leg and into his head and chest and heart.

He began to sweat. He vision was blurred, his breathing shallow. He shook uncontrollably. And he ran. He ran as fast as he could. He ran, not knowing where he was running.

Cars passed him at fifty miles an hour. It was the oncoming cars that attracted him. The ones with lights. Travis wanted to step into the light. He told himself if he did so, the car would kill him. His emotions said the light would save him. It was the only thing that could save him.

He resisted the urge, but for how long?

In the distance lights shined. Small shops. Hotels. Restaurants. Lights and more lights. Where to go? He ran down the sidewalk, the well-lit sidewalk. But even as illuminated as the street was, there were dogs of darkness living on the edges that nipped at his heels.

He needed a place he could stay. A well-lit place. A place that wouldn't close and turn off their lights and throw him out into the dark.

There! Perfect.

With his chest constricting and his limbs shaking so badly he could barely stand, Travis ran through the door like a sprinter breaking the tape at the end of the race. The women and children in the all-night Laundromat stared at him like he was crazy.

By about 12:30 a.m. Travis had the place to himself. He felt ridiculous, but it was a far sight better than what he'd feel if he were in the dark. Even now it lurked on the other side of the plate glass window, taunting him to come out.

A huge, burly man walked through the doorway carrying a basket of laundry. His shoulders nearly brushed both sides of the doorway simultaneously when he passed through it. He looked over at Travis and gave him a "Hey, dude" nod, then proceeded to empty his clothes into one of the coin-operated washing machines. He stopped midway.

"Golly!" he said.

Travis had been around a lot of guys, not surprising for a guy who just came back from Vietnam, but never in his life had he heard a man who looked like a bouncer or a professional wrestler use the word *golly*. He had to stifle a snicker lest the guy come over and offer to rearrange his face.

"Got any change?"

"Huh?"

The hulking clothes washer ambled toward him, all the while digging into his jean pockets. "I said, do you got any change? I have a buck here; wait a minute...." He smiled. "I didn't forget after all."

He pulled out two quarters and held them up for Travis to see. Travis was happy for him.

Now that the door of conversation was open, he took advantage of it. "I like this time of night. Hate it when you have to fight for a washer or a dryer, don't you?"

"Yeah."

The gentle giant looked up and down the rows of machines closest to Travis. All the lids were up.

"You doin' your laundry?" he asked.

"No," Travis said. "Just hangin' out."

The man eyed Travis suspiciously. "You're not waitin' to make a drug deal with someone, are you?"

"Nothing like that. Just a traveler. Thought I'd take a load off my feet for a while."

"Traveler, huh? Where you headin'?"

"No place in particular. Thought I'd just wander up Interstate 5 until I can find a place where the sun doesn't set."

The man screwed up his face, "Huh?"

Travis shook him off. "A private joke."

The guy closed the lid on the machine, snapped his fingers, reached into his basket for a box of powdered soap, and poured some in.

"You a veteran?"

"Why do you ask that?"

"No reason. Just thought you looked military, that's all. Been to 'Nam?"

"Just back."

"And now you're gonna travel, see the States."

"Something like that."

The large man loaded his quarters, pushed the coin slot mechanism, and stood back as the sound of water could be heard filling the machine.

"Here," he said. "Here's some reading material for you to take with you on the road."

He reached into his back pocket. A blank expression covered his face and was quickly replaced by one of surprise.

"Oh golly!" he said.

He threw open the lid of the machine and fished around in the washer looking for something. He pulled out a pair of jeans, reached into the pocket and retrieved a piece of printed paper. Apparently it was what he was looking for because finding it prompted a smile.

He walked over to Travis smoothing out the wrinkles and dusting off some soap granules. "Here," he said, handing it to Travis.

Travis took it and read: "God's Speed Doesn't Kill."

When Paige left the house with Del she was under the impression he had a very tight schedule.

"You lied to me!" she said.

"It was just a little lie," Del replied. "It got you to come with me, didn't it?"

"You lied to me!"

"Hey, cool it! What difference does it make? It didn't hurt anybody, did it?"

The '55 Ford rode down the sloping on-ramp, picking up speed as it headed south on Interstate 5. The Garnet Avenue off-ramp and Pacific Beach were only a couple of miles down the road.

"Where'd you get the car?"

"Traded Allen's van for it in Albuquerque."

"You traded Allen's van? Then this car is his?"

"How do you figure?"

"How do you figure it's yours? You used a van that didn't belong to you to get this one."

Del shook his head. "The way I figure it, Allen owed me."

"How so?"

"He agreed to take us to Chicago and back, right?"

"Yeah."

"Well, he didn't. His stinkin' van broke down in Albuquerque. I swapped a van that was broken for a car that runs."

"A van that you stole!"

"Stole? What are you talkin' about? I waited for Allen for three days. He never showed up."

"And you stranded Natalie and me."

"Stranded nothing. I couldn't get to you with all the rioting going on."

Paige was getting nowhere. She didn't even want to get into Natalie's death, which Del probably didn't even know about. There was only one reason she was even with him right now. She felt a moment of compassion for him.

She thought that maybe, if she could convince Del to see Allen, then Allen could witness to him. Del needed Jesus more than anybody else she knew. Only she hadn't told Del she was staying at a *Jesus* commune, just that she and Allen were staying at *a* commune.

"This is it?"

Del pulled up in front of the Catacombs.

"Where's all the activity?"

Unlike Shores Drive where there was always someone coming or going, the Catacombs looked like every other house on the quiet residential street. Paige led Del inside.

Del's first comment inside was, "Looks like my grandma's living room."

"Wait right here, I'll go get Allen."

She didn't have to. Allen walked into the room as if on cue. For a moment the two men stood and stared at one another. Paige thought she'd made a mistake bringing Del here.

"Look who showed up at my house, Allen!" she said.

Allen smiled. It was a genuine smile. He walked toward Del and—instead of extending his hand—he hugged him.

Del was speechless.

"Welcome to the Catacombs, Del."

"The Catacombs?"

Allen nodded. "It was named after the hiding place of the early Christians in Rome."

"I know what the catacombs are," Del said. "Are you people hiding from Nero or something?"

Allen laughed. "Nothing like that. It's a tie to our spiritual heritage."

From the growing humor on Del's face, Paige could see he was beginning to guess what kind of place this was.

There was a familiar sound of feet bounding down the stairs. Terri burst into the room.

"Del!" she said. She ran across the room and threw her arms around him.

"Terri! You're here, too?"

She nodded excitedly.

Del burst out laughing. "This is rich!" he said. "This is really rich. Be honest with me ... you guys are Jesus freaks, aren't you?"

"We're Christians, if that's what you mean," Allen said.

"This is great! Let me tell you, this is rich!" Del howled. "Who would've thought that Allen here would grow up to be a dyed-in-the-wool, Scripture-totin', hands-in-the-air, shoutin'-hallelujah preacher!"

Allen himself seemed amused. He looked at Paige and said, "You didn't tell him, did you?"

Feeling a little sheepish, Paige said, "He showed up at my house. I thought this would be a good place to bring him."

"You did the right thing," Allen said.

"What? You're gonna try to convert me?" Del said.

"You need the Lord, Del," Allen said.

"They whacked you on the head good in Chicago, didn't they?"

"Listen to him, Del," Paige said.

Terri nodded. "Please, Del, just listen. What could it hurt?"

Del wiped a tear of laughter from his eye. "Well, Paige, I gotta tell you. You really made my day. But I'm outta here. Let's go, babe."

Paige looked at Allen. "Del wants me back. He came down to take me back with him to Shores Drive."

"I see," Allen said.

"Let's go, babe," Del said. "These two probably have a lot of praying to catch up on."

Allen stepped in. "Del, for old times sake. Let me tell you what happened to me when I was in that Chicago jail cell."

Del threw up both hands. "I'll pass. I always knew you were weak in the head, buddy. But you really went off the deep end with this one."

"Come on, Paige. Let's get outta here."

"I'm staying."

"Cute. Now let's go. We have some world-changing plans to make. Berkeley is where it's really happening. There are some guys there …"

"Del, I'm staying here."

He looked confused.

"I'm one of them. I'm a Jesus freak."

He let out an exasperated noise. "They've played with your mind! Give me ten minutes on the road and I'll have you all straightened out again."

"No, Del. This is where I belong."

"With them? Don't make me laugh. Remember the dreams we had? We're going to change the world! We're going to bring this nation to its knees and build a country that is worth living in. Do you mean to tell me that you'd rather stay here with them and hand out punch and cookies to a bunch of drunks at the rescue mission? What a waste!"

"It's not a waste!" Paige said. "We're doing more here to change the world than you'll ever do!"

"Yeah? How?"

"One life at a time, Del. One life at a time. A revolution that starts in the heart and changes a person from within. A revolution based on love, not hate and destruction."

"Opium of the masses," Del said. "They're convincing you to sell out to the establishment by putting your mind to sleep, Paige."

"No, Del. For the first time in my life, I'm thinking for myself. I know who I am. And I know where I belong. I belong here."

"You're serious."

"Yes."

"You're really serious!"

"Jesus loves you, Del."

If she'd slapped him in the face, he wouldn't have reeled backward any harder. "I can't believe this!" he shouted. "You're throwing away everything we've dreamed about! And for what?"

"For a better revolution, Del. One that has a chance of making the changes we dreamed about."

"Well, you're right about one thing," he screamed. "You belong here. You're nothing! Nothing! They're nothing!" Pointing to Allen, Paige, and Terri, he shouted, "A loser, a groupie, and a whore! What better place for you than in a convent!"

He stormed out the door.

Allen went to Paige and put his arm around her. Terri did, too.

"Paige, what you just said to Del ..."

"Yes?"

"It was the most unchameleon thing I've ever seen you do."

He knew the angle was worth another shot. He was so sure, in fact, he'd already started doing some of the legwork for the story. Nat's editor loved the way the search for his son turned out. The picture of Travis curled up around the infant, laying in the rippling grass, would be a two-page spread for the cover story in the next issue. So it came as no surprise to Nat that his editor would go for this new idea, too.

"It's similar to the Vietnam piece, only this time a concerned father goes after a daughter who has run away to join a religious cult." That's how he'd described the story.

He was given the green light to do the piece.

Nat flipped through his notebook. He already had several quotes ready to attach to his pictures:

A utility company representative told him: "The house and people living in it were filthy. According to their neighbors, they'd wander around during the day, sleep late, and rarely open the doors to visitors. When I called on them to ask for payment on their overdue bill, some guy who identified himself as an elder cussed me out."

One long-standing church woman who tried to help them encountered drugs and free sex in the place. She said, "Those Jesus kids have just baptized their old habits!"

A member of a prominent church denomination had a similar experience. He said, "They asked to stay a few days. There were only a few so we let them use our building. A month later when we finally drove them out, there were thirty of them in there."

One church member lamented, "What's wrong with us? They believe the same doctrines as we do, they don't seem to be angry at anybody, they take church money to underwrite their programs— but they won't come to our church! Our church is losing even the few kids we had! That's not right!"

A deaconess of one church asked, "If they really are Christians, why don't they look like Christians?"

And a pastor in Ocean Beach said, "The Jesus movement is a fad. The shallowness and quackery of it ought to be exposed."

Nat closed his notepad. *It ought to be exposed.* That's exactly what he was setting out to do.

32

"My brother disappeared two weeks ago," Paige said. "It was only his second day home after returning from Vietnam."

"Bummer."

Paige didn't see who made the response. It didn't matter. She sat cross-legged on the floor of the Catacombs. The commune had gathered for family prayers.

"He had a pretty rough time over there. His entire squad was wiped out. Only he and his squad leader survived. Another time he was nearly overrun by VC when he was sucked into the belly of the earth. For a long time he hid out in that cave knowing that the Viet Cong were nearby. He finally was rescued. Then, one day when his new squad was interrogating a Vietnamese village, his squad leader snapped and ordered everyone killed and the village burned to the ground. My brother refused to do it. He also refused to kill a tiny Vietnamese baby. So his squad leader—a former boyfriend of mine and someone my brother looked up to—started shooting at him. Driven into the jungle, he was reported MIA. My brother hid underground. And if it weren't for my dad going over there to find him, he'd probably still be there today."

"So why did he run away from home?" Terri asked.

"No one knows for sure. At church that morning some of the people held him responsible for Keith's court-martial—Keith was the squad leader. Ever since Keith was little, he was sort of the golden boy of the congregation."

"Who saw him last?" Allen asked.

"We all did. Well, I guess, actually my mother did. All of us were sitting down for Sunday lunch—that's when Del came over. My dad had a phone call. And my mom and brother were left alone at the table. He said something like, 'I can't do this,' and that he was going to the beach to clear his head."

"And that was two weeks ago?" Allen asked.

"Two weeks ago Sunday."

Allen looked at the assembled faithful and said, "Let's lift up Paige's brother ..." he turned to Paige, "... what's his name?"

"Travis."

"Let's lift up Travis to the Lord. Jesus knows where he is. Jesus knows what's going on inside his head. This boy needs Jesus."

"If I can say one more thing ..." Paige said.

"Yes?"

"There's another reason why I'm asking for prayer in this matter," she said. She took a deep breath before continuing. "One of the reasons God brought me here was to show me that my life had no direction. No purpose. I always adopted someone else's passion."

Terri was smiling at her. Encouraging her.

"And thanks to Jesus, through the prayer of the elders and Terri ..." Her emotions began to spill over. She paused a moment to rein them in. "... I was able to see that. And so, to make a long story short, I've been seeking God's purpose for my life. And now I think I've found at least part of it."

There was a chorus of Amens.

Paige took another deep breath before continuing. "Jesus told me that if I really loved him, I would tend his sheep. I didn't know exactly what he meant by that at first, by I think now I do. My brother is a lost sheep. He has wandered away from the flock. I believe God is telling me to go find him and bring him home."

※

Nat squeezed himself into the cramped bathroom trying to get a halfway decent camera angle. Wall-to-wall people jammed the tiny room. They were there to witness what they called, "a toilet service."

A young blonde—Nat guessed her to be sixteen or seventeen—approached the toilet, pulled a plastic bag out of her jeans pocket and emptied its contents into the toilet bowl. Ten to twenty pills plopped into the water.

FLASH!

Nat captured the image.

The girl pushed the handle and the toilet flushed. The room erupted with cheers and Amens and Praise the Lords.

A bare-chested young man with a beard flushed marijuana joints. Others flushed LSD and every other street drug imaginable. The line of kids waiting to flush their drugs down the toilet stretched down the hallway and out the front door.

This was a regular activity of the Jesus House in Hollywood following conversions. Kids by the hundreds were turning away from drugs and turning to Jesus.

Nat had never seen anything like it before in his life. And if he hadn't witnessed it himself, he wouldn't have believed it.

FLASH!

His camera strobe was getting a workout that night. He wanted to record everything so that people could see what he was seeing. When he stopped listening to what other people were saying about the Jesus movement and began witnessing some of the results himself, he became a convert.

His notebook was crammed with story after story of kids being saved from a culture that was luring them to destruction with a promise of getting high. Every story was a conversion testimony.

One girl described how she was a lesbian before she gave her heart to Christ. She also credited Jesus for breaking her barbiturate habit and saving her from an overdose.

A guy described how he came out of what he called the good life—"I had enough dope, some nice chicks, a good home, but something was missing. Now I love what God is making of me, and I want to give it to others."

One young man Nat interviewed said, "When I met these Christians, I couldn't believe it. I was stoned on grass; they were stoned on God."

"Do you see that girl over there?" a buddy of his said, pointing to a long-haired brunette who was praying with another girl in the corner of the room. "She had an eighty-dollar-a-day habit before she came to Christ. When she was converted, she didn't even go through withdrawal."

"I used to be into Satan," one guy said, "and it was hard to get away. It was getting me down because I was wearing myself out trying to fight what was too much for me. Alone, I was incapable of handling the power that Satan had over me. I had to trust the Lord because he had already overcome Satan. I knew that Satan couldn't win against him."

Referring to the former Satan worshipper, one girl said, "You never see him without his Bible."

Nat talked to one lovely young girl, a member of a Jesus commune, who was sitting alone quietly reading the Bible.

"What do your parents say? Doesn't your mother object to you being in this house with all these other people?"

The girl smiled sweetly and replied, "My mother knows what I used to be, before I met Jesus."

"Are you happy here?"

Her face lit up. "Oh wow! Are you serious?"

Being a photojournalist, however, Nat couldn't discount the earlier quotes he'd recorded, those who spoke against the Jesus kids. He found, however, that while there were some failures in the movement, there were also plenty of successes.

He interviewed a neighbor of one of the Jesus communes who confessed that he considered selling his house when a bunch of long-haired freaks rented the place next door. But he changed his mind when he saw so many hours being put into yard work and painting. According to the neighbor, the "normal" family that had rented the house before had let it run down terribly. The Jesus kids had the place looking better than it had in years.

In another city he discovered a Jesus commune where police regularly brought delinquents. They figured the Jesus kids just might be able to help them. One elder produced a letter of recommendation from the municipal police chief, commending them for helping out teenage runaways.

But it was the little fourteen-year-old girl in a Fullerton commune who first convinced him that the Jesus movement was real. He watched her for much of one afternoon, concerned that she was so young and not living with her parents. Yet she seemed so happy and contented at the Jesus house. He watched as she listened to an elder teaching her about how Jesus was the fulfillment of Old Testament promises while she was mending a pair of blue jeans. He learned that she'd been living there for several months, that she hadn't started high school yet, but that the house was providing her with a tutor to help her meet the state's educational requirements.

Nat asked one of the elders, "Is this really any life for a fourteen-year-old girl? Shouldn't she be home with her parents?"

"Are you kidding?" the elder replied. "She was riding with the Hell's Angels when she was twelve."

Following the toilet service in Hollywood, Nat jumped onto the freeway and headed south. He had one stop that evening before going home. Billy Graham was preaching in Anaheim, and Nat had heard that a lot of the Jesus people would be in attendance. He thought it would be interesting for his story to see how well a traditional Southern Baptist evangelist and a bunch of Jesus street people got along together.

His mind turned to Travis. When he got to the stadium, he'd find a phone and call home to see if anything had come of the missing persons report they'd filed on their son.

Nat's heart was heavy. Somehow finding a runaway in Southern California seemed a lot more daunting than finding an MIA in Vietnam. Then he thought of all the runaways he'd been interviewing these past two weeks.

He prayed, "Lord, I have a runaway. Could you steer him toward one of these Jesus homes?"

As the prayer meeting was breaking up, Moose joined Terri, Allen, and Paige.

"If you need a bodyguard," he said, "I'll go with you."

"Thanks, Moose, that's really sweet of you," Paige said. "But Allen has already volunteered."

"Where will you start looking?" Terri asked.

Paige shrugged. "I guess at the beaches. Travis has always loved the beach."

Moose shook his head. "You know, I've come across so many guys who come back from 'Nam with their heads all messed up. Just the other night I was doing my laundry and there was this guy who said he'd just come back from 'Nam. He was just sittin' there on top of the counter in the corner. At first

I thought he was waitin' to make a drug deal. Of course, I gave him a tract."

"Did he read it?" Allen asked.

Moose nodded. "He looked at it, then stuffed it in his pocket. Wasn't hostile, but he didn't seem interested, either."

Paige said, "If we're going to do anything tonight, we'd better hit the road."

Allen agreed. Terri said, "Moose and I will start praying for you right now."

"Thanks, you two, we're going to need it."

"He kept staring at the window," Moose said.

"Who?" Paige asked.

"The guy at the Laundromat. You know, I really think he was in there because he was afraid to go out in the dark. Can you imagine what he must have seen in 'Nam to make a grown man …"

"… be afraid of the dark?" Paige finished his sentence.

A startled Moose answered, "Yeah, why?"

"Moose, what did he look like?"

Moose described a young man with bleach-blond hair, good upper-body development, clean-shaven.

"That sounds like him!" Paige shouted. Her body began to tingle with anticipation. She tried to control it, but she found it difficult to stand still.

"When? When did you see him?"

Moose looked at the ceiling. His fingers and lips moved as he calculated the days. "It was Sunday. Two weeks ago."

"The night Travis disappeared!" Allen said. "But why do you think this might be your brother?"

"The dark. Travis developed a phobia that has to do with the dark. Mom said the first night he was home, he insisted that every light in the house be turned on. Then, when he went to sleep that night, he slept with his room light on."

Now they were all beginning to get excited.

"Moose," Paige said, "did he say anything to you that might be a clue to his whereabouts?"

Moose squinted so hard Paige feared he might burst a blood vessel. *Bless him, dear Lord, he wants so much to help.*

"He said he was just hangin' out … wandering … oh! He called himself a traveler, and I asked, 'Where are you traveling?'"

They waited for more.

"Well?" Terri said. "Did he say he was traveling to someplace?"

"I'm thinking!"

Moose was even grunting now he was trying so hard. Finally, he exhaled and shook his head. "Sorry, that's all I can remember."

The other three patted him on his back.

"That's more than we had a few minutes ago," Allen said.

"You did good, Moose," Terri said, adding a smile that had something a little more to it than usual.

"You're terrific, Moose," Paige said.

Allen turned to Paige. "Are you ready to go?"

"North!" Moose shouted. "He said he was heading north! Um … up Interstate 5."

"Great, Moose!" Paige said.

"Wait! Wait, there's more. He said something really strange … Wait, I'll get it, I'll get it …"

The three waited on the big guy expectantly. It was as though his head could hold only so much information at a time and he had to dispense some to make room for more. They were waiting for more to pour in.

"I got it! He said something like he was lookin' for a place where the sun didn't set."

Moose opened his eyes and grinned.

The three stared at him.

"That's it!" he said. "Hey, I don't make this stuff up, I just remember it."

"His fear of the dark again," Paige said. "Before we go, Allen, I want to call my mother and tell her that we think Moose saw Travis."

"Good idea." He looked at his watch. "It's going to be late by the time we head up the road. Maybe we should get a fresh start in the morning."

Paige checked her watch, too. "That might not be a bad ... no, we have to go tonight."

"Why tonight?"

"Because it's dark. If we find Travis, we'll find him in a place that's well lit."

※

Nat pulled into the parking lot. An hour before the revival service was to begin, and already he found it difficult to find a place to park.

Getting out of the car, he checked his camera bag for film and batteries. He slung the bag over his shoulder and began walking through row after row of parked cars. The distinctive A-shaped scoreboard towered high over the edge of the stadium.

When it wasn't being used for revivals, a professional baseball team used the park. They were called the Angels. Nat thought the name fitting for a religious revival.

※

Allen and Paige rode up Interstate 5 looking out the windows on both sides. Allegra sat quietly in the back seat, asking them to elaborate on their hmms, and Looks! and How about theres!

When Paige called her, she insisted on coming along, saying she'd had enough time to cry and pray, she wanted to do something to help find her son no matter how great the odds were that their search would amount to nothing.

As they passed through Oceanside and entered the Camp Pendleton area where the marines were trained, the landscape grew depressingly dark.

"He may not have even come this way," Paige said.

"We'll just have to pray and let the Holy Spirit make it plain to us."

They traveled on through San Juan Capistrano and Irvine and began entering the southern portion of the Los Angeles metroplex.

"He might be at Disneyland," Paige offered. "There are a lot of lights there."

"A lot of dark places, too," Allen said. "From the way Moose described him, he'll want something brighter."

"We'll find him even if we have to search every all-night laundry place between San Diego and San Francisco," Allegra said.

They continued up the road and passed under the overpass of a major intersection. A glow appeared in the distance. The farther they went, the brighter it became.

"What's that?" Paige asked.

"Interesting," Allen replied.

"What? What?" Allegra asked.

As they continued on, Allen said, "I know what that is!"

"What?" both Paige and Allegra said in chorus.

"Anaheim Stadium."

"You think Travis went to a baseball game?" Allegra asked.

"Let's get closer and see what's going on," Allen replied.

"It's certainly bright," Paige said. "What better place for a guy to go who's afraid of the dark?"

"Ahhhh!" Allen groaned.

"What is it?" Allegra shouted from the back.

"It's not a baseball game," he said. "It's a Billy Graham revival."

Paige laughed.

"What?" Allegra asked.

"The place where Billy Graham is preaching. It's called Angel Stadium."

"It's a sign," Allegra said.

᛭

Nat had worked his way up to the nose-bleed section of the stadium. The revival service was well under way. Hymns had been sung, local dignitaries and celebrities introduced, George Beverly Shea had completed his solo, and now the world-famous evangelist was preaching. His message was a simple one in which he emphasized that more than ever before the times indicated our need for a personal Savior.

Nat had found several groups of Jesus people, pockets of them sitting in the midst of mainstream America. Now he wanted to get a few shots of the entire stadium with a wide-angle lens.

Lifting the camera, he looked through the eyepiece and composed his shot. He focused on the A-framed scoreboard. It had to be something large since, with a wide-angle lens, he could get the entire stadium into the picture, which meant that individuals were very small.

He changed lenses as the evangelist began to extend his invitation to the people. Organ music started playing, "Just As I Am." Already people were leaving their seats as the evangelist directed them and were coming down onto the playing field to make a decision for Christ. Counselors were already standing there waiting for them. The evangelist told the people that their friends and family would wait for them if they came.

And they did. Hundreds upon hundreds of them streamed down every aisle. The playing field was filling quickly.

Nat raised the camera to his eye and peered into the viewfinder. He was looking through a telephoto lens now. With it, he was far enough away from people that he could take candid shots. He trained the lens on the rows of stadium stairs across the field. Everything was blurry. He pulled the people into focus.

People of all ages and races were coming down the stairs. He focused on a woman wearing a blue suit. In front of her was a little girl wearying a white frilly dress. Just behind her and to one side was …

"Travis!" Nat shouted.

He looked again. There was no mistaking his son.

"Thank you, God!" Nat shouted.

"And Hallelujah!" the man next to him replied.

Nat began running down the stairs, slowed by those who were going to make a decision. He excused himself a hundred times as he worked his way down to the playing field. All the time he kept looking at the stairs opposite him, keeping an eye on his son. He didn't want to lose him now.

"There he is!" Paige shouted. "I see him!"

Allegra lifted her hands to her mouth. "Thank you, God," she cried. "Thank you."

They had nearly given up. The stadium was packed with faces. Neither Paige nor Allen had heard a single word of testimony or song or sermon. They spent the entire time scanning the crowd and praying.

Allegra had just finished saying, "In all my life I never regretted not being able to see. Until now."

"Mother, wait here. I'll go get him," Paige said.

"Not on your life!" Allegra declared. "That's my son!"

Allen turned to Paige. "You bring your mother, I'll run ahead and get him!"

Paige nodded and Allen bounded down the stairs. He didn't get far. Turning around, he came back.

"What's wrong?" Paige asked.

"This is your mission, Paige," he said. "I'll help your mother. You go get your brother."

Paige gave him a hug. Then she bounded down the stairs as fast as her legs would carry her.

Just before reaching the playing field, Paige paused and took one last look to get her bearings. She knew that once she was on the same level as Travis, she would lose sight of him.

"Dear God," she prayed, "please guide me."

She waded into the sea of humanity. Person after person was talking with a counselor, listening, praying, weeping, laughing; some were kneeling, others held their hands toward heaven.

Paige made her way through the human maze to the point where she expected to find Travis.

He wasn't there.

She turned on her heels three hundred and sixty degrees. Still no Travis. She jumped up to get a look over people's heads. She still didn't see him.

Panic began to set in.

Which way to go now?

Maybe she should just stand there and shout and let him find her. She even considered going to the platform and trying to talk Billy Graham into calling Travis forward.

Then she saw him.

Thank you, God. Thank you!

With the calm assurance that she was fulfilling a divinely inspired purpose in her life, she headed confidently toward her brother.

He didn't see her coming.

"Good evening, young man," she said. "Do you know that Jesus loves you? And so do I?"

Travis turned toward her.

Shocked. He began to weep.

Paige threw her arms around her brother. She had found the

sheep that had wandered away.

"Travis!"

"Dad?"

Now it was Paige's turn to be shocked as her father came running up to them.

"Son!" he cried, throwing his arms around Travis's neck. With a huge grin, he said to Paige, "What are you doing here?"

"There they are!" It was Allen's voice.

"Travis? Travis, where are you?" Allegra called.

Nat turned around, surprised. "Good Lord, the whole family's here!"

"Mother?"

Allegra embraced her son. "Travis, don't you know how much we love you?" she said.

Travis began to tremble. His knees gave way. He sank to the ground.

"Thank you, God," he said, his face wet with tears. "Thank you! Thank you!"

Paige got on her knees beside her brother and held him. He was so overcome he could barely speak. When he could finally form words, he said, "I've been so scared. So scared. I saw these lights and came here not knowing that it was a revival service. But then, I knew that God had led me here. And I began to pray. I asked him to send me someone. Someone to help me. Because I'm scared and all alone. Oh, God, I feel so alone."

Nat got on his knees beside his son. Allen helped Allegra to her knees. There, on the playing field of Anaheim Stadium, the Morgans were reunited.

"Son," Nat said, "there is nothing we can't face together as a family with God's help. That's the way it's always been with us Morgans, and that's the way it will always be."

Paige said, "Amen."

EPILOGUE

Allegra hugged the Morgan family Bible against her chest and listened to all the busy noise around her. People were scurrying everywhere, talking, taking and giving directions, getting their equipment ready, checking costumes and makeup.

"Exciting, isn't it?" Nat said.

Allegra laughed. "I can't begin to tell you."

"Why do you have that?"

"The family Bible?"

"Yeah."

"Paige told me that Brad wanted to see it."

"Well, of course," Nat said. "*Brad* wanted to see it. So now we're on a first-name basis?"

Allegra laughed. "Oh, stop it! Besides, it's fitting, don't you think? The Bible's come full circle."

※

Nat and Allegra stood in the courtyard of Windsor Castle. The sun was shining warmly, reflecting heat off the stone walls. Everywhere Nat looked there were cables and cameras and light reflectors and actresses and actors and cameramen and directors and a hundred other people who work behind the scenes on a movie set.

There was something exciting about standing here, on location in London. Allegra was right. This was where it all began for the Morgans over three hundred years previous. Who would have thought that anyone would want to make a major motion picture of the Morgan family?

Everything started falling into place about two years after Travis returned from Vietnam. It was during a Thanksgiving dinner that Allegra revealed to the family the secret project she'd been working on. It was a novel based on the actual history of the Morgan family. But the news got even better. She'd just received a letter from a publisher. They wanted to publish it!

Sales were brisk from the start, which the marketing people partially attributed to the stunning cover, which featured an original oil painting by Paige. And two months after Allen and Paige were married, Allegra's agent called her and told her that her book had reached the top of the *New York Times* best-seller list. Six months after that, he called again to tell her he'd sold the movie rights.

"Isn't this place beautiful?" Paige said, joining her parents. Allen was by her side. Nat looked at his son-in-law. Had he hand-selected a partner for his daughter, he couldn't have chosen a better one.

Terri and Moose, newlyweds themselves, decided to honeymoon in London so they could say they saw a motion picture being made.

"Mom?"

Travis approached his mother. A young man dressed in fifteenth-century garb accompanied him. "Mom, I'd like you to meet Glen Campbell," Travis said. "He's the actor who will be playing the part of Drew Morgan."

Allegra extended her hand. "It's a pleasure to meet you, Mr. Campbell," she said.

"The pleasure is mine, Mrs. Morgan," Campbell said. "After reading your book, I immediately called my agent and told him that if he heard a movie was going to be made of it, I wanted to be in it."

"How kind of you," Allegra said.

"And this is the actual Morgan family Bible?"

"Yes it is." She handed it to him.

With great care he thumbed through the pages. Then he opened the front cover and read each name on the list.

The director called for the actors to take their places. The Bible was given back to Allegra. When everything was ready, the call was given: "Quiet on the set."

Nat stood next to his wife. "This is exciting," he said.

One of the workers turned and shushed him.

Nat didn't care. He glanced at Travis with pride. The boy still had his bad days, but for the most part, the old Travis had finally returned.

When Nat had found out the reason Travis had run away, the two of them had a long talk. Things were better now, and Travis understood that heroism was nothing more than having the courage to live your beliefs.

Later that night, in a London hotel, he would pass the Morgan Bible to his son in keeping with the family tradition.

"ACTION!"

Allegra leaned toward her husband. "Tell me what you see," she whispered.

"Brad is running across the green," he said. "He's reached the huge wooden door. He's looking both ways, pulling on it. It opens, and he slips inside."

Allegra smiled contentedly. She said, "The story begins at Windsor Castle, the day Drew Morgan met Bishop Laud. For it was on that day his life began its downward direction...."

AFTERWORD

I don't know which book was more difficult to write, the first book in this series or the last. Since *The Puritans* was the first novel I ever wrote, it was a learning experience each step of the way. One would think that, seven novels later, I would have a handle on how to write these things. Such is not the case. Each book in this series was an adventure unique to itself.

With *The Peacemakers*, the challenges began early on. First of all this is the first book in the series that is set in a time period in which I had personal experience. I remember the '60s. In 1968—the specific time frame for the bulk of this novel—I was a sophomore in high school. I remember scenes from Vietnam intruding into our living room via television; I remember drugs on campus, underground newspapers, and hearing about the demonstrations and riots on the college campuses; I remember the day Bobby Kennedy was shot.

I was attracted to the youthfulness and antiwar sentiment of the younger brother of JFK. During the California primaries Bobby Kennedy was scheduled to come to San Diego. I was going to skip school to go see him. For some reason his schedule changed and I didn't get to see him, but I followed the primary returns on television, and when I went to bed at eleven o'clock the race was still undecided. The next morning my father woke me up for school. He told me the news. "Bobby Kennedy took the California primary, then somebody shot him."

I remember JFK being assassinated; I remember Martin Luther King Jr. being assassinated; I remember George Wallace being shot; I remember Kent State and My Lai. I remember wondering what had gone wrong with our country so that we felt hatred and violence was the answer to everything. I was disturbed that my generation was making such a black mark on history. I remember wondering if our nation would even exist by the turn of the century. Now I think of the '60s and wonder how we survived them.

As a rule of thumb, historical fiction deals with time periods fifty years previous and beyond. This novel falls somewhere in between an historical novel and a contemporary novel. While *The Victors*, set during World War II, was the first novel I wrote in which people were still alive who can remember the time period, it seems everybody remembers the '60s. This is both a blessing and a curse. The blessing is that there are plenty of firsthand accounts upon which to draw. That's the curse, too. There are so many of them.

More than once when I guest-preach for an absent pastor, after telling the congregation about the project I was working on, a person would slip me either his business card or his name and phone number on a piece of paper and say, "Call me. I was in 'Nam. I can tell you stories you won't believe."

On an airline flight to a writers conference, an elderly man struck up a conversation with me when he saw I was reading a book on Berkeley as background for this project. He said, "My son was there. Ran away from home. Hitchhiked his way from New York to California. Was into the drug and demonstration scene. Now he's an executive in an aeronautical plant in San

Diego." The man gave me his son's phone number and told me to call him. He said, "I don't know if he'll be willing to help you or not. I doubt if he's even told his children what he did in the '60s."

At another writers conference I had the good fortune to meet Roger and Andrea Palms. Roger is former editor of *Decision* magazine produced by the Billy Graham Evangelistic Association. When sharing the status of our current projects, I learned he had written a book on the Jesus movement, that he had traveled extensively interviewing the people involved in it. He graciously sent me a copy of the book and searched his garage for original research materials. Unfortunately, having recently retired, he'd thrown the materials away. But the offer was appreciated nonetheless.

Family and friends all knew someone who'd been in Vietnam whom I could talk to. And on and on it went. Add to these sources thousands of books, audio and video cassettes of interviews, film clips, news reports of Vietnam and life in the United States in the 1960s, and I was literally buried in material. The question I faced was, "How can I possibly write a single novel that even begins to capture this turbulent decade?"

With the project done now, I can look back on it and explain why I chose the segments I chose and lament not having enough space to include other things. Had I included everything, the story of the '60s would undoubtedly be an eight-book series in itself.

As in the previous afterword sections of my books I will attempt to explain my approach to this novel, the characters I chose and why, and what elements of the story are fictional and which are historical.

The focus of the novel is 1968. I chose this year because it was the most turbulent in the decade—with the Tet Offensive, the assassination of Bobby Kennedy, the My Lai massacre, and the Democratic National Convention riots.

This leads into the historical elements of the novel:

The Tet Offensive struck a serious blow to the American sense of superiority in Vietnam and was a turning point in the war.

As for the Bobby Kennedy assassination, I followed the historical account studiously, since it provided its own drama and pathos without any help from me.

The same is true of the Democratic National Convention. Speech quotes, candidate personalities, Chicago Mayor Richard Daley, the balloting, and the riots in the parks and the streets are all based on historical accounts. Furthermore, the personalities Abbie Hoffman, Jerry Rubin, and Tom Hayden are historical.

The settings in Vietnam, the towns, villages, jungle descriptions, military tactics, and the underground network of caves are all based on historical research. The large cave in which Travis stumbled upon a cache of American military supplies is based on an actual find during the war. The massacre of the village, while fictional, is representative of the My Lai massacre only on a much smaller scale. The My Lai massacre of March 16, 1968, resulted in the deaths of 504 men, women, and children. It is without doubt one of the army's blackest days.

A further note is needed here regarding the military story line. As with the previous books in this series, I avoided much use of military designations, jargon, company names, acronyms, and weapons designations. This I did to emphasize the human drama. While those who were in the military might object to my decision, those who are unfamiliar with these terms will not be unduly distracted. Each profession has its own jargon; had this been a story about lawyers and the legal system, I would have limited the use of legal terms and generally unfamiliar references. In addition I chose not to dwell on the rampant drug and alcohol use in the military at that time, or the racism problem. I chose not to use derogatory names for the enemy, or to use the ever-present cursing that is so prevalent in the military. These choices were made taking evangelical readership into consideration. Once again I prefer to emphasize the human and spiritual drama. For those who feel my portrayal lacks a sense of reality by omitting these things, while I understand your position, I hope you will respect my choice to let other authors explore those areas.

The representation of the Jesus movement is largely historical. While the Catacombs in this novel is a fictional house, it is representational of Jesus houses across the nation. Many of the scenes are based on real events. The quotes are real. My research into the Jesus people was one of the joys of writing this novel. Their raw faith and zeal are refreshing. I hope to write a much fuller treatment representing the people of this movement in the future.

Billy Graham held a revival in Anaheim Stadium in 1968. It was one of those serendipitous finds for me. I was pleased that it could become the setting for the story's climax and the reuniting of the Morgan family.

La Jolla and vicinity, the shores, and Pacific Beach are actual locations in San Diego County. I spent many a happy summer day at La Jolla Shores and have fond memories of church youth group outings there.

Fictitious elements of the story include UCRD, Rancho Diego, and the Shores Drive commune, though the house was based on various college houses of its kind. And while Rancho Diego is just a product of my imagination, its geographical location as described in the book actually resides just south of the city of San Clemente, more popularly known as the site of Richard Nixon's western White House. In picking a site, I thought that location was humorously ironic considering the nature of the events that took place there both fictionally and historically.

While the shooting at UCRD was fictional, it was representative of the Kent State shooting, which came later in 1970.

For this story I chose three major point-of-view characters: Nat, Paige, and Travis.

Nat represents the World War II veteran who finds in the '60s a generation with values totally different from those he fought for in the 1940s. He is the establishment.

Paige represents the younger generation's search for a better world. She finds the political rebellion to be self-defeating and the Jesus movement to be self-fulfilling. Both had similar goals—to change the world; but while one based its revolution on hatred and destruction, the other based its revolution on love and spiritual renewal.

Travis, obviously, represents the average patriot-male who was thrust into a disillusioning war. So many good kids came home injured physically, psychologically, emotionally, and spiritually. And they were the lucky ones. At least they came home.

Of the minor characters, Allegra is my favorite. This is the third book in which she appears, and each time I've found myself at the end of the story wishing I had spent more time with her character. Only with one other character have I felt that way— Abigail, the wax sculptress in *The Patriots*. In that book I had a similar feeling, a wish that I could have introduced her earlier in the work, but the story wouldn't allow me. Because these two characters—strong women each—share a common desire in my heart, I tied them together in a small, but significant way in chapter 17.

Regarding the other minor characters:

Del Gilroy is the quintessential radical with no moral base.

Terri is an unlikely heroine and, later, a wonderful Christian role model. She is like so many so-called minor characters in life who lead interesting and surprisingly heroic lives.

Allen, like Paige, becomes part of two revolutions and is lucky enough to survive the one to find the power of the other.

Finally, while there are, and forever will be, numerous debates on the '60s between radicals and liberals and conservatives, doves and hawks, and evangelical and mainstream believers, it was never my attempt to do what they attempt to do and interpret this decade in light of their biases. As with every novel in this series, my sincere attempt has been to portray the kinds of struggles Christians faced in that time in keeping with their personalities and beliefs as they interact with other characters, events, and philosophies.

And so concludes the Morgan family saga. They have been a significant part of my life for nearly a decade. And while I welcome new challenges in writing, I know that I shall miss them.

Jack Cavanaugh
Chula Vista, 1999

The Morgan Family
The Puritans—The Adversaries

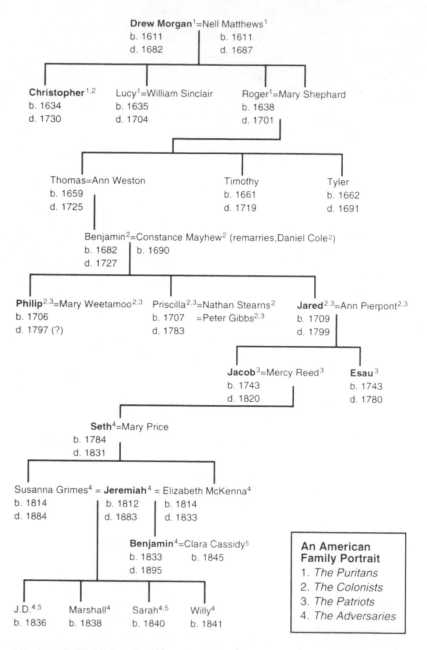

Drew Morgan[1]=Nell Matthews[1]
b. 1611   b. 1611
d. 1682   d. 1687

Christopher[1,2]   Lucy[1]=William Sinclair   Roger[1]=Mary Shephard
b. 1634   b. 1635   b. 1638
d. 1730   d. 1704   d. 1701

Thomas=Ann Weston   Timothy   Tyler
b. 1659   b. 1661   b. 1662
d. 1725   d. 1719   d. 1691

Benjamin[2]=Constance Mayhew[2] (remarries,Daniel Cole[2])
b. 1682   b. 1690
d. 1727

Philip[2,3]=Mary Weetamoo[2,3]   Priscilla[2,3]=Nathan Stearns[2]   **Jared**[2,3]=Ann Pierpont[2,3]
b. 1706   b. 1707   =Peter Gibbs[2,3]   b. 1709
d. 1797 (?)   d. 1783   d. 1799

Jacob[3]=Mercy Reed[3]   Esau[3]
b. 1743   b. 1743
d. 1820   d. 1780

Seth[4]=Mary Price
b. 1784
d. 1831

Susanna Grimes[4] = **Jeremiah**[4] = Elizabeth McKenna[4]
b. 1814   b. 1812   b. 1814
d. 1884   d. 1883   d. 1833

Benjamin[4]=Clara Cassidy[5]
b. 1833   b. 1845
d. 1895

J.D.[4,5]   Marshall[4]   Sarah[4,5]   Willy[4]
b. 1836   b. 1838   b. 1840   b. 1841

**An American
Family Portrait**
1. *The Puritans*
2. *The Colonists*
3. *The Patriots*
4. *The Adversaries*

---

* Names in **bold** appear in the Morgan family Bible.
* Superscript numbers indicate which characters appear in which books.

The Morgan Family
The Pioneers–The Peacemakers

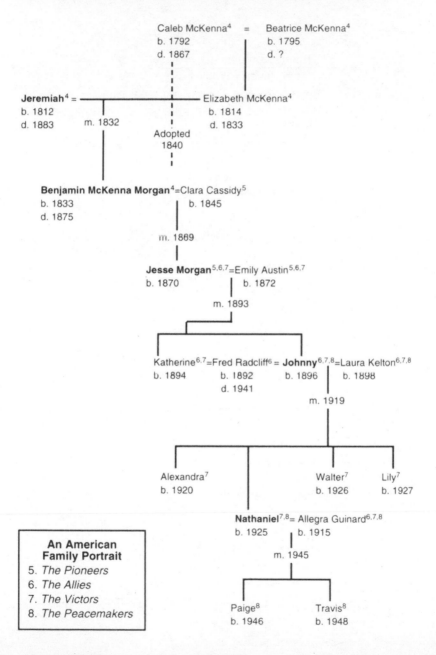

Caleb McKenna[4] = Beatrice McKenna[4]
b. 1792   b. 1795
d. 1867   d. ?

Jeremiah[4] =   Elizabeth McKenna[4]
b. 1812   b. 1814
d. 1883   m. 1832   d. 1833

Adopted
1840

Benjamin McKenna Morgan[4]=Clara Cassidy[5]
b. 1833   b. 1845
d. 1875

m. 1869

Jesse Morgan[5,6,7]=Emily Austin[5,6,7]
b. 1870   b. 1872

m. 1893

Katherine[6,7]=Fred Radcliff[6] = Johnny[6,7,8]=Laura Kelton[6,7,8]
b. 1894   b. 1892   b. 1896   b. 1898
              d. 1941

m. 1919

Alexandra[7]   Walter[7]   Lily[7]
b. 1920   b. 1926   b. 1927

Nathaniel[7,8]= Allegra Guinard[6,7,8]
b. 1925   b. 1915

m. 1945

Paige[8]   Travis[8]
b. 1946   b. 1948

**An American
Family Portrait**
5. *The Pioneers*
6. *The Allies*
7. *The Victors*
8. *The Peacemakers*

* Names in **bold** appear in the Morgan family Bible.
* Superscript numbers indicate which characters appear in which books.

Additional copies of this and other titles in the
American Family Portrait series
and other RiverOak titles are available
wherever good books are sold.

If you have enjoyed this book,
or if it has had an impact on your life,
we would like to hear from you.

Please contact us at:

RiverOak Books
Cook Communications Ministries, Dept. 201
4050 Lee Vance View
Colorado Springs, CO 80918

Or visit our Web site:
www.cookministries.com

RiverOak®
Good News in Fiction